# THE
# TENTH
# CIRCLE

# Also by Jodi Picoult

Vanishing Acts
My Sister's Keeper
Second Glance
Perfect Match
Salem Falls
Plain Truth
Keeping Faith
The Pact
Mercy
Picture Perfect
Harvesting the Heart
Songs of the Humpback Whale

# THE TENTH CIRCLE

*Jodi Picoult*

Illustrations by Dustin Weaver

DOUBLEDAY LARGE PRINT HOME LIBRARY EDITION
**ATRIA** BOOKS
NEW YORK   LONDON   TORONTO   SYDNEY

This Large Print Edition, prepared especially for Doubleday Large Print Home Library, contains the complete, unabridged text of the original Publisher's Edition.

**ATRIA** BOOKS
1230 Avenue of the Americas
New York, NY 10020

ISBN-13: 978-0-7394-6578-3
ISBN-10: 0-7394-6578-3

This Atria Books hardcover edition March 2006

**ATRIA** BOOKS is a trademark of Simon & Schuster, Inc.

Manufactured in the United States of America

For Nick and Alex Adolph
(and their parents, Jon and Sarah)
because I promised that one day I would.

# ACKNOWLEDGMENTS

This was a massive undertaking, and it would have been an impossible one without the help of my Dream Team of research helpers.

My usual suspects: Betty Martin, Lisa Schiermeier, Nick Giaccone, Frank Moran, David Toub, Jennifer Sternick, Jennifer Sobel, Claire Demarais, JoAnn Mapson, Jane Picoult.

Two ladies with the grace to help rape victims find a fragile peace: Laurie Carrier and Annelle Edwards.

Three terrific young women who let me peek into the life of a teenager: Meredith Olsen, Elise Baxter, and Andrea Desaulniers.

The entire team at Atria Books and Goldberg McDuffie Communications, especially Judith Curr, Karen Mender, Jodi Lipper, Sarah Branham, Jeanne Lee, Angela Stamnes, Justin Loeber, and Camille McDuffie.

Laura Gross, who goes above and beyond the call of agent duty on a daily basis.

Emily Bestler, who said all the wonderful, right things I needed to hear when I gave her a book that was like nothing she'd ever seen before.

Joanne Morrissey, who gave me a refresher course on Dante and whom I'd most like to be stranded with in hell.

My own personal comic book superheroes: Jim Lee, Wyatt Fox, and Jake van Leer.

Pam Force, for the opening poem.

My Alaskan hosts: Annette Rearden, and Rich and Jen Gannon.

Don Rearden, who is not only an excellent writer (one who probably regrets ever saying, "Hey, if you ever want to go to the Alaskan bush . . .") but also generous to a fault with his own knowledge and experience. And who guided me into the bush and, months later, to my last page.

Dustin Weaver, the comic book penciler who said he thought this might be fun. Quite simply: You drew the soul of this book.

And finally, thanks to Tim, Kyle, Jake, and Sammy, who give me my happy endings.

In the very earliest time,
when both people and animals lived on earth,
a person could become an animal if he wanted
    to and an animal could become a human be-
    ing.
Sometimes they were people
and sometimes animals
and there was no difference.
All spoke the same language.
That was the time when words were like magic.
The human mind had mysterious powers.
A word spoken by chance
might have strange consequences.
It would suddenly come alive
and what people wanted to happen could
    happen—
all you had to do was say it.
Nobody could explain this:
That's the way it was.
                    —"Magic Words," by Edward
                    Field
                    Inspired by the Inuit

# PROLOGUE

*December 23, 2005*

This is how it feels when you realize your child is missing: The pit of your stomach freezes fast, while your legs go to jelly. There's one single, blue-bass thud of your heart. The shape of her name, sharp as metal filings, gets caught between your teeth even as you try to force it out in a shout. Fear breathes like a monster into your ear: *Where did I see her last? Would she have wandered away? Who could have taken her?* And then, finally, your throat seals shut, as you swallow the fact that you've made a mistake you will never be able to fix.

The first time it happened to Daniel Stone, a decade ago, he had been visiting Boston. His wife was at a colloquium at Harvard; that was a good enough reason to take a family vacation. While Laura sat on her panel, Daniel pushed Trixie's stroller the cobbled length of the Freedom Trail.

They fed the ducks in the Public Garden; they watched the sloe-eyed sea turtles doing water ballet at the aquarium. After that, when Trixie announced that she was hungry, Daniel headed toward Faneuil Hall and its endless food court.

That particular April day was the first one warm enough for New Englanders to unzip their jackets, to remember that there was any season other than winter. In addition to the centipedes of school groups and the shutter-happy tourists, it seemed that the whole of the financial district had bled out, men Daniel's age in suits and ties, who smelled of aftershave and envy. They sat with their gyros and chowder and corned beef on rye on the benches near the statue of Red Auerbach. They sneaked sideways glances at Daniel.

He was used to this—it was unusual for a father to be the primary caretaker of his four-year-old daughter. Women who saw him with Trixie assumed that his wife had died, or that he was newly divorced. Men who saw him quickly looked the other way, embarrassed on his behalf. And yet Daniel would not have traded his setup for the world. He enjoyed molding his job around Trixie's schedule. He liked her questions: Did dogs *know* they were naked? Is *adult supervision* a power grown-ups use to fight bad guys? He loved the fact that when Trixie was spacing out in her car seat and wanted attention, she always started with "Dad . . . ?" even if Laura happened to be driving the car.

"What do you want for lunch?" Daniel asked

Trixie that day in Boston. "Pizza? Soup? A burger?"

She stared up at him from her stroller, a miniature of her mother with the same blue eyes and strawberry hair, and nodded yes to all three. Daniel had hefted the stroller up the steps to the central food court, the scent of the salted ocean air giving way to grease and onions and stir-fry. He would get Trixie a burger and fries, he decided, and for himself, he'd buy a fisherman's platter at another kiosk. He stood in line at the grill, the stroller jutting out like a stone that altered the flow of human traffic. "A cheeseburger," Daniel yelled out to a cook he hoped was listening. When he was handed the paper plate he juggled his wallet free so that he could pay and then decided that it wasn't worth a second tour of duty just to get himself lunch, too. He and Trixie could share.

Daniel maneuvered the stroller into the stream of people again, waiting to be spit out into the cupola. After a few minutes, an elderly man sitting at a long table shuffled his trash together and left. Daniel set down the burger and turned the stroller so that he could feed Trixie—but the child inside was a dark-haired, dark-skinned infant who burst into tears when he saw the stranger in front of him.

Daniel's first thought: Why was this baby in Trixie's stroller? His second: *Was* this Trixie's stroller? Yes, it was yellow and blue with a tiny repeating bear print. Yes, there was a carrying basket underneath. But Graco must have sold millions of these, thousands alone in the Northeast. Now, at closer inspection, Daniel realized that this particular stroller had a plastic activity bar attached on the front. Trixie's ratty security blanket was not folded up in the bottom, just in case of crisis.

Such as now.

Daniel looked down at the baby again, the baby that was not his, and immediately grabbed the stroller and starting running to the grill. Standing there, with a cabbage-cheeked Boston cop, was a hysterical mother whose sights homed in on the stroller Daniel was using to part the crowd like the Red Sea. She ran the last ten feet and yanked her baby out of the safety restraint and into her arms while Daniel tried to explain, but all that came out of his mouth was, "Where is she?" He thought, hysterical, of the fact that this was an open-air market, that there was no way to seal the entrance or even make a general public announcement, that by now five minutes had passed and his daughter could be with the psychopath who stole her on the T heading to the farthest outskirts of the Boston suburbs.

Then he noticed the stroller—*his* stroller—kicked over onto its side, the safety belt undone. Trixie had gotten proficient at this just last week. It had gotten comical—they would be out walking and suddenly she was standing up in the fabric hammock, facing Daniel, grinning at her own clever expertise. Had she freed herself to come looking for him? Or had someone, seeing a golden opportunity for abduction, done it for her?

In the moments afterward, there were tracts of

time that Daniel couldn't remember even to this day. For example, how long it took the swarm of police that converged on Faneuil Hall to do a search. Or the way other mothers pulled their own children close to their side as he passed, certain bad luck was contagious. The detective's hammered questions, a quiz of good parenting: *How tall is Trixie? What does she weigh? What was she wearing? Have you ever talked to her about strangers?* This last one, Daniel couldn't answer. *Had* he, or had he just been *planning* to? Would Trixie know to scream, to run away? Would she be loud enough, fast enough?

The police wanted him to sit down, so that they'd know where to find him if necessary. Daniel nodded and promised, and then was on his feet the moment their backs were turned. He searched behind each of the food kiosks in the central court. He looked under the tables in the cupola. He burst into the women's bathroom, crying Trixie's name. He checked beneath the ruffled skirts of the pushcarts that sold rhinestone earrings, moose socks, your name written on a grain of rice. Then he ran outside.

The courtyard was full of people who didn't know that just twenty feet away from them the world had been overturned. Oblivious, they shopped and milled and laughed as Daniel stumbled past them. The corporate lunch hour had ended, and many of the businessmen were gone. Pigeons pecked at the crumbs they'd left behind, caught between the cobblestones. And huddled beside the seated bronze of Red Auerbach, sucking her thumb, was Trixie.

Until Daniel saw her, he didn't truly realize how much of himself had been carved away by her absence. He felt—ironically—the same symptoms that had come the moment he knew she was missing: the shaking legs, the loss of speech, the utter immobility. "Trixie," he said finally, then she was in his arms, thirty pounds of sweet relief.

Now—ten years later—Daniel had again mistaken his daughter for someone she wasn't. Except this time, she was no longer a four-year-old in a stroller. This time, she had been gone much longer than twenty-four minutes. And *she* had left *him*, instead of the other way around.

Forcing his mind back to the present, Daniel cut the throttle of the snow machine as he came to a fork in the path. Immediately the storm whipped into a funnel—he couldn't see two feet in front of himself, and when he took the time to look behind, his tracks had already been filled, a seamless stretch. The Yup'ik Eskimos had a word for this kind of snow, the kind that bit at the back of your eyes and landed like a hail of arrows on your bare skin: *pirrelvag.* The term rose in Daniel's throat, as startling as a second moon, proof that he had been here before, no matter how good a job he'd done of convincing himself otherwise.

He squinted—it was nine o'clock in the morning, but in December in Alaska, there wasn't much sunlight. His breath hung before him like lace. For a moment, through the curtain of snow, he thought he could see the bright flash of her hair—a fox's tail peeking from a snug woolen cap—but as quickly as he saw it, it was gone.

The Yupiit also had a word for the moments when it was so cold that a mug of water thrown into the air would harden like glass before it ever hit the frozen ground: *cikuq'erluni. One wrong move,* Daniel thought, *and everything will go to pieces around me.* So he closed his eyes, gunned the machine, and let instinct take over. Almost immediately, the voices of elders he used to know came back to him—*spruce needles stick out sharper on the north side of trees; shallow sandbars make the ice buckle*—hints about how to find yourself, when the world changed around you.

He suddenly thought back to the way, at Faneuil Hall, Trixie had melted against him when they were reunited. Her chin had notched just behind his shoulder, her body went boneless with faith. In spite of what he'd done, she'd still trusted him to keep her safe, to bring her home. In hindsight, Daniel could see that the real mistake he'd made that day hadn't been turning his back momentarily. It had been believing that you could lose someone you loved in an instant, when in reality it was a process that took months, years, her lifetime.

It was the kind of cold that made your eyelashes freeze the minute you walked outside and the insides of your nostrils feel like shattered glass. It was the kind of cold that went through you as if you were no more than a mesh screen. Trixie Stone shivered on the frozen riverbank beneath the school building that was checkpoint headquarters in Tuluksak, sixty miles from the spot where her father's borrowed snow machine was carving a signature across the tundra, and tried to think up reasons to stay right where she was.

Unfortunately, there were more reasons—*better* reasons—to leave. First and foremost, it was a mistake to stay in one place too long. Second, sooner or later, people were going to figure out that she wasn't who they thought she was, especially if she kept screwing up every task they gave her. But then again, how was she supposed to know that all the mushers were entitled to complimentary straw for their sled dogs at several points during the K300 racecourse, including here in Tuluksak? Or that you could take a musher to the spot where food and water was stored . . . but you weren't allowed to help feed the dogs? After those two fiascoes, Trixie was demoted to babysitting the dogs that were dropped from a team, until the bush pilots arrived to transport them back to Bethel.

So far the only dropped dog was a husky named Juno. Frostbite—that was the official reason given by the musher. The dog had one brown eye and one blue eye, and he stared at Trixie with an expression that spoke of being misunderstood.

In the past hour, Trixie had managed to sneak Juno an extra handful of kibble and a couple of biscuits, stolen from the vet's supply. She wondered if she could buy Juno from the musher with some of the money left over in the stolen wallet.

She thought maybe it would be easier to keep running if she had someone else to confide in, someone who couldn't possibly tell on her.

She wondered what Zephyr and Moss and anyone else back home in the other Bethel—Bethel, Maine—would say if they saw her sitting in a snowbank and eating salmon jerky and listening for the crazy fugue of barking that preceded the arrival of a dog team. Probably, they would think she had lost her mind. They'd say, *Who are you, and what have you done with Trixie Stone?* The thing is, she wanted to ask the same question.

She wanted to crawl into her favorite flannel pajamas, the ones that had been washed so often they were as soft as the skin of a rose. She wanted to open up the refrigerator and not be able to find anything on its stocked shelves worth eating. She wanted to get sick of a song on the radio and smell her father's shampoo and trip over the curly edge of the rug in the hallway. She wanted to go back—not just to Maine, but to early September.

Trixie could feel tears rising in her throat like the watermarks on the Portland dock, and she was afraid someone would notice. So she lay down on the matted straw, her nose nearly touching Juno's. "You know," she whispered, "I got left behind once, too."

Her father didn't think she remembered what had happened that day in Faneuil Hall, but she did—bits and pieces cropped up at the strangest times. Like when they went to the beach in the summer and she smelled the ocean: It suddenly got harder to breathe. Or how at hockey games and movie theaters and other places where she got mixed up in a crowd, she sometimes felt sick to her stomach. Trixie remembered, too, that they had abandoned the stroller at Faneuil Hall—her father simply carried her back in his arms. Even after they returned from vacation and bought a new stroller, Trixie had refused to ride in it.

Here's what she *didn't* remember about that day: the getting-lost part. Trixie could not recall unbuckling the safety harness or pushing through the shifting sea of legs to the doors that led outside. Then, she saw the man who looked like he might be her father but who actually turned out to be a statue sitting down. Trixie had walked to the bench and climbed up beside him only to realize that his metal skin was warm, because the sun had been beating down on it all day. She'd curled up against the statue, wishing with every shaky breath that she would be found.

This time around, that's what scared her most.

# #5
## DANIEL STONE

# THE IMMORTAL
# WILDCLAW

## IN: THE TENTH CIRCLE

DIRECT EDITION

$3.95 US $5.25 CAN

7 59606 05503 6

001111

I HAVE BEEN CALLED A *HERO.*

MAYBE *THAT'S* WHAT I AM.

I'VE BEEN CALLED A *BEAST.*

MAYBE *THAT'S* WHAT I AM.

ALL I KNOW FOR CERTAIN...

KNOCK KNOCK KNOCK

DAD! IF YOU DON'T LET ME USE THE *BATHROOM,* LIKE, FIVE *MINUTES AGO,* I'M GOING TO KILL YOU!

...IS THAT I'M A *FATHER.*

IT'S THE *ONLY* THING I'M SURE OF.

# 1

Laura Stone knew exactly how to go to hell.

She could map out its geography on napkins at departmental cocktail parties; she was able to recite all of the passageways and rivers and folds by heart; she was on a first-name basis with its sinners. As one of the top Dante scholars in the country, she taught a course in this very subject and had done so every year since being tenured at Monroe College. English 364 was also listed in the course handbook as Burn Baby Burn (or: What the Devil is the Inferno?), and it was one of the most popular courses on campus in the second trimester even though Dante's epic poem the *Divine Comedy* wasn't funny at all. Like her husband Daniel's artwork, which was neither *comic* nor a *book*, the *Inferno* covered every genre of pop culture: romance, horror, mystery, crime. And like all of the best stories, it had at its center an ordinary, everyday hero who simply didn't know how he'd ever become one.

She stared at the students packing the rows in the utterly silent lecture hall. "Don't move," she instructed. "Not even a twitch." Beside her, on the podium, an egg timer ticked away one full minute. She hid a smile as she watched the undergrads, all of whom suddenly had gotten the urge to sneeze or scratch their heads or wriggle.

Of the three parts of Dante's masterpiece, the *Inferno* was Laura's favorite to teach—who better to think about the nature of actions and their consequences than teenagers? The story was simple: Over the course of three days—Good Friday to Easter Sunday—Dante trekked through the nine levels of hell, each filled with sinners worse than the next, until finally he came through the other side. The poem was full of ranting and weeping and demons, of fighting lovers and traitors eating the brains of their victims—in other words, graphic enough to hold the interest of today's college students . . . and to provide a distraction from her real life.

The egg timer buzzed, and the entire class exhaled in unison. "Well?" Laura asked. "How did that feel?"

"Endless," a student called out.

"Anyone want to guess how long I timed you for?"

There was speculation: Two minutes. Five.

"Try sixty seconds," Laura said. "Now imagine being frozen from the waist down in a lake of ice for eternity. Imagine that the slightest movement would freeze the tears on your face and the water surrounding you. God, according to Dante, was all about motion and energy, so the ultimate punishment for Lucifer is to not be able to move at all. At the very bottom of hell, there's no fire, no brimstone, just the utter inability to take action." She cast her gaze across the sea of faces. "Is Dante right? After all, this is the very bottom of the barrel of hell, and the devil's the worst of the lot. Is taking away your ability to do whatever you want, *whenever* you want, the very worst punishment you can imagine?"

And that, in a nutshell, was why Laura loved Dante's *Inferno.* Sure, it could be seen as a study of religion or politics. Certainly it was a narrative of redemption. But when you stripped it down, it was also the story of a guy in the throes of a midlife crisis, a guy who was reevaluating the choices he'd made along the way.

Not unlike Laura herself.

As Daniel Stone waited in the long queue of cars pulling up to the high school, he glanced at the stranger in the seat beside him and tried to remember when she used to be his daughter.

"Traffic's bad today," he said to Trixie, just to fill up the space between them.

Trixie didn't respond. She fiddled with the radio, running through a symphony of static and song bites before punching it off entirely. Her red hair fell like a gash over her shoulder; her hands were burrowed in the sleeves of her North Face jacket. She turned to stare out the window, lost in a thousand thoughts, not a single one of which Daniel could guess.

These days it seemed like the words between them were there only to outline the silences. Daniel understood better than anyone else that, in the blink of an eye, you might reinvent yourself. He understood that the person you were yesterday might not be the person you are tomorrow. But this time, he was the one who wanted to hold on to what he had, instead of letting go.

*"Dad,"* she said, and she flicked her eyes ahead, where the car in front of them was moving forward.

It was a complete cliché, but Daniel had assumed that the traditional distance that came between teenagers and their parents would pass by him and Trixie. They had a different relationship, after all, closer than most daughters and their fathers, simply because he was the one she came home to every day. He had done his due diligence in her bathroom medicine cabinet and her desk drawers and underneath her mattress—there were no drugs, no accordion-pleated condoms. Trixie was just growing away from him, and somehow that was even worse.

For years she had floated into the house on the wings of her own stories: how the butterfly they were hatching in class had one of its antennae torn off by a boy who wasn't gentle; how the school lunch that day had been pizza when the notice *said* it was going to be chicken chow mein and how if she'd *known* that, she would have bought instead of bringing her own; how the letter *l* in cursive is nothing like you'd think. There had been so many easy words between them that Daniel was guilty of nodding every now and then and tuning out the excess. He hadn't known, at the time, that he should have been hoarding these, like bits of sea glass hidden in the pocket of his winter coat to remind him that once it had been summer.

This September—and here was another cliché—Trixie had gotten a boyfriend. Daniel had had his share of fantasies: how he'd be casually cleaning a pistol when she was picked up for her first date; how he'd buy a chastity belt on the Internet. In none of those scenarios, though, had he ever really considered how the sight of a boy with his proprietary hand around his daughter's waist might make him want to run until his lungs burst. And in none of these scenarios had he seen Trixie's face fill with light when the boy came to the door, the same way she'd once looked at Daniel. Overnight, the little girl who vamped for his home videos now moved like a vixen when she wasn't even trying. Overnight, his daughter's actions and habits stopped being cute and started being something terrifying.

His wife reminded him that the tighter he kept Trixie on a leash, the more she'd fight the choke hold. After all, Laura pointed out, rebelling against the system was what made her start dating Daniel. So when Trixie and Jason went out to a movie, Daniel forced himself to wish her a good time. When she escaped to her room to talk to her boyfriend privately on the phone, he did not hover at the door. He gave her breathing space, and somehow, that had become an immeasurable distance.

*"Hello?!"* Trixie said, snapping Daniel out of his reverie. The cars in front of them had pulled away, and the crossing guard was furiously miming to get Daniel to drive up.

"Well," he said. "Finally."

Trixie pulled at the door handle. "Can you let me out?"

Daniel fumbled with the power locks. "I'll see you at three."

"I don't need to be picked up."

Daniel tried to paste a wide smile on his face. "Jason driving you home?"

Trixie gathered together her backpack and jacket. "Yeah," she said. "Jason." She slammed the truck door and blended into the mass of teenagers funneling toward the front door of the high school.

"Trixie!" Daniel called out the window, so loud that several other kids turned around with her. Trixie's hand was clenched into a fist against her chest, as if she were holding tight to a secret. She looked at him, waiting.

There was a game they had played when Trixie was little, and would pore over the comic book collections he kept in his studio for research when he was drawing. *Best transportation?* she'd challenge, and Daniel would say the Batmobile. *No way*, Trixie had said. *Wonder Woman's invisible plane.*

*Best costume?*

*Wolverine*, Daniel said, but Trixie voted for the Dark Phoenix.

Now he leaned toward her. "Best superpower?" he asked.

It had been the only answer they agreed upon: *flight.* But this time, Trixie looked at him as if he were crazy to be bringing up a stupid game from a thousand years ago. "I'm going to be late," she said and started to walk away.

Cars honked, but Daniel didn't put the truck into gear. He closed his eyes, trying to remember what he had been like at her age. At fourteen, Daniel had been living in a different world and doing everything he could to fight, lie, cheat, steal, and brawl his way out of it. At fourteen, he had been someone Trixie had never seen her father be. Daniel had made sure of it.

"Daddy."

Daniel turned to find Trixie standing beside his truck. She curled her hands around the lip of the open window, the glitter in her pink nail polish catching the sun. "Invisibility," she said, and then she melted into the crowd behind her.

Trixie Stone had been a ghost for fourteen days, seven hours, and thirty-six minutes now, not that she was officially counting. This meant that she walked around school and smiled when she was supposed to; she pretended to listen when the algebra teacher talked about commutative properties; she even sat in the cafeteria with the other ninth-graders. But while they laughed at the lunch ladies' hairstyles (or lack thereof), Trixie studied her hands and wondered whether anyone else noticed that if the sun hit your palm a certain way, you could see right through the skin, to the busy tunnels with blood moving around inside. Corpuscles. She slipped the word into her mouth and tucked it high against her cheek like a sucking candy, so that if anyone happened to ask her a question she could just shake her head, unable to speak.

Kids who knew (and who didn't? the news had traveled like a forest fire) were waiting to see her lose her careful balance. Trixie had even overheard one girl making a *bet* about when she might fall apart in a public situation. High school students were cannibals; they fed off your broken heart while you watched and then shrugged and offered you a bloody, apologetic smile.

Visine helped. So did Preparation H under the eyes, as disgusting as it was to imagine. Trixie would get up at five-thirty in the morning, carefully select a double layer of long-sleeved T-shirts and a pair of flannel pants, and gather her hair into a messy ponytail. It took an hour to make herself look like she'd just rolled out of bed, like she'd been losing no sleep at all over what had happened. These days, her entire life was about making people believe she was someone she wasn't anymore.

Trixie crested the hallway on a sea of noise—lockers gnashing like teeth, guys yelling out afternoon plans over the heads of underclassmen, change being dug out of pockets for vending machines. She turned into a doorway and steeled herself to endure the next forty-eight minutes. Psychology was the only class she had with Jason, who was a junior. It was an elective. Which was a fancy way of saying: *You asked for this.*

He was already there; she knew by the way the air had taken a charge around her body, an electric field. He was wearing the faded denim shirt she'd borrowed once when he spilled Coke on her while they were studying, and his black hair was a mess. *You need a part*, she used to tell him, and he'd laugh. *I've got better ones*, he'd say.

She could smell him—shampoo and peppermint gum and, believe it or not, the cool white mist of utter ice. It was the same smell on the T-shirt she'd hidden in the bottom of her pajama drawer, the one he didn't know she had, the one she wrapped around her pillow each night before she went to sleep. It kept the details in her dreams: a callus on the edge of Jason's wrist, rubbed raw by his hockey glove. The flannel-covered sound of his voice when she called him on the phone and woke him. The way he twirled a pencil around the fingers of one hand when he was nervous or thinking too hard.

He'd been doing that when he broke up with her.

She took a deep breath and headed past the seat where Jason slouched, his eyes focused on the four-letter words students had worn into the desktop through years of boredom. She could feel his face heat up with the effort he was making to avoid looking at her. It felt unnatural to walk past, to not have him tug on the straps of her backpack until she gave him her full attention. "You're coming to practice," he'd say, "right?" As if there had ever been any question.

Mr. Torkelson had assigned seating, and Trixie had been placed in the first row—something she had hated for the first three months of the school year and now was supremely grateful for, because it meant she could stare at the board and not have to see Jason or anyone else out of the corner of her eye. She slipped into the chair and opened her binder, her eyes avoiding the big Wite-Out centipede that used to be Jason's name.

When she felt a hand on her shoulder—a warm, broad, guy's hand—all the breath left her body. Jason was going to apologize; he'd realized that he'd made a mistake; he wanted to ask her if she'd ever forgive him. She turned around, the word *yes* playing over her lips like the call of a flute, but instead found herself staring at Moss Minton, Jason's best friend.

"Hey." He glanced back over his shoulder to where Jason was still hunched over his own desk. "You okay?"

Trixie smoothed the edges of her homework. "Why wouldn't I be?"

"I just want you to know we all think he's an idiot."

*We.* We could be the state champion hockey team, of which Moss and Jason were cocaptains. It could be the whole of the junior class. It could be anyone who wasn't her. That part of it was almost

as hard as the not having Jason: trying to negotiate through the minefield of the friends they'd
shared, to learn who still belonged to her.

"I think she's just something he needs to get out
of his system," Moss said, his words a handful of
stones dropped from a cliff.

Trixie's handwriting started to swim on the page
before her. *Please leave*, she thought, praying
fiercely for the telekinetic power to cause a distraction, and for once in her life something went right.
Mr. Torkelson walked in, slammed the door, and
came to the front of the classroom. "Ladies and
gentlemen," he announced, "why do we dream?"

A stoner in the back row answered. "Because
Angelina Jolie doesn't go to Bethel High."

The teacher laughed. "Well, that's one reason.
Sigmund Freud might even agree with you. He
called dreams a 'royal road' into the unconscious,
made up of all the forbidden wishes you had and
wished you didn't."

Dreams, Trixie thought, were like soap bubbles.
You could look at them from a distance, and they
were lovely. It's when you stuck your face too close
that your eyes wound up stinging. She wondered if
Jason had the same dreams she did, the kind
where you wake up with all your breath gone and
your heart as flat as a dime.

"Ms. Stone?" the teacher repeated.

Trixie blushed. She had no idea what Torkelson
had asked. She could feel Jason's gaze rising like
a welt on the back of her neck.

"I've got one, Mr. T," Moss called out from

somewhere behind her. "I'm skating out at the regionals, and a pass comes my way, but all of a sudden my stick is like a piece of spaghetti—"

"As blatantly Freudian as that is, Moss, I'd really like to hear from Trixie."

Like one of her father's superheroes, Trixie's senses narrowed. She could hear the girl in the back of the class scratching out a secret note to her friend across the aisle, Torkelson clasping his hands together, and worst of all, that broken connection as Jason closed his eyes. She scribbled on her thumbnail with her pen. "I don't remember any dreams."

"You spend a sixth of your life dreaming, Ms. Stone. Which in your case amounts to about two and a half years. Certainly you haven't blocked out two and a half years of your life?"

She shook her head, looked up at the teacher, and opened her mouth. "I . . . I'm going to be sick," Trixie managed, and with the classroom wheeling around her, she grabbed her books and fled.

In the bathroom, she flung her backpack under the row of square white sinks that looked like a giant's dentures and crouched in front of one of the toilets. She vomited, although she would have wagered that there was nothing inside of her. Then she sat on the floor and pressed her hot cheek against the metal wall of the stall.

It was not that Jason had broken up with her on their three-month anniversary. It was not that Trixie—a freshman who'd seemed to have hit the jackpot, a nobody elevated to the level of queen by association—had lost her Cinderella status. It was that she truly believed you could be fourteen when you learned how love could change the speed your blood ran through you, how it made you dream in kaleidoscope color. It was that Trixie knew she couldn't have loved Jason this hard if he hadn't loved her that way too.

Trixie came out of the stall and turned the water on in the sink. She splashed her face, wiped it with a brown paper towel. She didn't want to go back to class, not ever, so she took out her eyeliner and mascara, her lip gloss and her compact mirror. She had her mother's rich copper hair, her father's dark complexion. Her ears were too pointed and her chin was too round. Her lips were okay, she guessed. Once, in art class, a teacher had said they were classic and made the rest of the students draw them. It was her eyes, though, that scared her. Although they used to be a dark mossy color, nowadays they were a frosted green so pale it was barely a color at all. Trixie wondered if you could cry away the pigment.

She snapped shut her compact and then, on second thought, opened it and set it on the floor. It took three stomps before the mirror inside shattered. Trixie threw out the plastic disc and all but one shard of glass. It was shaped like a tear, rounded on one end and sharp as a dagger on the other.

She slid down along the tiled wall of the bathroom until she was sitting underneath the sink.

Then she dragged the makeshift knife over the white canvas of her inner arm. As soon as she did it, she wished she could take it back. Crazy girls did this, girls who walked like zombies through YA novels.

But.

Trixie felt the sting of the skin as it split, the sweet welling rise of blood.

It hurt, though not as much as everything else.

"You have to do something pretty awful to wind up in the bottom level of hell," Laura said rhetorically, surveying her class. "And Lucifer used to be God's right-hand man. So what went wrong?"

It had been a simple disagreement, Laura thought. Like almost every other rift between people, that's how it started. "One day God turned to his buddy Lucifer and said that he was thinking of giving those cool little toys he created—namely, people—the right to choose how they acted. Free will. Lucifer thought that power should belong only to angels. He staged a coup, and he lost big-time."

Laura started walking through the aisles—one downside of free Internet access at the college was that kids used lecture hours to shop online and download porn, if the professor wasn't vigilant. "What makes the *Inferno* so brilliant are the *contrapassi*—the punishments that fit the crime. In Dante's mind, sinners pay in a way that reflects what they did wrong on earth. Lucifer didn't want man to have choices, so he winds up literally paralyzed in ice. Fortune-tellers walk around with their heads on backward. Adulterers end up joined to-gether for eternity, without getting any satisfaction from it." Laura shook off the image that rose in her mind. "Apparently," she joked, "the clinical trials for Viagra were done in hell."

Her class laughed as she headed toward her podium. "In the 1300s—before Italians could tune in to *The Revenge of the Sith* or *Lord of the Rings*—this poem was the ultimate battle of good versus evil," she said. "I like the word *evil.* Scramble it a little, and you get *vile* and *live. Good*, on the other hand, is just a command to *go do.*"

The four graduate students who led the class sections for this course were all sitting in the front row with their computers balanced on their knees. Well, three of them were. There was Alpha, the self-christened retrofeminist, which as far as Laura could tell meant that she gave a lot of speeches about how modern women had been driven so far from the home they no longer felt comfortable inside it. Beside her, Aine scrawled on the inside of one alabaster arm—most likely her own poetry. Naryan, who could type faster than Laura could breathe, looked up over his laptop at her, a crow poised for a crumb. Only Seth sprawled in his chair, his eyes closed, his long hair spilling over his face. Was he *snoring*?

She felt a flush rise up the back of her neck. Turning her back on Seth Dummerston, she glanced up at the clock in the back of the lecture hall. "That's it for today. Read through the fifth canto," Laura instructed. "Next Wednesday, we'll be talking about poetic justice versus divine retribution. And have a nice weekend, folks."

The students gathered their backpacks and laptops, chattering about the bands that were playing later on, and the BΘΠ party that had brought in a truckload of real sand for Caribbean Night. They wound scarves around their necks like bright bandages and filed out of the lecture hall, already dismissing Laura's class from their minds.

Laura didn't need to prepare for her next lecture; she was living it. *Be careful what you wish for*, she thought. *You just might get it.*

Six months ago, she had been so sure that what she was doing was right, a liaison so natural that stopping it was more criminal than letting it flourish. When his hands roamed over her, she transformed: no longer the cerebral Professor Stone but a woman for whom feeling came before thought. Now, though, when Laura realized what she had done, she wanted to blame a tumor, temporary insanity, anything but her own selfishness. Now all she wanted was damage control: to break it off, to slip back into the seam of her family before they had a chance to realize how long she'd been missing.

When the lecture hall was empty, Laura turned off the overhead lights. She dug in her pocket for her office keys. Damn, had she left them in her computer bag?

*"Veil."*

Laura turned around, already recognizing the soft Southern curves of Seth Dummerston's voice.

He stood up and stretched, unfolding his long body after that nap. "It's another anagram for *evil*," he said. "The things we hide."

She stared at him coolly. "You fell asleep during my lecture."

"I had a late night."

"Whose fault is that?" Laura asked.

Seth stared at her the way she used to stare at him, then bent forward until his mouth brushed over hers. "You tell me," he whispered.

Trixie turned the corner and saw them: Jessica Ridgeley, with her long sweep of blond hair and her dermatologist's-daughter skin, was leaning against the door of the AV room kissing Jason.

Trixie became a rock, the sea of students parting around her. She watched Jason's hands slip into the back pockets of Jessica's jeans. She could see the dimple on the left side of his mouth, the one that appeared only when he was speaking from the heart.

Was he telling Jessica that his favorite sound was the thump that laundry made when it was turning around in a dryer? That sometimes he could walk by the telephone and think she was going to call, and sure enough she did? That once, when he was ten, he broke into a candy machine because he wanted to know what happened to the quarters once they went inside?

Was she even *listening*?

Suddenly, Trixie felt someone grab her arm and start dragging her down the hall, out the door, and into the courtyard. She smelled the acrid twitch of a match, and a minute later, a cigarette had been stuck between her lips. "Inhale," Zephyr commanded.

Zephyr Santorelli-Weinstein was Trixie's oldest friend. She had enormous doe eyes and olive skin and the coolest mother on the planet, one who bought her incense for her room and took her to get her navel pierced like it was an adolescent rite. She had a father, too, but he lived in California with his new family, and Trixie knew better than to bring up the subject. "What class have you got next?"

"French."

"Madame Wright is senile. Let's ditch."

Bethel High had an open campus, not because the administration was such a fervent promoter of teen freedom but because there was simply nowhere to go. Trixie walked beside Zephyr along the access road to the school, their faces ducked against the wind, their hands stuffed into the pockets of their North Face jackets. The crisscross pattern where she'd cut herself an hour earlier on her arm wasn't bleeding anymore, but the cold made it sting. Trixie automatically started breathing through her mouth, because even from a distance, she could smell the gassy, rotten-egg odor from the paper mill to the north that employed most of the adults in Bethel. "I heard what happened in psych," Zephyr said.

"Great," Trixie muttered. "Now the whole world thinks I'm a loser *and* a freak."

Zephyr took the cigarette from Trixie's hand and

smoked the last of it. "What do you care what the whole world thinks?"

"Not the whole world," Trixie admitted. She felt her eyes prickle with tears again, and she wiped her mitten across them. "I want to kill Jessica Ridgeley."

"If I were you, I'd want to kill Jason," Zephyr said. "Why do you let it get to you?"

Trixie shook her head. "I'm the one who's supposed to be with him, Zephyr. I just *know* it."

They had reached the turn of the river past the park-and-ride, where the bridge stretched over the Androscoggin River. This time of year, it was nearly frozen over, with great swirling art sculptures that formed as ice built up around the rocks that crouched in the riverbed. If they kept walking another quarter mile, they'd reach the town, which basically consisted of a Chinese restaurant, a mini-mart, a bank, a toy store, and a whole lot of nothing else.

Zephyr watched Trixie cry for a few minutes, then leaned against the railing of the bridge. "You want the good news or the bad news?"

Trixie blew her nose in an old tissue she'd found in her pocket. "Bad news."

"Martyr," Zephyr said, grinning. "The bad news is that my best friend has officially exceeded her two-week grace period for mourning over a relationship, and she will be penalized from here on in."

At that, Trixie smiled a little. "What's the good news?"

"Moss Minton and I have sort of been hanging out."

Trixie felt another stab in her chest. Her best friend, and Jason's? "Really?"

"Well, maybe we weren't actually *hanging out.* He waited for me after English class today to ask me if you were okay . . . but still, the way I figure it, he could have asked *anyone*, right?"

Trixie wiped her nose. "Great. I'm glad my misery is doing wonders for your love life."

"Well, it's sure as hell not doing anything for *yours.* You can't keep crying over Jason. He knows you're obsessed." Zephyr shook her head. "Guys don't want high maintenance, Trix. They want . . . Jessica Ridgeley."

"What the fuck does he see in her?"

Zephyr shrugged. "Who knows. Bra size? Neanderthal IQ?" She pulled her messenger bag forward, so that she could dig inside for a pack of M&M's. Hanging from the edge of the bag were twenty linked pink paper clips.

Trixie knew girls who kept a record of sexual encounters in a journal, or by fastening safety pins to the tongue of a sneaker. For Zephyr, it was paper clips. "A guy can't hurt you if you don't let him," Zephyr said, running her finger across the paper clips so that they danced.

These days, having a boyfriend or a girlfriend was not in vogue; most kids trolled for random hookups. The sudden thought that Trixie might have been that to Jason made her feel sick to her stomach. "I can't be like that."

Zephyr ripped open the bag of candy and passed it to Trixie. "Friends with benefits. It's what the guys want, Trix."

"How about what the girls want?"

Zephyr shrugged. "Hey, I suck at algebra, I can't sing on key, and I'm always the last one picked for a team in gym . . . but apparently I'm quite gifted when it comes to hooking up."

Trixie turned, laughing. "They *tell* you that?"

"Don't knock it until you've tried it. You get all the fun without any of the baggage. And the next day you just act like it never happened."

Trixie tugged on the paper clip chain. "If you're acting like it never happened, then why are you keeping track?"

"Once I hit a hundred, I can send away for the free decoder ring." Zephyr shrugged. "I don't know. I guess it's just so I remember where I started."

Trixie opened her palm and surveyed the M&M's. The food coloring dye was already starting to bleed against her skin. "Why do you think the commercials say they won't melt in your hands, when they always do?"

"Because everyone lies," Zephyr replied.

All teenagers knew this was true. The process of growing up was nothing more than figuring out what doors hadn't yet been slammed in your face. For years, Trixie's own parents had told her that she could be anything, have anything, do anything. That was why she'd been so eager to grow up— until she got to adolescence and hit a big, fat wall of reality. As it turned out, she *couldn't* have any-thing she wanted. You didn't get to be pretty or smart or popular just because you wanted it. You didn't control your own destiny; you were too busy trying to fit in. Even now, as she stood here, there were a million parents setting their kids up for heartbreak.

Zephyr stared out over the railing. "This is the third time I've cut English this week."

In French class, Trixie was missing a quiz on *le subjonctif.* Verbs, apparently, had moods too: They had to be conjugated a whole different way if they were used in clauses to express want, doubt, wishes, judgment. She had memorized the red-flag phrases last night: *It is doubtful that. It's not clear that. It seems that. It may be that. Even though. No matter what. Without.*

She didn't need a stupid *leçon* to teach her something she'd known for years: Given anything negative or uncertain, there were rules that had to be followed.

If he had the choice, Daniel would draw a villain every time.

There just wasn't all that much you could do with heroes. They came with a set of traditional standards: square jaw, overdeveloped calves, per-fect teeth. They stood half a foot taller than your average man. They were anatomical marvels, intri-cate displays of musculature. They sported ridicu-lous knee-high boots that no one without superhu-man strength would be caught dead wearing.

On the other hand, your average bad guy might have a face shaped like an onion, an anvil, a pancake. His eyes could bulge out or recess in the folds of his skin. His physique might be meaty or cadaverous, furry or rubberized, or covered with lizard scales. He could speak in lightning, throw fire, swallow mountains. A villain let your creativity out of its cage.

The problem was, you couldn't have one without the other. There couldn't be a bad guy unless there was a good guy to create the standard. And there couldn't be a good guy until a bad guy showed just how far off the path he might stray.

Today Daniel sat hunched at his drafting table, procrastinating. He twirled his mechanical pencil; he kneaded an eraser in his palm. He was having a hell of a time turning his main character into a hawk. He had gotten the wingspan right, but he couldn't seem to humanize the face behind the bright eyes and beak.

Daniel was a comic book penciler. While Laura had built up the academic credentials to land her a tenured position at Monroe College, he'd worked out of the home with Trixie at his feet as he drew filler chapters for DC Comics. His style got him noticed by Marvel, which asked him numerous times to come work in NYC on Ultimate X-Men, but Daniel put his family before his career. He did graphic art to pay the mortgage—logos and illustrations for corporate newsletters—until last year, just before his fortieth birthday, when Marvel signed him to work from home on a project all his own.

He kept a picture of Trixie over his workspace—not just because he loved her, but because for this particular graphic novel—*The Tenth Circle*—she was his inspiration. Well, Trixie *and* Laura. Laura's obsession with Dante had provided the barebones plot of the story; Trixie had provided the impetus. But it was Daniel who was responsible for creating his main character—Wildclaw—a hero that this industry had never seen.

Historically, comics had been geared toward teenage boys. Daniel had pitched Marvel a different concept: a character designed for the demographic group of adults who had been weaned on comic books yet who now had the spending power they'd lacked as adolescents. Adults who wanted sneakers endorsed by Michael Jordan and watched news programs that looked like MTV segments and played Tetris on a Nintendo DS during their business-class flights. Adults who would immediately identify with Wildclaw's alter ego, Duncan: a fortysomething father who knew that getting old was hell, who wanted to keep his family safe, whose powers controlled him, instead of the other way around.

The narrative of the graphic novel followed Duncan, an ordinary father searching for his daughter, who had been kidnapped by the devil into Dante's circles of hell. When provoked, through rage or fear, Duncan would morph into Wildclaw—literally becoming an animal. The catch was this: Power always involved a loss of humanity. If Duncan turned into a hawk or a bear or a wolf to elude a dangerous creature, a piece of him would stay that way. His biggest fear was that if and when he *did* find his missing daughter, she would no longer recognize who he'd become in order to save her.

Daniel looked down at what he had on the page so far, and sighed. The problem wasn't drawing the hawk—he could do that in his sleep—it was making sure the reader saw the human behind it. It was not new to have a hero who turned into an animal—but Daniel had come by the concept honestly. He'd grown up as the only white boy in a native Alaskan village where his mother was a schoolteacher and his father was simply gone. In Akiak, the Yupiit spoke freely of children who went to live with seals, of men who shared a home with black bears. One woman had married a dog and given birth to puppies, only to peel back the fur to see they were actually babies underneath. Animals were simply nonhuman people, with the same ability to make conscious decisions, and humanity simmered under their skins. You could see it in the way they sat together for meals, or fell in love, or grieved. And this went both ways: Sometimes, in a human, there would turn out to be a hidden bit of a beast.

Daniel's best and only friend in the village was a Yup'ik boy named Cane, whose grandfather had taken it upon himself to teach Daniel how to hunt and fish and everything else that his own father should have. For example, how after killing a rabbit, you had to be quiet, so that the animal's spirit could visit. How at fish camp, you'd set the bones of the salmon free in the river, whispering *Ataam taikina.* Come back again.

Daniel spent most of his childhood waiting to leave. He was a *kass'aq*, a white kid, and this was reason enough to be teased or bullied or beaten. By the time he was Trixie's age, he was getting drunk, damaging property, and making sure the rest of the world knew better than to fuck with him. But when he wasn't doing those things, he was drawing—characters who, against all odds, fought and won. Characters he hid in the margins of his schoolbooks and on the canvas of his bare palm. He drew to escape, and eventually, at age seventeen, he did.

Once Daniel left Akiak, he never looked back. He learned how to stop using his fists, how to put rage on the page instead. He got a foothold in the comics industry. He never talked about his life in Alaska, and Trixie and Laura knew better than to ask. He became a typical suburban father who coached soccer and grilled burgers and mowed the lawn, a man you'd never expect had been accused of something so awful that he'd tried to outrun himself.

Daniel squeezed the eraser he was kneading and completely rubbed out the hawk he'd been attempting to draw. Maybe if he started with Duncan-the-man, instead of Wildclaw-the-beast? He took his mechanical pencil and started sketching the loose ovals and scribbled joints that materialized into his unlikely hero. No spandex, no high boots, no half mask: Duncan's habitual costume was a battered jacket, jeans, and sarcasm. Like Daniel, Duncan had shaggy dark hair and a dark complexion. Like Daniel, Duncan had a teenage daughter. And like Daniel, everything Duncan did or didn't do was linked to a past that he refused to discuss.

When you got right down to it, Daniel was secretly drawing himself.

Jason's car was an old Volvo that had belonged to his grandmother before she died. The seats had been reupholstered in pink, her favorite color, by his grandfather for her eighty-fifth birthday. Jason had told Trixie he used to think about changing them back to their original flesh tone, but how could you mess with that kind of love?

Hockey practice had ended fifteen minutes ago. Trixie waited in the cold, her hands tucked into the sleeves of her jacket, until Jason came out of the rink. His enormous hockey bag was slung over his shoulder, and he was laughing as he walked beside Moss.

Hope was a pathological part of puberty, like acne and surging hormones. You might sound cynical to the world, but that was just a defense mechanism, cover-up coating a zit, because it was too embarrassing to admit that in spite of the bum deals you kept getting, you hadn't completely given up.

When Jason noticed her, Trixie tried to pretend

she didn't see the look that ghosted over his face—regret, or maybe resignation. She concentrated instead on the fact that he was walking toward her alone. "Hey," she said evenly. "Can you give me a ride home?"

He hesitated, long enough for her to die inside all over again. Then he nodded and unlocked the car. She slid into the passenger seat while Jason stowed his gear, turned over the ignition, and blasted the heater. Trixie thought up a thousand questions—*How was practice? Do you think it'll snow again? Do you miss me?*—but she couldn't speak. It was too much, sitting there on the pink seats, just a foot away from Jason, the way she'd sat beside him in this car a hundred times before.

He pulled out of the parking spot and cleared his throat. "You feeling better?"

Than *what*? she thought.

"You left psych this morning," Jason reminded her.

That class seemed like forever ago. Trixie tucked her hair behind her ear. "Yeah," she said, and glanced down. Trixie thought of how she used to grasp the stick shift, so that when Jason reached for it, he would automatically be holding her hand. She slid her palm beneath her thigh and gripped the seat so she wouldn't do anything stupid.

"What are you doing here, anyway?" Jason said.

"I wanted to ask you something." Trixie took a deep breath for courage. "How do you do it?"

"Do what?"

"All of it. You know. Go to class and practice. Make it through the day. Act like . . . like none of it mattered."

Jason swore beneath his breath and pulled the car over. Then he reached across the seat and brushed his thumb over her cheek; until then, she hadn't been aware she was crying. "Trix," he sighed, "it mattered."

By now, the tears were coming faster. "But I *love* you," Trixie said. There was no easy switch that she could flip to stem the flow of feelings, no way to drain the memories that pooled like acid in her stomach because her heart no longer knew what to do with them. She couldn't blame Jason; she didn't like herself like this, either. But she couldn't go back to being the girl she'd been before she met him; that girl was gone. So where did *that* leave her?

Jason was wavering, she could tell. When he reached over the console to pull her into his arms, she tucked her head against his neck and rounded her mouth against the salt of his skin. *Thank you*, she murmured, to God or Jason or maybe both.

His words stirred the hair beside her ear. "Trixie, you've got to stop. It's over."

The sentence—and that's exactly what it was, in every sense of the word—fell between them like a guillotine. Trixie disengaged herself, wiping her eyes on the puffy sleeve of her coat. "If it's *us*," she whispered, "how come *you* get to decide?"

When he didn't answer—*couldn't* answer—she turned and stared out the front window. As it turned out, they were still in the parking lot. They hadn't gotten anywhere at all.

The entire way home, Laura planned the way she was going to break the news to Seth. As flattering as it was to have a twentysomething man find a thirty-eight-year-old woman attractive, it was also wrong: Laura was his professor; she was married; she was a mother. She belonged in a reality made up of faculty meetings and papers being published and think tanks conducted at the home of the dean of humanities, not to mention parent-teacher conferences at Trixie's school and worries about her own metabolism slowing down and whether she could save money on her cellular service if she switched companies. She told herself that it did not matter that Seth made her feel like summer fruit about to drop from a vine, something she could not remember experiencing anytime in the last decade with Daniel.

Doing something wrong, it turned out, packed a heady adrenaline rush. Seth was dark and uneven and unpredictable and—oh, God, just thinking about him was making her drive too fast on this road. On the other hand, Laura's husband was the most solid, dependable, mild-mannered man in all of Maine. Daniel never forgot to put out the recycling bin; he set the coffee to brew the night before because she was a bear when she didn't have any in the morning; he never once complained about the fact that it had taken a good decade longer than he'd liked to make a name for himself in the comics industry because he was the stay-at-home parent. Sometimes, ridiculously, the more perfect he was the angrier she got, as if his generosity existed only to highlight her own selfishness. But then, she had only herself to blame for that—wasn't she the one who'd given him the ultimatum, who'd said he had to change?

The problem was (if she was going to be honest with herself) that when she asked him to change, she was focusing on what she thought she needed. She'd forgotten to catalog all the things she'd lose. What she had loved most about Seth—the thrill of doing something forbidden, the understanding that women like her did not connect with men like him—was exactly what had once made her fall for Daniel.

She had toyed with the idea of telling Daniel about the affair, but what good would that do, except hurt him? Instead, she would overcompensate. She would kill him with kindness. She would be the best wife, the best mother, the most attentive lover. She would give him back what she hoped he never realized had been missing.

Even Dante said that if you walked through hell, you could climb your way to paradise.

In the rearview mirror, Laura saw a carnival of flashing lights. "God*damn*," she muttered, pulling over as the police cruiser slid neatly behind her Toyota.

A tall officer walked toward her, silhouetted by the headlights of his vehicle. "Good evening, ma'am, did you know you were speeding?"

*Apparently not*, thought Laura.

"I'm going to need your license and . . . Professor Stone? Is that you?"

Laura peered up at the officer's face. She couldn't place it, but he was young enough; she might have taught him. She offered her most humble expression. Had he gotten a high enough grade in her class to keep her from getting a ticket?

"Bernie Aylesworth," he said, smiling down at Laura. "I took your Dante class my senior year, back in 2001. Got shut out of it the year before."

She knew she was a popular teacher—her Dante course was rated even higher than the Intro to Physics lectures where Jeb Wetherby shot monkeys out of cannons to teach projectile motion. The *Unauthorized Guide to Monroe College* named her the prof students most wanted to take out for a beer. *Had Seth read that?* she thought suddenly.

"I'm just gonna give you a warning this time," Bernie said, and Laura wondered where he had been six months ago, when she truly needed one. He passed her a crisp piece of paper and smiled. "So where were you hurrying off to?"

Not *to*, she thought, just *back.* "Home," she told him. "I was headed home." She waited until he was back in the cruiser to put on her signal—a penitent motion if ever there was one—and pulled into the gentle bend of the road. She drove well within the speed limit, her eyes focused ahead, as careful as you have to be when you know someone is watching.

• • •

"I'm leaving," Laura said the minute she walked through the door. Daniel looked up from the kitchen counter, where he was chopping broccoli in preparation for dinner. On the stove, chicken was simmering in garlic.

"You just got here," he said.

"I know." Laura lifted the lid on the skillet, breathed in. "Smells really good. I wish I *could* stay."

He could not pinpoint what was different about her, but he thought it had to do with the fact that when she'd just said she wanted to be home, he believed her—most of the time, if she apologized for leaving, it was only because it was expected. "What's going on?" he asked.

She turned her back to Daniel and began to sort through the mail. "That departmental thing I told you about."

She had not told him; he *knew* she hadn't told him. She unwound her scarf and shrugged out of her coat, draped them over a chair. She was wearing a black suit and Sorel boots, which were tracking snow in small puddles all over the kitchen floor. "How's Trixie?"

"She's in her room."

Laura opened the refrigerator and poured herself a glass of water. "The crazy poet is trying to stage a coup," she said. "She's been talking to the tenured professors. I don't think she knows that—" Suddenly, there was a crash, and Daniel turned in time to see the glass explode against the tile floor.

Water spread in a puddle, seeping beneath the edge of the refrigerator. "Damn it!" Laura cried, kneeling to pick up the pieces.

"I've got it," Daniel said, tossing down paper towels to absorb the spill. "You've got to slow down. You're bleeding."

Laura glanced down at the gash on the pad of her thumb as if it belonged to someone else. Daniel reached for her and wrapped her hand in a clean dish towel. They knelt inches apart on the tile floor, watching her blood soak through the checkered fabric.

Daniel couldn't remember the last time he and Laura had been this close to each other. He couldn't remember a lot of things, like the sound of his wife's breathing when she gave herself over to sleep, or the half smile that slipped out like a secret when something took her by surprise. He had tried to tell himself that Laura was busy, the way she always got at the beginning of a trimester. He did not ask if it could be anything more than that, because he did not want to hear the answer.

"We need to take care of that," Daniel said. The bones of her wrist were light and fine in his hand, delicate as china.

Laura tugged herself free. "I'm fine," she insisted, and she stood up. "It's a scratch." For a moment she stared at him, as if she knew, too, that there was another entire conversation going on here, one they had chosen *not* to have.

"Laura." Daniel got to his feet, but she turned away.

"I really have to go change," she said.

Daniel watched her leave, heard her footsteps on the stairs overhead. *You already have*, he thought.

"You *didn't*," Zephyr said.

Trixie pushed her sleeves up and stared down at the cuts on her arms, a red web of regret. "It seemed like a good idea at the time," she said. "I started walking, and I wound up at the rink . . . I figured it was a sign. If we could just talk—"

"Trixie, right now Jason doesn't want to talk. He wants to take out a restraining order." Zephyr sighed. "You are *so Fatal Attraction*."

"Fatal what?"

"It's an old movie. Don't you ever watch anything that doesn't have Paul Walker in it?"

Trixie tucked the phone between her shoulder and her ear and carefully unwound the screw neck of the X-Acto knife that she'd taken from her father's office. The blade came out, a tiny silver trapezoid. "I'd do anything to get him back." Closing her eyes, Trixie scored the blade over her left arm. She sucked in her breath and imagined she was opening up a vent, allowing some of the enormous pressure to ease.

"Are you going to complain about this until we graduate?" Zephyr asked. "Because if that's the case, then I'm taking matters into my own hands."

What if her father knocked on the door right now? What if anyone, even Zephyr, found out that she was doing stuff like this? Maybe it wasn't relief she was feeling, but shame. Both made you burn from the inside out.

"So, do you want my help?" Zephyr asked.

Trixie clapped her hand over the cut, stanching the flow.

"Hello?" Zephyr said. "Are you still there?"

Trixie lifted her hand. The blood was rich and bright against her palm. "Yeah," she sighed. "I guess I am."

"Good timing," Daniel said, as he heard Trixie's footsteps pounding down the stairs. He set two plates on the kitchen table and turned around to find her waiting in her coat, carrying a backpack. Her cascade of hair spilled out from beneath a striped stocking cap.

"Oh," she said, blinking at the food. "Zephyr invited me for a sleepover."

"You can go after you eat."

Trixie bit her lower lip. "Her mom thinks I'm coming for dinner."

Daniel had known Zephyr since she was seven. He used to sit in the living room while she and Trixie performed the cheerleading moves they'd made up during an afternoon of play, or lip-synched to the radio, or presented tumbling routines. He could practically still hear them doing a hand-clapping game: *The spades go eeny-meeny pop zoombini . . .*

Last week, Daniel had walked in with a bag of groceries to find someone unfamiliar in the kitchen, bent over a catalog. *Nice ass*, he thought, until she straightened and turned out to be Zephyr. "Hey, Mr. Stone," she'd said. "Trixie's in the bathroom."

She hadn't noticed that he went red in the face, or that he left the kitchen before his own daughter returned. He sat on the couch with the grocery bag in his hands, the ice cream inside softening against his chest, as he speculated whether there were other fathers out there making the same mistake when they happened upon Trixie.

"Well," he said now, "I'll just save the leftovers." He stood up, fishing for his car keys.

"Oh, that's okay. I can walk."

"It's dark out," Daniel said.

Trixie met his gaze, challenging. "I think I can manage to get to a house three blocks away. I'm not a baby, Dad."

Daniel didn't know what to say. She *was* a baby, to him. "Then maybe before you go to Zephyr's you could go vote, join the army, and rent us a car . . . oh, hang on, that's right. You *can't.*"

Trixie rolled her eyes, took off her hat and gloves, and sat down.

"I thought you were eating at Zephyr's."

"I will," she said. "But I don't want you to have to eat all by yourself."

Daniel sank into the chair across from her. He had a sudden flashback of Trixie in ballet class, the two of them struggling to capture her fine hair in a netted bun before the session began. He had always been the sole father present; other men's wives would rush forward to help him figure out how to secure the bobby pins, how to slick back the bangs with hair spray.

At her first and only ballet performance, Trixie had been the lead reindeer, drawing out the sleigh that held the Sugar Plum Fairy. She wore a white leotard and an antler headband and had a painted red nose. Daniel hadn't taken his eyes off her, not for any of the three minutes and twenty-two seconds that she stood on that stage.

He didn't want to take his eyes off her now, but part of this new routine of adolescence meant a portion of the dance took place offstage.

"What are you guys going to do tonight?" Daniel asked.

"I don't know. Rent a movie off the dish, I guess. What are *you* going to do?"

"Oh, the same thing I always do when I'm alone in the house. Dance around naked, call the psychic hotline, cure cancer, negotiate world peace."

Trixie smiled. "Could you clean my room too?"

"Don't know if I'll have time. It depends on whether the North Koreans are being cooperative." He pushed his food around his plate, took a few bites, and then dumped the rest into the trash. "Okay, you're officially free."

She bounced up and grabbed her pack, heading toward the front door. "Thanks, Daddy."

"Any time," Daniel said, but the words turned up at the end, as if he were asking her for minutes that were no longer hers to give.

• • •

She wasn't lying. Not any more than her father had when Trixie was little and he said one day they'd get a dog, although they didn't. She was just telling him what he wanted—needed—to hear. Everyone always said the best relationships between parents and kids involved open communication, but Trixie knew that was a joke. The best relationships were the ones where both sides went out of their way to make sure the other wasn't disappointed.

She wasn't lying, not really. She *was* going to Zephyr's house. And she *did* plan to sleep over.

But Zephyr's mother had gone to visit her older brother at Wesleyan College for the weekend, and Trixie wasn't the only one who'd been invited for the evening. A bunch of people were coming, including some hockey players.

Like Jason.

Trixie ducked behind the fence at Mrs. Argobath's house, opened up her backpack, and pulled out the jeans that were so low rise she had to go commando. She'd bought them a month ago and had hidden them from her father, because she knew he'd have a heart attack if he saw her wearing them. Shimmying out of her sweatpants and underwear—Jesus, it was cold out—she skimmed on the jeans. She rummaged for the items she'd stolen from her mother's closet—they were the same size now. Trixie had wanted to borrow the killer black-heeled boots, but she couldn't find them. Instead, Trixie had settled for a chain-link belt and a sheer black blouse her mother had worn one year over a velvet camisole to a faculty Christmas dinner. The sleeves weren't see-through enough that you could see the Ace bandage she'd wrapped around the cuts on her arm, but you could totally tell that all she had on underneath was a black satin bra.

She zipped up her coat again, jammed on her hat, and started walking. Trixie honestly wasn't sure she'd be able to do what Zephyr had suggested. *Make him come to you*, Zephyr had said. *Get him jealous.*

Maybe if she was hammered enough, or totally stoned.

Now *there* was a thought. When you were high, you were hardly yourself.

Then again, maybe it would be easier than she expected. Being someone else—*anyone* else, even for one night—would beat being Trixie Stone.

A human heart breaks harder when it's dropped from a greater height. Seth lay on the sheets of his futon, the ones that smelled of the cigarettes he rolled and—he loved this—of Laura. He still felt her words like the recoil from a shotgun. *It's over.*

Laura had gone to pull herself together in the bathroom. Seth knew there was a hairline fracture between duty and desire; that you might think you were walking on one side of it and then find yourself firmly entrenched on the other. He just also had believed—stupidly—that it wasn't that way for them. He'd believed that even with the age difference, he could be Laura's future. He hadn't counted on the chance that she might want her past instead.

"I can be whatever you want me to be," he'd promised. *Please*, he had said, half question, half command.

When the doorbell rang, he nearly didn't answer. This was the last thing he needed right now. But the bell rang again, and Seth opened the door to find the kid standing in the shadows. "Later," Seth said, and he started to shut the door.

A twenty-dollar bill was pressed into his hand. "Look," Seth said with a sigh, "I'm out."

"You've got to have *something*." Two more twenties were pushed at him.

Seth hesitated. He hadn't been lying—he really didn't have any weed—but it was hard to turn down sixty bucks when you had eaten ramen noodles every night that week. He wondered how much time he had before Laura came out of the bathroom. "Wait here," he said.

He kept his stash in the belly of an old guitar with half its strings missing. The battered case had travel stamps on it, from Istanbul and Paris and Bangkok, and a bumper sticker that said, IF YOU CAN READ THIS, GET THE FUCK AWAY.

The first time Laura had visited his apartment he'd come back from digging up a bottle of wine to find her strumming the remaining strings, the guitar still cradled inside its open case. *Do you play?* she had asked.

He had frozen, but only for a moment. He took

the case, snapped it shut, and put it off to the side. *Depends on the game*, he had answered.

Now he reached into the sound hole and rummaged around. He considered his sidelight vocation philosophically: Grad school cost a fortune; his tech job at the vet's office barely paid his rent; and selling pot wasn't much different from buying a six-pack for a bunch of teenagers. It wasn't like he went around selling coke or heroin, which could really mess you up. But he still didn't want Laura to know this about him. He could tell you how she felt about politics or affirmative action or being touched along the base of her delicate spine, but he didn't know what she'd say if she discovered that he was dealing.

Seth found the vial he was looking for. "This is powerful shit," he warned, passing it outside.

"What does it do?"

"It takes you away," Seth answered. He heard the water stop running in the bathroom. "Do you want it or not?"

The kid took the vial and shrank back into the night. Seth shut the door just as Laura walked out of the bathroom, her eyes red and her face swollen. Immediately, she froze. "Who were you talking to?"

Although Seth would have gladly crowed to the world that he loved Laura, she had too much at stake to lose—her job, her family. He should have known that someone trying so hard to keep from being noticed would never really be able to see him.

"No one," Seth said bitterly. "Your little secret's still safe."

He turned away so that he would not have to bear witness as she left him. He heard the door open, felt the gasp of cold air. "You're not the one I'm ashamed of," Laura murmured, and she walked out of his life.

Zephyr was handing out tubes of lipstick—hot pink, Goth black, scarlet, plum. She pressed one into Trixie's hand. It was gold, and Trixie turned it upside down to read the name: All That Glitters. "You know what to do, right?" Zephyr murmured.

Trixie did. She'd never played Rainbow before, she'd never had to. She'd always been with Jason instead.

As soon as Trixie had arrived at Zephyr's, her friend had laid out the guidelines for Trixie's sure-fire success that night. First, look hot. Second, drink whenever, whatever. Third—and most impor-tant—do not break the two-and-a-half-hour rule. That much time had to pass at the party before Trixie was allowed to talk to Jason. In the mean-time, Trixie had to flirt with everyone but him. Ac-cording to Zephyr, Jason expected Trixie to still be pining for him. When the opposite happened— when he saw other guys checking Trixie out and telling him he'd blown it—it would shock him into realizing his mistake.

However, Jason hadn't showed up yet. Zephyr told Trixie just to carry on with points one and two of the plan, so that she'd be good and wasted by

the time Jason arrived and saw her enjoying herself. To that end, Trixie had spent the night dancing with anyone who wanted to, and by herself
when she couldn't find a partner. She drank until
the horizon swam. She fell down across the laps of
boys she could not care less about and let them
pretend she liked it.

She looked at her reflection in the plate-glass
window and applied the gold lipstick. It made her
look like a model in an MTV video.

There were three games that had been making
the rounds at parties recently. Daisy-chaining
meant having sex like a conga line—you'd do it
with a guy, who'd do it with some girl, who'd do it
with another guy, and so on, until you made your
way back to the beginning. During Stoneface, a
bunch of guys sat at a table with their pants pulled
down and their expressions wiped clean of emotion, while a girl huddled underneath giving one of
them a blow job—and they all had to try to guess
the lucky recipient.

Rainbow was a combination of the two. A dozen
or so girls were given different colored lipsticks before having oral sex with the guys, and the boy
who sported the most colors at the end of the
night was the winner.

An upperclassman that Trixie didn't know
threaded his fingers through Zephyr's and tugged
her forward. Trixie watched him sit on the couch,
watched her wilt like a flower at his feet. She
turned away, her face flaming.

*It doesn't mean anything*, Zephyr had said.

*It only hurts if you let it.*

"Hey."

Trixie turned around to find a guy staring at her. "Um," she said. "Hi."

"You want to . . . go sit down?"

He was blond, where Jason had been so dark. He had brown eyes, not blue ones. She found herself studying him not in terms of who he was, but who he wasn't.

She imagined what would happen if Jason walked in the door and saw her going at it with someone. She wondered if he'd recognize her right away. If the stake through his heart would hurt as much as the one Trixie felt every time she saw him with Jessica Ridgeley.

Taking a deep breath, she led this boy—what was his name? did it even matter?—toward a couch. She reached for a beer on the table beside them and chugged the entire thing. Then she knelt between the boy's legs and kissed him. Their teeth scraped.

She reached down and unbuckled his belt, looking down long enough to register that he wore boxers. She closed her eyes and tried to imagine what it would be like if the bass in the music could beat through the pores of her skin.

His hand tangled in her hair, drawing her down, head to a chopping block. She smelled the musk of him and heard the groan of someone across the room and he was in her mouth and she imagined the flecks of gold on her lips ringing him like fairy dust.

Gagging, Trixie wrenched herself away and rocked back on her heels. She could still taste him, and she scrambled out of the pulsing living room and out the front door just in time to throw up in Mrs. Santorelli-Weinstein's hydrangea bush.

When you fooled around without the feelings attached, it might not mean anything . . . but then again, neither did you. Trixie wondered if there was something wrong with her, for not being able to act like Zephyr—cool and nonchalant, like none of this mattered anyway. Is that really what guys wanted? Or was it just what the girls *thought* the guys wanted?

Trixie wiped a shaking hand across her mouth and sat down on the front steps. In the distance, a car door slammed. She heard a voice that haunted her each moment before she fell asleep: "Come on, Moss. She's a *freshman.* Why don't we just call it a night?"

Trixie stared at the sidewalk until Jason came into view, haloed by a streetlight as he walked beside Moss toward Zephyr's front door.

She spun around, took the lipstick out of her pocket, and reapplied a fresh coat. It sparkled in the dark. It felt like wax, like a mask, like none of this was real.

Laura had called to say that since she was on campus, she was going to stay there and catch up on some grading. She might even just crash overnight in her office.

*You could work at home*, Daniel said, when what

he really meant was, *Why does it sound like you've been crying?*

*No, I'll get more done here*, Laura answered, when what she really meant was, *Please don't ask.*

*Love you*, Daniel said, but Laura didn't.

When your significant other was missing, it wasn't the same bed. There was a void on the other side, a cosmic black hole, one that you couldn't roll too close to without falling into a chasm of memories. Daniel lay with the covers drawn up to his chin, the television screen still glowing green.

He had always believed that if someone in this marriage was going to cheat, it would have been himself. Laura had never done anything wayward, had never even gotten a damn traffic ticket. On the other hand, he had a long history of behavior that would have surely landed him in jail eventually, had he not fallen in love instead. He assumed you could hide infidelity, like a wrinkle in your clothing stuffed underneath a belt line or a cuff, a flaw you knew existed but could conceal from the public. Instead, cheating had its own smell, one that clung to Laura's skin even after she'd stepped out of the shower. It took Daniel a while longer to recognize this sharp lemon scent for what it was: a late and unexpected confidence.

At dinner a few nights ago, Trixie had read them a logic problem from her psych homework: *A woman is at the funeral of her mother. There, she meets a man she doesn't know and has never met, who she thinks is her dream partner. But because of the circumstances, she forgets to ask for his number, and she can't find him afterward. A few days later, she kills her own sister. Why?*

Laura guessed that the sister had been involved with the man. Daniel thought it might be something to do with an inheritance. Congratulations, Trixie had said, neither one of you is a psychopath. The reason she murdered her sister was because she hoped the guy would show up at *that* funeral, too. Most serial killers who had been asked this question had given the right answer.

It was later, while he was lying in bed with Laura sleeping soundly beside him, that Daniel came up with a different explanation. According to Trixie, the woman at the funeral had fallen in love. And like any accelerant, that would change the equation. Add love, and a person might do something crazy. Add love, and all the lines between right and wrong were bound to disappear.

It was two-thirty in the morning, and Trixie was bluffing.

By now, the party had wound down. Only four people remained: Zephyr and Moss and Trixie and Jason. Trixie had managed to avoid finishing out the Rainbow game by playing Quarters in the kitchen instead with Moss and Jason. When Zephyr found her there, she had pulled Trixie aside, furious. Why was Trixie being such a prude? Wasn't this whole night supposed to be about making Jason jealous? And so Trixie had marched back to Moss and Jason, and suggested the four of them play strip poker.

They had been at it long enough for the stakes to be important. Jason had folded a while ago; he stood against the wall with his arms crossed, watching the rest of the game develop.

Zephyr laid out her cards with a flourish: two pairs—threes and jacks. On the couch across from her, Moss tipped his hand and grinned. "I have a straight."

Zephyr had already taken off her shoes, her socks, and her pants. She stood up and started to peel off her shirt. She walked toward Moss in her bra, draping her T-shirt around his neck and then kissing him so slowly that all the pale skin on his face turned bright pink.

When she sat back down, she glanced at Trixie, as if to say, *That's how you do it.*

"Stack the deck," Moss said. "I want to see if she's really a blonde."

Zephyr turned to Trixie. "Stack the deck. I want to see if he's really a guy."

"Hey, Trixie, what about you?" Moss asked.

Trixie's head was cartwheeling, but she could feel Jason's eyes on her. Maybe this was where she was supposed to go in for the kill. She looked to Zephyr, hoping for a cue, but Zephyr was too busy hanging on Moss to pay attention to her.

*Oh, my God, it was brilliant.*

If the goal of this entire night was to get Jason jealous, the surest way to do it would be to come on to his best friend.

Trixie stood up and tumbled right into Moss's lap. His arms came around her, and her cards spilled onto the coffee table: two of hearts, six of diamonds, queen of clubs, three of clubs, eight of spades. Moss started to laugh. "Trixie, that's the worst hand I've ever seen."

"Yeah, Trix," Zephyr said, staring. "You're asking for it."

Trixie glanced at her. She knew, didn't she, that the only reason she was flirting with Moss was to make Jason jealous? But before she could tele-graph this with some kind of ESP, Moss snapped her bra strap. "I think you lost," he said, grinning, and he sat back to see what piece of clothing she was going to take off.

Trixie was down to her black bra and Ace ban-dage and her low-rise jeans—the ones she was wearing without underwear. She wasn't planning on parting with any of *those* items. But she had a plan—she was going to remove her earrings. She lifted her left hand up to the lobe, only to realize that she'd forgotten to put them on. The gold hoops were sitting on her dresser, in her bedroom, just where she'd left them.

Trixie had already removed her watch, and her necklace, and her barrette. She'd even cut off her macramé anklet. A flush rose up her shoulders—her bare shoulders—onto her face. "I fold."

"You can't fold *after* the game," Moss said. "Rules are rules."

Jason pushed away from the wall and walked closer. "Give her a break, Moss."

"I think she'd rather have something else . . ."

"I'm out," Trixie said, her voice skating the thin edge of panic. She held her hands crossed in front of herself. Her heart was pounding so hard she thought it would burst into her palm. Suddenly, this seemed even worse than Rainbow, because the anonymity was gone. Here, if she acted like a slut, everyone knew her by name.

"I'll pinch-strip for her," Zephyr suggested, leaning into Moss.

But at that moment, Trixie looked at Jason and remembered why she had come to Zephyr's in the first place. *It's worth it*, she thought, *if it brings him back.* "I'll do it," she said. "But just for a second."

Turning her back to the three of them, she slipped the straps of her bra down her arms and felt her breasts come free. She took a deep breath and spun around.

Jason was staring down at the floor. But Moss was holding up his cell phone, and before Trixie could understand why, he'd snapped a picture of her.

She fastened her bra and lunged for the phone. "Give me that!"

He stuffed it in his pants. "Come and get it, baby."

Suddenly Trixie found herself being pulled off Moss. The sound of Jason's fist hitting Moss made her cringe. "Jesus Christ, lay off!" Moss cried. "I thought you said you were finished with her."

Trixie grabbed for her blouse, wishing that it was something flannel or fleece that would completely obliterate her. She held it in front of her and ran into the bathroom down the hall. Zephyr followed, coming into the tiny room and closing the door behind her.

Shaking, Trixie slipped her hands into the sleeves of the blouse. "Make them go home."

"But it's just getting interesting," Zephyr said.

Trixie looked up, stunned. *"What?"*

"Well, for God's sake, Trixie. So he had a camera phone, big fucking deal. It was a joke."

"Why are you taking his side?"

"Why are you being such an asshole?"

Trixie felt her cheeks grow hot. "This was *your* idea. You told me that if I did what you said, I'd get Jason back."

"Yeah," Zephyr shot back. "So why were you all over *Moss*?"

Trixie thought of the paper clips on Zephyr's backpack. Random hookups weren't random, no matter what you told yourself. Or your best friend.

There was a knock on the door, and then Moss opened it. His lip was split, and he had a welt over his left eye. "Oh, my God," Zephyr said. "Look at what he did to you."

Moss shrugged. "He's done worse during a scrimmage."

"I think you need to lie down," she said. "Preferably with me." As she tugged Moss out of the bathroom and upstairs, she didn't look back.

Trixie sat down on the lid of the toilet and buried her face in her hands. Distantly, she heard the music being turned off. Her temples throbbed, and her arm where she'd cut it earlier. Her throat was dry as leather. She reached for a half-empty can of Coke on the sink and drank it. She wanted to go home.

"Hey."

Trixie glanced up to find Jason staring down at her. "I thought you left."

"I wanted to make sure you were all right. You need a ride?"

Trixie wiped her eyes, a smear of mascara coming off on the heel of her hand. She had told her father she would be staying overnight, but that was before her fight with Zephyr. "That would be great," she said, and then she began to cry.

He pulled her upright and into his arms. After tonight, after everything that had happened and how stupid she'd been, all she wanted was a place where she fit. Everything about Jason was *right*, from the temperature of his skin to the way that her pulse matched his. When she turned her face into the bow of his neck, she pressed her lips against his collarbone: not quite a kiss, not quite not one.

She thought, hard, about lifting her face up to his before she did it. She made herself remember what Moss had said: *I thought you were done with her.*

When Jason kissed her, he tasted of rum and of indecision. She kissed him back until the room spun, until she couldn't remember how much time had passed. She wanted to stay like this forever. She wanted the world to grow up around them, a mound in the landscape where only violets bloomed, because that was what happened in a soil too rich for its own good.

Trixie rested her forehead against Jason's. "I don't have to go home just yet," she said.

Daniel was dreaming of hell. There was a lake of ice and a run of tundra. A dog tied to a steel rod, its nose buried in a dish of fish soup. There was a mound of melting snow, revealing candy wrappers, empty Pepsi cans, a broken toy. He heard the hollow thump of a basketball on the slick wooden boardwalk and the tail of a green tarp rattling against the seat of the snow machine it covered. He saw a moon that hung too late in the sky, like a drunk unwilling to leave the best seat at the bar.

At the sound of the crash, he came awake immediately to find himself still alone in bed. It was three thirty-two A.M. He walked into the hall, flipping light switches as he passed. "Laura," he called, "is that you?"

The hardwood floors felt cold beneath his bare feet. Nothing seemed to be out of the ordinary downstairs, yet by the time he reached the kitchen he had nearly convinced himself that he was about to come face-to-face with an intruder. An old wariness rose in him, a muscle memory of fight or flight that he'd thought he'd long forgotten.

There was no one in the cellar, or the half bath, or the dining room. The telephone still slept on its cradle in the living room. It was in the mudroom that he realized Trixie must have come home early:

Her coat was here, her boots kicked off on the brick floor.

"Trixie?" he called out, heading upstairs again.

But she wasn't in her bedroom, and when he reached the bathroom, the door was locked. Daniel rattled it, but there was no response. He threw his entire weight against the jamb until the door burst free.

Trixie was shivering, huddled in the crease made by the wall and the shower stall. "Baby," he said, coming down on one knee. "Are you sick?" But then Trixie turned in slow motion, as if he were the last person she'd ever expected to see. Her eyes were empty, ringed with mascara. She was wearing something black and sheer that was ripped at the shoulder.

"Oh, Daddy," she said, and started to cry.

"Trixie, what happened?"

She opened her mouth to speak, but then pressed her lips together and shook her head.

"You can tell me," Daniel said, gathering her into his arms as if she were small again.

Her hands were knotted together between them, like a heart that had broken its bounds. "Daddy," she whispered. "He raped me."

# 2

She had kissed him back. They must have both fallen asleep for a while, because Trixie woke up with him leaning over her, his lips against her neck. She'd felt her skin burn where he touched her.

She was jerked back to the present as her father reached for the controls of the heater on the dashboard. "Are you too hot?"

Trixie shook her head. "No," she said. "It's okay." But it wasn't, not anymore, not by a long shot.

Daniel fiddled with the knob for another moment. This was the nightmare that sank its teeth into every parent's neck. *Your child is hurt. How quickly can you make it better?*

*What if you can't?*

Beneath the tires, he heard the name that he couldn't get out of his head, not since the moment he'd found Trixie in the bathroom.

*Who did this to you?*

*Jason. Jason Underhill.*

In a tornado of pure fury, Daniel had grabbed the first thing he could lay hold of—a soap dish—and hurled it into the bathroom mirror. Trixie had started shrieking, shaking so hard it took him five minutes to calm her down. He didn't know who'd been more shocked at the outburst: Trixie, who'd never seen him like this, or Daniel himself, who'd forgotten. After that, he'd been careful which questions he asked his daughter. It wasn't that he didn't want to talk to her; he was just afraid to hear her answer, and even more afraid he would again do the wrong thing. He had never learned the protocol for this. It went beyond comfort; it went beyond parenting. It meant transforming all the rage he felt right now—enough to breathe fire and blow out the windshield—into words that spread like balm, invisible comfort for wounds too broad to see.

Suddenly, Daniel braked hard. The logging truck in front of them was weaving over the median line of the divided highway. "He's going to kill someone," Daniel said, and Trixie thought, *Let it be me.* She felt numb from the waist down, a mermaid encased in ice. "Will Mom meet us there?"

"I hope so, baby."

It was after her father had wrapped her in a blanket and rocked her and told her they were going to the hospital, when Trixie was still crying softly for her mother, that her father admitted Laura wasn't home. *But it's three-thirty in the morning*, Trixie had said. *Where did she go?* There had been a moment where the pain had stopped belonging to Trixie and started to belong to her father instead, but then he'd turned away to get her another blanket, and that was when Trixie realized she wasn't the only casualty of the night.

The logging truck veered sharply to the left. HOW AM I DOING? read the bumper sticker on its back door, the one that encouraged motorists to report reckless driving to an 800 number. *I am doing fine*, Daniel thought. *I am hale and whole, and next to me the person I love most in this world has broken into a thousand pieces.*

Trixie watched the side of the logging truck as her father accelerated and passed it, holding down his horn. It sounded too loud for this hour of the morning. It seemed to rip the sky in half. She covered her ears, but even then she could still hear it, like a scream that started from inside.

Weaving back into the right-hand lane of the highway, Daniel stole a glance at Trixie across the front seat. She was curled into a ball. Her face was pale. Her hands were hidden in her sleeves. Daniel bet she didn't even know she was crying.

She'd forgotten her coat, and Daniel realized this was his fault. He should have reminded her. He should have brought one of his own.

Trixie could feel the weight of her father's worry. Who knew that the words you never got around to saying could settle so heavy? Suddenly, she remembered a blown-glass candy dish she had broken when she was eleven, an heirloom that had belonged to her mother's grandmother. She had gathered all the pieces and had glued them together seamlessly—and she still hadn't been able to fool her mother. She imagined the same would be true, now, of herself.

If this had been an ordinary day, Daniel thought, he would have been getting Trixie up for school about now. He'd yell at her when she spent too much time in the bathroom doing her hair and tell her she was going to be late. He'd put a cereal bowl out for her on the breakfast table, and she'd fill it with Life.

From the moment it was over until the moment she entered her own home, Trixie had said only two words, uttered as she got out of his car. *Thank you.*

Daniel watched the logging truck recede in his rearview mirror. Danger came in different packages, at different points in a lifetime. There were grapes and marbles and other choking hazards. There were trees too tall for climbing. There were matches and scooters and kitchen knives left lying on the counter. Daniel had obsessed about the day Trixie would be able to drive. He could teach her how to be the most defensive driver on the planet, but he couldn't vouch for the moron truckers who hadn't slept for three days, who might run a red light. He couldn't keep the drunk from having one more before he got behind the wheel of his car to head home.

Out the passenger window, Trixie watched the scenery stream by without registering a single image. She couldn't stop wondering: If she had not kissed him back, would it never have happened?

• • •

The phone rang ten times in Laura's office, a room the size of a walk-in closet, but Daniel couldn't seem to hang up. He had tried everything, everywhere. Laura was not answering the phone in the office; she was not at home; her cell automatically rolled over to the voice message system. She had disconnected herself, on purpose.

Daniel had made excuses for his wife on his own behalf, but he couldn't make them for Trixie's sake. Because for the first time in his life, he didn't think he could be everything his daughter needed right now.

He cursed out loud and called Laura's office again to leave a message. "It's Daniel. It's four in the morning. I've got Trixie at Stephens Memorial, in the ER. She was . . . she was raped last night." He hesitated. "Please come."

Trixie wondered if this was what it felt like to be shot. If, even after the bullet went through flesh and bone, you would look down at yourself with detachment, assessing the damage, as if it wasn't you who had been hit but someone else you were asked to appraise. She wondered if numbness qualified as a chronic ache.

Sitting here, waiting for her father to come back from the restroom, Trixie cataloged her surroundings: the squeak of the nurse's white shoes, the urgent chatter of a crash cart being rolled across linoleum, the underwater-green cinder block of the walls and the amoeba shapes of the chairs where they had been told to wait. The smell of linen and metal and fear. The garland and stockings hung behind the triage nurse, the afterthought of a Christmas tree that sat next to the wire box holding patient charts. Trixie didn't just notice all these things, she absorbed them, and she decided she was saturating herself with sensation to make up for the thirty minutes she had blocked out of her consciousness.

She realized, with a start, that she had already begun to divide her life into *before* and *after.*

*Hi, you've reached Laura Stone*, her voice said. *Leave me a message and I'll get back to you.*

*Leave me.*

*I'll get back to you.*

Daniel hung up again and walked back inside the hospital, where cell phones were prohibited. But when he got back to the waiting area, Trixie was gone. He approached the triage nurse. "Which room is my daughter in? Trixie Stone?"

The nurse glanced up. "I'm sorry, Mr. Stone. I know she's a priority case, but we're short staffed and—"

"She hasn't been called in yet?" Daniel said. "Then where is she?" He knew he shouldn't have left her alone, knew even as she was nodding at him when she asked if she'd be all right by herself for a moment that she hadn't heard him at all. Backing away from the horseshoe desk, he started through the double doors of the ER, calling Trixie's name.

"Sir," the nurse said, getting to her feet, "you can't go in there!"

"Trixie?" Daniel yelled, as patients stared at him from the spaces between privacy curtains, their faces pale or bloodied or weak. "Trixie!"

An orderly grabbed his arm; he shook the massive man off. He turned a corner, smacking into a resident in her ghost-white coat before he came to a dead end. Whirling about, he continued to call out for Trixie, and then—in the interstitial space between the letters of her name—he heard Trixie calling for *him.*

He followed the thread of her voice through the maze of corridors and finally saw her. "I'm right here," he said, and she turned to him and burst into tears.

"I got lost," she sobbed against his chest. "I couldn't breathe. They were staring."

"Who was?"

"All the people in the waiting room. They were wondering what was wrong with me."

Daniel took both of her hands. "There's nothing wrong with you," he said, that first lie a fissure crack in his heart.

A woman wearing a trowel's layer of cosmetics approached. "Trixie Stone?" she said. "My name's Janice. I'm a sexual assault advocate. I'm here to answer questions for you and your family, and to help you understand what's going to be happening."

Daniel couldn't get past the makeup. If this woman had been called in for Trixie, how much time had been lost applying those false eyelashes, that glittery blush? How much faster might she have come?

"First things first," Janice said, her eyes on Trixie. "This wasn't your fault."

Trixie glanced at her. "You don't even know what happened."

"I know that no one deserves to be raped, no matter who she is and what she's been doing," Janice said. "Have you taken a shower yet?"

Daniel wondered how on earth she could even think this. Trixie was still wearing the same torn blouse, had the same raccoon circles of mascara under her eyes. She had wanted to shower—that was why, when he'd found her, she was in the bathroom—but Daniel knew enough to keep her from doing it. *Evidence.* The word had swum in his mind like a shark.

"What about the police?" Daniel heard, and he was stunned to realize he'd been the one to say it.

Janice turned. "The hospital automatically reports any sexual assault of a minor to the police," she said. "Whether or not Trixie wants to press charges is up to her."

*She will press charges against that son of a bitch*, Daniel thought, *even if I have to talk her into it.*

And on the heels of that: If he forced Trixie to do something she didn't want to, then how was he any different from Jason Underhill?

As Janice outlined the specifics of the upcoming examination, Trixie shook her head and folded her arms around herself. "I want to go home," she said, in the smallest of voices. "I've changed my mind."

"You need to see a doctor, Trixie. I'll stay with you, the whole time." She turned to Daniel. "Is there a Mrs. Stone . . . ? "

*Excellent question*, Daniel thought, before he could remember not to. "She's on her way," he said. Maybe this was not even a lie by now.

Trixie grabbed onto his arm. "What about my father? Can he come in with me?"

Janice looked from Daniel to Trixie and then back again. "It's a pelvic exam," she said delicately.

The last time Daniel had seen Trixie naked, she had been eleven and about to take a bubble bath. He had walked into the bathroom, thinking she was only brushing her teeth, and together they had stared at her blossoming body in the reflection of the mirror. After that, he was careful to knock on doors, to draw an invisible curtain of distance around her for privacy.

When he was a kid in Alaska, he had met Yu'pik Eskimos who hated him on sight, because he was a *kass'aq.* It didn't matter that he was six or seven, that he hadn't been the particular Caucasian who had cheated that person out of land or reneged on a job or any of a hundred other grievances. All they saw was that Daniel was white, and by association, he was a magnet for their anger. He imagined, now, what it would be like to be the only male in the room during a sexual assault examination.

"Please, Daddy?"

Behind the fear in Trixie's eyes was the understanding that even with this stranger, she would be alone, and she couldn't risk that again. So Daniel took a deep breath and headed down the hall between Trixie and Janice. Inside the room, there was a gurney; he helped Trixie climb onto it. The doctor entered almost immediately, a small woman wearing scrubs and a white coat. "Hi, Trixie," she said, and if she seemed surprised to see a father in the room, instead of a mother, she said nothing. She came right up to Trixie and squeezed her hand. "You're already being very brave. All I'm going to ask you to do is keep that up."

She handed a form to Daniel and asked him to sign it, explaining that because Trixie was a minor, a parent or guardian had to authorize the collection and release of information. She took Trixie's blood pressure and pulse and made notes on her clipboard. Then she began to ask Trixie a series of questions.

*What's your address?*

*How old are you?*

*What day did the assault occur? What approximate time?*

*What was the gender of the perpetrator? The number of perpetrators?*

Daniel felt a line of sweat break out under the collar of his shirt.

*Have you douched, bathed, urinated, defecated since the assault?*

*Have you vomited, eaten or drunk, changed clothes, brushed your teeth?*

He watched Trixie shake her head no to each of these. Each time before she spoke, she would glance at Daniel, as if he had the answer in his eyes.

*Have you had consensual intercourse in the last five days?*

Trixie froze, and this time, her gaze slid away from his. She murmured something inaudible. "Sorry," the doctor said. "I didn't quite get that?"

"This was the first time," Trixie repeated.

Daniel felt the room swell and burst. He was vaguely aware of excusing himself, of Trixie's face—a white oval that bled at the edges. He had to try twice before he could maneuver his fingers in a way that would open the latch of the door.

Outside, he balled his hand into a fist and struck it against the cinder-block wall. He pummeled the cement again and again. He did this even as the tears came and a nurse led him away, to wash the blood off his knuckles and to bandage the scrapes on his palm. He did this until he knew Trixie wasn't the only one hurting.

Trixie wasn't where everyone thought she was. She might have physically been in the examination room, but mentally she was floating, hovering in the top left corner of the ceiling, watching the doctor and that other woman minister to the poor, sad, broken girl who used to be her.

She wondered if they knew that their patient

was a husk, a shell left behind by a snail because home didn't fit anymore. You'd think someone who'd been to medical school would be able to hear through a stethoscope that somebody was empty inside. Trixie watched herself step onto a sheet of white paper with stiff, jerky movements. She listened as Dr. Roth asked her to remove her clothes, explaining that there might be evidence on the fabric that the detectives could use. "Will I get them back?" Trixie heard herself say.

"I'm afraid not," the doctor answered.

"Your dad is going to run home and get you something to wear," Janice added.

Trixie stared down at her mother's sheer blouse. *She's going to kill me*, Trixie thought, and then she almost laughed—would her mother really be paying attention to the freaking *blouse* when she found out what had happened? With slow movements, Trixie mechanically unbuttoned the shirt and pulled it off. Too late, she remembered the Ace bandage around her wrist.

"What happened there?" Dr. Roth asked, gently touching the metal pins holding the wrap in place.

Trixie panicked. What would the doctor say if she knew Trixie had taken to carving her own arm up? Could she get thrown into a psych ward for that?

"Trixie," Dr. Roth said, "are there bruises under there?"

She looked down at her feet. "They're more like cuts."

When Dr. Roth began to unravel the bandage on

her left wrist, Trixie didn't fight her. She thought about what it would be like in an institution. If, in the aftermath of all this, it might not be such a bad thing to be sealed away from the real world and totally overmedicated.

Dr. Roth's gloved hands skimmed over a cut, one so new that Trixie could see the skin still knitting together. "Did he use a knife?"

Trixie blinked. She was still so disconnected from her body that it took her a moment to understand what the doctor was implying, and another moment after that to understand that she had just been given a way out.

"I . . . I don't think so," Trixie said. "I think he scratched me when I was fighting."

Dr. Roth wrote something down on her clipboard, as Trixie kept getting undressed. Her jeans came next, and then she stood shivering in her bra and panties. "Were you wearing that pair of underwear when it happened?" the doctor asked.

Trixie shook her head. She'd put them on, along with a big fat sanitary napkin, once she saw that she was bleeding. "I wasn't wearing underwear," Trixie murmured, and immediately she realized how much that made her sound like a slut. She glanced down at the floor, at the see-through blouse. Was that why it had happened?

"Low-rise jeans," Janice commiserated, and Trixie nodded, grateful that she hadn't been the one to have to explain.

Trixie couldn't remember ever being so tired. The examination room was runny at the edges, like a breakfast egg that hadn't been cooked quite long enough. Janice handed her a hospital johnny, which was just as good as being naked with the way it was hanging open in the back. "You can take a seat," Dr. Roth said.

The blood samples were next. It was just like when they'd had to pair up in eighth-grade science to try to analyze their own blood type. Trixie had nearly passed out at the sight of the blood, and her teacher had sent her to the nurse to breathe into a paper bag for a half hour, and she was so mortified that she'd called her father and said she was sick even though physically she was feeling much better. She and her father had had a Monopoly tournament, and like always, Trixie bought Park Place and Boardwalk and set up hotels and creamed her father.

This time, though, when the needle went in, Trixie watched from above. She didn't feel the prick, she didn't feel woozy. She didn't feel anything at all, of course, because it wasn't her.

When Dr. Roth turned off the lights in the room, Janice stepped forward. "The doctor's going to use a special light now, a Woods lamp. It won't hurt."

It could have been a thousand needles—Trixie knew she still wouldn't feel it. But instead, this turned out to be like a tanning booth, except creepier. The light glowed ultraviolet, and when Trixie glanced down at her own bare body, it was covered with purple lines and blotches that hadn't been visible before. Dr. Roth moistened a long cotton swab and touched it to a spot on her shoulder. She left it on the counter to air-dry, and as it did, Trixie watched her write on the paper sleeve that the swab had been packaged in: *Suspected saliva from right shoulder.*

The doctor took swabs from the inside of her cheek and off her tongue. She gently combed Trixie's hair over a paper towel, folding up the comb inside the towel when she was finished. Dr. Roth slipped another towel underneath her, using a different comb to work through her pubic hair. Trixie had to turn away—it was *that* embarrassing to watch. "Almost done," Janice murmured.

Dr. Roth pulled a pair of stirrups from the end of the examination table. "Have you ever been to a gynecologist, Trixie?" she asked.

Trixie had an appointment, scheduled for next February, with her mother's doctor. *It's a health thing*, her mother had assured her, which was just fine because Trixie wasn't planning on discussing her sex life out loud, especially not with her mother. Months ago, when the appointment had been made, Trixie hadn't even ever kissed a guy.

"You're going to feel a little pressure," Dr. Roth said, folding Trixie's legs into the stirrups, a human origami that left her stark and open.

In that instant, Trixie felt what was left of her spirit sinking down from where it had been watching near the ceiling, to take dark root in her beaten body. She could feel Janice's hand stroking her arm, could feel the doctor's rubber glove parting the heart of her. For the first time since she'd entered the hospital, she was completely, violently aware of who she was and what had been done to her.

There was cold steel, and a rasp of flesh. A push from the outside, as her body struggled to keep the speculum out. Trixie tried to kick out with one foot, but she was being held down at the thighs and then there was pain and force and *you are breaking me in two.*

"Trixie," Janice said fiercely. "Trixie, honey, stop fighting. It's okay. It's just the doctor."

Suddenly the door burst open and Trixie saw her mother, lion-eyed and determined. "Trixie," Laura said, two syllables that broke in the center.

Now that Trixie could feel, she wished she couldn't. The only thing worse than not feeling anything was feeling *everything.* She started shaking uncontrollably, an atom about to split beneath its own compounded weight; and then she found herself anchored in her mother's embrace, their hearts beating hard against each other as the doctor and Janice offered to give them a moment of privacy.

"Where *were* you?" Trixie cried, an accusation and a question all at once. She started to sob so hard she could not catch her breath.

Laura's hands were on the back of Trixie's neck, in her hair, around the bound of her ribs. "I should have been home," her mother said. "I'm sorry. I'm so sorry."

Trixie wasn't sure if her mother was apologizing, or just acknowledging her own errors. She *should* have been home. Maybe then Trixie wouldn't have chanced lying about going to Zephyr's; maybe she never would have had the opportunity to steal the sheer blouse. Maybe she would have spent the night in her own bed. Maybe the worst hurt she would have had to nurse was another razor stripe, a self-inflicted wound.

Her anger surprised her. Maybe none of this had been her mother's fault, but Trixie pretended it was. Because a mother was supposed to protect her child. Because if Trixie was angry, there was no room left for being scared. Because if it was her mother's mistake, then it couldn't be *hers.*

Laura folded her arms around Trixie so tight that there was no room for doubt between them. "We'll get through this," she promised.

"I know," Trixie answered.

They were both lying, and Trixie thought maybe that was the way it would be, now. In the wake of a disaster, the last thing you needed to do was set off another bomb; instead, you walked through the rubble and told yourself that it wasn't nearly as bad as it looked. Trixie bit down on her lip. After tonight, she couldn't be a kid anymore. After tonight, there was no more room in her life for honesty.

Daniel was supremely grateful to have been given a job. "She needs a change of clothes," Janice had said. He was worried about not getting back in time before Trixie was ready, but Janice promised that they would be a while yet.

He drove back home from the hospital as quickly as he'd driven to it, just in case.

By the time he reached Bethel, morning had cracked wide open. He drove by the hockey rink and watched it belch out a steady stream of tiny Mites, each followed by a parent-Sherpa lugging an outsized gear bag. He passed an old man skating down the ice of his driveway in his bedroom slippers, out to grab the newspaper. He wove around the parked rigs of hunters culling the woods for winter deer.

His own house had been left unlocked in the hurry to leave it. The light on the stove hood—the one he'd kept on last night in case Laura came home late—was still burning, although there was enough sunshine to flood the entire kitchen. Daniel turned it off and then headed upstairs to Trixie's room.

Years ago, when she'd told him she wanted to fly like the men and women in his comic book drawings, he had given her a sky in which to do it. Trixie's walls and ceiling were covered with clouds; the hardwood floors were an ethereal cirrus swirl. Somehow, as Trixie got older, she hadn't outgrown the murals. They seemed to compliment her, a girl too vibrant to be contained by walls. But right now, the clouds that had once seemed so liberating made Daniel feel like he was falling. He anchored himself by holding on to the furniture, weaving from bed to dresser to closet.

He tried to remember what Trixie liked to wear on weekends when it was snowing, when the single event on the docket was to read the Sunday paper and doze on the couch, but the only outfit he could picture was the one she had been dressed in when he'd found her last night. Gilding the lily, that's what Laura had called it when Trixie and Zephyr got into her makeup drawer as kids and then paraded downstairs looking like the worst prostitutes in the Combat Zone. Once, he remembered, they'd come with their mouths pale as corpses and asked Laura why she had white lipstick. *That's not lipstick*, she'd said, laughing, *that's concealer. It hides zits and dark circles, all the things you don't want people to see.* Trixie had only shaken her head: *But why wouldn't you want people to see your lips?*

Daniel opened a dresser drawer and pulled out a bell-sleeved shirt that was tiny enough to have fit Trixie when she was eight. Had she ever worn this in public?

He sank down onto the floor, holding the shirt, wondering if all this had been his own fault. He'd forbidden Trixie to buy certain clothes, like the pants she had had on last night, in fact, and that she must have purchased and hidden from him. You saw outfits like those in fashion magazines, outfits so revealing they bordered on porn, in Daniel's opinion. Women glanced at those photo spreads and wished they looked that way, men glanced at them and wished for women who looked that way, and the sad reality was that most of those models were not women at all, but girls about Trixie's age.

Girls who might wear something to a party thinking it was sexy, without considering what it would mean if a guy thought that too.

He had assumed that a kid who slept with stuffed animals would not also be wearing a thong, but now it occurred to Daniel that long before any comic book penciler had conceived of Copycat or The Changeling or Mystique, shape-shifters existed in the form of teenage girls. One minute you might find your daughter borrowing a cookie sheet to go sledding in the backyard, and the next she'd be online IMing a boy. One minute she'd lean over to kiss you good night, the next she'd tell you she hated you and couldn't wait to go away to college. One minute she'd be putting on her mother's makeup, the next she'd be buying her own. Trixie had morphed back and forth between childhood and adolescence so easily that the line between them had gone blurry, so indistinct that Daniel had simply given up trying for a clearer vision.

He dug way into the back of one of Trixie's drawers and pulled out a pair of shapeless fleece sweatpants, then a long-sleeved pink T-shirt. With his eyes closed, he fished in her underwear drawer for panties and a bra. As he hurried back to the hospital, he remembered a game he and Trixie used to play when they were stuck in traffic at the Maine tolls, trying to come up with a superhero power for every letter of the alphabet. Amphibious, bulletproof, clairvoyant. Danger sensitive, electromagnetic. Flight. Glow-in-the-dark. Heat vision. Invincibility.

Jumping over tall buildings. Kevlar skin. Laser sight. Mind control. Never-ending life. Omniscience.

Pyrokinesis. Quick reflexes. Regeneration. Superhuman strength. Telepathy.

Underwater breathing. Vanishing. Weather control. X-ray vision. Yelling loud.

Zero gravity.

Nowhere in that list was the power to keep your child from growing up. If a superhero couldn't do it, how could any ordinary man?

There was a knock on the examination room door. "It's Daniel Stone," Laura heard. "I, um, have Trixie's clothes."

Before Janice could reach the door, Laura opened it. She took in Daniel's disheveled hair, the shadow of beard on his face, the storm behind his eyes, and thought for a moment she had fallen backward fifteen years.

"You're here," he said.

"I got the message on my cell." She took the stack of clothing from his hands and carried it over to Trixie. "I'm just going to talk to Daddy for a minute," Laura said, and as she moved away, Janice stepped forward to take her place.

Daniel was waiting outside the door for Laura. "*Jason* did this?" she turned to him, fever in her eyes. "I want him caught. I want him *punished.*"

"Take a number." Daniel ran a hand down his face. "How is she?"

"Nearly finished." Laura leaned against the wall beside him, a foot of space separating them.

"But how *is* she?" Daniel repeated.

"Lucky. The doctor said there wasn't any internal injury."

"Wasn't she . . . she was bleeding."

"Only a tiny bit. It's stopped now." Laura glanced up at Daniel. "You never told me she was sleeping at Zephyr's last night."

"She got invited after you left."

"Did you call Zephyr's mother to—"

"No," Daniel interrupted. "And you wouldn't have, either. She's gone to Zephyr's a hundred times before." His eyes flashed. "If you're going to accuse me of something, Laura, just do it."

"I'm not accusing you—"

"People in glass houses," Daniel murmured.

*"What?"*

He moved away from the wall and approached her, backing her into a corner. "Why didn't you answer when I called your office?"

Excuses rose inside Laura like bubbles: *I was in the restroom. I had taken a sleeping pill. I accidentally turned the ringer off.* "I don't think now is the time—"

"If this isn't the time," Daniel said, his voice aching, "maybe you could give me a number at least. A place I can reach you, you know, in case Trixie gets raped again."

Laura stood perfectly still, immobilized by equal parts shame and anger. She thought of the deepest level of hell, the lake of ice that only froze harder the more you tried to work yourself free.

"Excuse me?"

Grateful for a distraction, Laura turned toward the voice. A tall, sad-eyed man with sandy hair stood behind her, a man who'd most likely heard every word between her and Daniel. "I'm sorry. I don't mean to interrupt. I'm looking for Mr. and Mrs. Stone?"

"That's us," Laura said. *In name, at least.*

The man held out a badge. "I'm Detective Mike Bartholemew. And I'd really like to speak to your daughter."

Daniel had been inside the Bethel police station only once, when he'd chaperoned Trixie's second-grade class there on a field trip. He remembered the quilt that hung in the lobby, stars sewn to spell out PROTECT AND SERVE, and the booking room, where the whole class had taken a collective grinning mug shot. He had not seen the conference room until this morning—a small, gray cubicle with a reverse mirrored window that some idiot contractor had put in backward, so that from inside, Daniel could see the traffic of cops in the hallway checking their reflections.

He focused on the winding wheels of the tape recorder. It was easier than concentrating on the words coming out of Trixie's mouth, an exhaustive description of the previous night. She had already explained how, when she left home, she changed into a different outfit. How there was a posse of players from the hockey team present when she arrived at Zephyr's, and how, by the end of the evening, it was only the four of them.

One parent was allowed in with Trixie when she gave her statement. Because Laura had been at the hospital exam—or maybe because of what Daniel had said to her in the hall—she had decided that he should be the one to go. It was only after he was inside that he realized this was more of a trial than an advantage. He had to sit very still and listen to Trixie's story in excruciating detail, smiling at her in encouragement and telling her she was doing great, when what he really wanted was to grab the detective and ask him why the hell he hadn't locked up Jason Underhill yet.

He wondered how, in just an hour's time, he'd regressed back to being the kind of person he'd been a lifetime ago—someone for whom feeling came before thought, for whom reason was a postscript. He wondered if this happened to all fathers: as their daughters grew up, they slid backward.

Bartholemew had brewed coffee. He'd brought in a box of tissues, which he put near Trixie, just in case. Daniel liked thinking that Bartholemew had been through this before. He liked knowing that *someone* had.

"What were you drinking?" the detective asked Trixie.

She was wearing the pink shirt and sweatpants that Daniel had brought, plus his coat. He'd forgotten to bring hers back, even when he went home again. "Coke," Trixie said. "With rum."

"Were you using any drugs?"

She looked down at the table and shook her head.

"Trixie," the detective said. "You're going to have to speak up."

"No," she answered.

"What happened next?"

Daniel listened to her describe a girl he didn't know, one who lap-danced and played strip poker. Her voice flattened under the weight of her bad judgment. "After Zephyr went upstairs with Moss, I figured everyone was gone. I was going to go home, but I wanted to sit down for a minute, because I had a really bad headache. And it turned out Jason hadn't left. He said he wanted to make sure I was all right. I started to cry."

"Why?"

Her face contorted. "Because we broke up a couple of weeks ago. And being that close to him again . . . it hurt."

Daniel's head snapped up. "Broke up?"

Trixie turned at the same time the detective stopped the tape. "Mr. Stone," Bartholemew said, "I'm going to have to ask you to remain silent." He nodded at Trixie to continue.

She let her gaze slide beneath the table. "We . . . we wound up kissing. I fell asleep for a little while, I guess, because when I woke up, we weren't near the bathroom anymore . . . we were on the carpet in the living room. I don't remember how we got there. That was when he . . . when he raped me."

The last drink that Daniel had had was in 1991, the day before he convinced Laura that he was worth marrying. But before that, he'd had plenty of firsthand knowledge about the faulty reasoning and slurred decisions that swam at the bottom of a bottle. He'd had his share of mornings where he woke up in a house he could not recall arriving at. Trixie might not remember how she got into the living room, but Daniel could tell her exactly how it had happened.

Detective Bartholemew looked squarely at Trixie. "I know this is going to be difficult," he said, "but I need you to tell me exactly what happened between you two. Like whether either of you removed any clothing. Or what parts of your body he touched. What you said to him and what he said to you. Things like that."

Trixie fiddled with the zipper of Daniel's battered leather jacket. "He tried to take off my shirt, but I didn't want him to. I told him that it was Zephyr's house and that I didn't feel right fooling around there. He said I was breaking his heart. I felt bad after that, so I let him unhook my bra and touch me, you know . . . my breasts. He was kissing me the whole time, and that was the good part, the part I wanted, but then he put his hand down my pants. I tried to pull his hand away, but he was too strong." Trixie swallowed. "He said, 'Don't tell me you don't want this.' "

Daniel gripped the edge of the table so hard that

he thought he would crack the plastic. He took a deep breath in through his mouth and held it. He thought of all the ways it would be possible to kill Jason Underhill.

"I tried to get away, but he's bigger than I am, and he pushed me down again. It was like a game to him. He held my hands up over my head and he pulled down my pants. I said I wanted him to stop and he didn't. And then," Trixie said, stumbling over the words. "And then he pushed me down hard and he raped me."

There was a bullet, Daniel thought, but that would be too easy.

"Had you ever had sex before?"

Trixie glanced at Daniel. "No," she answered. "I started screaming, because it hurt so much. I tried to kick him. But when I did, it hurt more, so I just stayed still and waited for it to be over."

Drowning, Daniel thought. Slowly. In a sewer.

"Did your friend hear you screaming?" Detective Bartholemew asked.

"I guess not," Trixie said. "There was music on, pretty loud."

No—a rusty knife. A sharp cut to the gut. Daniel had read about men who'd had to live for days, watching their insides being eaten out by infection.

"Did he use a condom?"

Trixie shook her head. "He pulled out before he finished. There was blood on the carpet, and on me, too. He was worried about that. He said he didn't mean to hurt me."

Maybe, Daniel mused, he would do all of these things to Jason Underhill. Twice.

"He got up and found a roll of paper towels so I could clean myself up. Then he took some rug cleaner from under the kitchen sink, and he scrubbed the spot on the carpet. He said we were lucky it wasn't ruined."

And what about Trixie? What magical solution would take away the stain he'd left on her forever?

"Mr. Stone?"

Daniel blinked, and he realized that he had become someone else for a moment—someone he hadn't been for years—and that the detective had been speaking to him. "Sorry."

"Could I see you outside?"

He followed Bartholemew into the hallway of the police station. "Look," the detective said, "I see this kind of thing a lot."

This was news to Daniel. The last rape he could remember in their small town happened over a decade ago and was perpetrated by a hitchhiker.

"A lot of girls think they're ready to have sex . . . but then change their mind, after the fact."

It took Daniel a minute to find his voice. "Are you saying . . . that my daughter's lying?"

"No. But I want you to understand that even if Trixie is willing to testify, you might not get the outcome you're hoping for."

"She's fourteen, for God's sake," Daniel said.

"Kids younger than that are having sex. And according to the medical report, there wasn't significant internal trauma."

"She wasn't hurt *enough*?"

"I'm just saying that given the details—the alcohol, the strip poker, the former relationship with Jason—rape could be a hard sell to a jury. The boy's going to say it was consensual."

Daniel clenched his jaw. "If a murder suspect told you he was innocent, would you just let him walk away?"

"It's not quite the same—"

"No, it's not. Because the murder victim's dead and can't give you any information about what really happened. As opposed to my *daughter*, the one who's inside there telling you exactly how she was *raped*, while you aren't fucking *listening* to her." He opened the door to the conference room to see Trixie with her arms folded on the table, her head resting on her hands.

"Can we go home?" she asked, groggy.

"Yes," Daniel said. "The detective can call us if he needs anything else." He anchored his arm around Trixie. They were halfway down the hall when Daniel turned around again to face Bartholemew. In the reflection of the backward mirror, he could see their faces, white ovals that hovered like ghosts. "You have any kids?" he asked.

The detective hesitated, then shook his head.

"I didn't think so," Daniel said, and shepherded Trixie through the door.

At home, Laura stripped the sheets off Trixie's bed and remade it with fresh ones. She found a plaid flannel quilt in the cedar chest in the attic and used that, instead of Trixie's usual quilt. She picked up the clothes that were tossed on the floor and straightened the books on the nightstand and tried to turn the room into something that would not remind Trixie of yesterday.

At the last minute, Laura walked toward a shelf and pulled down the stuffed moose that Trixie had slept with until she was ten. Bald in some spots and missing one eye, it had been retired, but Trixie hadn't quite been able to bring herself to put it into a garage sale pile. Laura settled this squarely between the pillows, as if it might be just that easy to take Trixie back to childhood.

Then she hauled the laundry downstairs and began to stir it into the washing machine. It was while she was waiting for the barrel to fill with water that she spilled bleach on her skirt, one of her work skirts, part of an expensive suit. Laura watched the color leach from the wool, a scar in the shape of a tear. She swore, then tried to reverse the damage by holding the hem of the skirt under running water in the sink. Finally, defeated, she sank down in front of the humming belly of the Kenmore and burst into tears.

Had she been so busy keeping her own secret that she didn't have the time or the inclination to dissolve Trixie's? What if, instead of seeing Seth, Laura had been here every night? What if she'd quizzed her on her French vocabulary, or carried a cup of hot chocolate to her room, or invited her to sit on the couch and make fun of the hairstyles on

an old sitcom? What if Laura had given Trixie a reason to stay home?

She knew, on some level, that it would not have
worked that way. Just because Laura felt like playing übermother did not mean Trixie would choose
to join the game: At her age, a mother's touch
couldn't compare to the brush of a boy's hand
down the valley of your spine. Laura forced herself
to picture Jason Underhill's face. He was a good-
looking boy—a tangle of black hair, aquamarine
eyes, an athlete's body. Everyone in Bethel knew
him. Even Laura, who wasn't a devotee of hockey,
had seen Jason's name splashed all over the
sports pages of the newspaper. When Daniel had
worried about an older boy dating Trixie, Laura had
been the one to tell him to relax. She saw kids
nearly that age every single day, and she knew that
Jason was a catch. He was smart, polite, and
crazy about Trixie, she'd told Daniel. What more
could you want for your daughter's first crush?

But now, when she thought of Jason Underhill,
she considered how persuasive those blue eyes
might be. How strong an athlete was. She started
to twist her thinking, boring it deep as a screw, so
that it would truly take hold.

If all the blame could be pinned on Jason Underhill, then it wasn't Laura's fault.

Trixie had been awake now for twenty-eight hours
straight. Her eyes burned, and her head was too
heavy, and her throat was coated with the residue
of the story she'd been telling over and over. Dr.

Roth had given her a prescription for Xanax, telling her that no matter how exhausted Trixie was, she was most likely going to find it difficult to sleep, and that this was perfectly normal.

She had, finally, wonderfully, been able to take a shower. She stayed in long enough to use an entire bar of soap. She had tried to scrub *down there*, but she couldn't get all the way inside where she still felt dirty. When the doctor had said there was no internal trauma, Trixie had nearly asked her to check again. For a moment, she'd wondered if she'd dreamed the whole thing, if it had never really happened.

"Hey," her father said, poking his head into her bedroom door. "You ought to be in bed."

Trixie pulled back the covers—her mother had changed her sheets—and crawled inside. Before, getting into bed had been the highlight of her day; she'd always imagined it like some kind of cloud or gentle nest where she could just let go of all the stress of acting cool and looking perfect and saying the right things. But now, it loomed like a torture device, a place where she'd close her eyes and have to replay what had happened over and over, like a closed-circuit TV.

Her mother had left her old stuffed moose on top of the pillows. Trixie squeezed it against her chest. "Daddy?" she asked. "Can you tuck me in?"

He had to work at it, but he managed to smile. "Sure."

When Trixie was little, her father had always left her a riddle to fall asleep on, and then he'd give her the answer at breakfast. *What gets bigger the more you take away from it? A hole. What's black when you buy it, red when you use it, and gray when you throw it away? Charcoal.*

"Could you maybe talk to me for a little while?" Trixie asked.

It wasn't that she wanted to talk, really. It was that she didn't want to be left alone in this room with only herself for company.

Trixie's father smoothed back her hair. "Don't tell me you're not exhausted."

*Don't tell me you don't want this*, Jason had said.

She suddenly remembered one of her father's nighttime riddles: *The answer is yes, but what I mean is no. What is the question?*

And the solution: *Do you mind?*

Her father notched the covers beneath her chin. "I'll send Mom in to say good night," he promised, and he reached over to turn off the lamp.

"Leave it on," Trixie said, panicking. "Please."

He stopped abruptly, his hand hovering in the air. Trixie stared at the bulb, until she couldn't see anything but the kind of brilliant light everyone says comes for you when you're about to die.

The absolute worst job, if you asked Mike Bartholemew, was having to go tell a parent that his or her kid had been in a fatal car crash or had committed suicide or OD'd. There just weren't words to hold up that kind of pain, and the recipient of the news would stand there, staring at him, certain she'd heard wrong. The second absolute worst job, in his opinion, was dealing with rape victims. He couldn't listen to any of their statements without feeling guilty for sharing the same gender as the perp. And even if he could collect enough evidence to merit a trial, and even if there was a conviction, you could bet it wouldn't be for very long. In most cases, the victim was still in therapy when the rapist got done serving his sentence.

The thing that most people didn't understand, if they weren't in his line of work, was that a rape victim and a victim of a fatal accident were both gone, forever. The difference was that the rape victim still had to go through the motions of being alive.

He climbed the stairs over the smoothie bar to the interim apartment he'd rented after the divorce, the one he swore he'd live in for only six months but that had turned out to be his home for six years. It wasn't furnished—the less appealing it was, the easier Mike figured it would be to get motivated to leave it—but he had a futon that he usually left open as a bed, and a beanbag chair and a TV that he left running 24/7 so that Ernestine would have something to listen to when he was at work.

"Ernie?" he called out as soon as his keys turned in the lock. "I'm back."

She wasn't on the futon, where he'd left her when the call came in this morning. Mike stripped off his tie and walked toward the bathroom. He drew back the shower curtain to find the potbellied pig asleep in the bottom of the tub. "Miss me?" he asked.

The pig opened one eye and grunted.

"You know, the only reason I came home was to take you for a walk," Mike said, but the pig had fallen back asleep.

He had a warrant in his pocket—Trixie's statement, plus the presence of semen, was enough probable cause to arrest Jason Underhill. He even knew where the kid was, just like everyone in the town who was following the high school hockey team's stellar exploits. But he had to come home first to let Ernie out. At least that's what he'd told himself.

*Do you have any kids?* Daniel Stone had asked.

Mike turned off the television and sat in silence for a few moments. Then he went to the one closet in the apartment and pulled down a cardboard box.

Inside the box was a pillow from Mike's daughter's bed, one that he'd stuffed into an enormous plastic evidence bag. He broke the ziplocked seal and inhaled deeply. It hardly smelled like her anymore at all, in spite of the great care he had taken.

Suddenly, Ernestine came running. She skidded across the floor, scrambling over to the futon where Mike sat. Her snout went into the plastic bag with the pillow, and Mike wondered if she could scent something he couldn't. The pig looked up at Mike.

"I know," he said. "I miss her, too."

• • •

Daniel sat in the kitchen with a bottle of sherry in front of him. He hated sherry, but it was the only liquid with alcoholic content in this house right now. He had already burned through half the bottle, and it was a large one, something Laura liked to use when she made stir-fry chicken. He didn't feel drunk, though. He only felt like a failure.

Fatherhood was the entire foundation Daniel had reinvented himself upon. When he thought about being a parent, he saw a baby's hand spread like a star on his chest. He saw the tightness between the kite and the spool of string that held it. Finding out that he'd fallen short of his responsibility for protecting his daughter made him wonder how he'd gone so long fooling himself into believing he had truly changed.

The part of himself that he'd thought he'd exorcised turned out to have been only lying in the shallow grave where old personalities went to be discarded. With the sherry lighting his way, Daniel could see that now. He could feel anger building like steam.

The new Daniel, the *father* Daniel, had answered the detective's questions and trusted the police to do what they were supposed to, because that was the best way to ensure the safety of his child. But the old Daniel . . . well, he never would have trusted anyone else to complete a job that rightfully belonged to him. He would have fought back in revenge, kicking and screaming.

In fact, he often had.

Daniel stood up and shrugged on his jacket just

as Laura walked into the kitchen. She took one look at the bottle of sherry on the table, and then at him. "You don't drink."

Daniel stared at her. "Didn't," he corrected.

"Where are you going?"

He didn't answer her. He didn't owe her an explanation. He didn't owe anyone anything. This was not about payment, it was about payback.

Daniel opened the door and hurried out to his truck. Jason Underhill would be at the town rink, right now, getting dressed for the Saturday afternoon game.

Because Trixie asked, Laura waited for her to fall asleep. She came downstairs in time to see Daniel leave, and he didn't have to tell her where he was headed. Even worse, Laura wasn't sure she would have stopped him.

Biblical justice was antiquated, or so she had been taught. You couldn't hack off the hand of a thief; you couldn't stone a murderer to death. A more advanced society took care of its justice in a courtroom—something Laura had advocated until about five hours ago. A trial might be more civilized, but emotionally, it couldn't possibly pack as much satisfaction.

She tried to imagine what Daniel might do if he found Jason, but she couldn't. It had been so long since Daniel had been anything but quiet and mild-mannered that she had completely forgotten the shadow that had once clung to him, so dark and unpredictable that she'd had to come closer for a second glance. Laura felt the same way she had last Christmas when she'd hung one of Trixie's baby shoes on the tree as an ornament: wistful, aware that her daughter had once been tiny enough to fit into this slipper but unable to hold that picture in her head along with the one in front of her eyes—a teenage Trixie dancing around the balsam in her bare feet, stringing white lights in her wake.

She tried to sit down with a book, but she reread the same page four times. She turned on the television but could not find the humor in any canned jokes.

A moment later, she found herself at the computer, Googling the word *rape.*

There were 10,900,000 hits, and immediately that made Laura feel better. Strength in numbers: She was not the only mother who'd felt this way; Trixie was not the only victim. The Web sites rooted this godawful word, and all the suffocating aftershocks that hung from it like Spanish moss.

She started clicking: One out of every six American women has been the victim of an attempted or a completed rape in her lifetime, adding up to 17.7 million people.

Sixty-six percent of rape victims know their assailant. Forty-eight percent are raped by a friend.

Twenty percent of rapes take place at the home of a friend, neighbor, or relative.

More than half occur within a mile of the victim's home.

Eighty percent of rape victims are under age

thirty. Girls between ages sixteen and nineteen are four times more likely than the general population to be victims of sexual assault.

Sixty-one percent of rapes are not reported to the police. If a rape is reported, there's a 50.8 percent chance that an arrest will be made. If an arrest is made, there's an 80 percent chance of prosecution. If there's a prosecution, there's a 58 percent chance of felony conviction. If there's a felony conviction, there's a 69 percent chance that the rapist will actually spend time in jail. Of the 39 percent of rapes that are reported to police, then, there's only a 16.3 percent chance that the rapist will wind up in prison. If you factor in all the unreported rapes, 94 percent of rapists walk free.

Laura stared at the screen, at the cursor blinking on one of the multiple percent signs. Trixie was one of these numbers now, one of these percents. She wondered how it was that she'd never truly studied this statistical symbol before: a figure split in two, a pair of empty circles on either side.

Daniel had to park far away from the entrance to the municipal rink, which wasn't surprising on a Saturday afternoon. High school hockey games in Bethel, Maine, drew the same kind of crowds high school football did in Midwestern communities. There were girls standing in the lobby, fixing their lipstick in the reflection of the plate-glass windows, and toddlers weaving through the denim forest of grown-up legs. The grizzled man who sold hot dogs and nachos and Swiss Miss cocoa had taken up residence behind the kitchenette and was singing Motown as he ladled sauerkraut into a bun.

Daniel walked through the crowd as if he were invisible, staring at the proud parents and spirited students who had come to cheer on their home-town heroes. He followed the swell of the human tide through the double doors of the lobby, the ones that opened into the rink. He didn't have a plan, really. What he wanted was to feel Jason Underhill's flesh under his fists. To smack his head up against the wall and scare him into contrition.

Daniel was just about to swing inside the home team's locker room when the door opened beneath his hand. He flattened himself up against the boards in time to see Detective Bartholemew leading Jason Underhill out. The kid was still wearing his hockey gear, in his stocking feet, carrying his skates in one hand. His face was flushed and his eyes were trained on the rubber mats on the floor. The coach followed close behind, yelling, "If it's just a chat, damn it, you could wait till after the game!"

Gradually, the people in the stands noticed Jason's departure and grew quiet, unsure of what they were watching. One man—Jason's father, presumably—pushed down from the bleachers and started running toward his son.

Daniel stood very still for a moment, certain that Bartholemew hadn't seen him, until the detective turned back and looked him straight in the eye. By now the crowd was buzzing with speculation; the air around Daniel's ears was pounding like a timpani—but for that moment, the two men existed in a vacuum, acknowledging each other with the smallest of nods and the quiet understanding that each of them would do what he had to.

"You went to the rink, didn't you," Laura said, as soon as Daniel stepped through the door.

He nodded and busied himself with unzipping his coat, hanging it carefully on one of the pegs in the mudroom.

"Are you going to tell me what happened?"

Vengeance was a funny thing: You wanted the satisfaction of knowing it had occurred, but you never wanted to actually hear the words out loud, because then you'd have to admit to yourself that you'd wanted proof, and that somehow made you baser, less civilized. Daniel found himself staring at Laura as he sank to the stairs. "Shouldn't I be asking you that?" he said quietly.

Just that quickly, this had become a different conversation, a train run off its course. Laura stepped back as if he'd struck her, and bright spots of color rose on her cheeks. "How long have you known?"

Daniel shrugged. "A while, I guess."

"Why didn't you say anything?"

He had asked himself the same question in the last few days a hundred times over. He'd pretended not to see all the late nights, the disconnections, because then he'd have been forced to make a choice: Could you really love someone who was capable of falling in love with somebody else?

But there had been a point in his relationship with Laura where Daniel had been irredeemable, and she had believed he could change. Did he owe her any less? And for that matter, if he let his anger and his shame get the best of him and threw her out of the house, wouldn't he be acting on adrenaline, the way he used to when he lost control?

It was this simple: If he couldn't forgive Laura—if he let himself be consumed by this—he was behaving like the kind of man he used to be.

But he did not have the words to say all this. "If I'd said something about it," Daniel said, "then you would have told me it was true."

"It's over, if that means anything."

He looked up at Laura, his gaze narrow. "Because of Trixie?"

"Before." She moved across the brick floor, her arms folded across her chest, and stood in a shaft of fading light. "I broke it off the night that she . . . that Trixie . . ." Her sentence unraveled at its edge.

"Were you fucking him the night our daughter was raped?"

"Jesus, Daniel—"

"*Were* you? Is that why you didn't answer the phone when I was trying to tell you about Trixie?" A muscle tightened along the column of Daniel's throat. "What's his name, Laura? I think you owe me that much. I think I ought to know who you wanted when you stopped wanting me."

Laura turned away from him. "I want to stop talking about this."

Suddenly, Daniel was on his feet, pinning Laura against the wall, his body a fortress, his anger an electric current. He grabbed Laura's upper arms and shook her so hard that her head snapped back and her eyes went wide with fear. He threw her own words back at her: "What *you* want," he said, his voice raw. "What *you* want?"

Then Laura shoved at him, stronger than he'd given her credit for being. She circled him, never losing eye contact, a lion tamer unwilling to turn her back on the beast. It was enough to bring Daniel to his senses. He stared down at his hands—the ones that had seized her—as if they belonged to someone else.

In that instant, he was standing again in the spring bog behind the school in Akiak, striped with mud and blood, holding his fists high. During the fight, he'd broken two ribs, he had lost a tooth, he had opened a gash over his left eye. He was weaving, but he wasn't about to give in to the pain. *Who else*, Daniel had challenged, until one by one, their hot black gazes fell to the ground like stones.

Shaken, Daniel tried to shove the violence back from wherever it had spilled, but it was like repacking a parachute—part of it trailed between him and Laura, a reminder that the next time he jumped off that cliff of emotion, he might not wind up safe. "I didn't mean to hurt you," he muttered. "I'm sorry."

Laura bowed her head, but not before he saw

the tears in her eyes. "Oh, Daniel," she said. "Me too."

Trixie slept through Jason Underhill's unofficial interrogation in the lobby of the hockey rink, and the moment shortly thereafter when he was officially taken into custody. She slept while the secretary at the police department took her lunch break and called her husband on the phone to tell him who'd been booked not ten minutes before. She slept as that man told his coworkers at the paper mill that Bethel might not win the Maine State hockey championship after all, and why. She was still sleeping when one of the millworkers had a beer on the way home that night with his brother, a reporter for the *Augusta Tribune*, who made a few phone calls and found out that a warrant had indeed been sworn out that morning, charging a minor with gross sexual assault. She slept while the reporter phoned the Bethel PD pretending to be the father of a girl who'd been in earlier that day to give a statement, asking if he'd left a hat behind. "No, Mr. Stone," the secretary had said, "but I'll call you if it turns up."

Trixie continued to sleep while the story was filed, while it was printed. She stayed asleep while the paper was bound with string and sent off in newspaper vans, tossed from the windows of the delivery boys' ratty Hondas. She was asleep still the next morning when everyone in Bethel read the front page. But by then, they already knew why Jason Underhill had been summoned away from a

Bethel High School hockey game the previous day. They knew that Roy Underhill had hired his son a Portland lawyer and was telling anyone who'd listen that his son had been framed. And even though the article was ethical enough never to refer to her by name, everyone knew that it was Trixie Stone, still asleep, who had set this tragedy in motion.

Because Jason was seventeen, the district court judge was sitting as a juvenile judge. And because Jason was seventeen, the courtroom was closed to spectators. Jason was wearing the brand-new blazer and tie his mother had bought him for college interviews. He'd gotten a haircut. His attorney had made sure of that, said sometimes a judge's decisions could hinge on something as frivolous as whether or not he could see your eyes.

Dutch Oosterhaus, his lawyer, was so smooth that every now and then Jason was tempted to look at the floor as he walked by, to see if he'd left a slick trail. He wore shoes that squeaked and the kind of shirts that required cuff links. But his father said Dutch was the best in the state and that he'd be able to make this mess go away.

Jason didn't know what the hell Trixie was trying to pull. They had been going at it, full force—*consensual*, Dutch called it. If that was how she communicated no, then it was a foreign language Jason had never learned.

And yet. Jason tried to hide the way his hands were shaking under the table. He tried to look confident and maybe a little bit pissed off, when in fact he was so scared he felt like he could throw up at any moment.

The district attorney made him think of a shark. She had a wide, flat face and blond hair that was nearly white, but it was the teeth that did it—they were pointy and large and looked like they'd be happy to rip into a person. Her name was Marita Soorenstad, and she had a brother who'd been a legend about ten years ago on the Bethel hockey team, although it hadn't seemed to soften her any toward Jason himself. "Your Honor," she said, "although the State isn't asking for the defendant to be held at a detention facility, there are several conditions we'd ask for. We'd like to make sure that he has no contact with the victim or her family. We'd prefer that he enter a drug and alcohol treatment program. With the exception of the academic school day, the State would like to request that the defendant not be allowed to leave his house—which would include attending sporting events."

The judge was an older man with a bad comb-over. "I'm going to pick and choose the conditions of release, Mr. Underhill. If you violate any of them, you're going to be locked up in Portland. You understand?"

Jason swallowed hard and nodded.

"You are not to have any contact with the victim or her family. You are to be in bed, alone, by ten P.M. You will steer clear of alcohol and drugs, and will begin mandatory substance abuse counseling.

But as for the State's request for house arrest . . . I'm disinclined to agree to that. No need to ruin the Buccaneers' chance for a repeat state championship when there will be plenty of other people around the rink in a supervisory context." He closed the folder. "We're adjourned."

Behind him, Jason could hear his mother weeping. Dutch started packing up his files and stepped across the aisle to speak to the Shark. Jason thought of Trixie, kissing him first that night at Zephyr's. He thought of Trixie hours before that, sobbing in his car, saying that without him, her life was over.

Had she been planning, even then, to end his?

Two days after being sexually assaulted, Trixie felt her life crack, unequally, along the fault line of the rape. The old Trixie Stone used to be a person who dreamed of flying and wanted, when she got old enough, to jump out of a plane and try it. The new Trixie couldn't even sleep with the light off. The old Trixie liked wearing T-shirts that hugged her tight; the new Trixie went to her father's dresser for a sweatshirt that she could hide beneath. The old Trixie sometimes showered twice a day, so that she could smell like the pear soap that her mother always put in her Christmas stocking. The new Trixie felt dirty, no matter how many times she scrubbed herself. The old Trixie felt like part of a group. The new Trixie felt alone, even when she was surrounded by people. The old Trixie would have taken one look at the new Trixie and dismissed her as a total loser.

There was a knock on her door. That was new, too—her father used to just stick his head in, but even he'd become sensitive to the fact that she jumped at her own shadow. "Hey," he said. "You feel up to company?"

She didn't, but she nodded, thinking he meant himself, until he pushed the door wider and she saw that woman Janice, the sexual assault advocate who'd been at the hospital with her. She was wearing a sweater with a jack-o'-lantern on it, although it was closer to Christmas, and enough eyeshadow to cover a battalion of supermodels. "Oh," Trixie said. "It's you."

She sounded rude, and there was something about that that made a little spark flare under her heart. Being a bitch felt surprisingly good, a careful compromise that nearly made up for the fact that she couldn't ever be herself again.

"I'll just, um, let you two talk," Trixie's father said, and even though she tried to send him silent urgent messages with her eyes to keep him from leaving her alone with this woman, he couldn't hear her SOS.

"So," Janice said, after he closed the door. "How are you holding up?"

Trixie shrugged. How had she not noticed at the hospital how much this woman's voice annoyed her? Like a Zen canary.

"I guess you're still sort of overwhelmed. That's perfectly normal."

"Normal," Trixie repeated sarcastically. "Yeah, that's *exactly* how I'd describe myself right now."

"Normal's relative," Janice said.

If it was relative, Trixie thought, then it was the crazy uncle that nobody could stand to be around at family functions, the one who talked about himself in the third person and ate only blue foods and whom everyone else made fun of on the way home.

"It's a whole bunch of baby steps. You'll get there."

For the past forty-eight hours, Trixie had felt like she was swimming underwater. She would hear people talking and it might as well have been Croatian for all that she could understand the words. When it got to be too quiet, she was sure that she heard Jason's voice, soft as smoke, curling into her ear.

"It gets a little easier every day," Janice said, and Trixie all of a sudden hated her with a passion. What the hell did Janice know? She wasn't sitting here, so tired that the insides of her bones ached. She didn't understand how even right now, Trixie wished she could fall asleep, because the only thing she had to look forward to was the five seconds when she woke up in the morning and hadn't remembered everything, yet.

"Sometimes it helps to get it all out," Janice suggested. "Play an instrument. Scream in the shower. Write it all down in a journal."

The last thing Trixie wanted to do was write

about what had happened, unless she got to burn it when she was done.

"Lots of women find it helpful to join a survivors' group . . ."

"So we can all sit around and talk about how we feel like shit?" Trixie exploded. Suddenly she wanted Janice to crawl back from whatever hole good Samaritans came from. She didn't want to make believe that she had a snowball's chance in hell of fitting back into her room, her life, this world. "You know," she said, "this has been real, but I think I'd rather contemplate suicide or something fun like that. I don't need you checking up on me."

"Trixie—"

"You have no idea what I feel like," Trixie shouted. "So don't stand here and pretend we're in this together. *You* weren't there that night. That was just me."

Janice stepped forward, until she was close enough for Trixie to touch. "It was 1972 and I was fifteen. I was walking home and I took a shortcut through the elementary school playground. There was a man there and he said he'd lost his dog. He wanted to know if I'd help him look. When I was underneath the slide, he knocked me down and raped me."

Trixie stared at her, speechless.

"He kept me there for three hours. The whole time, all I could think about was how I used to play there after school. The boys and the girls always kept to separate sides of the jungle gym. We used to dare each other. We'd run up to the boys' side, and then back to safety."

Trixie looked down at her feet. "I'm sorry," she whispered.

"Baby steps," Janice said.

That weekend, Laura learned that there are no cosmic referees. Time-outs do not get called, not even when your world has taken a blow that renders you senseless. The dishwasher still needs to be emptied and the hamper overflows with dirty clothes and the high school buddy you haven't spoken to in six months calls to catch up, not realizing that you cannot tell her what's been going on in your life without breaking down. The twelve students in your class section still expect you to show up on Monday morning.

Laura had anticipated hunkering down with Trixie, protecting her while she licked her wounds. However, Trixie wanted to be by herself, and that left Laura wandering a house that was really Daniel's domain. They were still dancing around each other, a careful choreography that involved leaving a room the moment he entered, lest they have to truly communicate.

"I'm going to take a leave of absence from the college," she had told Daniel on Sunday, when he was reading the newspaper. But hours later, when they were lying on opposite sides of the bed—that tremendous elephant of the affair snug between them—he had brought it up again. "Maybe you shouldn't," he said.

She had looked at him carefully, not sure what he was trying to imply. Did he not want her around 24/7, because it was too uncomfortable? Did he think she cared more about her career than her daughter?

"Maybe it will help Trixie," he added, "if she sees that it's business as usual."

Laura had looked up at the ceiling, at a watermark in the shape of a penguin. "What if she needs me?"

"Then I'll call you," Daniel replied coolly. "And you can come right home."

His words were a slap—the last time he'd called her, she hadn't answered.

The next morning, she fished for a pair of stockings and one of her work skirts. She packed a breakfast she could eat in the car and she left Trixie a note. As she drove, she became aware of how the more distance she put between herself and her home, the lighter she felt—until by the time she reached the gates of the college, she was certain that the only thing anchoring her was her seat belt.

When Laura arrived at her classroom, the students were already clustered around the table, involved in a heated discussion. She'd missed this easy understanding of who she was, where she belonged, the comfort of intellectual sparring. Snippets of the conversation bled into the hallway. *I heard from my cousin, who goes to the high school . . . crucified . . . had it coming.* For a moment Laura hesitated outside the door, wondering how she could have been naïve enough to believe this horrible thing had happened to Trixie, when in truth it had happened to all three of them. Taking a deep breath, she walked into the room, and twelve pairs of eyes turned to her in utter silence.

"Don't stop on my account," she said evenly.

The undergraduates shifted uncomfortably. Laura had so badly wanted to settle into the comfort zone of academia—a place so fixed and immutable that Laura would be assured she could pick up just where she left off—but to her surprise, she no longer seemed to fit. The college was the same; so were the students. It was Laura herself who'd changed.

"Professor Stone," one of the students said, "are you okay?"

Laura blinked as their faces swam into focus before her. "No," she said, suddenly exhausted by the thought of having to deceive anyone else anymore. "I'm not." Then she stood up—leaving her notes, her coat, and her baffled class—and walked into the striking snow, heading back to where she should have been all along.

"Do it," Trixie said, and she squeezed her eyes shut.

She was at Live and Let Dye, a salon within walking distance of her home that catered to the blue-haired set and that, under normal circumstances, she wouldn't have been caught dead in. But this was her first venture out of the house, and in spite of the fact that Janice had given her father a pamphlet about how *not* to be overprotective, he was reluctant to let Trixie go too far. "If you're not back in an hour," her father had said, "I'm coming after you."

She imagined him, even now, waiting by the bay window that offered the best view of their street, so that he'd see her the minute she came back into view. But she'd made it this far, and she wasn't going to let the outing go to waste. Janice had said that when it came to making a decision, she should make a list of pros and cons—and as far as Trixie could tell, anything that made her forget the girl she used to be could only be a good thing.

"You've got quite a tail here," the ancient hairdresser said. "You could donate it to Locks of Love."

"What's that?"

"A charity that makes wigs for cancer patients."

Trixie stared at herself in the mirror. She liked the idea of helping someone who might actually be worse off than she was. She liked the idea of someone who was worse off than she was, period.

"Okay," Trixie said. "What do I have to do?"

"We take care of it," the hairdresser said. "You just give me your name, so that the charity can send you a nice thank-you card."

If she'd been thinking clearly—which, let's face it, she wasn't—Trixie would have made up an alias. But maybe the staff at Live and Let Dye didn't read the newspapers, or ever watch anything but *The Golden Girls*, because the hairdresser didn't bat a fake eyelash when Trixie told her who she was.

She fastened a string around Trixie's waist-length hair and tied it to a little card printed with her name. Then she held up the scissors. "Say good-bye," the hairdresser said.

Trixie drew in her breath at the first cut. Then she noticed how much lighter she felt without all that hair to weigh her down. She imagined what it would be like to have her hair so short that she could feel the wind rushing past the backs of her ears. "I want a buzz cut," Trixie announced.

The hairdresser faltered. "Darlin'," she said, "that's for *boys.*"

"I don't care," Trixie said.

The hairdresser sighed. "Let me see if I can make us both happy."

Trixie closed her eyes and felt the hairdresser's scissors chatter around her head. Hair tumbled down in soft strawberry tufts, like the feathers of a bird shot out of the sky. "Good-bye," she whispered.

They had bought the king-sized bed when Trixie was three and spent more time running from nightmares in her own bed straight into the buffer zone of their own. It had seemed a good idea at the time. Back then, they had still been thinking about having more kids, and it seemed to say *married* with a finality that you couldn't help but admire. And yet, they had fallen in love in a dormitory bed, on a twin mattress. They had slept so close to each other that their body heat would rise each night like a spirit on the ceiling, and they'd wake up with the covers kicked off on the floor. Given that, it was amazing to think that with all the space between them now, they were still too close for comfort.

Daniel knew that Laura was still awake. She had come home from the college almost immediately after she'd left, and she hadn't given him an explanation why. As for Daniel, she'd spoken to him only sporadically, economic transactions of information: had Trixie eaten (no); did she say anything else (no); did the police call (no, but Mrs. Walstone from the end of the block had, as if this was any of her business). Immediately, she'd thrown herself into a tornado of activity: cleaning the bathrooms, vacuuming underneath the couch cushions, watching Trixie come back through the door with that hatchet job of a haircut and swallowing her shock enough to suggest a game of Monopoly. It was, he realized, as if she was trying to make up for her absence these past few months, as if she'd judged herself and meted out a sentence.

Now, lying in bed, he wondered how two people could be just a foot of distance away from each other but a million miles apart. "They knew," Laura said.

"Who?"

"Everyone. At school." She rolled toward him, so that in the plush dark he could make out the green of her eyes. "They all were talking about it."

Daniel could have told her that none of this would go away, not until he and Laura and even Trixie could get past it. He had learned this when he was eleven years old, and Cane's grandfather took him on his first moose hunt. At dusk, they'd set out on the Kuskokwim River in the small aluminum boat. Daniel was dropped off at one bend, Cane at another, to cover more ground.

He had huddled in the willows, wondering how long it would be before Cane and his grandfather came back, wondering if they ever would. When the moose stepped delicately out of the greenery—spindled legs, brindled back, bulbous nose—Daniel's heart had started to race. He'd lifted his rifle and thought, *I want this, more than anything.*

At that moment, the moose slipped into the wall of willows and disappeared.

On the ride home, when Cane and his grandfather learned what had happened, they muttered *kass'aq* and shook their heads. Didn't Daniel know that if you thought about what you were hunting while you were hunting it, you might as well be telegraphing to the animal that you were there?

At first, Daniel had shrugged this off as Yup'ik Eskimo superstition—like having to lick your bowl clean so you wouldn't slip on ice, or eating the tails of fish to become a fast runner. But as he grew older, he learned that a word was a powerful thing. An insult didn't have to be shouted at you to make you bleed; a vow didn't have to be whispered to you to make you believe. Hold a thought in your head, and that was enough to change the actions of anyone and anything that crossed your path.

"If we want things to be normal," Daniel said, "we have to act like we're already there."

"What do you mean?"

"Maybe Trixie should go back to school."

Laura came up on an elbow. "You *must* be joking."

Daniel hesitated. "Janice suggested it. It isn't much good to sit around here all day, reliving what happened."

"She'll see him, in school."

"There's a court order in place; Jason can't go near her. She has as much right to be there as he does."

There was a long silence. "If she goes back," Laura said finally, "it has to be because she wants to."

Daniel had the sudden sense that Laura was speaking not only of Trixie but also herself. It was as if Trixie's rape was a constant fall of leaves they were so busy raking away they could ignore the fact that beneath them, the ground was no longer solid.

The night pressed down on Daniel. "Did you bring him here? To this bed?"

Laura's breathing caught. "No."

"I picture him with you, and I don't even know what he looks like."

"It was a mistake, Daniel—"

"Mistakes are something that happen by accident. You didn't walk out the door one morning and fall into some guy's bed. You thought about it, for a while. You made that choice."

The truth had scorched Daniel's throat, and he found himself breathing hard.

"I made the choice to end it, too. To come back."

"Am I supposed to *thank* you for that?" He flung an arm across his eyes, better to be blind.

Laura's profile was cast in silver. "Do you . . . do you want me to move out?"

He had thought about it. There was a part of him that did not want to see her in the bathroom brushing her teeth, or setting the kettle on the stove. It was too ordinary, a mirage of a marriage. But there was another part of him that no longer remembered who he used to be without Laura. In fact, it was because of her that he'd become the kind of man he now was. It was like any other dual dynamic that was part and parcel of his art: You couldn't have strength without weakness; you couldn't have light without dark; you couldn't have love without loss. "I don't think it would be good for Trixie if you left right now," Daniel said finally.

Laura rolled over to face him. "What about you? Would it be good for you?"

Daniel stared at her. Laura had been inked onto his life, as indelible as any tattoo. It wouldn't matter if she was physically present or not; he would carry her with him forever. Trixie was proof of that. But he'd folded enough loads of laundry during Oprah and Dr. Phil to know how infidelity worked. Betrayal was a stone beneath the mattress of the bed you shared, something you felt digging into you no matter how you shifted position. What was the point of being able to forgive, when deep down, you both had to admit you'd never forget?

When Daniel didn't respond to her, Laura rolled onto her back. "Do you hate me?"

"Sometimes."

"Sometimes I hate myself, too."

Daniel pretended that he could hear Trixie's breathing, even and untroubled, through the bedroom wall. "Was it really so bad? The two of us?"

Laura shook her head.

"Then why did you do it?"

For a long time, she did not answer. Daniel assumed she'd fallen asleep. But then her voice pricked on the edges of the stars strung outside the window. "Because," she said, "he reminded me of you."

Trixie knew that at the slightest provocation, she could stand up and walk out of class and head down to the office for refuge without any teacher even blinking. She had been given her father's cell phone. *Call me anytime*, he said, *and I will be there before you hang up.* She had stumbled through an awkward conversation with the school principal, who phoned to tell her that he would certainly do his best to make Bethel High a haven of safety for her. To that end, she was no longer taking psych with Jason; she had an independent study instead in the library. She could write a report on anything. Right now, she was thinking of a topic: Girls Who Would Rather Disappear.

"I'm sure that Zephyr and your other friends will be happy to see you," her father said. Neither of them mentioned that Zephyr hadn't called, not once, to see how she was doing. Trixie tried to convince herself that was because Zephyr felt guilty, with the fight they'd had and what had happened afterward as a direct result. She didn't explain to her father that she didn't really have any other friends in the ninth grade. She'd been too busy filling her world with Jason to maintain old relationships, or to bother starting new ones.

"What if I've changed my mind?" Trixie asked softly.

Her father looked at her. "Then I'll take you home. It's that easy, Trix."

She glanced out the car window. It was snowing, a fine fat-flaked dusting that hung in the trees and softened the edges of the landscape. The cold seeped through the stocking cap she wore—who knew her hair had actually kept her so warm? She kept forgetting she'd cut it all off in all the smallest ways: when she looked in the mirror and got the shock of her life, when she tried to pull a long nonexistent ponytail out from beneath the collar of her coat. To be honest, she looked horrible—the short cap of hair made her eyes look even bigger and more anxious; the severity of the cut was better suited to a boy—but Trixie liked it. If people were going to stare, she wanted to know it was because she *looked* different, not because she *was* different.

The gates of the school came into view through the windshield wipers, the student parking lot to the right. Under the cover of snow, the cars looked like a sea of beached whales. She wondered which one was Jason's. She imagined him inside the building already, where he'd been for two whole days longer than her, sowing the seeds of his side of the story that by now, surely, had grown into a thicket.

Her father pulled to the curb. "I'll walk you in," he said.

All live wires inside Trixie tripped. Could there be anything that screamed out *loser!* more than a rape victim who had to be walked into school by her daddy? "I can do it myself," she insisted, but when she went to unbuckle her seat belt she found that her mind couldn't make her fingers do the work they needed to.

Suddenly she felt her father's hands on the fastenings, the harness coming free. "If you want to go home," he said gently, "that's okay."

Trixie nodded, hating the tears that welled at the base of her throat. "I know."

It was stupid to be scared. What could possibly happen inside that school that was any worse than what already had? But you could reason with yourself all day and still have butterflies in your stomach.

"When I was growing up in the village," Trixie's father said, "the place we lived was haunted."

Trixie blinked. She could count on one hand the number of times in her life that her father had talked about growing up in Alaska. There were certain remnants of his childhood that labeled him as different—like the way, if it got too loud, he'd have to leave the room, and the obsession he had with conserving water even though they had an endless supply through their home well. Trixie knew this much: Her father had been the only white boy in a native Yup'ik Eskimo village called Akiak. His mother, who raised him by herself, had taught school there. He had left Alaska when he was eighteen, and he swore he'd never go back.

"Our house was attached to the school. The last person who'd lived in it was the old principal, who'd hanged himself from a beam in the kitchen. Everyone knew about it. Sometimes, in the school, the audiovisual equipment would turn on even when it was unplugged. Or the basketballs lying on the floor of the gym would start to bounce by themselves. In our house, drawers would fly open every now and then, and sometimes you could smell aftershave, out of nowhere." Trixie's father looked up at her. "The Yupiit are afraid of ghosts. Sometimes, in school, I'd see kids spit into the air, to check if the ghost was close enough to steal their saliva. Or they'd walk around the building three times so that the ghost couldn't follow them back to their own homes."

He shrugged. "The thing is . . . I was the white kid. I talked funny and I looked funny and I got picked on for that on a daily basis. I was terrified of that ghost just like they were, but I never let anyone know it. That way, I knew they might call me a lot of awful names . . . but one of them wasn't *coward*."

"Jason's not a ghost," Trixie said quietly.

Her father tugged her hat down over her ears.

His eyes were so dark she could see herself shining in them. "Well, then," he said, "I guess you've got nothing to be afraid of."

Daniel nearly ran after Trixie as she navigated the slippery sidewalk up to the front of the school. What if he was wrong about this? What if Janice and the doctors and everyone else didn't know how cruel teenagers could be? What if Trixie came home even *more* devastated?

Trixie walked with her head down, bracing against the cold. Her green jacket was a stain against the snow. She didn't turn back to look at him.

When she was little, Daniel had always waited for Trixie to enter the school building before he drove away. There was too much that could go wrong: She might trip and fall; she could be approached by a bully; she might be teased by a pack of girls. He'd liked to imagine that just by keeping an eye on her, he could imbue her with the power of safety, much like the way he'd draw it onto one of his comics panels in a wavy, flowing force field.

The truth was, though, that Daniel had needed Trixie far more than Trixie had ever needed him. Without realizing it, she'd put on a show for him every day: hopping, twirling, spreading her arms and taking a running leap, as if she thought that one of these mornings she might actually get airborne. He'd watch her and he'd see how easy it was for kids to believe in a world different from the one presented to them. Then he'd drive home and translate that stroke by stroke onto a fresh page.

He could remember wondering how long it would take for reality to catch up to his daughter. He could remember thinking: *The saddest day in the world will be the one when she stops pretending.*

Daniel waited until Trixie slipped through the double doors of the school, and then pulled carefully away from the curb. He needed a load of sand in the back of his pickup to keep it from fishtailing in the snow. Whatever it took, right now, to keep his balance.

# 3

Trixie knew the story behind her real name, but that didn't mean she hated it any less. Beatrice Portinari had been Dante's one true love, the woman who'd inspired him to write a whole batch of epic poems. Her mother the classics professor had single-handedly filled out the birth certificate when her father (who'd wanted to name his newborn daughter Sarah) was in the bathroom.

Dante and Beatrice, though, were no Romeo and Juliet. Dante met her when he was only nine and then didn't see her again until he was eighteen. They both married other people and Beatrice died young. If that was everlasting love, Trixie didn't want any part of it.

When Trixie had complained to her father, he said Nicolas Cage had named his son Kal-el, Superman's Kryptonian name, and that she should be grateful. But Bethel High was brimming with Mallorys, Dakotas, Crispins, and Willows. Trixie had spent most of her life pulling the teacher aside on the first day of school, to make sure she said *Trixie* when she read the attendance sheet, instead of *Beatrice*, which made the other kids crack up. There was a time in fourth grade when she started calling herself Justine, but it didn't catch on.

Summer Friedman was in the main office with Trixie, signing into school late. She was tall and blonde, with a perpetual tan, although Trixie knew for a fact she'd been born in December. She turned around, clutching her blue hall pass. "Slut," she hissed at Trixie as she walked past.

"Beatrice?" the secretary said. "The principal's ready for you."

Trixie had been in the principal's office only once, when she made honor roll during the first quarter of freshman year. She'd been sent during homeroom, and the whole time she'd been shaking, trying to figure out what she'd done wrong. Principal Aaronsen had been waiting with a Cookie Monster grin on his face and his hand extended. "Congratulations, Beatrice," he had said, and he'd handed her a little gold honor roll card with her own disgusting name printed across it.

"Beatrice," he said again this time, when she went into his office. She realized that the guidance counselor, Mrs. Gray, was waiting there for her too. Did they think that if she saw a man alone she might freak out? "It's good to have you back," Mr. Aaronsen said.

*It's good to be back.* The lie sat too sour on Trixie's tongue, so she swallowed it down again.

The principal was staring at her hair, or lack of it,

but he was too polite to say anything. "Mrs. Gray and I just want you to know that our doors are open any time for you," the principal said.

Trixie's father had two names. She had discovered this by accident when she was ten and snooping in his desk drawers. Wedged into the back of one, behind all the smudged erasers and tubes of mechanical pencil leads, was a photograph of two boys squatting in front of a cache of fish. One of the boys was white, one was native. On the back was written: Cane & Wass, fish camp. Akiak, Alaska—1976.

Trixie had taken the photo to her father, who'd been out mowing the lawn. *Who are these people?* she had asked.

Her father had turned off the lawn mower. *They're dead.*

"If you feel the slightest bit uncomfortable," Principal Aaronsen was saying. "If you just want a place to catch your breath . . ."

Three hours later, Trixie's father had come looking for her. *The one on the right is me,* he'd said, showing her the photo again. *And that's Cane, a friend of mine.*

*Your name's not Wass,* Trixie had pointed out.

Her father had explained that the day after he'd been born and named, a village elder came to visit and started calling him Wass—short for Wassilie—after her husband, who'd fallen through the ice and died a week before. It was perfectly normal for a Yup'ik Eskimo who had recently died to take up residence in a newborn. Villagers would laugh when they met Daniel as a baby, saying things like, *Oh, look. Wass has come back with blue eyes!* or *Maybe that's why Wass took that English as a Second Language class!*

For eighteen years, he'd been known as Daniel to his white mother and as Wass to everyone else. In the Yup'ik world, he told Trixie, souls get recycled. In the Yup'ik world, no one ever really gets to leave.

". . . a policy of zero tolerance," the principal said, and Trixie nodded, although she hadn't really been listening.

The night after her father told Trixie about his second name, she had a question ready when he came to tuck her in. *How come when I first asked, you said those boys were dead?*

*Because,* her father answered, *they are.*

Principal Aaronsen stood up, and so did Mrs. Gray, and that was how Trixie realized that they intended to accompany her to class. Immediately she panicked. This was way worse than being walked in by her father; this was like having fighter jets escort a plane into a safe landing: Was there any person at the airport who wouldn't be watching out the windows and trying to guess what had happened on board?

"Um," Trixie said, "I think I'd kind of like to go by myself."

It was almost third period, which meant she'd have time to go to her locker before heading to English class. She watched the principal look at the guidance counselor. "Well," Mr. Aaronsen said, "if that's what you want."

Trixie fled the principal's office, blindly navigating the maze of halls that made up the high school. Class was still in session, so it was quiet—the faint jingle of a kid with a bathroom pass, the muted click of high heels, the wheezy strains of the wind instruments upstairs in the band room. She twisted the combination on her own locker, 40-22-38. *Hey*, Jason had said, a lifetime ago. *Aren't those Barbie's measurements?*

Trixie rested her forehead against the cool metal. All she had to do was sit in class for another four hours. She could fill her mind with *Lord of the Flies* and $A = \pi r^2$ and the assassination of Archduke Franz Ferdinand. She didn't have to talk to anyone if she didn't want to. All of her teachers had been briefed. She would be an army of one.

When she pulled open the door of her locker, a sea of snakes poured out of the narrow cubby, spilling over her feet. She reached down to pick one up. Eight small foil squares, accordion-pleated at the perforations.

*Trojan*, Trixie read. *Twisted Pleasure Lubricated Latex Condoms.*

"They're all having sex," Marita Soorenstad said, tilting her head and pouring the last of the lime-colored powder into her mouth. In the fifteen minutes that Mike Bartholemew had been sitting with the assistant district attorney, she'd consumed three Pixy Stix. "Teenage girls want guys to be attracted to them, but no one's taught them how to deal with the emotions that come with that stuff. I see this all the time, Mike. Teenage girls wake up to find someone having sex with them, and they don't say a word." She crushed the paper straw in her fist and grimaced. "Some judge told me these were a godsend when he was trying to quit smoking. But I swear all I'm getting is a sugar high and a green tongue."

"Trixie Stone said *no*," the detective pointed out. "It's in her statement."

"And Trixie Stone was drinking. Which the defense attorney will use to call her judgment into question. Oosterhaus is going to say that she was intoxicated, and playing strip poker, and saying *yes yes yes* all the way up till afterward, which is about when she decided to say *no.* He's going to ask her what time it was when she said it and how many pictures were on the walls of the room and what song was playing on the stereo and whether the moon was in Scorpio—details she won't be able to remember. Then he'll say that if she can't remember particulars like this, how on earth could she be sure of whether she told Jason to stop?" Marita hesitated. "I'm not saying that Trixie Stone wasn't raped, Mike. I'm just telling you that not everyone is going to see it as clearly."

"I think the family knows that," Bartholemew said.

"The family never knows that, no matter what they say." Marita opened the file on Trixie Stone.

"What the hell else did they think their kid was out doing at two in the morning?"

Bartholemew pictured a car overturned on the side of the road, the rescue crews clustered around the body that had been thrown through the windshield. He imagined the EMT who pulled up the sleeve of his daughter's shirt and saw the bruises and needle marks along the map of her veins. He wondered if that tech had looked at Holly's long-sleeved shirt, worn on the hottest night of July, and asked himself what this girl's parents had been thinking when they saw her leave the house in it.

The answer to this question, and to Marita's: *We weren't thinking. We didn't let ourselves think, because we didn't want to know.*

Bartholemew cleared his throat. "The Stones thought their daughter was having a parent-supervised sleepover at a friend's house."

Marita ripped open a yellow Pixy Stix. "Great," she said, upending the contents into her mouth. "So Trixie's already lied once."

Even though parents don't want to admit it, school isn't about what a kid absorbs while she's sitting at a cramped desk, but what happens around and in spite of that. It's the five minutes between bells when you find out whose house is hosting the party that evening; it's borrowing the right shade of lip gloss from your friend before you have French with the cute guy who moved here from Ohio; it's being noticed by everyone else and pretending you are above that sort of celebrity.

Once all this social interaction was surgically excised from Trixie's school day, she noticed how little she cared about the academic part. In English, she focused on the printed text in her book until the letters jumped like popcorn in a skillet. From time to time she would hear a snide comment: *What did she do to her hair?* Only once did someone have the guts to actually speak to her in class. It was in phys ed, during an indoor soccer game. A girl on her own team had come up to her after the teacher called a time-out. "Someone who got raped for real," she'd whispered, "wouldn't be out here playing soccer."

The part of the day that Trixie was most dreading was lunch. In the cafeteria, the mass of students split like amoebas into socially polarized groups. There were the drama kids and the skateboarders and the brains. There were the Sexy Seven—a group of girls who set the school's unwritten fashion rules, like what months you should wear shorts to school and how flip-flops were totally passé. There were the caffies, who hung out all morning drinking java with their friends until the voc-tech bus came to ferry them to classes on hairstyling and child care. And then there was the table where Trixie used to belong—the one with the popular kids, the one where Zephyr and Moss and a carefree knot of hockey players hung out pretending they didn't know that everyone else was looking at them and saying they were so fake, when in reality those same kids went home and wished that their own group of friends could be as cool.

Trixie bought herself french fries and chocolate milk—her comfort lunch, for when she screwed up on a test or had period cramps—and stood in the middle of the cafeteria, trying to find a place for herself. Since Jason had broken up with Trixie, she'd been sitting somewhere else, but Zephyr had always joined her in solidarity. Today, though, she could see Zephyr sitting at their old table. One sentence rose from the collective din: "She wouldn't dare."

Trixie held her plastic tray like a shield. She finally moved toward the Heater Hos, congregating near the radiator. They were girls who wore white pants with spandex in them and had boyfriends who drove raised I-Rocs; girls who got pregnant at fifteen and then brought the ultrasounds to school to show off.

One of them—a ninth-grader in what looked like her ninth month—smiled at Trixie, and the action was so unexpected, she nearly stumbled. "There's room," the girl said, and she slid her backpack off the table so that Trixie could sit down.

A lot of kids at Bethel High made fun of the Heater Hos, but Trixie never had. She found them too depressing to be the butt of jokes. They seemed to be so nonchalant about throwing their lives away—not that their lives were the kind that anyone would have wanted in the first place, but still. Trixie had wondered if those belly-baring

T-shirts they wore and the pride they took in their situation were just for show, a way to cover up how sad they really were about what had happened to them. After all, if you acted like you really wanted something even when you didn't, you just might convince yourself along with everyone else.

Trixie ought to know.

"I asked Donna to be Elvis's godmother," one of the girls said.

"Elvis?" another answered. "I thought you were going to name him Pilot."

"I was, but then I thought, what if he's born afraid of heights? That would suck for him."

Trixie dipped a french fry into a pool of ketchup. It looked weak and watery, like blood. She wondered how many hours it had been since she'd talked out loud. If you didn't use your voice, ever, would it eventually shrivel up and dry away? Was there a natural selection involved in not speaking up?

"Trixie."

She looked up to see Zephyr sliding into the seat across from her. Trixie couldn't contain her relief—if Zephyr had come over here, she couldn't be mad anymore, could she? "God, I'm glad to see you," Trixie said. She wanted to make a joke, to let Zephyr know it was okay to treat her like she wasn't a freak, but she couldn't think of a single thing to say.

"I would have called," Zephyr said, "but I've sort of been grounded until I'm forty."

Trixie nodded. It was enough, really, that Zephyr was sitting here now.

"So . . . you're *okay*, right?"

"Yeah," Trixie said. She tried to remember what her father had said that morning: If you think you're fine, you'll start to believe it.

"Your hair . . ."

She ran her palm over her head and smiled nervously. "Crazy, isn't it?"

Zephyr leaned forward, shifting uncomfortably. "Look, what you did . . . well, it worked. No question—you got Jason back."

"What are you *talking* about?"

"You wanted payback for getting dumped, and you got it. But Trixie . . . it's one thing to teach someone a lesson . . . and a whole different thing to get him *arrested.* Don't you think you can stop now?"

"You think . . ." Trixie's scalp tightened. "You think I made this up?"

"Trix, everyone knows you wanted to hook up with him again. It's kind of hard to rape someone who's *willing.*"

"You're the one who came up with the plan! You said I should make him jealous! But I never expected . . . I didn't . . ." Trixie's voice was as thin as a wire, vibrating. "He *raped* me."

A shadow fell across the table as Moss approached. Zephyr looked up at him and shrugged. "I tried," she said.

He pulled Zephyr out of her chair. "Come on."

Trixie stood up, too. "We've been friends since kindergarten. How could you believe him over me?"

Something in Zephyr's eyes changed, but before she could speak, Moss slid an arm around her shoulders, anchoring her to his side. *So,* Trixie thought. *It's like that.*

"Nice hair, *G.I. Ho,*" Moss said as they walked off.

It had gotten so quiet in the cafeteria that even the lunch ladies seemed to be watching. Trixie sank down into her seat again, trying not to notice the way that everyone was staring at her. There was a one-year-old she used to babysit for who liked to play a game: He'd cover his face with his hands and you'd say, "Where's Josh?" She wished it was that simple: Close your eyes, and you'd disappear.

Next to her, one of the Heater Hos cracked her bubble gum. "I wish Jason Underhill would rape *me,*" she said.

Daniel had made coffee for Laura.

Even after what she had done, even after all the words that fell between them like a rain of arrows, he had still done this for her. It might not have been anything more than habit, but it brought her to the verge of tears.

She stared at the carafe, its swollen belly steaming with French roast. It occurred to Laura that in all the years they had been married, she could literally not remember it being the other way around: Daniel had been a student of her likes and dislikes;

in return, Laura had never even signed up for the proverbial course. Was it complacency that had made her restless enough to have an affair? Or was it because she hadn't wanted to admit that even *had* she applied herself, she would not be as good a wife as Daniel was a husband?

She had come into the kitchen to sit down at the table, spread out her notes, prepare for her afternoon class. Today, thank God, was a lecture, an impersonal group where she got to do all the talking, not a smaller class where she might have to face the questions of students again. In her hands was a book, open to the famous Doré illustration for Canto 29, where Virgil—Dante's guide through hell—berated his curiosity. But now that Laura could smell the grounds, inhale that aromatic steam, she couldn't for the life of her remember what she was going to say about this drawing to her students.

Explaining hell took on a whole new meaning when you'd been recently living smack in the middle of it, and Laura envisioned her own face on the sketch, instead of Dante's. She took a sip of her coffee and imagined drinking from the River Lethe, which ran back to its source, taking all your sins with it.

There was a fine line between love and hate, you heard that cliché all the time. But no one told you that the moment you crossed it would be the one you least expected. You'd fall in love and crack open a secret door to let your soul mate in. You just never expected such closeness, one day, to feel like an intrusion.

Laura stared down at the picture. With the exception of Dante, nobody chose to go willingly to hell. And even Dante would have lost his way if he hadn't found a guide who'd already been through hell and come out the other side.

Reaching up to the cabinet, Laura took out a second mug and poured another cup of coffee. In all honesty, she had no idea if Daniel took it with milk or sugar or both. She added a little of each, the way she liked to drink it.

She hoped that was a start.

In the latest issue of *Wizard* magazine, on the list of top ten comic book artists, Daniel was ranked number nine. His picture was there, eight notches below Jim Lee's number one smiling face. Last month, Daniel had been number ten; it was the growing anticipation for *The Tenth Circle* that was fueling his fame.

It was actually Laura who had told Daniel when he was becoming famous. They'd gone to a Christmas party at Marvel in New York, and when they entered the room, they were separated in the crush. Later, she told him that as he walked through the crowd, she could hear everyone talking in his wake. *Daniel*, she had said, *people definitely know you.*

When he'd first been given a test story to draw, years ago—a god-awful piece that took place inside a cramped airplane—he'd worried about things that he never would have given a second thought to now: having F lead in his pencil instead of something too soft, testing the geometry of arches, mapping the feel of a ruler in his hand. If anything, he had drawn more from the gut when he was starting out—emotional art, instead of cerebral. The first time he'd penciled Batman for DC Comics, for example, he'd had to reimagine the hero. Daniel's rendition had a certain length ear and a certain width belt that had little to do with the historical progression of art on that character and far more to do with poring over the comic as a kid, and remembering how Batman had looked at his coolest.

Today, though, drawing wasn't bringing him any joy or relief. He kept thinking about Trixie and where she would be at this hour of the day and if it was a good thing or a bad thing that she hadn't called him yet to say how it was going. Ordinarily, if Daniel was restless, he'd get up and walk around the house, or even take a run to jog his brain and recover his lost muse. But Laura was home—she had no classes until this afternoon—and that was enough to keep him holed up in his office. It was easier to face down a blank page than to pull from thin air the right words to rebuild a marriage.

His task today was to draw a series of panels in hell with adultery demons—sinners who had lusted for each other in life, and in death couldn't be separated from each other. The irony of having to draw this, given his own situation, had not been lost on Daniel. He imagined a male and a female torso, each growing out of the same root of a body. He pictured one wing on each of their backs. He saw claws that would reach in to steal a hero's heart, because that was exactly how it felt.

He was cheating today, drawing the action sequences, because they were the most engaging. He always jumped around the story, to keep himself from overdoing it on the first panel he drew. But just in case he started running out of time on a deadline, it was easier to draw straight lines and buildings and roads than to dynamically draw a figure.

Daniel began sketching the outline of an ungainly, birdlike creature, half man and half woman. He roughed in a wing—no, too batlike. He was just blowing the eraser rubbings off the Miraweb paper when Laura walked into his office, holding a cup of coffee.

He set down his pencil and leaned back in his chair. Laura rarely visited him in his office. Most of the time, she wasn't home. And when she was, it was always Daniel seeking *her* out, instead of the other way around.

"What are you drawing?" she asked, peering down at the panels.

"Nothing good."

"Worried about Trixie?"

Daniel rubbed a hand down his face. "How couldn't I be?"

She sank down at his feet, cross-legged. "I know. I keep thinking I hear the phone ring." She glanced down at her coffee cup, as if she was surprised to find herself clutching it. "Oh," she said. "I brought this for you."

She never brought him coffee before. He didn't even really *like* coffee. But there was Laura with her hand outstretched, offering the steaming mug— and in that instant, Daniel could imagine her fingers reaching like a dagger between his ribs. He could see how a wing that grew from between her shoulder blades might sweep over the muscles of her trapezius, wrapping over her arm like a shawl.

"Do me a favor?" he asked, taking the mug from her. He grabbed a quilt that he kept on the couch in his office and leaned down to pull it around Laura.

"God," she said. "I haven't modeled for you in years."

When he was just starting out, he'd pose her a hundred different ways: in her bra and panties holding a water gun; tossed halfway off the bed; hanging upside down from a tree in the yard. He would wait for the moment when that familiar skin and structure stopped being Laura and became, instead, a twist of sinew and a placement of bone, one he could translate anatomically into a character sprawled just the same way on the page.

"What's the quilt for?" Laura asked, as he picked up his pencil and started to draw.

"You have wings."

"Am I an angel?"

Daniel glanced up. "Something like that," he said.

The moment Daniel stopped obsessing about

drawing the wing, it took flight. He drew fast, the lines pouring out of him. This quick, art was like breath. He couldn't have told you why he placed the fingers at that angle instead of the more conventional one, but it made the figure seem to move across the panel. "Lift the blanket up a little, so it covers your head," he instructed.

Laura obliged. "This reminds me of your first story. Only drier."

Daniel's first paid gig had been a Marvel fill-in for the Ultimate X-Men series. In the event that a regular artist didn't make deadline, his stand-alone piece would be used without breaking the continuity of the ongoing saga.

He'd been given a story about Storm as a young child, harnessing the weather. In the name of research, he and Laura had driven to the shore during a thunderstorm, with Trixie still in her infant seat. They left the sleeping baby in the car and then sat on the beach in the pouring rain with a blanket wrapped around their shoulders, watching the lightning write notes on the sand.

Later that night, on his way back to the car, Daniel had tripped over the strangest tube of glass. It was a fulgurite, Laura told him, sand fused the moment it was struck by lightning. The tube was eight inches long, rough on the outside and smooth through its long throat. Daniel had tucked it into the side of Trixie's car seat, and even today it was still delicately displayed on her bookshelf.

It had amazed him: that utter transformation, the

understanding that radical change could come in a heartbeat.

Finally, Daniel finished drawing. He put down his pencil, flexed his hand, and glanced down at the page: This was good; this was better than good. "Thanks," he said, standing up to take the blanket off Laura's shoulders.

She stood, too, and grabbed two corners of the quilt. They folded it in silence, like soldiers with a casket's flag. When they met in the middle, Daniel went to take the blanket from her, but Laura didn't let go. She slid her hands along its folded seam until they rested on top of Daniel's, and then she lifted her face shyly and kissed him.

He didn't want to touch her. Her body pressed against his through the buffer of the quilt. But instinct broke over him, a massive wave, and he wrapped his arms so tightly around Laura he could feel her struggling to breathe. His kiss was hungry, violent, a feast for what he'd been missing. It took a moment, and then she came to life beneath him, grabbing fistfuls of his shirt, pulling him closer, consuming him in a way he could not ever remember her doing before.

*Before.*

With a groan, Daniel dragged his mouth from hers, buried his face in the curve of her neck. "Are you thinking about him?" he whispered.

Laura went utterly still, and her arms fell away. "No," she said, her cheeks bright and hot.

Between them on the floor, the quilt was now a heap. Daniel saw a stain on it that he hadn't noticed before. He bent down and gathered it into his arms. "Well, *I* am."

Laura's eyes filled with tears, and a moment later she walked out of his office. When he heard the door close, Daniel sank down into his chair again. He kept brushing up against the fact that his wife had cheated on him. It was a little like a scar on a polished wooden table—you'd try to see the rest of the gleaming surface, but your eyes and your fingers would be drawn to the pitted part, the one thing that kept it from being perfect.

It was two-fifteen; only another half hour until he picked up Trixie at school. Only a half hour until she could serve as the cushion that kept him and Laura from rubbing each other raw.

But in a half hour, lightning could strike. Wives could fall in love with men who weren't their husbands. Girls could be raped.

Daniel buried his face in his hands. Between his splayed fingers, he could see the figure he'd sketched. Half of a demon, she was wrapped in her own single wing. She was the spitting image of Laura. And she was reaching for a heart Daniel couldn't draw, because he'd forgotten its dimensions years ago.

Jason was missing practice. He sat in the swanky law offices of Yargrove, Bratt & Oosterhaus, wondering what drills Coach was putting the team through. They had a game tomorrow against Gray–New Gloucester, and he was on the starting line.

Trixie had come back to school today. Jason hadn't seen her—someone had made damn sure of that—but Moss and Zephyr and a dozen other friends had run into her. Apparently, she'd practically shaved her head. He'd wondered, on the drive down to Portland, what it would have been like if he *had* crossed paths with Trixie. The judge at the arraignment had said that was enough cause to have Jason sent to a juvy prison, but he must have meant Jason would be in trouble if he sought Trixie out . . . not if Fate tossed her in his path.

Which is sort of what had happened in the first place.

He still couldn't believe that this was real, that he was sitting in a lawyer's office, that he had been charged with rape. He kept expecting his alarm clock to go off any minute now. He'd drive to school and catch Moss in the hallway and say, *Man, you wouldn't believe the nightmare I had.*

Dutch Oosterhaus was talking to his parents, who were wearing their church clothes and were looking at Dutch as if he were Jesus incarnate. Jason knew his parents were paying the lawyer with money they'd scrimped together to send him for a PG year at a prep school, so that he'd have a better chance of making a Division I college hockey team. Gould Academy scouts had already come to watch him play; they'd said he was as good as in.

"She was crying," Dutch said, rolling a fancy pen between his fingers. "She was begging you to get back together with her."

"Yeah," Jason replied. "She didn't . . . she didn't take the breakup very well. There were times I thought she was losing it. You know."

"Do you know if Trixie was seeing a psychiatrist?" Dutch made a note to himself. "She might even have talked to a rape crisis counselor. We can subpoena those records for evidence of mental instability."

Jason didn't know what Trixie was up to, but he'd never thought she was crazy. Until Friday night's party, Trixie had been so easy to read that it set her apart from the dozens of girls he'd hooked up with who were in it for the status or the sex or the head games. It was nuts—and this wasn't something he'd ever admit to his friends—but the best part about being with Trixie had not been the fact that she was, well, hot. It had been knowing that even if he'd never been an athlete or an upperclassman or popular, she still would have wanted to be with him.

He'd liked her, but he hadn't really loved her. At least he didn't think he had. There were no lightning bolts across his vision when he saw her across a room, and his general feeling when he was with her was one of comfort, not of blood boiling and fire and brimstone. The reason he'd broken up with her was, ironically, for her own good. He knew that if he'd asked Trixie to drop everything and follow him across the earth, she'd do it; if the roles were reversed, though, he wouldn't. They were at different places in that same relationship, and like anything that's out of alignment, they were destined to crash sooner or later. By taking care of it early—gently, Jason liked to think—he was only trying to keep Trixie from getting her heart broken even harder.

He certainly felt bad about doing it, though. Just because he didn't love Trixie didn't mean he didn't like her.

And as for the other, well. He *was* a seventeen-year-old guy, and you didn't throw away something that was handed to you on a silver platter.

"Walk me through what happened after you found her in Zephyr's bathroom?"

Jason scrubbed his hands over his head, making his hair stand on end. "I offered her a ride home, and she said yes. But then she started crying. I felt bad for her, so I kind of hugged her."

"Hugged her? How?"

Jason lifted up his arms and folded them awkwardly around himself. "Like that."

"What happened next?"

"She came on to me. She kissed me."

"What did you do?" Dutch asked.

Jason stole a glance at his mother, whose cheeks were candy-apple red with embarrassment. He couldn't believe that he had to say these things in front of her. She'd be saying Rosaries for a week straight on his behalf. "I kissed her back. I mean, it was like falling into an old habit, you know? And she clearly was interested—"

"Define that," Dutch interrupted.

"She took off her own shirt," Jason said, and his

mother winced. "She unbuckled my belt and went down on me."

Dutch wrote another note on his pad. "She initiated oral sex?"

"Yeah."

"Did you reciprocate?"

"No."

"Did she say anything to you?"

Jason felt himself getting hot beneath the collar of his shirt. "She said my name a lot. And she kept talking about doing this in someone's living room. But it wasn't like she was freaked out about it—it was more like it was exciting for her, hooking up in someone else's house."

"Did she tell you she was interested in having intercourse?"

Jason thought for a second. "She didn't tell me she *wasn't*," he replied.

"Did she ask you to stop?"

"No," Jason said.

"Did you know she was a virgin?"

Jason felt all the thoughts in his head solidify into one hard, black mass, as he understood that he'd been played the fool. "Yeah," he said, angry. "Back in October. The first time we had sex."

Trixie looked like she'd been fighting a war. The minute she threw herself into the truck beside Daniel, he was seized with the urge to storm into the school and demand retribution from the student body that had done this to her. He imagined himself raging through the halls, and then, quickly, shook the vision out of his mind. The last thing Trixie needed, after being raped, was to see that violence could beget more violence.

"Do you want to talk about it?" he said after they had driven for a few moments.

Trixie shook her head. She drew her knees up and wrapped her arms around them, as if she was trying to make herself as small as possible.

Daniel pulled off the road. He reached over the console to awkwardly draw Trixie into his arms. "You don't have to go back," he promised. "Ever." Her tears soaked through his flannel shirt. He would teach Trixie at home, if he had to. He would find her a tutor. He would pick up the whole family and move.

Janice, the sexual assault advocate, had warned him against just that. She said that fathers and brothers always wanted to protect the victim after the fact, because they felt guilty about not doing it right the first time. But if Daniel fought Trixie's battles, she might never figure out for herself how to be strong again.

Well, fuck Janice. She didn't have a daughter who'd been raped. And even if she *did*, it wasn't Trixie.

Suddenly there was the sound of glass breaking, as a car drove by and the boys inside threw a six-pack of empty beer bottles at the truck. *"Whore!"* The word was yelled through open windows. Daniel saw the retreating taillights of a Subaru. The backseat passenger reached through his window to high-five the driver.

Daniel let go of Trixie and stepped out of the car onto the shoulder of the road. Beneath his shoes, glass crunched. The bottles had scratched the paint on the door of the truck, had shattered under his tires. The word they'd called his daughter still hung in the air.

He had an artist's vision—of Duncan, his hero, turning into Wildclaw . . . this time in the shape of a jaguar. He imagined what it would be like to run faster than the wind, to race around the tight corner and leap through the narrow opening of the driver's side window. He pictured the car, careening wildly. He smelled their fear. He went for blood.

Instead, Daniel leaned down and picked up the biggest pieces of glass. He carefully cleared a path, so that he could get Trixie back home.

The night that Trixie met Jason, she'd had the flu. Her parents had been at some fancy shindig at Marvel headquarters in New York City, and she was spending the night at Zephyr's house. Zephyr had wangled her way into an upperclass party that evening, and it had been all the two of them could talk about. But no sooner had school let out than Trixie started throwing up.

"I think I'm going to die," Trixie had told Zephyr.

"Not before you hang out with seniors," Zephyr said.

They told Zephyr's mother that they were going to study for an algebra test with Bettina Majura-dee, the smartest girl in ninth grade, who in reality wouldn't have given them the time of day. They walked two miles to the house party, which was being held by a guy named Orson. Twice, Trixie had to double up at the side of the road and barf into some bushes. "Actually, this is cool," Zephyr had told her. "They're going to think you're already trashed."

The party was a writhing, pulsing mass of noise and bodies and motion. Trixie moved from a quartet of gyrating girls to a table of faceless guys playing the drinking game Beirut, to a posse of kids trying to make a pyramid out of empty cans of Bud. Within fifteen minutes, she felt feverish and dizzy and headed to the bathroom to be sick.

Five minutes later, she opened up the door and started down the hallway, intent on finding Zephyr and leaving. "Do you believe in love at first sight," a voice asked, "or should I ask you to walk by me again?"

Trixie glanced down to find a guy sitting on the floor, his back to the wall. He was wearing a T-shirt so faded she couldn't read the writing on it. His hair was jet-black, and his eyes were the color of ice, but it was his smile—lopsided, as if it had been built on a slope—that made her heart hitch.

"I don't think I've seen you before," he said.

Trixie suddenly lost the power of conversation.

"I'm Jason."

"I'm sick," Trixie blurted out, cursing herself the minute she heard the words. Could she sound any stupider if she tried?

But Jason had just grinned, off-kilter, again.

"Well, then," he'd said, and started it all. "I guess I need to make you feel better."

Zephyr Santorelli-Weinstein worked at a toy store. She was affixing UPC codes for prices onto the feet of stuffed animals when Mike Bartholemew arrived to talk to her. "So," he said, after introducing himself. "Is now a good time?" He looked around the store. There were science kits and dress-up clothes and Legos, marble chutes and paint-your-own beanbag chair kits and baby dolls that cried on command.

"I guess," Zephyr said.

"You want to sit down?" But the only place to sit was a little kid-sized tea table, set with Madeline china and plastic cupcakes. Bartholemew could imagine his knees hitting his chin or, worse, getting down and never getting back up again.

"I'm good," Zephyr said. She put down the gun that affixed the UPC labels and folded her arms around a fluffy polar bear.

Bartholemew looked at her stretch button-down shirt and stacked heels, her eye makeup, her scarlet nail polish, the toy in her arms. He thought, *This is exactly the problem.* "I appreciate you talking to me."

"My mother's making me do it."

"Guess she wasn't thrilled to find out about your little party."

"She's less thrilled that you turned the living room into some kind of crime scene."

"Well," Bartholemew said, "it *is* one."

Zephyr snorted. She picked up the sticker gun and started tagging the animals again.

"I understand that you and Trixie Stone have been friends for a while."

"Since we were five."

"She mentioned that just before the incident occurred, you two were having an argument." He paused. "What were you fighting about?"

She looked down at the counter. "I don't remember."

"Zephyr," the detective said, "if you've got details for me, it might help corroborate your friend's story."

"We had a plan," Zephyr sighed. "She wanted to make Jason jealous. She was trying to get him back, to hook up with him. That was the whole *point.* Or at least that's what she told me."

"What do you mean?"

"Well, I guess she meant to screw Jason in more ways than one."

"Did she say she intended to have intercourse that night?"

"She told me she was willing to do whatever it took," Zephyr said.

Bartholemew looked at her. "Did you see Trixie and Jason having sex?"

"I'm not into peep shows. I was upstairs."

"Alone?"

"With a guy. Moss Minton."

"What were you doing?"

Zephyr glanced up at the detective. "Nothing."

"Were you and Moss having sex?"

"Did my mother ask you to ask me that?" she said, narrowing her eyes.

"Just answer the question."

"No, all right?" Zephyr said. "We were going to. I mean, I figured we were going to. But Moss passed out first."

"And you?"

She shrugged. "I guess I fell asleep eventually, too."

"When?"

"I don't know. Two-thirty? Three?"

Bartholemew looked at his notes. "Could you hear the music in your bedroom?"

Zephyr stared at him dully. "*What* music?"

"The CDs you were playing during your party. Could you hear that upstairs?"

"No. By the time we got upstairs, someone had turned them off." Zephyr gathered the stack of stuffed animals, holding them in her arms like a bounty, and walked toward an empty shelf. "That's why I figured Jason and Trixie had gone home."

"Did you hear Trixie scream for help?"

For the first time since he'd started speaking to her, Bartholemew saw Zephyr at a loss for words. "If I'd heard that," Zephyr said, her voice wavering the tiniest bit, "I would have gone downstairs." She set the bears down side by side, so that they were nearly touching. "But the whole night, it was dead quiet."

Until Laura met Daniel, she had never done anything wrong. She'd gotten straight A's in school.

She'd been known to pick up *other* people's litter. She'd never had a cavity.

She was a graduate student at ASU, dating an MBA named Walter who had already taken her to three jewelry stores to get her feedback on engagement rings. Walter was attractive, secure, and predictable. On Friday nights, they always went out to dinner, switched their entrees halfway through the meal, and then went to see a movie. They alternated picking the films. Afterward, over coffee, they talked about the quality of the acting. Then Walter would drive her back to her apartment in Tempe and after a bout of predictable sex he'd go home because he didn't like to sleep in other people's beds.

One Friday, when they went to the movie theater, it was closed because of a burst water main. She and Walter decided to walk down Mill Avenue instead, where on warm nights buskers littered the streets with their violin cases and their impromptu juggling.

There were several artists too, sketching in pencil, sketching in charcoal, making caricatures with Magic Markers that smelled like licorice. Walter gravitated toward one man, bent over his pad. The artist had black hair that reached down to the middle of his back and ink all over his hands. Behind him was a makeshift cardboard stand, onto which he'd pinned dynamic drawings of Batman and Superman and Wolverine. "These are amazing," Walter said, and Laura had thought at the time that she'd never seen him get so excited about something. "I used to collect comics as a kid."

When the artist looked up, he had the palest blue eyes, and they were focused on Laura. "Ten bucks for a sketch," he said.

Walter put his arm around Laura. "Can you do one of her?"

Before she knew it, she'd been seated on an overturned milk crate. A crowd gathered to watch as the sketch took shape. Laura glanced over at Walter, wishing that he hadn't suggested this. She startled when she felt the artist's fingers curl around her chin, turning her face forward again. "Don't move," he warned, and she could smell nicotine and whiskey.

He gave the drawing to Laura when he was finished. She had the body of a superhero—muscular and able—but her hair and face and neck were all her own. A galaxy swirled around her feet. There were people sketched into the background—the crowd that had gathered. Walter's face was nearly off the edge of the page. Beside the figure of Laura, however, was a man who looked just like the artist. "So that you'll be able to find me one day," he said, and she felt as if a storm had blown up inside her.

Laura looked at Walter, holding out his ten-dollar bill. She lifted her chin. "What makes you think I'll be looking?"

The artist grinned. "Wishful thinking."

When they left Mill Avenue, Laura told Walter it was the worst sketch she'd ever seen—her calves weren't that big, and she'd never be caught dead wearing thigh-high boots. She planned to go home and throw it in the trash. But instead, that night, Laura found herself staring at the bold strokes of the artist's signature: *Daniel Stone.* She examined the picture more closely and noticed what she hadn't the first time around: In the folds of the cape the man had drawn were a few lines darker than the rest, which clearly spelled out the word MEET.

In the toe of the left boot was ME.

She scrutinized the sketch, scanning the crowd for more of the message. She found the letters AT on the rings of the planet in the upper left corner. And in the collar of the shirt worn by the man who looked like Walter was the word HELL.

It felt like a slap in the face, as if he knew she'd be reading into the drawing he'd made. Angry, Laura buried the sketch in her kitchen trash can. But she tossed and turned all night, deconstructing the language in the art. You wouldn't say *meet me* at *hell*; you'd say *meet me* in *hell. In* suggested submersion, *at* was an approach to a place. Had this not been a rejection, then, but an invitation?

The next day, she pulled the sketch out from the trash, and sat down with the Phoenix area phone book.

Hell was at 358 Wylie Street.

She borrowed a magnifying glass from an ASU biology lab but couldn't find any more clues in the drawing regarding a time or date. That afternoon, once she finished her classes, Laura made her way to Wylie Street. Hell turned out to be a narrow space between two larger buildings—one a head shop with bongs in the window, the other a XXX video store. The jammed little frontage had no windows, just a graffiti-riddled door. In lieu of a formal sign, there was a plank with the name of the establishment hand-lettered in blue paint.

Inside, the room was thin and long, able to accommodate a bar and not much else. The walls were painted black. In spite of the fact that it was three in the afternoon, there were six people sitting at the bar, some of whom Laura could not assign to one gender or the other. As the sunlight cracked through the open doorway, they turned to her, squinting, moles coming up from the belly of the earth.

Daniel Stone sat closest to the door. He raised one eyebrow and stubbed out his cigarette on the wood of the bar. "Have a seat."

She held out her hand. "I'm Laura Piper."

He looked at her hand, amused, but didn't shake it. She crawled onto the stool and folded her purse into her lap. "Have you been waiting long?" she asked, as if this were a business meeting.

He laughed. The sound made her think of summer dust, kicked up by tires on a dirt road. "My whole life."

She didn't know how to respond to that. "You didn't give me a specific time . . ."

His eyes lit up. "But you found the rest. And I pretty much live here, anyway."

"Are you from Phoenix?"

"Alaska."

To a girl who'd grown up on the outskirts of the desert, there was nothing more remarkable or idealistically romantic. She pictured snow and polar bears. Eskimos. "What made you come here?"

He shrugged. "Up there, you learn the blues. I needed to see reds." It took Laura a moment to realize that he was talking about colors and his drawing. He lit another cigarette. It bothered her—she wasn't used to people smoking around her—but she didn't know how to ask him not to. "So," he said. "Laura."

Nervous, she began to fill in the silence between them. "There was a poet who had a Laura as his muse. Petrarch. His sonnets are really beautiful."

Daniel's mouth curved. "Are they, now."

She didn't know if he was making fun of her, and now she was conscious of other people in the bar listening to their conversation, and frankly, she couldn't remember why she'd ever come here in the first place. She was just about to get up when the bartender set a shot of something clear in front of her. "Oh," she said. "I don't drink."

Without missing a beat, Daniel reached over and drained the shot glass.

She was fascinated by him, in the same way that an entomologist would be fascinated by an insect from the far side of the earth, a specimen she had read about but never imagined she'd hold in the palm of her hand. There was an unexpected thrill to being this close to the type of person she'd avoided her whole life. She looked at Daniel Stone and didn't see a man whose hair was too long and who hadn't shaved in days, whose T-shirt was threadbare underneath his battered jacket, whose fingertips were stained with nicotine and ink. Instead, she saw who she might have been if she hadn't made the conscious choice to be someone else.

"You like poetry," Daniel said, picking up the thread of conversation.

"Well, Ashbery's okay. But if you've read Rumi—" She broke off, realizing that what she really should have said, in response, was *Yes.* "I guess you probably didn't invite me here to talk about poetry."

"It's all bullshit to me, but I like the way your eyes look when you talk about it."

Laura put a little more distance between them, as much as she could while sitting on a bar stool.

"Don't you want to know why I invited you here?" Daniel asked.

She nodded and forgot to breathe.

"Because I knew you were smart enough to find the invitation. Because your hair's got all the colors of fire." He reached out and put his hand on her chin, trailing it down her throat. "Because when I touched you here the other night, I wanted to taste you."

Before she realized what he was doing, Laura found herself in his arms, with his mouth moving hot across hers. On his breath, there were traces of alcohol and cigarettes and seclusion.

Shoving him away, she stumbled off her bar stool. "What are you doing?"

"What you came here for," Daniel said.

The other men at the bar were whistling. Laura felt her face burn. "I don't know why I came here," she said, and she started to walk toward the door.

"Because of everything we have in common," Daniel called out.

She couldn't simply let that one pass. Turning around, she said, "Believe me. We don't have *anything* in common."

"Don't we?" Daniel approached her, pinning the door shut with one arm. "Did you tell your boyfriend you were coming to see me?" When Laura remained stone-silent, he laughed.

Laura stilled underneath the weight of the truth: She had lied—not only to Walter but also to herself. She had come here of her own free will; she had come here because she couldn't stand the thought of not coming. But what if the reason Daniel Stone fascinated her had nothing to do with difference . . . but similarity? What if she recognized in him parts of herself that had been there all along, underneath the surface?

What if Daniel Stone was right?

She stared up at him, her heart hammering. "What would you have done if I hadn't come here today?"

His blue eyes darkened. "Waited."

She was awkward, and she was self-conscious, but Laura took a step toward him. She thought of Madame Bovary and of Juliet, of poison running through your bloodstream, of passion doing the same.

• • •

Mike Bartholemew was pacing around near the emergency room's Coke machine when he heard his name being called. He glanced up to find a tiny woman with a cap of dark hair facing him, her hands buried in the pockets of her white physician's coat. *C. Roth, M.D.* "I was hoping to talk to you about Trixie Stone," he said.

She nodded, glancing at the crowd around them. "Why don't we go into one of the empty exam rooms?"

There was nowhere Mike wanted to be less. The last time he'd been in one, it was to ID his daughter's body. He had no sooner walked across the threshold than he started to weave and feel the room spin. "Are you all right?" the doctor asked, as he steadied himself against the examination table.

"It's nothing."

"Let me get you something to drink."

She was gone for only a few seconds and came back bearing a paper cone from a water cooler. When Mike finished drinking, he crushed the cup in his hand. "Must be a flu going around," he said, trying to dismiss his own weakness. "I've got a few follow-up questions based on your medical report."

"Fire away."

Mike took a pad and pen out of his coat pocket. "You said that Trixie Stone's demeanor was calm when she was here?"

"Yes, until the pelvic exam—she got a bit upset

at that. But during the rest of the exam she was very quiet."

"Not hysterical?"

"Not all rape victims come in that way," the doctor said. "Some are in shock."

"Was she bleeding?"

"Minimally."

"Shouldn't there have been more, if she was a virgin?"

The doctor shrugged. "A hymen can break when a girl is eight years old, riding a bike. There doesn't have to be blood the first time there's intercourse."

"But you also said there was no significant internal trauma," Mike said.

The doctor frowned at him. "Aren't you supposed to be on *her* side?"

"I don't take sides," Mike said. "But I do try to make sense of the facts, and before we have a rape case, I need to make sure that I've ruled out inconsistencies."

"Well, you're talking about an organ that's made for accommodation. Just because there wasn't visible internal trauma doesn't mean there wasn't intercourse without consent."

Mike looked down at the examination table, uncomfortable, and suddenly could see the still, swathed form of his daughter's battered body. One arm, which had slipped off to hang toward the floor, with its black user's bruise in the crook of the elbow.

"Her arm," Mike murmured.

"The cuts? I photographed them for you. The

lacs were still oozing when she came in," the doctor said, "but she couldn't remember seeing a weapon during the attack."

Mike took the Polaroid out of his pocket, the one that showed Trixie's left wrist. There was the deep cut that Dr. Roth was describing, still angry and red as a mouth, but if you looked carefully you could also see the silver herringbone pattern of older scars. "Is there any chance Trixie Stone did this to herself?"

"It's a possibility. We see a lot of cutting in teenage girls these days. But it still doesn't preclude the fact that Trixie was sexually assaulted."

"You'd be willing to testify to that?" Mike asked.

The doctor folded her arms. "Have you ever sat in on a female rape kit collection, Detective?"

She knew, of course, that Mike hadn't. He couldn't, as a man.

"It takes over an hour and involves not just a thorough external examination but a painfully thorough internal one as well. It involves having your body scrutinized under UV light and swabbed for evidence. It involves photography. It involves being asked intimate details about your sexual habits. It involves having your clothes confiscated. I've been an ER OB/GYN for fifteen years, Detective, and I have yet to see the woman who'd be willing to suffer through a sexual assault exam just for the hell of it." She glanced up at Mike. "Yes," Dr. Roth said. "I'll testify."

• • •

Janice didn't just have tea in her office. She had oolong, Sleepytime, and orange pekoe. Darjeeling, rooibos, and sencha. Dragon Well, macha, gunpowder, jasmine, Keemun. Lapsang souchong and Assam: Yunnan and Nilgiri. "What would you like?" she asked.

Trixie hugged a throw pillow to her chest. "Coffee."

"Like I haven't heard that before."

Trixie had come to this appointment reluctantly. Her father had dropped her off and would be back to get her at five. "What if I have nothing to say?" Trixie had asked him the minute before she got out of the car. But as it turned out, since she'd sat down, she hadn't shut up. She'd told Janice about her conversation with Zephyr and the way Moss had looked through her like she was a ghost. She'd talked about the condoms in her locker and why she hadn't reported them to the principal. She talked about how, even when people weren't whispering behind her back, she could still hear them doing it.

Janice settled down onto a heap of pillows on the floor—her office was shared by four different sexual assault advocates and was full of soft edges and things you could hug if you needed to. "It sounds to me like Zephyr's a little confused right now," Janice said. "She thinks she has to pick between you and Moss, so she isn't going to be a viable form of support."

"Well," Trixie said, "that leaves my mom and

dad, and I can't quite go dragging *them* to school with me."

"What about your other friends?"

Trixie worried the fringe of the pillow on her lap. "I sort of stopped spending time with them when I started hanging out with Jason."

"You must have missed them."

She shook her head. "I was so wrapped up in Jason, there wasn't room for anything else." Trixie looked up at Janice. "That's love, isn't it?"

"Did Jason ever tell you he loved you?"

"I told him once." She sat up and reached for the tea that Janice had given her, even though she'd said she didn't want any. The mug was smooth in her palms, radiant with heat. Trixie wondered if this was what it felt like to hold a heart. "He said he loved me too."

"When was that?"

October fourteenth, at nine thirty-nine P.M. They had been in the back row of a movie theater holding hands, watching a teen slasher flick. She had been wearing Zephyr's blue mohair sweater, the one that made her boobs look bigger than they actually were. Jason had bought Sour Patch Kids and she was drinking Sprite. But Trixie thought that telling Janice the details that had been burned into her mind might make her sound too pathetic, so instead she just said, "About a month after we got together."

"Did he tell you he loved you after that?"

Trixie had waited for him to say it first, without prompting, but Jason hadn't. And she hadn't said it again, because she was too afraid he wouldn't say it back.

She had thought she heard him whisper it *after-ward*, the other night, but she was so numb by then she still was not entirely sure she hadn't just made it up to soften the blow of what had happened.

"How did you two break up?" Janice asked.

They had been standing in Jason's kitchen, eating M&M's out of a bowl on the table. *I think it might be a good thing if we saw other people*, he had said, when five seconds earlier they had been talking about a teacher who was taking the rest of the year off to be with the baby she'd adopted from Romania. Trixie hadn't been able to breathe, and her mind spun frantically to figure out what she had done wrong. *It isn't you*, Jason had said. But *he* was perfect, so how could that be true?

He said he wanted them to stay friends, and she nodded, even though she knew it was impossible. How was she supposed to smile as she passed by him at school, when she wanted to collapse? How could she unhear his promises?

The night Jason broke up with her, they had gone to his house to hook up—his folks were out. Afraid that her parents might do something stupid, like call, Trixie had told them that a whole bunch of kids were going to a movie. And so, after Jason dropped the bomb, Trixie was forced to spend another two hours in his company, until the time the movie would have been over, when all she really wanted to do was hide underneath her covers and cry herself dry.

"When Jason broke up with you," Janice asked, "what did you do to make yourself feel better?"

*Cut.* The word popped into Trixie's mind so fast that only at the very last moment did she press her lips together to keep it inside. But at the same time, she subconsciously slid her right hand over her left wrist.

Janice had been watching too closely. She reached for Trixie's arm and inched up the cuff of her shirt. "So that didn't happen during the rape."

"No."

"Why did you tell the doctor in the emergency room that it did?"

Trixie's eyes filled with tears. "I didn't want her to think I was crazy."

After Jason broke up with her, Trixie lost any semblance of emotional control. She'd find herself sobbing when a certain song came on the car radio and have to make up excuses to her father. She would walk by Jason's locker in the hope that she might accidentally cross paths with him. She'd find the one computer in the library whose screen in the sunlight mirrored the table behind her, and she'd watch Jason in its reflection while she pretended to type. She was swimming in tar, when the rest of the world, including Jason, had so seamlessly moved on.

"I was in the bathroom one day," Trixie confessed, "and I opened up the medicine cabinet and saw my father's razor blades. I just did it without thinking. But it felt so good to take my mind off everything else. It was a kind of pain that made sense."

"There are constructive ways to deal with depression—"

"It's crazy, right?" Trixie interrupted. "To love someone who's hurt you?"

"It's crazier to think that someone who hurts you loves you," Janice replied.

Trixie lifted her mug. The tea was cold now. She held it in a way that blocked her face, so that Janice wouldn't be able to look her in the eye. If she did, surely she'd see the one last secret Trixie had managed to keep: that after That Night, she hated Jason . . . but she hated herself more. Because even after what had happened, there was a part of Trixie that still wanted him back.

From the *Letters to the Editor* page of the *Portland Press Herald:*

To the Editors:
We would like to express our shock and anger at the allegations leveled against Jason Underhill. Anyone who knows Jason understands that he doesn't have a violent bone in his body. If rape is a crime of violence and dominance over another person, shouldn't there then be signs of violence?

While Jason's life has been brought to a screeching halt, the so-called victim in this case continues to walk around undeterred.

While Jason is being redrawn as a monster, this victim is seemingly absent of the symptoms associated with a sexual assault. Might this not be a rape after all . . . but a case of a young girl's remorse after making a decision she wished she hadn't?

If the town of Bethel was to pass judgment on this case, Jason Underhill would surely be found innocent.

Sincerely,

Thirteen anonymous educators from Bethel H.S. . . . and fifty-six additional signatories

Superheroes were born in the minds of people desperate to be rescued. The first, and arguably the most legendary, arrived in the 1930s, care of Shuster and Siegel, two unemployed, apprehensive Jewish immigrants who couldn't get work at a newspaper. They imagined a loser who only had to whip off his glasses and step into a phone booth to morph into a paragon of manliness, a world where the geek got the girl at the end. The public, reeling from the Depression, embraced Superman, who took them away from a bleak reality.

Daniel's first comic book had been about leaving, too. It had grown from a Yup'ik story about a hunter who stupidly set out alone and speared a walrus. The hunter knew he couldn't haul it in by himself, yet if he didn't let go of the rope it would drag him down and kill him. The hunter decided to release the line, but his hands had frozen into position and he was pulled underwater. Instead of drowning, though, he sank to the bottom of the sea and became a walrus himself.

Daniel started to draw the comic book at recess one day, after he was kept inside because he'd punched a kid who teased him for his blue eyes. He'd absently picked up a pencil and drew a figure that started in the sea—all flippers and tusks—and evolved toward shore to standing position, gradually developing the arms and legs and face of a man. He drew and he drew, watching his hero break away from his village in a way that Daniel couldn't himself.

He couldn't seem to escape these days, either. In the wake of Trixie's rape, Daniel had gotten precious little drawing done. At this point, the only way he would make his deadline was if he stayed awake 24/7 and managed to magically add a few hours to each day. He hadn't called Marvel, though, to break the bad news. Explaining *why* he had been otherwise occupied would somehow make what had happened to Trixie more concrete.

When the phone rang at seven-thirty A.M., Daniel grabbed for it. Trixie was not going to school today, and Daniel wanted her to stay blessedly unconscious for as long as humanly possible. "You got something to tell me?" the voice on the other end demanded.

Daniel broke out in a cold sweat. "Paulie," he said. "What's up?"

Paulie Goldman was Daniel's longtime editor, and a legend. Known for his ever-present cigar and red bow tie, he'd been a crony of all the great men in the business: Stan Lee, Jack Kirby, Steve Ditko. These days, he'd be just as likely to be found grabbing a Reuben at his favorite corner deli with Alan Moore, Todd McFarlane, or Neil Gaiman.

It had been Paulie who'd jumped all over Daniel's idea to bring a graphic novel back to former comic book fans who were now adults, and to let Daniel not only pencil the art but also write a story line that might appeal to them. He'd gotten Marvel on board, although they were leery at first. Like all publishers, trying something that hadn't been done before was considered anathema—unless you succeeded, in which case you were called *revolutionary.* But given the marketing that Marvel had put behind the Wildclaw series, to miss a deadline would be catastrophic.

"Have you happened to read the latest *Lying in the Gutters*?" Paulie asked.

He was referring to an online trade gossip column by Rich Johnston. The title was a double entendre—gutters were the spaces between panels, the structure that made a comic illustration a comic illustration. Johnston encouraged "gutterati" to send him scoop to post in his articles, and "guttersnipes" to spread the word across the Internet. With the phone crooked against his shoulder, Daniel pulled up the Web page on his computer and scanned the headlines.

*A Story That's Not About Marvel Editorial*, he read.

*The DC Purchase of Flying Pig Comics That Isn't Going to Happen.*

*You Saw It Here Second:* In The Weeds, *the new title from Crawl Space, will be drawn by Evan Hohman . . . but the pages are already popping up on eBay.*

And on the very bottom: *Wildclaw Sheathed?*

Daniel leaned toward the screen. *I understand that Daniel Stone, It Kid of the Moment, has drawn . . . count 'em, folks . . . ZERO pages toward his next* Tenth Circle *deadline. Was the hype really just a hoax? What good's a great series when there's nothing new to read?*

"This is bullshit," Daniel said. "I've been drawing."

"How much?"

"It'll get done, Paulie."

"How *much*?"

"Eight pages."

"Eight pages? You've got to get me twenty-two by the end of the week if it's going to get inked on time."

"I'll ink it myself if I have to."

"Yeah? Will you run it off on Xerox machines and take it to the distributor too? For God's sake, Danny. This isn't high school. The dog isn't allowed to eat your homework." He paused, then said, "I know you're a last-minute guy, but this isn't like you. What's going on?"

How do you explain to a man who'd made a life out of fantasy that sometimes reality came crashing down? In comics, heroes escaped and villains lost and not even death was permanent. "The series," Daniel said quietly. "It's taking a little bit of a turn."

"What do you mean?"

"The story line. It's becoming more . . . family oriented."

Paulie was silent for a moment, thinking this over. "Family's good," he mused. "You mean a plot that would bring parents and their kids together?"

Daniel pinched the bridge of his nose between his thumb and forefinger. "I hope so," he said.

Trixie was systematically removing all traces of Jason from her bedroom. She tossed into the trash the first note he'd passed her in class. The goofy reel of pictures they'd taken at a booth at Old Orchard Beach. The green felt blotter on her desk, where she could feel the impression of his name, after writing it dozens of times on paper.

It was when she went to throw the blotter out in the recycle bin that she saw the newspaper, the page open to the letter her parents had not wanted her to see.

"If the town of Bethel was to pass judgment on this case," Trixie read, "Jason Underhill would surely be found innocent."

What they hadn't said, in that awful editorial letter, was that this town had already tried and judged the wrong person. She ran upstairs again, to her computer, and connected to the Internet. She looked up the Web page for the *Portland Press Herald* and started to type a rebuttal letter.

*To Whom It May Concern*, Trixie wrote.

*I know it is the policy of your paper to keep victims who are minors anonymous. But I'm one of those minors, and instead of having people guess, I want them to know my name.*

She thought of a dozen other girls who might read this, girls who had been too scared to tell anyone what had happened to them. Or the dozen girls who *had* told someone and who could read this and find the courage they needed to get through one more day of the hell that was high school. She thought of the boys who would think twice before taking something that wasn't theirs.

*My name is Trixie Stone*, she typed.

She watched the letters quiver on the page; she read the spaces between the words—all of which reminded her that she was a coward. Then she hit the delete button.

The phone rang just as Laura walked into the kitchen. By the time she'd picked up, so had Daniel on an upstairs connection. "I'm looking for Laura Stone," the caller said, and she dropped the glass she was holding into the sink.

"I've got it," Laura said. She waited for Daniel to hang up.

"I miss you," Seth replied.

She didn't answer right away; she couldn't. What if she hadn't picked up the phone? Would Seth have started chatting up Daniel? Would he have introduced himself? "Do not ever call here again," Laura whispered.

"I need to talk to you."

Her heart was beating so hard she could barely hear her own voice. "I can't."

"Please. Laura. It's important."

Daniel walked into the kitchen and poured himself some water. "Please take me off your call list," Laura said, and she hung up.

In retrospect Laura realized that she'd dated Daniel through osmosis, taking a little of his recklessness and making it part of herself. She broke up with Walter and began sleeping through classes. She started smoking. She peppered Daniel with questions about the past he wouldn't discuss. She learned how her own body could be an instrument, how Daniel could play a symphony over her skin.

Then she found out she was pregnant.

At first, she thought that the reason she didn't tell Daniel was because she feared he'd run. Gradually, though, she realized that she hadn't told Daniel because *she* was the one considering flight. Reality kicked at Laura with a vengeance, now that responsibility had caught up to her. At twenty-four years old, what was she doing staying up all night to bet on cockfights in the basement of a tenement? What good would it be in the long run if she could lay claim to finding the best tequila over the border but her doctoral thesis was dead in the water? It had been one thing to flirt with the dark side; it was another thing entirely to set down roots there.

Parents didn't take their baby trolling the streets

after midnight. They didn't live out of the back of a car. They couldn't buy formula and cereal and clothes with the happenstance cash that dribbled in from sketches done here and there. Although Daniel could currently pull Laura like a tide to the moon, she couldn't imagine them together ten years from now. She was forced to consider the startling fact that the love of her life might not actually be someone with whom she could spend a lifetime.

When Laura broke up with Daniel, she convinced herself she was doing both of them a favor. She did not mention the baby, although she had known all along she would keep it. Sometimes she'd find herself losing hours at a time, wondering if her child would have the same pale wolf-eyes as its father. She threw out her cigarettes and started wearing sweater sets again and driving with her seat belt fastened. She folded Daniel neatly away in her mind and pretended not to think about him.

A few months later, Laura came home to find Daniel waiting at her condo. He took one look at her maternity top and then, furious, grabbed her by her upper arms. "How could you not tell me about this?"

Laura panicked, wondering if she'd misinterpreted the jagged edge of his personality all along. What if he wasn't just wild, but truly dangerous? "I figured it was best if—"

"What were you going to tell the baby?" Daniel said. "About me?"

"I . . . hadn't gotten that far."

Laura watched him carefully. Daniel had turned into someone she couldn't quite recognize. This wasn't just some Bad Boy out to buck the system—this was someone so deeply upset that he'd forgotten to cover the scars.

He sank down onto the front steps. "My mother told me that my dad died before I was born. But when I was eleven, the mail plane brought a letter addressed to me." Daniel glanced up. "You don't get money from ghosts."

Laura crouched down beside him.

"The postmarks were always different, but after that first letter he'd send cash every month. He never talked about why he wasn't there, with us. He'd talk about what the salt mountains looked like in Utah, or how cold the Mississippi River was when you stepped into it barefoot. He said that one day he'd take me to all those places, so I could see for myself," Daniel said. "I waited for years, you know, and he never came to get me."

He turned to Laura. "My mother said she'd lied because she thought it would be easier to hear that my father was dead than to hear he hadn't wanted a family. I don't want our baby to have a father like that."

"Daniel," she confessed, "I'm not sure if I want our baby to have a father like *you.*"

He reared back, as if he'd been slapped. Slowly, he got to his feet and walked away.

Laura spent the next week crying. Then one morning, when she went out to get the newspaper, she found Daniel asleep on the front steps of her condo. He stood up, and she could not stop staring: His shoulder-length hair had been cut military-short; he was wearing khaki pants and a blue oxford cloth shirt with the sleeves rolled up. He held out a stub of paper. "It's the check I just deposited," Daniel explained. "I got a job working at Atomic Comics. They gave me a week's salary in advance."

Laura listened, her resolve cracking wide open. What if she was not the only one who had been fascinated by a personality different from her own? What if all the time that she'd been absorbing Daniel's wildness, he'd been looking to her for redemption?

What if love wasn't the act of finding what you were missing but the give-and-take that made you both match?

"I don't have enough cash yet," Daniel continued, "but when I do, I'm going to take art courses at the community college." He reached for Laura, so that their child was balanced between them. "Please," he whispered. "What if that baby's the best part of me?"

"You don't want to do this," Laura said, even as she moved closer to him. "You'll hate me one day, for ruining your life."

"My life was ruined a long time ago," Daniel said. "And I'll never hate you."

They got married at the city hall, and Daniel was completely true to his word. He quit smoking and drinking, cold turkey. He came to every OB appointment. Four months later, when Trixie was born, he doted over her as if she were made of sunlight. While Laura taught undergrads during the day, Daniel played with Trixie in the park and at the zoo. At night, he took classes and began doing freelance graphic art, before working for Marvel. He followed Laura from a teaching position in San Diego to one at Marquette to the current one in Maine. He had dinner waiting when she came home from lecturing; he stuffed caricatures of Trixie as SuperBaby in the pockets of her brief-case; he never forgot her birthday. He was, in fact, so perfect that she wondered if the wild in Daniel had only been an act to attract her. But then she would remember the strangest things out of the blue: a night when Daniel had bitten her so hard during sex he'd drawn blood; the sound of him fighting off imaginary enemies in the thick of a nightmare; the time he had tattooed Laura's body with Magic Markers—snakes and hydras down her arms, a demon in flight at the small of her back. A few years ago, wistful, she had gone so far as to bring one of his inking pens to bed. "You know how hard it is to get that stuff off your skin?" Daniel had said, and that was the end of that.

Laura knew she had no right to complain. There were women in this world whose husbands beat them, who cried themselves to sleep because their spouses were alcoholics or gamblers. There were women in this world whose partners had said "I love you" fewer times in a lifetime than Daniel would in a week. Laura could shift the blame any old way she liked, but the stiff wind of truth would send it back to her: She hadn't ruined Daniel's life by asking him to change. She had ruined her own.

Mike Bartholemew glanced at the tape recorder to make sure it was still running. "She was all over me," Moss Minton said. "Putting her hands in my hair, lap dancing, that kind of stuff."

The kid had come down willingly, at Mike's request, to talk. But less than five minutes into the conversation, it was clear that anything that came out of Moss's mouth was going to be unduly colored by his allegiance to Jason Underhill.

"I don't know how to say this without sounding like a total jerk," Moss said, "but Trixie was asking for it."

Bartholemew leaned back in his chair. "You know this for a fact."

"Well . . . yeah."

"Did you have intercourse with Trixie that night?"

"No."

"Then you must have been in the room when your friend was having sex with her," Bartholemew said. "Or how else would you have heard her consent?"

"I wasn't in the room, dude," Moss said. "But neither were you. Maybe I didn't hear her say yes, but you didn't hear her say no, either."

Bartholemew turned off the tape recorder. "Thanks for coming in."

"We're done?" Moss said, surprised. "That's it?"

"That's it." The detective took a card out of his pocket and handed it to Moss. "If you happen to think of anything else you need to tell me, just call."

"Bartholemew," Moss read aloud. "I used to have a babysitter named Holly Bartholemew. I think I was around nine or ten."

"My daughter."

"No kidding? Does she still live around here?"

Mike hesitated. "Not anymore."

Moss stuffed the business card in his pocket. "Tell her I said hi the next time you see her." He gave the detective a half wave and then walked out.

"I will," Mike said, as his voice unraveled like lace.

Daniel opened the door to find Janice, the sexual assault advocate, on the other side. "Oh, I didn't know Trixie made plans to see you."

"She didn't," Janice replied. "Can I speak to you and Laura for a second?"

"Laura's at the college," he said, just as Trixie poked her head over the railing from upstairs. Before, Trixie would not have hung back like that; she would have bounded down like lightning, certain that the visitor was for her.

"Trixie," Janice said, spotting her. "I need to tell you something you're not going to like."

Trixie came downstairs, sidling up beside Daniel, the way she used to do when she was tiny and saw something frightening.

"The defense attorney representing Jason Underhill has subpoenaed the records of my conversations with Trixie."

Daniel shook his head. "I don't understand. Isn't that a violation of privacy?"

"Only when you're talking about the defendant. Unfortunately, if you're the *victim* of a crime, it's a different story. You can wind up with your diary as evidence, or the transcripts of your psychiatric sessions." She looked at Trixie. "Or your discussions with a rape crisis counselor."

Daniel had no idea what went on during the times Janice had met with Trixie, but beside him, his daughter was shaking. "You can't turn over the records," she said.

"If we don't, our director will be sent to jail," Janice explained.

"I'll do it," Daniel said. "I'll go to jail in her place."

"The court won't accept that. Believe me, you're not the first father to volunteer."

*You're not the first.* Daniel slowly put the words together. "This happened before?"

"Unfortunately, yes," Janice admitted.

"You said what I told you didn't leave that room!" Trixie cried. "You said you'd help me. How is *this* supposed to help me?"

As Trixie flew up the stairs, Janice started after her. "Let me go talk to her."

Daniel stepped forward, blocking her way. "Thanks," he said. "But I think you've done enough."

• • •

*The law says that Jason Underhill has the right to mount a defense*, Detective Bartholemew explained on the phone. *The law says that a victim's credibility can be questioned. And with all due respect*, he added, *your daughter already has some credibility issues.*

*She was involved with this boy beforehand.*

*She was drinking.*

*She's made some inconsistent statements.*

Daniel's response: *Like what?*

Now that he'd finished talking to the detective, Daniel felt numb. He walked upstairs and opened Trixie's bedroom door. She lay on her bed, facing away from him.

"Trixie," he said as evenly as he could. "Were you really a virgin?"

She went still. "What, now *you* don't believe me either?"

"You lied to the police."

Trixie rolled over, stricken. "You're going to listen to some stupid detective instead of—"

*"What were you thinking?"* Daniel exploded.

Trixie sat up, taken aback. "What were *you* thinking?" she cried. "You *knew*. You had to know what was going on."

Daniel thought of the times he had watched Trixie pull up in Jason's car after a date, when he had moved away from the window. He'd told himself it was for her privacy, but was that true? Had he really turned a blind eye because he couldn't bear to see that boy's face close to his daughter's, to see his hand graze the bottom of Trixie's breast?

He'd seen towels in the wash smeared with heavy eye makeup he couldn't remember Trixie wearing out of the house. He'd kept silent when he heard Laura complain because her favorite pair of heels or shirt or lipstick had gone missing, only to find them underneath Trixie's bed. He'd pretended not to notice how Trixie's clothes fit tighter these days, how her stride shimmered with confidence.

Trixie was right. Just because a person didn't admit that something had changed didn't mean it hadn't happened. Maybe Trixie had screwed up . . . but so had he.

"I knew," he said, stunned to speak the words aloud. "I just didn't *want* to."

Daniel looked at his daughter. There were still traces of Trixie as a stubborn little girl—in the curve of her chin when her jaw clenched, in the dusky length of her lashes, in her much-maligned freckles. She wasn't all gone, not yet.

As he pulled Trixie into his arms and felt her unspool, Daniel understood: The law was not going to protect his daughter, which meant that *he* had to.

"I couldn't tell them," Trixie sobbed. "*You* were standing right there."

That was when Daniel remembered: When the doctor asked Trixie if she'd ever had intercourse before, he'd still been in the examination room.

Her voice was small, the truth curled tight as a snail. "I didn't want you to be mad at me. And I thought if I told the doctor that Jason and I had already done it, she wouldn't believe I got raped. But it could still happen, couldn't it, Daddy? Just because I said yes before doesn't mean I couldn't say no this time . . . ? " She convulsed against him, crying hard.

You signed no contract to become a parent, but the responsibilities were written in invisible ink. There was a point when you had to support your child, even if no one else would. It was your job to rebuild the bridge, even if your child was the one who burned it in the first place. So maybe Trixie had danced around the truth. Maybe she had been drinking. Maybe she had been flirting at the party. But if Trixie said she had been raped, then Daniel would swear by it.

"Baby," he said, "I believe you."

A few mornings later, when Daniel was out at the dump, Laura heard the doorbell ring. But by the time she reached the hallway to answer it, Trixie was already there. She stood in her flannel pajama bottoms and T-shirt, staring at a man standing on the porch.

Seth was wearing work boots and a fleece vest and looked as if he hadn't slept in several days. He was looking at Trixie with confusion, as if he couldn't quite place her. When he saw Laura approach, he immediately started to speak. "I've got to talk to you," he began, but she cut him off.

She touched Trixie's shoulder. "Go upstairs," she said firmly, and Trixie bolted like a rabbit. Then Laura turned to Seth again. "I cannot *believe* you had the nerve to come to my house."

"There's something you need to know—"

"I know that I can't see you anymore," Laura said. She was shaking, partly with fear, partly because of Seth's proximity. It had been easier to convince herself that this was over when he wasn't standing in front of her. "Don't do this to me," she whispered, and she closed the door.

Laura rested against it for a second, eyes closed. What if Daniel had not been at the dump, if he'd opened the door, instead of Trixie? Would he have recognized Seth on sight, simply by the way his face changed when he looked at Laura? Would he have gone for Seth's throat?

If they'd fought, she'd have sided with the victim. But which man *was* that?

Gathering her composure, Laura walked up the stairs toward Trixie's room. She wasn't sure what Trixie knew, or even what she suspected. Surely she had noticed that her parents barely spoke these days, that her father had taken to sleeping on the couch. She had to wonder why, the night of the rape, Laura had been staying overnight in her office. But if Trixie had questions, she'd kept them to herself. It was as if she instinctively understood what Laura was only just figuring out: Once you admitted to a mistake, it grew exponentially, until there was no way to get it back under wraps.

Laura was tempted to pretend that Seth was a Fuller Brush salesman or any other stranger but decided she would take her cues from Trixie herself. Laura opened the door to find Trixie pulling a shirt over her head. "That guy," she said, her face hidden. "What was he doing here?"

*Well.*

Laura sat down on the bed. "He wasn't here because of you. I mean, he's not a reporter or anything like that. And he's not coming back. Ever." She sighed. "I wish I didn't have to have this conversation."

Trixie's head popped through the neck of the shirt. "What?"

"It's finished, completely, one hundred percent. Your father knows, and we're trying . . . well, we're trying to figure this out. I screwed up, Trixie," Laura said, choking over the words. "I wish I could take it back, but I can't."

She realized that Trixie was staring at her, the same way she used to gaze hard at a math problem she simply couldn't puzzle into an answer. "You mean . . . you and him . . ."

Laura nodded. "Yeah."

Trixie ducked her head. "Did you guys ever talk about me?"

"He knew you existed. He knew I was married."

"I can't believe you'd do this to Daddy," Trixie said, her voice rising. "He's, like, *my* age. That's *disgusting.*"

Laura's jaw clenched. Trixie deserved to have this moment of rage; it was owed to her as part of Laura's reparation. But that didn't make it any easier.

"I wasn't thinking, Trixie—"

"Yeah, because you were too busy being a *slut.*"

Laura raised her palm, coming just short of slapping Trixie across the face. Her hand shook inches away from Trixie's cheek, rendering both of them speechless for a moment. "No," Laura breathed. "Neither of us should do something we won't be able to take back."

She stared Trixie down, until the fury dissolved and the tears came. Laura drew Trixie into her arms, rocked her. "Are you and Daddy going to get a divorce?" Her voice was small, childlike.

"I hope not," Laura said.

"Did you . . . love him?"

She closed her eyes and imagined Seth's poetry, placed word by word onto her own tongue, a gourmet meal mixed with rhythm and description. She felt the immediacy of a single moment, when unlocking a door took too long, when buttons were popped instead of slipped open.

But here was Trixie, who had nursed with her hand fisted in Laura's hair. Trixie, who sucked her thumb until she was ten but only when no one could see. Trixie, who believed that the wind could sing and that you could learn the songs if you just listened carefully enough. Trixie, who was the proof that at one time, she and Daniel had achieved perfection together.

Laura pressed her lips against her daughter's temple. "I loved you more," she said.

She had nearly turned her back once on this family. Had she really been stupid enough to come close to doing it again? She was crying just as hard as Trixie was now, to the point where it was impossible to tell which one of them was clinging to the other. Laura felt, in that moment, like the survivor of the train wreck, the woman who steps outside the smoking wreckage to realize that her arms and legs still work, that she has somehow come through a catastrophe unscathed.

Laura buried her face in the curve of her daughter's neck. It was possible she'd been wrong on several counts. It was possible that a miracle was not something that happened to you, but rather something that didn't.

The first place it appeared was on the screen at the school library computer terminal where you could look books up by their Dewey decimal number. From there, it spread to the twenty iBooks and ten iMacs in the computer lab, while the ninth-graders were in the middle of taking their typing skills test. Within five more minutes, it was on the monitor of the desk of the school nurse.

Trixie was in an elective, School Newspaper, when it happened. Although her parents had tried to talk her out of going to school, it turned out to be the lesser of two evils. Home was supposed to be a safe place, but had become a minefield full of explosions waiting to happen. School, she already knew, wouldn't be comfortable at all. And right now, she really needed to function in a world where nothing took her by surprise.

In class, Trixie was sitting beside a girl named Felice with acne and beaver breath, the only one who would volunteer these days to be her partner.

They were using desktop-publishing software to move columns of text about the losing basketball team, when the computer blue-screened. "Mr. Watford," Felice called out. "I think we crashed . . ."

The teacher came over, reaching between the girls to hit Control-Alt-Delete a few times, but the machine wouldn't reboot. "Hmm," he said. "Why don't you two edit the advice column by hand instead?"

"No, wait, it's coming back," Felice said, as the screen blossomed into Technicolor. Smack in the middle was Trixie, standing half naked in Zephyr's living room—the photo Moss had taken the night she was raped.

"Oh," Mr. Watford said faintly. "Well, then."

Trixie felt as if a pole had been driven through her lungs. She tore herself away from the computer screen, grabbed her backpack, and ran to the main office. There, she threw herself on the mercy of the secretary. "I need to talk to the principal—"

Her voice snapped like an icicle, as she glanced down at the computer on the secretary's desk and saw her own face staring back at her.

Trixie flew out of the office, out the front doors of the school. She didn't stop running until she was standing on the bridge over the river, the same bridge where she and Zephyr had stood the day before she became someone different. She dug in her backpack through loose pencils and crumpled papers and makeup compacts until she found the cell phone her father had given her—his own, for emergencies. "Daddy," she sobbed, when he answered, "please come get me."

It wasn't until her father assured her he would be there in two minutes flat that she hung up and noticed what she hadn't when she first placed the call: Her father's phone screen saver—once a graphic of Rogue, from the X-Men—was now the topless picture of Trixie that had spread to three-quarters of the cell phone users in Bethel, Maine.

The knock on Bartholemew's door caught him off guard. It was his day off—although he'd already been to Bethel High and back. He had just finished changing into pajama pants and an old police academy sweatshirt with a sleeve that Ernestine had chewed a hole through. "Coming," he called out, and when he opened the door he found Daniel Stone standing on the other side of it.

It wasn't surprising to him that Stone was there, given what had happened at the school. It also wasn't surprising that Stone knew where Bartholemew lived. Like most cops, he didn't have a listed address and phone number, but Bethel was small enough for most people to know other people's business. You could drive down the street and recognize folks by the cars they drove; you could pass a house and know who resided inside.

He was aware, for example, even before Trixie Stone's case came to his attention that a comic book artist of some national renown lived in the area. He hadn't read the comics, but some of the other guys at the station had. Supposedly, unlike his violence-prone hero Wildclaw, Daniel Stone was a mild-mannered guy who didn't mind signing an autograph if you stood behind him in the grocery store checkout line. In his few dealings with Stone so far, the guy had seemed protective of his daughter and frustrated beyond belief. Unlike some of the men Bartholemew had run across in his career, who put their fists through glass walls or drowned their wrath in alcohol, Daniel Stone seemed to have a handle on his emotions—until now. The man was standing at the threshold of Bartholemew's door, literally shaking with rage.

Stone thrust a printout of the now-infamous picture of Trixie into Bartholemew's hand. "Have you seen this?"

Bartholemew had. For about three straight hours this morning, at the high school, on the computers at the town offices, everywhere he looked.

"Hasn't my daughter been victimized enough?"

Bartholemew instinctively went into calming mode, softening his voice. "I know you're upset, but we're doing everything we can."

Stone scraped his gaze over Bartholemew's off-duty attire. "Yeah. You look like you're working your ass off." He looked up at the detective. "You told us that Underhill's not supposed to have anything to do with Trixie."

"Our computer tech guys traced the photo to Moss Minton's cell phone, not Jason Underhill's."

"It doesn't matter. My daughter's not the one who's supposed to be on trial." Stone set his jaw. "I want the judge to know this happened."

"Then he's also going to know that your daughter was the one who took off her clothes. He's going to know that every eyewitness at that party I've interviewed says Trixie was coming on to a whole bunch of different guys that night," Bartholemew said. "Look. I know you're angry. But you don't want to press this right now, when it might wind up backfiring."

Daniel Stone ripped the printed photo from the detective's grasp. "Would you be saying that if this was *your* daughter?"

"If it was my daughter," Bartholemew said, "I'd be thrilled. I'd be fucking delirious. Because it would mean she was still alive."

The truth rolled like mercury, and like any poison, it was the last thing either of them wanted to touch. You'd think, in this age of technology, there'd be some kind of network between fathers, one that let a guy who was in danger of losing his daughter instinctively recognize someone who'd already walked that barren road. As it turned out, hell wasn't watching the people you love get hurt; it was coming in during the second act, when it was already too late to stop it from happening.

He expected Daniel Stone to offer his condolences, to tell Bartholemew he was sorry for mouthing off. But instead, the man threw the printed photo onto the ground between them like a gauntlet. "Then of all people," he said, "you should understand."

● ● ●

She didn't have a lot of time.

Trixie's mother's voice swam up the stairs. Her mom was on babysitting detail and hadn't let Trixie out of her sight until she had headed for the bathroom. Her father, right now, was chewing out Detective Bartholemew or the superintendent of schools or maybe even both of them. And what difference would it make? They could burn every last copy of that awful picture of her, and a few months from now, someone else would have a chance to strip her naked in court.

Sitting on the closed lid of the toilet, she accidentally banged her funny bone against the wall. "Fuck!" she cried, tears springing to her eyes.

Once, Trixie had had her mouth washed out with soap for road-testing four-letter words. She was four years old, at the supermarket with her father, and she repeated what he'd whispered under his breath when the cashier couldn't do the math to make change: *Use the damn register.*

She knew all sorts of four-letter words now; they just weren't the ones that most people considered foul language.

*Love.*
*Help.*
*Rape.*
*Stop.*
*Then.*

As a child, she'd been afraid of the dark. The closet door had to be shut tight, with her desk chair wedged under the knob, to keep the monsters from getting out. Her blanket had to be pulled up to her neck, or the devil might get her. She had to sleep on her belly, or a vampire could come and put a stake through her heart.

She was still afraid, years later—not of the dark but of the days. One after another, and no end in sight.

"Trixie?"

Trixie heard her mother again and swiftly reached into the medicine cabinet. The hilarious thing—the thing that no one bothered to tell you—was that being raped wasn't the worst part of everything she'd been through. In fact, that first frantic fall didn't hurt nearly as much as getting back on your feet afterward.

It was the kind of doorknob that needed only a straightened wire hanger to pop the bolt. The minute Laura stepped inside the bathroom, she saw it—blood smearing the white wall of the sink, blood pooling beneath Trixie on the floor, blood covering Trixie's shirt as she hugged her slashed wrists to her chest. "Oh, my God," Laura cried, grabbing Trixie's arms to try to stop the flow. "Oh, Trixie, no . . ."

Trixie's eyelids fluttered. She looked at Laura for a half second and then sank into unconsciousness. Laura held her daughter's limp body up against her own, knowing that she had to get to a phone and equally sure that if she left Trixie alone, she'd never see her alive again.

The paramedics who came minutes later asked Laura a barrage of questions: How long had Trixie been unconscious? Had Trixie been suicidal before? Did Laura know where the razor blade had come from? Laura answered each of these, but they didn't ask the question she was expecting, the one she didn't have a response for: What if Jason Underhill wasn't the biggest threat to Trixie? What if that was Trixie herself?

Trixie had been doing this for a while. Not in-your-face suicide attempts but recreational cutting. Ironically, the doctors said, that might have been what saved her. Most girls who cut did so horizontally across the wrist, in light little lines. Today, Trixie had cut a deeper slash, but in the same direction. People who meant business, or who knew better, killed themselves by cutting vertically, which meant they'd bleed out faster.

Either way, if Laura hadn't gone in when she did, they probably would have been standing over their daughter's grave instead of her hospital bed.

The lights were turned off in the room, and there was a glowing red clamp on one of Trixie's fingers, keeping tabs on her oxygen levels. Someone—a nurse?—had put Trixie in a hospital gown. Daniel had no idea what had happened to her clothes. Did they get saved as evidence, like the ones she had been wearing the night she was raped? As proof of a girl who desperately wanted to trade in her title of *survivor*?

"Did you know?" Laura asked softly, her voice reaching through the dark.

Daniel looked up at her. All he could see was the shine of her eyes. "No."

"Do you think we should have?"

She wasn't blaming him; that note wasn't in her voice. She was asking if there had been clues missed, trails ignored. She was trying to pinpoint the moment that it all started to disintegrate.

Daniel knew there was no answer to that. It was like a trapeze act: How could you really tell at what second the acrobat pushed away, at what moment the anchor let go? You couldn't, and that was that. You made your deductions from the outcome: a successful landing or a spiraling fall. "I think Trixie was doing her best to make sure we *didn't* know."

He had a sudden memory of Trixie dressed as a bunch of grapes for Halloween one year. She was five and had been so excited about the costume— they'd spent a month making papier-mâché globes in the basement and painting them purple—but when the time came to trick-or-treat, she refused to get dressed.

It was dark outside, there were trolling monsters and witches—plenty of reasons, in short, that a kid might get cold feet. *Trix*, he had asked, *what are you scared of?*

*How are you going to know who I am*, she finally said, *if I don't look like me?*

Laura's head was bent over her folded hands, and her lips were moving. She didn't go to church anymore, but she'd been raised Catholic. Daniel had never been particularly religious. Growing up, he and his mother hadn't gone to church, although most of their neighbors had. The Yupiit got Christianity from the Moravian church, and it had stuck fast. For an Eskimo, it wasn't inconsistent to believe both that Jesus was his Savior, and that a seal's soul lived in its bladder until a hunter returned it to the sea.

Laura brushed Trixie's hair off her face. "Dante believed God punished suicides by trapping the person's spirit in a tree trunk. On Judgment Day, they were the only sinners who didn't get their souls back, because they tried to get rid of them once before."

Daniel knew this, actually. It was one of the few points of Laura's research that intrigued him. It had always struck him as ironic that in the Yup'ik villages, where there was such an epidemic of teen suicide, there weren't any trees.

Just then, Trixie stirred. Daniel watched her as the unfamiliar room came into focus. Her eyes widened, hopeful, and then dimmed with disappointment as she realized that in spite of her best intentions, she was still here.

Laura crawled onto the bed, holding Trixie tight. She was whispering to Trixie, words that Daniel wished came as easily to him. But he didn't have Laura's facility with language; he could not keep Trixie safe with promises. All he'd ever been able to do was repaint the world for her, until it became a place she wanted to be.

Daniel stayed long enough to watch Trixie reach for Laura, grab on with a sure, strong hold. Then he slipped out of the hospital room, moving past nurses and orderlies and patients who were too blind to witness the metamorphosis happening before their eyes.

This is what Daniel bought:
Work gloves and a roll of duct tape.
A pack of rags.
Matches.
A fisherman's fillet knife.
He drove thirty miles away, to a different town, and he paid in cash.
He was determined that there would be no evidence left behind. It would be his word against Daniel's, and as Daniel was learning, that meant a victim would not win.

Jason found that the only time of day his mind was truly occupied was during hockey practice. He simply gave himself over to the game, cutting hard and skating fast and stick-handling with surety and grace. It was this simple: If you were giving a hundred percent at hockey, you didn't have room left for anything else—such as obsessing over the rumor going around school that Trixie Stone had tried to kill herself.

He'd been getting ready for practice in the locker room when he heard, and he started to shake so violently that he'd gone into a bathroom stall to sit down. A girl he'd cared for—a girl he'd *slept* with—had nearly died. It freaked him out to imagine Trixie laughing as her long hair fell over her face, and then the next minute to picture that face six feet underground and crawling with worms.

By the time he'd regained his composure, Moss was in the locker room, lacing up his skates. It had been Moss who, as a joke, had hacked into the computer system at the school and sent out the photo he'd taken of Trixie during the poker game. Jason had been totally furious, but he couldn't say that out loud to the kids who high-fived him and told him that they were on his side. His own attorney had even said Jason couldn't have asked for a better stroke of evidentiary luck. But what if that prank had been the one to put Trixie over the edge? He was already being blamed for something he didn't do. Would he have been blamed for her death?

"You are surely the most unlucky bastard on this planet," Moss had said, giving voice to the other thought in Jason's head. Had Trixie succeeded, then he'd have been off the hook.

Now practice was over, and with it came the casual conversation that would—inevitably—turn to Trixie. Jason hurried off the ice and pulled off the gladiator layers of his equipment. He was the first player out of the rink, the first player to his car. He slid into the driver's seat and turned the ignition, then rested his head on the wheel for a second. *Trixie*. "Jesus," he murmured.

Jason felt the blade of the knife on his Adam's apple before he heard the voice at his ear. "Close enough," Daniel Stone said. "Start praying."

• • •

Daniel made Jason drive to a bog near the river. He'd driven past once or twice and knew that local hunters liked it for deer and moose, and that their cars stayed well hidden while they were out in their stands. Daniel liked it especially because the evergreens marched thick to the edge of the water and had created enough cover to keep snow from blanketing the ground, which meant that their footsteps would be lost in the marsh instead of preserved.

He held the boy at knifepoint, backing Jason up against a pine tree until he was kneeling, securing his arms and ankles behind him with duct tape so that he was effectively trussed. The whole time, Daniel kept thinking of what Laura had said about Dante—of Trixie's soul trapped in that tree, with Jason's body wrapped around it. That image was all he needed to give him the strength to subdue a seventeen-year-old athlete when Jason started fighting back.

Jason struggled, pulling on the tape until his wrists and ankles were raw, while Daniel built a campfire. Finally, the boy sagged against the trunk and let his head fall forward. "What are you going to do to me?"

Daniel took his knife and slipped it under the hem of Jason's T-shirt. He dragged it up to the boy's throat in one long line, cutting the fabric in half. "This," he said.

Daniel systematically shredded Jason's clothing, until the kid was naked and shivering. He tossed the strips of fabric and denim into the flames.

By then, Jason's teeth were chattering. "How am I supposed to get home?"

"What makes you think I'm going to let you?"

Jason swallowed hard, his eyes on the knife Daniel still held in his hand. "How is she?" he whispered.

Daniel felt the granite gate of restraint burst inside him. How could this bastard think he had the right to ask after Trixie? Leaning down, Daniel pressed the blade against Jason's testicles. "Do you want to know what it's like to bleed out? Do you really want to know how she felt?"

"Please," Jason begged, going pale. "Oh, Jesus, don't."

Daniel pushed the slightest bit, until a line of blood welled up at the crease of Jason's groin.

"I didn't do anything to her, I swear it," Jason cried, trying to twist away from Daniel's hand. "I didn't. Stop. God. Please stop."

Daniel set his face an inch away from Jason's. "Why should I? *You* didn't."

In that moment between reason and rage, Trixie slipped into both of their minds. It was all Jason needed to break down, sobbing; it was all Daniel needed to remember himself. He looked down at his hand, holding the knife. He blinked at Jason. Then he shook his head to clear it.

Daniel was not in the bush anymore, and this was no village corporation store he was robbing for booze or cash. He was a husband, he was a father. Instead of having something to prove, he had everything to lose.

Lifting the blade, Daniel staggered to his feet. He hurled the knife the hundred feet it would take to land in the middle of the river and then walked back to Jason, who was fighting for breath. He took the boy's car keys from his own pocket and wrapped them tight in the only morsel of mercy he had left. These, he wedged into Jason's hand, still bound by duct tape.

It was not compassion that led to Daniel's change of heart, and it was not kindness. It was realizing that, against all odds, he had something in common with Jason Underhill. Like Daniel, Jason had learned the hard way that we are never the people we think we are. We are the ones we pretend, with all our hearts, we can't become.

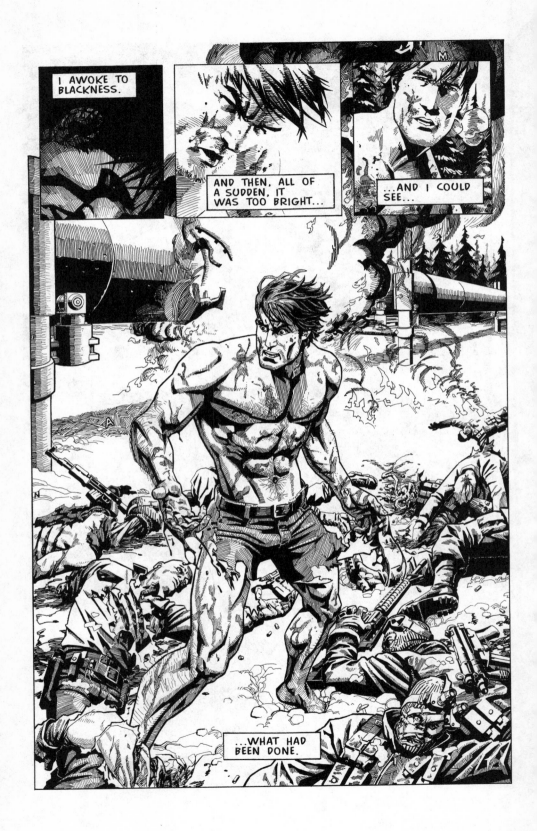

# 4

It took Jason a half hour to saw through the duct tape with his keys. When he could pull his arms forward again, the blood burned as it circulated, a severe pain that overtook the numbness caused by the cold. He stumbled to his feet, running toward the spot where Stone had made him leave the truck, praying it was still there.

The only clothes he had were in his hockey equipment bag, so he wound up dressing in a jersey and his padded pants. He kept expecting to be ambushed again at any moment. His hands shook so badly that it took four tries to get the key into the ignition.

He drove to the police station, thinking only that there was no way he was going to let Trixie's father get away with something like this. But as he pulled into the parking lot, he heard Daniel Stone's voice in his head again: *Tell anyone*, he'd said, *and I'll kill you.* Frankly, Jason could believe it. There had been something in the man's eyes—something inhuman—that made Jason think he was capable of anything.

He was so wrapped up in his thoughts that he didn't see the pedestrian walking across the parking lot. As Jason braked hard, the car lurched forward and stopped. Detective Bartholemew, the same man who'd arrested Jason, stood with one hand on the hood of his car, staring him down. And suddenly Jason remembered what the judge had said at the arraignment: If Jason had any contact whatsoever with Trixie Stone or her family, he'd be shipped off to the juvenile detention facility. He was already accused of rape. If he reported what had happened to the cops, would they even believe him? What if they confronted Daniel Stone— and he insisted it had been Jason who approached *him*?

The detective walked to the driver's side of the car. "Mr. Underhill," he said. "What brings you here?"

"I . . . I thought I might be getting a flat," he managed.

The detective walked around the vehicle. "Doesn't look that way." He leaned closer to the car; Jason could see him doing a quick visual assessment. "Anything else I can help you with?"

It was all right there, caught behind the fence of his teeth: *He dragged me off, he tied me up, he threatened me.* But Jason found himself shaking his head. "No, thanks," he said. He put the car into gear and drove at snail speed out of the parking lot, aware of Bartholemew's gaze following him.

In that moment, Jason made the decision to tell no one what happened: not his buddies, not his parents, not his lawyer. Not the police. He was too damn scared that telling the truth, in this case, would severely backfire on him.

He found himself wondering: Had Trixie felt that, too?

The way drunks kept a bottle of gin hidden in the toilet tank, and addicts tucked an emergency hit in the hem of a threadbare old coat, Daniel kept a pad and a pen in his car. In the parking lot of the hospital, he sketched. Instead of his comic book hero, however, he started penciling his daughter. He drew her when she was only minutes old, rolled into a blanket like sushi. He drew her taking her first steps. He froze moments—the birthday when she made him spaghetti for breakfast; the school play where she fell off the stage into the audience; the high-rise hotel they visited, where they spent hours pushing all the elevator buttons to see if the floors looked any different.

When his hand cramped so badly that he couldn't sketch another line, Daniel gathered up the pictures and got out of the car, heading toward Trixie's room.

Shadows reached across the bed like the fingers of a giant. Trixie had fallen asleep again; in a chair beside her, Laura dozed too. For a moment he stared at the two of them. No question about it: Trixie had been cut from the same cloth as her mother. It was more than just their coloring: Sometimes she'd toss him a glance or an expression that reminded him of Laura years ago. He'd wondered if the reason he loved Trixie so damn much was that, through her, he got to fall in love with his wife all over again.

He crouched down in front of Laura. The movement of the air against her skin made her stir, and her eyes opened and locked onto Daniel's. For a fraction of a second, she started to smile, having forgotten where she was, and what had happened to her daughter, and what had gone wrong between the two of them. Daniel found his hands closing into fists, as if he could catch that moment before it disappeared entirely.

She glanced over at Trixie, making sure she was still asleep. "Where *were* you?"

Daniel certainly couldn't tell her the truth. "Driving."

He took off his coat and began to lay the sketches he'd done over the pale green blanket on the hospital bed. There was Trixie sliding into his lap the day Daniel got the phone call about his mother's death, asking, *If everyone died, would the world just stop?* Trixie holding a caterpillar, wondering whether it was a boy or a girl. Trixie pushing his hand away as he brushed a tear off her cheek, and saying, *Don't wipe off my feelings.*

"When did you do these?" Laura whispered.

"Today."

"But there are so many . . ."

Daniel didn't answer. He knew no words big enough to explain to Trixie how much he loved her, so instead, he wanted her to wake up covered with memories.

He wanted to remember why he could not afford to let go.

It was from his friend Cane that Daniel learned language was a force to be reckoned with. Like most Yup'ik Eskimos, Cane lived by three rules. The first was that thoughts and deeds were inextricably linked. How many times had Cane's grandfather explained that you couldn't properly butcher a moose while you were yammering about which girl in the fifth grade had to mail-order for an honest-to-God bra? You had to keep the thought of the moose in your mind, so that you'd make way for them to come back to you another time, during another hunt.

The second rule was that individual thoughts were less important than the collective knowledge of the elders—in other words, do whatever you're told and stop complaining.

But it was the third rule that was the hardest for Daniel to understand: the idea that words were so powerful they had the ability to change someone else's mind . . . even if they remained unspoken. It was why, when the Moravian church moved into the bush and the reverend told the Yupiit they had to leave fish camp on a Sunday to attend services about Jesus, they agreed, without ever having any real intention of going. What the reverend saw as a blatant lie, the Yup'ik Eskimos saw as a measure of respect: They liked the reverend too much to tell him he was wrong; instead, they just acquiesced and pretended otherwise.

It was this rule, ultimately, that divided Daniel and Cane. "Tomorrow's going to be a good day for hunting," Cane would tell Daniel, and Daniel would agree. But the next day Cane would go off with his grandfather for caribou and never ask Daniel to join them. It took years for Daniel to get up the nerve to ask Cane why he wasn't invited. "But I *do* invite you," he said, confused. "Every time."

Daniel's mother tried to explain it to him: Cane never would have come right out and asked Daniel to go hunting, because Daniel might have had other plans. It would be disrespectful to issue a formal invitation, because simply putting the words out into the world might cause Daniel to change his mind about what he wanted to do the next day, and Cane liked Daniel too much to risk that. When you are thirteen, though, cultural differences hardly matter. What you feel is every minute of the Saturday you spend by yourself, wishing you'd been asked to tag along. What you notice is the loneliness.

Daniel started to isolate himself, because it hurt less than being pushed away. He never really considered that a Yup'ik boy who couldn't ask him to come hunting might have even more difficulty asking Daniel what he'd done to make him angry. Within two years' time, Daniel had taken to occupying himself—vandalizing the school building and getting drunk and stealing snow machines. Cane was just someone Daniel used to know.

It wasn't until a year later, when Daniel was standing over Cane's body in the gymnasium and his hands were covered with Cane's blood, that he realized the Yupiit had been right all along. One word might have changed everything. One word might have spread like fire.

One word might have saved them both.

Could you pinpoint the very moment when your life began to fall apart?

For Laura, it seemed like each instance she found had an antecedent. Trixie's rape. Her own affair with Seth. Her unexpected pregnancy. The decision she made to find Daniel after he drew her. The first time she laid eyes on him and knew that everything else she saw from then on would no longer look the same. Disaster was an avalanche, gathering speed with such acceleration that you worried more about getting out of its path, not finding the pebble at its center.

It was easier for Laura to find the moment Trixie's life had been ruined. It all started, and ended, with Jason Underhill. If she'd never met him, if she'd never dated him, none of this would have happened. Not the rape, not the cutting, not even the suicide attempt. Laura had given it serious thought today: Jason was to blame for all of it. He had been the root of Trixie's deceptions; he had been the reason Laura hadn't been able to see her own daughter clearly.

She lay alone in bed, wide awake. Sleep was out of the question, with Trixie still at the hospital.

The doctors had assured Laura that Trixie would be watched like a hawk, that if all was well, they could bring her home tomorrow—but that didn't keep Laura from wondering if she was comfortable, if there was a nurse taking care of her even now.

Daniel wasn't asleep either. She had been listening to his footsteps downstairs, moving like open-ended questions. But now she heard him heading upstairs. A moment later he stood by the side of the bed. "Are you still up?" he whispered.

"I was never asleep."

"Can I . . . can I ask you something?"

She kept her eyes trained on the ceiling. "Okay."

"Are you afraid?"

"Of what?"

"Forgetting?"

Laura understood what he was trying to say. Although talking about what had happened to Trixie was the hardest thing in the world, they had to do it. If they didn't, they ran the risk of losing—by comparison—the memory of who Trixie used to be.

It was a catch-22: If you didn't put the trauma behind you, you couldn't move on. But if you *did* put the trauma behind you, you willingly gave up your claim to the person you were before it happened.

It was why, even when they weren't actively discussing it, the word *rape* hung like smoke over all of their heads. It was why, even as they were making polite conversation, every other thought in Laura's and Daniel's heads was *unfaithful.*

"Daniel," Laura admitted, "I'm afraid all the time."

He sank to his knees, and it took her a moment to realize that he was crying. She could not remember ever seeing Daniel cry—he used to say that he'd used up his allotment of tears as a kid. Laura sat up in bed, the covers falling away from her. She put her hands on Daniel's bowed head and stroked his hair. "Sssh," she said, and she drew him up onto the bed and into her arms.

At first it was about comfort: Laura being able to give; Daniel softening under her hands. But then Laura felt the air move like liquid as Daniel's body pressed against hers, desperate, his actions full of *now* and *need.* She felt her pulse jump under his fingers, as she fell back in time, remembering him like this years ago, and herself reacting. Then just as abruptly as Daniel had begun, he stopped. In the dark, she could see only the shine of his eyes. "I'm sorry," he murmured, backing away.

"Don't be," she said, and she reached for him.

It was all Daniel needed to let loose the last thread of restraint. He laid siege to Laura; he took no quarter. He scratched her skin and bit her throat. He reached for her hands and pinned them over her head. "Look at me," he demanded, until her eyes flew open and locked on his. "Look at me," he said again, and he drove himself into her.

Daniel waited until she was underneath him, writhing, poised for each moment when he came into her. As his arms anchored her closer, she threw back her head and let herself break apart.

She felt Daniel's hesitation, and his glorious, reckless fall.

As his sweat cooled on her own body, Laura traced a message over Daniel's right shoulder blade. *S-O-R-R-Y*, she wrote, even though she knew that the truths that sneak up behind a person are the ones he's most likely to miss.

Once, the Yupiit say, there was a man who was always quarreling with his wife. They fought over everything. The wife said her husband was lazy. The husband said his wife only wanted to sleep with other men. Finally, the wife went to a shaman in the village and begged to be changed into another creature. *Anything but a woman*, she said.

The shaman turned her into a raven. She flew off and built a nest, where she mated with other ravens. But every night, she found herself flying back to the village. Now, ravens can't come inside dwellings, so she would sit on the roof and hope to catch a glimpse of her husband. She'd think of reasons for him to come outside.

One night, he stepped through the entry and stood under the stars. *Oh*, she thought, *how lovely you are.*

The words fell into her husband's outstretched hands, and just like that, the raven turned back into a woman. Just like that, the man wanted her once again to be his wife.

The next morning, a chill snaked its way into the house. Daniel found his teeth chattering as he headed downstairs to make a pot of coffee. He put a call in to the hospital: Trixie had had a good night.

Well. So had he. His mistake had been in not admitting just how much had gone wrong between him and Laura. Maybe you had to scrape the bottom before you could push your way back to the surface.

He was bent over the fireplace, feeding kindling to the paper he'd lit, when Laura came downstairs wearing a sweater over her flannel pajamas. Her hair was sticking up in the back, and her cheeks were still flushed with a dream. "Morning," she murmured, and she slipped by him to pour herself a glass of orange juice.

Daniel waited for her to say something about the previous night, to admit that things had changed between them, but Laura wouldn't even look him in the eye. Immediately, his boldness faded. What if this spiderweb connection they'd made last night was not, as he'd thought, a first step . . . but a mistake? What if the whole time she'd been with Daniel, she'd wished she wasn't? "The hospital says we can get Trixie at nine," he said neutrally.

At news of Trixie, Laura turned. "How is she?"

"Great."

"Great? She tried to kill herself yesterday."

Daniel sat back on his heels. "Well . . . compared to yesterday, then . . . I guess she *is* doing pretty damn great."

Laura looked down at the counter. "Maybe that's true for all of us," she said.

Her face was red, and Daniel realized she wasn't embarrassed but nervous. He stood up and walked into the kitchen until he was standing beside her. Sometime between when they had gone to bed last night and the sun coming up this morning, the world had shifted beneath them. It wasn't what they had said to each other but what they hadn't: that forgiving and forgetting were fused together—flip sides of the same coin—and yet they couldn't both exist at the same time. Choosing one meant that you sacrificed seeing the other.

Daniel slipped his arm around Laura's waist and felt her shiver. "Cold out," she said.

"Brutal."

"Did you hear anything about weather like this?"

Daniel faced her. "I don't think anyone predicted it."

He opened his arms, and Laura moved into them, her eyes closing as she leaned against him. "I guess these things happen," she replied, as a rogue burst of sparks rose up the chimney.

You could not walk out of the hospital, for insurance reasons. If you tripped before you crossed the threshold, you might sue. However, if you chose to throw yourself in front of a car the minute you stepped outside, no one would give a damn.

Trixie was thinking about it.

She'd already had to sit down with a shrink this morning, and apparently she was going to have to do that twice a week for the next five forevers, too, all because she had seen a brass ring in the bathroom and had tried to grab it. It didn't matter if, like Janice the rape counselor, these sessions could eventually wind up in court. She had to attend them, or she had to stay in the hospital on the psych floor with a roommate who ate her own hair. She was going to have to take medicine, too—under the watchful eye of her parents, who would actually check the sides of her mouth and under her tongue to make sure she didn't fake swallowing. Since arriving at the hospital this morning, her mother was trying so hard to smile that Trixie expected her face to crack, and her father kept asking her if she needed anything. *Yeah*, she felt like answering. *A life.*

Trixie seesawed between wishing everyone would leave her alone and wondering why everyone treated her like a leper. Even when that stupid psychiatrist had been sitting across from her, asking things like, *Do you think you're in danger of wanting to kill yourself right now?* she felt like she was watching the whole scene from a balcony, and it was a comedy. She kept expecting the girl who played her to say something smart, like, *Why yes, thanks, I would like to kill myself right now . . . but I'll restrain myself until the audience is gone.* Instead, she watched the actress who was really her fold like a fortune cookie and burst into tears.

What Trixie wanted, most of all, was what she couldn't have—to go back to being the kind of girl who worried about things like science tests and whether any college would admit her, instead of being the kind of girl everyone worried about.

She survived the ride home by closing her eyes almost immediately and pretending she'd fallen asleep. Instead, she listened to the conversation between her parents in the front seat:

*Do you think it's normal, the way her voice sounds?*

*How do you mean?*

*You know. Like most of the notes are missing.*

*Maybe it's the medicine.*

*They said that would take a few weeks to kick in.*

*Then how are we supposed to keep her safe in the meantime?*

Trixie almost would have felt sorry for her parents if she wasn't so sure that they'd brought this on themselves. After all, her mother didn't *have* to open the bathroom door yesterday.

She felt the truth that she'd been hiding, like an after-dinner mint that might last for ages, if you were careful enough; the truth that she hadn't told the shrink or the doctors or her parents, no matter how much they tried to pull it out of her. She would swallow it whole before she spit it out loud.

Trixie made a big show of stretching and yawning as they approached the turn to their street. Her mother turned around, that Halloween-mask smile still on her face. "You're awake!"

Her father glanced at her in the rearview mirror. "You need anything?"

Trixie turned and stared out the window. Maybe she *had* died, after all. And this was hell.

Just about when Trixie decided things couldn't get any worse, the car turned into the driveway and she saw Zephyr waiting. The last conversation they'd had wasn't one that invited future chats, and it had left Trixie feeling like she'd been quarantined from the rest of the earth. But right now, Zephyr was the one who looked nervous.

Zephyr knocked on the window. "Um, Mrs. Stone. I, was kind of, you know, hoping to talk to Trixie."

Her mother frowned. "I don't really think that now's the best time—"

"Laura," her father interrupted, and he glanced at Trixie in the rearview mirror: *It's up to you.*

Trixie got out of the backseat. She hunched her shoulders, so that her wrists were even more hidden by the sleeves of her coat. "Hey," she said cautiously.

Zephyr looked the way Trixie had felt for the past twenty-four hours—like she was completely made up of tears and trying to hold some semblance of human form together before someone noticed that she was actually just a puddle. She followed Trixie into the house, up to her bedroom. There was one terrifying moment when Trixie passed the bathroom—had anyone cleaned up since yesterday? But the door was closed, and she fled into her own room before she had to think about it anymore.

"Are you okay?" Zephyr said.

Trixie wasn't about to fall for the false sympathy routine. "Who dared you?"

"What?"

"Are you, like, supposed to come back with a

lock of my hair to prove you got close? Oh, *that's* right, I don't *have* any hair. I cut it off when I started to go psycho."

Zephyr swallowed. "I heard you almost died."

*Almost doesn't count*, Trixie's father used to say. *Except in horseshoes and hand grenades.*

What about in rape cases?

"Do you almost care?" Trixie said.

Suddenly Zephyr's face crumpled. "I've been a total asshole. I was mad at you, because I thought you planned this whole revenge thing for Jason and didn't trust me enough to tell me—"

"I never—"

"No, wait, let me finish," Zephyr said. "And I was mad at you for that night, when Moss paid more attention to you than to me. I wanted to get back at you, so I said—I said what they all were saying. But then I heard that you were in the hospital and I kept thinking about how awful it would have been if you . . . if you, *you know*, before I had a chance to tell you I believe you." Her face crumpled. "I feel like this was all my fault. I'd do anything to make it up to you."

There was no way to tell whether Zeph was telling the truth, and even if she was, that didn't mean Trixie trusted her anymore. There was every chance that Zephyr was going to run to Moss and Jason and the rest of the hockey team and regale them with tales of the freak. But then again . . . maybe she wasn't; maybe the reason Zephyr was here had nothing to do with guilt or her mom telling her to be here but simply because she remembered, like Trixie did, that once when they were five they had been the only two people in the world who knew that fairies lived inside the kitchen cabinets and hid under the pots and pans when you opened the doors.

Trixie looked at her. "Do you want to know how I did it?"

Zephyr nodded, drawn forward.

She slowly pulled the tape that sealed the bandage around her wrist and unraveled the gauze until the wound was visible: gaping and saw-edged, angry.

"Wow," Zephyr breathed. "That is *sick*. Did it hurt?"

Trixie shook her head.

"Did you see lights or angels or, like, God?"

Trixie thought about it, hard. The last thing she could remember was the rusted edge of the radiator, which she focused on before blacking out. "I didn't see anything."

"Figures," Zephyr sighed, and then she looked at Trixie and grinned.

Trixie felt like smiling back. For the first time in a long time, when she told her brain to do it, it actually worked.

Three days after Trixie tried to kill herself, Daniel and Laura found themselves in Marita Soorenstad's office, with Trixie between them. Detective Bartholemew was seated to their left, and behind the desk the DA was ripping open a Pixy Stix. "Help yourselves," she said, and then she turned to Trixie. "I'm certainly glad to see you're with us. From what I understand, that wasn't a sure thing a few days ago."

Daniel reached over and took his daughter's hand. It felt like ice. "Trixie's feeling much better."

"For how long?" the district attorney asked, folding her hands on the desk. "I don't mean to sound insensitive, Mr. Stone, but the only thing consistent in this case so far has been the lack of consistency."

Laura shook her head. "I don't understand . . ."

"As a prosecutor, my job is to present facts to a jury that make it possible for them to find, beyond a reasonable doubt, that your daughter was the victim of a rape perpetrated by Jason Underhill. However, the facts I'm presenting are the ones that your daughter presented to us. And that means our case is only as good as the information she's provided me with and as strong as the picture she paints on the stand."

Daniel felt his jaw tighten. "I'd think that when a girl tries to kill herself, it's a pretty good indicator that she's suffering from trauma."

"Either that, or mental instability."

"So, you just give up?" Laura said, incredulous. "You don't try a case if you think it's going to be a tough sell?"

"I never said that, Mrs. Stone. But I do have an ethical obligation not to bring a case to court if even *I'm* unsure a crime happened."

"You've got evidence," Daniel said. "That rape kit."

"Yes. The same rape kit that allowed a labora-tory to find evidence of semen in Trixie's mouth, when by her own statement she did not have oral sex that night. On the other hand, Jason Underhill alleges that the intercourse was consensual—and was both oral and vaginal." The DA turned over a page in a file. "According to Trixie, she screamed *no* while she was being raped but said that her friend Zephyr wouldn't have been able to hear her over the music. Yet according to other witnesses, no music was playing during the time of the as-sault."

"They're all lying," Daniel said.

Marita stared at him. "Or Trixie is. She lied to you about going to her friend's house for a quiet sleepover that night. She lied about losing her vir-ginity the night of the assault—"

*"What?"* Laura said, her jaw dropping, and at that moment Daniel remembered he'd never told her what the detective had said. Had he forgotten, or had he intended to forget all along?

"—she lied to the ER physician about the cuts on her wrist, some of which were made long before that Friday night," Marita continued. "Which begs the question: What else is Trixie lying about?"

"I want to speak to your boss," Laura de-manded.

"My boss will tell you that I have a hundred other cases to prosecute that could be commanding my attention. I don't have time for a victim who's cry-ing wolf."

Daniel couldn't look at Trixie. If he did, he thought

he might break down. Where he'd grown up, a Yup'ik boy who cried wolf would simply turn into that animal forever. His relatives would say he had it coming. He'd spend the rest of his life watching his old family through yellow eyes, from a distance.

Daniel turned to the detective, who'd been doing a good job of trying to blend into the 1970s paneling. "Tell her about the photo."

"He already has," Marita said. "And I'm going to have my hands full trying to keep that out of the courtroom as it is."

"It's a perfect example of how Trixie's being victimized—"

"It doesn't tell us anything about the night of the assault—except that Trixie wasn't a choirgirl before it happened."

*"Will you all just shut up!"* At the sound of Trixie's voice, all eyes turned. "I'm here, in case you hadn't noticed. So can you all stop talking about me like I'm *not*?"

"By all means, Trixie, we'd love to hear what you have to say. Today."

Trixie swallowed. "I didn't mean to lie."

"You're admitting you did?" the district attorney replied.

"There were so many . . . holes. I didn't think anyone would believe what happened if I couldn't remember the whole story." She pulled her sleeves down farther over her wrists. Daniel had noticed her doing that in the past few days, and every time it made his heart pleat. "I remember going to Zephyr's, and all the people who were there. I didn't know most of them. A bunch of the girls were playing Rainbow—"

"Rainbow?" Daniel said.

Trixie began to pick at the hem of her coat. "It's where everyone gets a different shade of lipstick, and the boys . . . you know, you go off with them . . ." She shook her head.

"The one with the most colorful penis at the end of the night wins," Marita said flatly. "Is that about right?"

Daniel heard Laura's intake of breath as Trixie nodded. "That's it," she whispered. "I didn't do it, though. I thought I could—I wanted to make Jason jealous—but I couldn't. Everyone went home after that, except for Jason and Moss and me and Zephyr, and that's when we started playing poker. Moss took the picture of me, and Jason got mad at him, and that's when it all goes blank. I know I was in the bathroom when he found me, but I can't remember how we got to the living room. I can't remember anything, really, until he was on top of me. I thought if I waited long enough, it would all come back. But it hasn't."

The district attorney and the detective exchanged a glance. "Are you saying," Marita clarified, "that you woke up to find him having intercourse with you?"

Trixie nodded.

"Do you remember any other details?"

"I had a really bad headache. I thought maybe he'd slammed my head on the floor or something."

Bartholemew walked toward the district attorney. He stood behind her shoulder, flipping over the contents of the file until he reached a certain page and pointed. "The ER doc noted a seemingly dissociated mental state. And during her initial interview at the PD, she was unresponsive."

"Mike," the district attorney said, "give me a break."

"If it's true, it would turn this into gross sexual assault," Bartholemew pressed. "And all of the inconsistencies in Trixie's story would actually work to the prosecution's advantage."

"We'd need proof. Date rape drugs stay in the bloodstream for only seventy-two hours, tops."

Bartholemew lifted a lab report out of the file folder. "Good thing you've got a sample, then, from six hours post."

Daniel was utterly lost. "What are you talking about?"

The prosecutor turned. "Right now, this case is being tried as a juvenile sexually assaulting a juvenile. That changes, however, if the assault is committed either while Trixie was unconscious, or if she was given a substance that impaired her ability to appraise or control the sexual act. In that case, by law, Jason Underhill would have to be tried as an adult."

"Are you saying Trixie was drugged?" Daniel said.

The district attorney fixed her gaze on Trixie. "Either that," she replied, "or your daughter is trying to dig herself out of yet another hole."

• • •

"Special K, Vitamin K, Kit Kat, Blind Squid, Cat Valium, Purple—it's got a dozen names on the street," Venice Prudhomme said, peeling off a pair of latex gloves and throwing them in the trash at Bartholemew's feet. "Ketamine's a nonbarbiturate, rapid-acting anesthetic used on both animals and humans—it's also allegedly a sexual stimulant. Kids like it as a club drug because, molecularly, it's very similar to angel dust—PCP. It produces a dissociative state, making them feel like their minds are separate from their bodies. We're talking hallucinations . . . amnesia."

Mike had begged Venice to run the test at the state lab, in spite of a two-month backlog of cases. He'd promised, in return, a pair of club-level Bruins tickets. Venice was a single mom with a hockey-crazy son, a woman who didn't get paid enough to spend $85 per ticket; he knew she wouldn't be able to turn down the offer. Where he was going to actually *get* two club-level Bruins tickets on his *own* salary, though, remained to be seen.

So far, Trixie had tested negative for GHB and Rohypnol, the two most common date rape drugs. At this point, Mike was close to conceding that Trixie had, again, duped them. He watched the computer screen, an incomprehensible run of numbers. "Who's dealing ketamine in Bethel, Maine?" he asked rhetorically.

"It's fully legal when it's Ketaset and sold to vets as a liquid. In that form, it's easy to use as a date rape drug. It's odorless and tasteless. You slip it into a girl's drink, and she's knocked out in less than a minute. For the next few hours, she's numb and willing . . . and best of all, she won't remember what happened." As the computer spit out the last analysis, Venice scanned it. "You say your victim's been lying to you?"

"Enough to make me wish I was working for the defense," Mike said.

She pulled a highlighter from her towering nest of braids and ran a yellow line across a field of results—a positive flag for ketamine. "Keep your day job," Venice replied. "Trixie Stone was telling the truth."

There were not, as most people believed, a hundred different Eskimo words for snow. Boil down the roots of the Yup'ik language, and you'd only have fifteen: *qanuk* (snowflake), *kanevvluk* (fine snow), *natquik* (drifting snow), *nevluk* (clinging snow), *qanikcaq* (snow on the ground), *muruaneq* (soft, deep snow on the ground), *qetrar* (crust on top of snow), *nutaryuk* (fresh fallen snow), *qanisqineq* (snow floating on water), *qengaruk* (snowbank), *utvak* (snow block), *navcaq* (snow cornice), *pirta* (snowstorm), *cellallir* (blizzard), and *pirrelvag* (severely storming).

When it came to snow, Daniel thought in Yup'ik. He'd look out the window and one of these words, or its derivatives, would pop into his mind ahead of the English. There were snows here in Maine, though, that didn't have equivalent terms in Alaska. Like a nor'easter. Or the kind of snow that landed like goose down, during mud season. Or the ice storm that made the needles on the pines look like they were fashioned out of crystal.

Times like those, Daniel's mind would simply go blank. Like now: There had to be a term for the kind of storm that he knew was going to be the first real measurable snow of the season. The flakes were the size of a toddler's fist and falling so fast that it seemed there was a rip in the seam of the gunmetal sky. It had snowed in October and November, but not like this. This was the sort of storm that would cause school superintendents to cancel afternoon basketball games, and create long lines at the Goodyear store; this was the kind of storm that made out-of-town drivers pull over on the highway and forced housewives to buy an extra gallon of milk.

It was the kind of snow that came so fast, it caught you unaware. You hadn't yet taken the shovels down from the attic where you'd put them last May; you didn't get a chance to cover the trembling rhododendrons with their ridiculous wooden tepees.

It was the kind of snow, Daniel realized, where you didn't have time to put away the errant rake and the clippers you'd used to trim back the black-berry bushes, so you'd find yourself walking in cir-cles, hoping you might trip over them before the blades rusted for good. But you never did. Instead, you were bound to lose the things you'd been careless with, and your punishment was not see-ing them again until the spring.

• • •

Trixie couldn't remember the last time she went out to play in the snow. When she was a kid, her father used to build a luge in the backyard that she'd slide down on a tube, but at some point it was no longer cool to look like a total spaz when she tipped over, and she'd traded her rubber-tread Sorels for fashionable stacked-heel boots.

She couldn't find her snow boots—they were buried under too much stuff in the closet. Instead, she borrowed her mother's, still drying in the mudroom, now that her mom had canceled her afternoon lecture in the wake of the storm. Trixie wrapped a scarf around her neck and jammed a hat onto her head that said DRAMA QUEEN across the front in red script. She pulled on a pair of her father's ski mittens and headed outside.

It was what her mother used to call snowman snow—the kind damp enough to stick together. Trixie packed it into a ball. She started to roll it across the lawn like a bandage, leaving behind a long brown tongue of matted grass.

After a while, she surveyed the damage. The yard looked like a crazy quilt, white stripes bordering triangles and squares made of lawn. Taking another handful of snow, Trixie began to roll a second snowball, and a third. A few minutes later, she was standing in the middle of them, wondering how they'd gotten so big so fast. There was no way she would be able to lift one onto the other. How had she managed to build a snowman when she was little? Maybe she hadn't. Maybe someone else had always done it for her.

Suddenly the door opened and her mother was standing there, screaming her name and trying to see through the flakes still coming down. She looked frantic, and it took Trixie a moment to understand: Her mother didn't know she'd come outside; her mother was still worried she'd kill herself.

"Over here," Trixie said.

Not that death-by-blizzard was a bad idea. When Trixie was tiny, she used to dig a hideout in the mountain of snow left behind by the plow. She called it her igloo, even though her father had told her that Eskimos in America did not and never had lived in those. But then she read a newspaper article about a kid in Charlotte, Vermont, who had done the same exact thing and the roof had collapsed on his head and smothered him before his parents even knew he was missing, and she never did it again.

Her mother walked outside and immediately sank ankle-deep in snow. She was wearing Trixie's boots, which she must have dug out of the closet wreckage after Trixie had commandeered her own Sorels. "You want help?" her mother asked.

Trixie didn't. If she'd wanted help, she would have invited someone outside with her in the first place. But she couldn't for the life of her imagine how she was going to get that stupid belly on top of the snowman's base. "All right," she conceded.

Her mother got on one side of the ball and pushed, while Trixie tried to pull it from the front.

Even together, they couldn't budge the weight. "Welcome to the Fourth Circle," her mother said, laughing.

Trixie fell onto her butt on the snow. Leave it to her mother to turn this into a classics lesson.

"You've got your tightwads on one side and your greedy folks on the other," her mother said. "They shove boulders at each other for all eternity."

"I was kind of hoping to finish this up before then."

Her mother turned. "Why, Trixie Stone. Was that a *joke*?"

Since coming home from the hospital, there had been precious few of those in the household. When a television sitcom came on, the channel was immediately changed. When you felt a smile coming on, you squelched it. Feeling happy didn't seem particularly appropriate, not with everything that had gone on lately. It was as if, Trixie thought, they were all waiting for someone to wave a magic wand and say, *It's okay, now. Carry on.*

What if *she* was the one who was supposed to wave that wand?

Her mother began to sculpt a snow ramp. Trixie fell into place beside her, pushing the middle snowball higher and higher until it tipped onto the bigger base. She packed snow between the seams. Then she lifted the head and perched it at the very top.

Her mother clapped . . . just as snowman listed and fell. His head rolled into one of the basement window gutters; his midsection cracked like an egg. Only the massive base sphere remained intact.

Frustrated, Trixie slapped a snowball against the side of it. Her mother watched and then packed her own snowball. Within seconds they were both firing shots at the boulder until it cleaved down the center, until it succumbed to the assault and lay between them in fat iceberg chunks.

By then, Trixie was lying on her back, panting. She had not felt—well, this *normal* in some time. It occurred to her that had things ended differently a week ago, she might not be doing any of this. She'd been so focused on what she had wanted to get away from in this world she forgot to consider what she might miss.

When you die, you don't get to catch snowflakes on your tongue. You don't get to breathe winter in, deep in your lungs. You can't lie in bed and watch for the lights of the passing town plow. You can't suck on an icicle until your forehead hurts.

Trixie stared up at the dizzy flakes. "I'm kind of glad."

"About what?"

"That it didn't . . . you know . . . *work out.*"

She felt her mother's hand reach over to grab her own. Their mittens were both soaked.

They'd go inside, stick their clothes inside the dryer. Ten minutes later, they'd be good as new.

Trixie wanted to cry. It was that beautiful, knowing what came next.

• • •

Because of the storm, hockey practice had been canceled. Jason came home after school, as per the conditions of his bail, and holed himself up in his bedroom listening to the White Stripes on his iPod. He closed his eyes and executed mental passes to Moss, wrist shots and slapshots and pucks that hit the top shelf.

One day, people would be talking about him, and not just because of this rape case. They'd say things like, *Oh, Jason Underhill, we always knew he'd make it.* They'd put up a replica jersey of his over the mirror behind the town bar, with his name facing out, and the Bruins games would take precedence over any other programming on the one TV mounted in the corner.

Jason had a lot of work cut out ahead of him, but he could do it. A year or two postgrad, then some college hockey, and maybe he'd even be like Hugh Jessiman at Dartmouth and get signed in the first round of the NHL draft. Coach had told Jason that he'd never seen a forward with as much natural talent as Jason. He'd said that if you wanted something bad enough, all you had to learn was how to go out and take it.

He was living out his fantasy for the hundredth time when the door to his room burst open. Jason's father strode in, fuming, and yanked the iPod's headphones out of Jason's ears.

"What the hell?" Jason said, sitting up.

"You want to tell me what you left out the first

time? You want to tell me where you got the god-damned drugs?"

"I don't *do* drugs," Jason said. "Why would I do something that's going to screw up my game?"

"Oh, I believe you," his father said, sarcastic. "I believe you didn't take any of those drugs your-self."

The conversation was spinning back and forth in directions Jason couldn't follow. "Then why are you flipping out?"

"Because Dutch Oosterhaus called me at work to discuss a little lab report he got today. The one they did on Trixie Stone's blood that proves some-one knocked her out by slipping her a drug."

Heat climbed the ladder of Jason's spine.

"You know what else Dutch told me? Now that drugs are in the picture, the prosecutor's got enough evidence to try you as an adult."

"I didn't—"

A vein pulsed in his father's temple. "You threw it all away, Jason. You fucking threw it all away for a small-town whore."

"I didn't drug her. I didn't rape her. She must have fooled around with that blood sample, be-cause . . . because . . ." Jason's voice dropped off. "Jesus Christ . . . you don't believe me."

"No one does," his father said, weary. He reached into his back pocket for a letter that had already been opened and passed it to Jason be-fore leaving the room.

Jason sank down onto his bed. The letter was embossed with a return address for Bethel Academy; the name of the hockey coach had been scrawled above it in pen. He began to read: *In lieu of recent circumstances . . . withdrawing its initial offer of a scholarship for a postgraduate year . . . sure you understand our position and its reflection on the academy.*

The letter dropped from his hands, fluttering to land on the carpet. The iPod, without its headphones, glowed a mute blue. Who would have imagined that the sound your life made as it disintegrated was total silence?

Jason buried his face in his hands and, for the first time since all this had begun, started to cry.

Once the storm had stopped and the streets were cleared, the storekeepers in Bethel came out to shovel their walkways and talk about how lucky they were that this latest blizzard hadn't caused the town manager to cancel the annual Winterfest.

It was always held the Friday before Christmas and was a direct ploy to boost the local economy. Main Street was blocked off by the spinning blue lights of police cars. Shops stayed open late, and hot cider was served for free in the inn. Christmas lights winked like fireflies in the bare branches of the trees. Some enterprising farmer carted in a sickly looking reindeer and set up portable fencing around it: a North Pole petting zoo. The bookstore owner, dressed as Santa, arrived at seven o'clock and stayed as long as it took to hear the holiday requests of all the children waiting in line.

This year, in an effort to connect local sports heroes to the community, the square in front of the town offices had been sealed and flooded to create a makeshift ice rink. The Ice CaBabes, a local competitive figure-skating team, had done an exhibition routine earlier that evening. Now the championship Bethel High School hockey team was slated to play pickup hockey with a local group of Boy Scouts.

After everything that had happened, Jason hadn't planned to go—until Coach called up and said he had an obligation to the team. What Coach hadn't done, however, was specify in what condition Jason had to arrive. It was a fifteen-minute ride downtown, and he drank a fifth of his dad's Jack Daniel's on the way.

Moss was already on the ice when Jason sat down on a bench and pulled out his skates. "You're late," Moss said.

Jason double-knotted the laces, grabbed his stick, and shoved hard past Moss. "You here to talk or play hockey?" He skated so fast down the center of the rink that he had to slalom around some of the wobbling kids. Moss met him and they passed the puck in a series of complicated handoffs. On the sidelines, the parents cheered, thinking this was all part of the exhibition.

Coach called for a face-off, and Jason skated into position. The kid he was opposing on the scout team came up as high as his hip. The puck was dropped, and the high school team let the kids win it. But Jason stick-checked the boy who was skating down the ice, stole the puck, and carried it down to the goal. He lifted it to the upper right corner of the net, where there was no chance of the tiny goalie being able to stop it. He pumped his stick in the air and looked around for his other teammates, but they were hanging back, and the crowd wasn't cheering anymore. "Aren't we *supposed* to score?" he yelled out, his words slurring. "Did the rules change here, too?"

Moss led Jason to the side of the rink. "Dude. It's just pond hockey, and they're just kids."

Jason nodded, shook it off. They met for another face-off, and this time when the kids took the puck Jason skated backward slowly, making no move to go after it. Unused to playing without the boards, he tripped over the plastic edge of the rink liner and fell into the arms of the crowd. He noticed Zephyr Santorelli-Weinstein's face, and a half-dozen others from school. "Sorry," he muttered, staggering to his feet.

When he stepped onto the ice again, Jason headed for the puck, hip-checking a player to get him out of the way. Except this time, his opponent was half his size and a third of his weight, and went flying.

The boy banged into his goalie, who slid into the net in a heap, crying. Jason watched the kid's father hurry onto the ice in his street shoes.

"What is *wrong* with you today?" Moss said, skating close.

"It was an accident," Jason answered, and his friend reared back, smelling the alcohol.

"Coach is going to rip you a new asshole. Get out of here. I'll cover for you."

Jason stared at him.

"Go," Moss said.

Jason took one last look at the boy and his father, then skated hard to the spot where he'd left his boots.

*I did not die, and yet I lost life's breath:*
*imagine for yourself what I became,*
*deprived at once of both my life and*
   *death.*

Laura read Lucifer's lines in the last canto of the *Inferno*, then closed the book. Hands down, Lucifer was the most fascinating character in the poem: waist-deep in the lake of ice, with his three heads gnawing on a feast of sinners. Having once been an archangel, he certainly had the freedom of choice—in fact, it was what got him to pick a fight with God in the first place. So if Lucifer had willingly chosen his course, had he known beforehand that he was going to end up suffering?

Did he think, on some level, that he deserved it?

Did anyone, who was cast in the role opposite the hero?

It occurred to Laura that she had sinned in every single circle. She'd committed adultery. She'd betrayed her benefactor—the university—by seducing a student . . . which could also be considered treachery, if you classified Seth as an innocent pawn in the game. She'd defied God by ignoring her wedding vows: She'd defied her family by distancing herself from Trixie when Trixie needed her most. She'd lied to her husband, she'd been angry and wrathful, she'd sowed discord, and she'd been a fraudulent counselor to a student who came looking for a mentor and wound up with a lover.

About the only thing Laura *hadn't* done was kill someone.

She reached behind her desk for an antique china human head she had found at a garage sale. It was smooth and white and divided into calligraphed subsections across the brain area: *wit, glory, revenge, bliss.* Over the skull she'd put a headband sporting two red devil horns, a gift from a student one Halloween. Now she took the headband off and tried it on for size.

There was a knock on her door, and a moment later Seth stepped into her office. "Are those horns on your head," he said, "or are you just happy to see me?"

She yanked off the headband.

"Five minutes." He closed the door, locked it. "You owe me that much."

Relationships always sounded so physically painful: You fell in love, you broke a heart, you lost your head. Was it any wonder that people came through the experience with battle scars? The problem with a marriage—or maybe its strength— was that it spanned a distance, and you were never the same person you started out being. If you were lucky, you could still recognize each other years later. If you weren't, you wound up in your office with a boy fifteen years younger than you were, pouring his heart into your open hands.

All right. If she was going to be honest, she had loved the way Seth knew what an anapest was, and a canzone. She loved seeing their reflection in a pane of glass as they passed a storefront and being surprised every time. She loved playing Scrabble on a rainy afternoon when she should have been grading papers or attending a departmental meeting. But just because she had called in sick that day didn't mean she wasn't still a professor. Just because she abandoned her family didn't mean she wasn't still a wife, a mother. Her biggest sin, when you got right down to it, was forgetting all that in the first place.

"Seth," she said, "I don't know how to make this any easier. But—"

She broke off, realizing the words she was about to say: *But I love my husband.*

*I always have.*

"We need to talk," Seth said quietly. He reached into the back pocket of his jeans and tossed a rolled newspaper onto the table.

Laura had seen it. The front page chronicled the newly filed charge by the district attorney. Jason Underhill would be tried as an adult, due to the presence of date rape drugs in the victim's bloodstream.

"Ketamine," Seth said.

Laura blinked at him. From what the prosecutor had said, the drug found in Trixie's system hadn't even been one of the more popular date rape drugs. It hadn't been listed in the newspaper, either. "How would you know that?"

Seth sat down on the edge of her desk. "There's something I have to tell you," he said.

"I'm coming!" Trixie yelled through the open door, as her father honked the horn for the third time. Jesus. It wasn't like she wanted to go into town right now, and it wasn't her fault that the pizza cheese he was using to cook dinner had grown enough mold to be classified as an antibiotic. She hadn't been doing anything earth-shattering that she couldn't interrupt, but it was the principle that was upsetting her: Neither parent felt comfortable letting Trixie out of sight.

She stomped into the first pair of boots she could find and headed outside to his idling truck. "Can't we just have soup?" Trixie said, slouching down in her seat, when what she really meant was: *What will it take to make you trust me again?*

Her father put the truck into first gear to go down a long hill. "I know you want me to leave you home alone. But I hope you also know why I can't do that."

Trixie rolled her eyes toward the window. "Whatever."

As they approached town, there was a glut of cars. People in bright parkas and scarves spilled across the street like a stream of confetti. Trixie felt her stomach turn over. "What's the date?" she murmured. She'd seen the signs all over school:

ICE = NICE. DON'T BE A SNOWFLAKE—COME TO WINTER-FEST.

Trixie shrank back in her seat as three girls she recognized from school came so close to the car they brushed the front bumper. *Everyone* came to the Winterfest. When she was little, her parents would take her to pat the sorry old reindeer idling near the camera store. She could remember seeing ordinary teachers and doctors and waitresses become Victorian carolers for a night. Last year, Trixie had been an elf along with Zephyr, the two of them wearing double layers of skating tights and handing out candy canes to the kids who sat on Santa's lap.

This year, walking down Main Street would be totally different. At first, no one would see her, because it was dark out. But then, someone would bump into her by accident. *Sorry*, they'd say, and then they'd realize who it was. They'd tap their friends. They would point. They'd lean close and whisper about how Trixie wasn't wearing any makeup and how her hair looked like it hadn't been washed in a week. Before she had made it to the other end of Main Street, their stares would have burned into the back of her coat like sunlight through a looking glass, starting a flash fire that reduced her to a pile of ashes.

"Daddy," she said, "can't we just go home?"

Her father glanced at her. He'd had to detour around Main Street and was now parked in a lot behind the grocery store. Trixie could see he was weighing the cost of reaching his destination against Trixie's extreme discomfort . . . and factoring in her suicide attempt to boot. "You stay in the car," her father conceded. "I'll be right back."

Trixie nodded and watched him cross the parking lot. She closed her eyes and counted to fifty. She listened to the sound of her own pulse.

Yet as it turned out, what Trixie had thought she wanted most of all—being left alone—turned out to be absolutely terrifying. When the door of the car beside her slammed, she jumped. The headlights swept over her as the car backed out, and she ducked her face against the collar of her coat so that the driver couldn't see.

Her father had been gone for three minutes when she started to actively panic. It didn't take much longer than that to buy some stupid cheese, did it? What if someone else came to this parking lot and saw her sitting there? How long before a crowd gathered, calling her a slut and a whore? Who would save her if they decided to pound on the windows, start a witch hunt, lynch her?

She peered out the windshield. It would take fifteen seconds, tops, to make it to the door of the grocery store. By now her father would be in line. She might run into someone she knew there, but at least she wouldn't be alone.

Trixie got out of the car and started to race across the parking lot. She could see the buttery windows of the grocery mart and the line of wire shopping carts shivering against its outer wall.

Someone was coming. She couldn't see whether it was her father—the figure seemed big enough, but the streetlamp was behind him, obscuring the features. If it was her father, he'd see her first, Trixie realized. And if it wasn't her father, then she was going to move past the stranger at the speed of light.

But as Trixie broke into a sprint, she hit a patch of black ice and her feet gave out from underneath her. One leg twisted, and she could feel herself falling. The moment before her left hip struck the pavement, she was wrenched upright by the very person she'd been trying to avoid. "You okay?" he said, and she looked up to find Jason holding her upper arm.

He let go almost as quickly as he'd grabbed her. Trixie's mother had said that Jason couldn't come near her, couldn't cross paths with her—if he did, he'd be shipped off to a juvenile detention center before the trial. But either her mother had been wrong or Jason had forgotten, because he shook off whatever fear had made him release her and began advancing on her instead. He smelled like a distillery, and his voice was raw. "What did you tell them? What are you trying to do to me?"

Trixie fought for breath. The cold was seeping through the back of her jeans and there was water in her boot where it had gone through the ice into a puddle. "I didn't . . . I'm not . . . ."

"You have to tell them the truth," Jason begged. "They don't believe me."

This was news to Trixie and cut clean as a knife through her fear. If they didn't believe *Jason*, and they didn't believe *her*, who *did* they believe?

He crouched in front of her, and that was all it took for Trixie to be whipped back to *then.* It was as if the rape was happening all over again, as if she couldn't control a single inch of her own body.

"Trixie," Jason said.

*His hands on her thighs, as she tried to pull away.*

"You *have* to."

*His body rising over hers, pinning her at the hips.* "Now."

Now, *he had said, throwing his head back as he pulled out and spilled hot across her belly.* Now, *he had said, but by then it was already too late.*

Trixie drew in a deep breath and screamed at the top of her lungs.

Suddenly Jason wasn't leaning over her anymore. Trixie glanced up to see him wrestling, trying to dodge her father's punches. "Daddy!" she screamed. "Stop!"

Her father turned, bleeding from a split lip. "Trixie, get in the car."

She didn't get in the car. She scrambled away from their brawl and stood in the halo of the streetlamp, watching as her father—the same man who caught the spiders in her bedroom and carried them outside in a Dixie cup, the same man who had never in his life spanked her—pummeled Jason. She was horrified and fascinated all at once. It was like meeting someone she'd never seen before and finding out that all this time, he'd been living next door.

The sound of flesh smacking flesh reminded

Trixie of the bluefish that got slapped hard against the docks in Portland by the fishermen, to still them before they were filleted. She covered her ears and looked down at the ground, at the plastic bag of shredded mozzarella that had fallen and been torn open under their boots during the fight.

"If you ever," her father panted, "*ever* . . ."

He landed a punch to Jason's gut.

". . . *ever* come near my daughter again . . ."

A blow across the right jaw.

"I will kill you." But just as he reared back his hand to strike again, a car drove past the parking lot, illuminating everything.

The last man Daniel had beaten up had already been dead. In the high school gym in Akiak, Daniel had slammed Cane against the floor, although his head already had a bullet hole in it. He'd done it because he wanted Cane to tell him to stop. He'd wanted Cane to sit up and take a swing back at him.

The principal had tiptoed gingerly into this nightmare, absorbing Daniel's sobs and the discarded rifle and the blood sprayed across the bleachers. *Daniel*, the principal had said, shocked. *What did you* do?

Daniel had run, because he was faster than the principal and faster than the police. For a few days he was a murder suspect, and he liked that. If Daniel had meant to kill Cane, then he couldn't feel as guilty about not keeping it from happening.

By the time he left town, the rumors surrounding

Daniel had died down. Everyone knew it was Cane's hunting rifle, and Daniel's fingerprints hadn't been on it. Cane had not left a suicide note—that was rare, in the village—but he'd left his basketball jersey on the table for his little sister. Daniel had been cleared as a suspect, but he left Alaska anyway. It wasn't that he'd been scared of his future; it was that he couldn't see one, period.

Every now and then, he still woke up with one thought caught like cotton on the roof of his mouth: Dead men don't bruise.

Tonight, he'd been stuck behind an old woman paying with pennies at the grocery mart. The whole time, he was second-guessing himself. At first, after the suicide attempt, Trixie had been distant and silent, but over the past few days her personality would bob to the surface every now and then. However, the minute they'd reached town, Trixie had gone still and blank—a relapse. Daniel hadn't wanted to leave her alone in the car but couldn't stand the thought of forcing her to leave that safety zone either. How long could it take to buy a single item? He'd hurried into the store, thinking only of Trixie and getting her back home as quickly as possible.

It was when he'd stepped under the streetlamp that he'd seen it: that bastard's hand on his daughter's arm.

For someone who has never given himself over to rage, it would be hard to understand. But for Daniel, it felt like shrugging on an old, soft suede coat that had been buried so deep in his closet he was certain it had long ago been given away to someone else who needed the cover. Lucid thought gave way to utter feeling. His body started to burn; his own anger buzzed in his ears. He saw through a crimson haze, he tasted his own blood, and still he knew he could not stop. As he gloried in the scrape of his knuckles and the adrenaline that kept him one step ahead, Daniel began to remember who he used to be.

Every brawl with a bully in Akiak, every fistfight with a drunk outside a bar, every window he'd smashed to get inside a locked door—it was as if Daniel had stepped completely outside his body and was watching the tornado that had taken up residence there instead. In the ferocity, he lost himself, which was what he'd hoped for all along.

By the time he was finished, Jason was shaking so hard that Daniel knew only his own hand at the boy's throat was keeping him upright. "If you ever . . . *ever* come near my daughter again," Daniel said, "I will kill you."

He stared at Jason, trying to commit to memory the way the boy looked when he knew he was defeated, because Daniel wanted to see it on his face again on the day they handed down a verdict in the courtroom. He drew back his arm, focusing his sights on the spot just under the boy's jaw—the spot where a good, strong blow would knock him unconscious—when suddenly the high beams of an oncoming car washed over him.

It was the opportunity Jason needed to throw Daniel off balance. He pushed away and took off at a dead run. Daniel blinked, his concentration shattered. Now that it was over, he could not stop his hands from trembling. He turned to the truck, where he'd told Trixie to wait, and he opened the door. "I'm sorry you had to see—" Daniel said, breaking off as he realized his daughter wasn't there.

"Trixie!" he yelled, searching the parking lot. "Trixie, where are you?"

It was too goddamned dark—Daniel couldn't see—so he started running up and down the aisles among the cars. Could Trixie have been so upset, watching him turn into an animal, that she'd been willing to jump from the frying pan into the fire, to get as far away from him as possible, even if that meant she'd have to run into town?

Daniel started sprinting down Main Street, calling for her. Frantic passed for festive in the dark. He pushed aside knots of carolers and divided families joined together at the hands. He barreled into a table with a sugar-on-snow display, kids rolling long strings of candied maple syrup around popsicle sticks. He climbed onto a sidewalk bench so that he could tower over the milling crowd and look around.

There were hundreds of people, and Trixie wasn't one of them.

He headed back to his car. It was possible that she had gone home, although it would take her a while to cover the four-mile distance on foot, in the snow. He could take his truck and start searching . . . but what if she *hadn't* left town? What if she came back looking for him, and he wasn't here?

Then again, what if she'd started home, and Jason found her first?

He reached into the glove compartment and fumbled for his cell phone. No one answered at the house. After a hesitation, he called Laura's office.

Last time he'd done this, she hadn't answered.

When she picked up on the first ring, Daniel's knees buckled with relief. "Trixie's missing."

*"What?"* He could hear the bright blue edge of panic in Laura's voice.

"We're in town . . . she was in the car waiting . . ." He was not making any sense, and he knew it.

"Where are you?"

"In the lot behind the grocery store."

"I'm on my way."

When the line went dead, Daniel slipped the phone into his coat pocket. Maybe Trixie would try to call him. He stood up and tried to replay the fight with Jason, but he could not dissect it: It could have been three minutes, it could have been thirty. Trixie might have run off at the first punch or after the last. He had been so single-minded about wanting to do harm that he'd lost sight of his daughter while she was still standing in front of him.

"Please," he whispered to a God he'd given up on years ago. "Please let her be all right."

Suddenly a movement in the distance caught his eye. He turned to see a shadow crossing behind the brush at the far end of the parking lot. Daniel stepped out of the circle of light thrown by the streetlamp and walked toward the spot where he'd seen the dark overlap itself. "Trixie," he called. "Is that you?"

Jason Underhill stood with his hands braced on the wooden railing of the trestle bridge, trying to see if the river had completely iced over yet. His face hurt like hell from where Trixie's father had beaten the crap out of him, his ribs throbbed, and he didn't have any idea how he was going to explain his battered face in the morning without revealing that he'd broken the conditions of his bail and interacted with not one but two members of the Stone family.

If they were going to try him as an adult, did that affect the rest? Once they found out that he'd approached Trixie, would he get sent to a real jail, instead of just some juvy facility?

Maybe it didn't matter, anyway. Bethel Academy didn't want him to play next year. His hopes to go professional one day were as good as dead. And why? Because he'd been considerate that night at Zephyr Santorelli-Weinstein's house and had gone back to make sure that Trixie was all right.

Three weeks ago, he had been the number one ranked high school hockey player in the state of Maine. He had a 3.7 grade point average and a penchant for hat tricks, and even kids who didn't know him pretended they did. He could have had his pick of high school girls and maybe even some from the local college, but he'd been stupid enough to fall for Trixie Stone: a human black hole who camouflaged herself as a girl with a heart so clear you might look at it and see yourself.

He was seventeen, and his life was as good as over.

Jason stared at the ice beneath the bridge. If his trial started before the spring came . . . if he *lost* . . . how long would it be before he saw the river running again?

He leaned down, his elbows on the wooden railing, and pretended that he could see it now.

Daniel was sitting underneath the streetlamp when Laura came running up to him. "Did she come back?"

"No," he said, getting slowly to his feet. "And she's not answering, if she's at the house."

"Okay," Laura said, pacing in a tight circle. "Okay."

"It's not okay. I got into a fight with Jason Underhill. He had his hands on her. And I . . . I . . . I snapped. I beat him up, Laura. Trixie saw every minute of it." Daniel took a deep breath. "Maybe we should call Bartholemew."

Laura shook her head. "If you call the police, you have to tell them you were fighting with Jason," she said flatly. "That's *assault*, Daniel. People get arrested for it."

Daniel fell silent, thinking of his previous encounter with Jason—the one in the woods, with a knife. As far as he knew, the boy hadn't said anything to anyone about it. But if it came out that Daniel had beaten him up, that other incident was bound to surface.

And it wasn't just assault—it qualified as kidnapping, too.

He turned to Laura. "So what do we do?"

She stepped closer, the light from the lamp falling over her shoulders like a cloak. "We find her ourselves," she said.

Laura ran into the house, calling for Trixie, but there was no answer. Shaking, she walked into the dark kitchen, still wearing her coat. She turned on the tap and splashed cold water on her face.

*This couldn't have happened.*

She and Daniel had plotted a strategy: He would search the streets for Trixie, while Laura went home in case she showed up. *You need to calm down*, she told herself. *This is all going to work out.*

When the phone rang, she grabbed it. *Trixie.* But in the moment it took for her to bring the receiver to her ear, she had another thought—what if it was the police?

Laura swallowed. "Hello?"

"Mrs. Stone . . . this is Zephyr. Is Trixie there? I've got to talk to her."

"Zephyr," she repeated. "No. Trixie's not— Have you seen her tonight?"

"Me? Um. No."

"Well." Laura closed her eyes. "I'll tell her you called," she said. She hung up the phone, sat down at the kitchen table, and steeled herself to wait for whatever came next.

Every summer, traveling fairs came through Maine. They arrived in caravans that popped open to reveal the baseball throw, the ringtoss, the balloon darts. A massive white truck unfolded, like a sleeping deer getting to its feet, to turn into the Tilt-A-Whirl; another transformed into the Indiana Jones Adventure House. There were kiddie rides—hot-air balloons that never left the ground, giant frogs with pink plaster tongues that chased flies in small circles, a carousel fit for a princess. But the ride Trixie looked forward to, year after year, was the Dragon Coaster.

The roller coaster had the enormous painted head of a Chinese New Year's dragon, five cars, and then an arched tail with gold curlicues painted on it. It mutated from one of those folding trucks: a tight loop of steel track that swung into a waystation. The carney who ran the coaster had a long, thin ponytail and so many tattoos on his arms that you had to get close to see they weren't just sleeves.

Trixie always tried to get the first car, the one that put you behind the dragon's mouth. For a kiddie ride, the roller coaster was surprisingly fast, and the front car was quicker than any other—you whipped harder around the corners. You lurched to a more jarring stop.

The summer Trixie was eleven, she climbed into the front car as usual and realized something was wrong. She couldn't pull the safety bar down over her knees. She had to turn sideways and jam herself along the side of the car. Trixie was convinced that this wasn't the same roller coaster—that they'd gotten an upgrade and skimped on the proportions—but the carney said nothing had changed.

He was lying. She knew this, because even as he said it, and pushed his ponytail out of the way, he was staring at the writing on her T-shirt: BETHEL FARM "A" SOFTBALL scrawled across her chest.

Until that moment, Trixie had been looking forward to going to middle school and the privileges that came with it. She'd held the word *adolescent* on her tongue, enjoying the way it fizzed like a bath bomb. Until then, she hadn't considered that there was a tradeoff, that she might not fit anymore in places where she'd been comfortable.

The next summer, when Trixie was twelve, she got dropped off at the fair with Zephyr. Instead of going on the rides, they bought an onion blossom and trolled through the crowd to find kids they knew.

Trixie was thinking about all this as she stood, shivering, in front of the Bank of Bethel. It was midnight, now, and the Winterfest was a memory. The police barriers blocking Main Street had been removed; the Christmas lights had been unplugged. The trash cans were stuffed with paper cups, plastic cider jugs, and broken candy canes.

The bank had a large mirrored window that had always fascinated Trixie. These days, when she passed by, she'd check herself out, or look to see if anyone else was doing the same. But as a kid, the mirror had taken her by surprise. For years she kept the secret from her parents that there was a girl in Bethel who looked exactly like her.

In the reflection, Trixie watched her father approach. She looked at him or, really, at the twin of him, standing beside the twin of her. The moment he touched her, it was as if a spell had broken. She could barely stand on her feet, she was that tired.

He caught her as she swayed. "Let's go home," he said, and he lifted her into his arms.

Trixie rested her head on his shoulder. She watched the stars shimmer and wink in patterns, an alphabet everyone else seemed to know but that she could not for the life of her read.

Laura's car was in the driveway when Daniel came back. That had been the plan: She'd drive back home and wait in the house, in case Trixie had made her way home. Daniel would walk the streets of Bethel, in case she hadn't. Trixie was sound asleep when he carried her out of the truck and brought her up to her bedroom. There, he unlaced her boots and unzipped her parka. He thought for a moment about helping her into pajamas but instead drew the covers up over Trixie, fully clothed.

When he stood up, Laura was standing in the doorway. Seeing Trixie, her eyes were wide, her face as white as chalk. "Oh, Daniel," she whispered, guessing the worst. "Something happened."

"Nothing happened," Daniel said softly, putting his arms around her.

Laura—who always seemed to know the right thing to do and the right thing to say—was at a complete loss. She wrapped her arms around Daniel's waist and burst into tears. He led her into the darkened hallway and closed Trixie's bedroom door so that she wouldn't be disturbed. "She's home," he said, forcing a smile, even though he could see the scrapes on his knuckles, could feel the bruises that bloomed beneath his skin. "That's all that counts."

The next morning, Daniel assessed the damage in the bathroom mirror. His lip was split; he had a shiner on his right temple; the knuckles of his right hand were swollen and raw. But that inventory didn't even begin to address the harm done to his relationship with his daughter. Because she'd fallen asleep, exhausted, Daniel still hadn't had the chance to explain what had happened to him last night, what beast he'd turned into.

He washed his face and toweled it dry. How did you go about explaining to your daughter—the victim of a *rape*, for God's sake—that violence in a man was like energy: transformed, but never destroyed? How did you tell a girl who was trying so hard to start fresh that you couldn't ever obliterate your past?

It was going to be one of those days when the temperature didn't climb above zero. He could tell, just by the bone-deep chill of the floorboards on his bare feet when he went downstairs and the way the icicles pointed like arrows from the outside overhang of the kitchen window. Trixie was standing at the refrigerator, wearing flannel pajama bottoms, a T-shirt that had gone missing from Daniel's own dresser, and a blue bathrobe that no longer fit. Her wrists and hands stuck out too far from the sleeves as she reached for the orange juice.

Laura glanced up from the table, where she was poring intently over the newspaper—looking, Daniel assumed, for a story about his brawl with Jason last night. "Morning," Daniel said hesitantly. Their eyes met, and they passed an entire conversation without speaking a word: *How is she? Did she say anything? Do I treat this as an ordinary day? Do I pretend last night never happened?*

Daniel cleared his throat. "Trixie . . . we have to talk."

Trixie didn't look at him. She unscrewed the Tropicana and began to pour some into a glass. "We're out of orange juice," she said.

The telephone rang. Laura stood up to answer it and carried the receiver into the living room that adjoined the kitchen.

Daniel sank down into the seat his wife had vacated and watched Trixie at the counter. He loved her, and in return she'd trusted him—and her reward was to see him turn into an animal before her eyes. It wasn't all that different, really, from what she must have experienced during the rape—and that alone was enough to make Daniel hate himself.

Laura came back into the room and hung up the phone. She moved stiffly, her features frozen.

"Who was it?" Daniel asked.

Laura shook her head, covered her hand with her mouth.

"Laura," he pressed.

"Jason Underhill committed suicide last night," she whispered.

Trixie shook the empty container. "We're out of orange juice," she repeated.

In the bathroom, Trixie ran the hot water for fifteen minutes before she stepped into the shower, letting the small space fill with enough steam that she wouldn't have to see her reflection in the mirror. The news had taken up residence in their house, and now, in the aftermath, nobody seemed to know what to do. Her mother had slipped out of the kitchen like a ghost. Her father sank down at the table with his head in his hands, his eyes squeezed shut. Distracted, he didn't notice when Trixie left. Neither parent was around to see her disappear into her bathroom or to ask her to leave the door wide open, as they had for the past week, so that they could check up on her.

What would be the point?

There would be no rape trial anymore. There was no need to make sure she didn't wind up in a mental hospital before she took the stand as a witness. She could go as crazy as she wanted to. She could secure herself a berth in a psych ward for the next thirty years, every minute of which she could spend thinking about what she'd done.

There was one Bic razor hidden away. It had fallen behind a crack in the sink cabinet and Trixie made sure to keep it there, in case of emergency. Now she fished for it and set it on the counter. She smacked it hard with a plastic bottle of bath gel, until the pink caddy cracked and the blade slipped out. She ran the tip of her finger over the edge, felt the skin peel back in an onion fold.

She thought about what it used to feel like when Jason kissed her, and she'd breathe in air that he'd breathed a moment before. She tried to imagine what it was like to not breathe anymore, ever. She thought of his head snapping back when her father hit him, of the last words he had said to her.

Trixie pulled off her pajamas and stepped into the shower. She crouched in the tub and let the water sluice over her. She cried great, damp, gray sobs that no one could hear over the roar of the plumbing, and she carved at her arm—not to kill herself, because she didn't deserve such an easy way out—just to release some of the pain before it exploded inside her. She cut three lines and a circle, inside the crook of her elbow:

*NO.*

Blood swirled pink between her feet. She looked down at her tattoo. Then she lifted the blade and slashed hatch marks through the letters, a grid of gashes, until not even Trixie could remember what she'd been trying to say.

# 5

When Jason Underhill's ghost showed up that night, Trixie was expecting him. He was transparent and white faced, with a gash in the back of his skull. She stared through him and pretended not to notice that he had materialized out of nowhere.

He was the first person Trixie knew who'd died. Technically, that wasn't quite accurate—her grandmother had died in Alaska when Trixie was four, but Trixie had never met her. She remembered her father sitting at the kitchen table with the telephone still in his hand even though the person on the other end had hung up, and silence landing on the house like a fat black crow.

Jason kept glancing at the ground, as if he needed to keep track of his footsteps. Trixie tried not to look at the bruises on his face or the blood on his collar. "I'm not scared of you," she said, although she was not telling the truth. "You can't do anything to me." She wondered if ghosts had the powers of superheroes, if they could see through linen and flannel to spot her legs shaking, if they could swallow her words and spit her lie back out like a bullet.

Jason leaned so close that his hand went right through Trixie. It felt like winter. He was able to draw her forward, as if he were magnetic and she had dissolved into a thousand metal filings. Pulling her upright in her bed, he kissed her full on the mouth. He tasted of dark soil and muddy currents. *I'm not through with you*, Jason vowed, and then he disappeared bit by bit, the pressure against her lips the last thing to go.

Afterward, Trixie lay in bed, shaking. She thought about the bitter cold that had taken up residence under her breastbone, like a second heart made of ice. She thought about what Jason had said and wondered why he'd had to die before he felt the same way she had felt about him all along.

Mike Bartholemew crouched in front of the boot prints that led up to the railing of the bridge from which Jason had jumped, a cryptic choreography of the boy's last steps. Placing a ruler next to the best boot print, he took a digital photo. Then he lifted an aerosol can and sprayed light layers of red wax over the area. The wax froze the snow, so that when he took the mixture of dental stone and water he'd prepared to make a cast, it wouldn't melt any of the ridge details.

While he waited for his cast to dry, he hiked down the slippery bank to the spot being combed by crime scene investigators. In his own tenure as a detective, he'd presided over two suicides in this very spot, one of the few in Bethel where you could actually fall far enough to do serious damage.

Jason Underhill had landed on his side. His head had cracked the ice on the river and was partially submerged. His hand was covered with dirt and matted leaves. The snow was still stained pink with blood that had pooled beneath his head.

For all intents and purposes, Jason had done the taxpayers a favor by saving them the cost of a trial and possible incarceration. Being tried as an adult for rape made the stakes higher—and more potentially devastating. Bartholemew had seen lesser motives that led folks to take their own lives.

He knelt beside Jerry, one of the forensic cops. "What have you got?"

"Maria DeSantos, only seventy degrees colder."

Maria DeSantos had been their last suicide plunger in this location, but she had been missing for three weeks in the heat of the summer before the stench of the decomposing body had attracted a kayaker on the river.

"Find anything?"

"A wallet and a cell phone. There could be more, but the snow's pretty deep." Jerry glanced up from his collection of blood on the body. "You see the kid play in the exhibition game last night in town?"

"I was on duty."

"I heard he was hammered . . . and that he was still a hell of a player." Jerry shook his head. "Damn shame, if you ask me."

"I didn't," Bartholemew said, and he stood up. He had already been to the Underhill house, to bring them the news of their son's death. Greta Underhill had opened the door, looked at his face, and burst into tears. Her husband had been only superficially composed. He thanked Bartholemew for bringing the information and said he'd like to see Jason now. Then he'd walked outside into the snow, without a coat, barefoot.

Bartholemew's own boss had brought him the news about Holly. He'd known that the worst had happened when he saw the chief of police standing on his porch in the middle of the night. He remembered demanding to be driven to the scene, where he stood at the guardrail her car had smashed through. He remembered, too, going to identify Holly's body in the hospital morgue. Bartholemew had pulled aside the sheet to see the tracks on her arms, the ones he'd been blind to as a parent. He'd put his hand over Holly's heart, just to make sure.

The Underhills wanted to see Jason; they'd be given that privilege before the autopsy began. In this sense, accidents, suicides, and murders were all the same—any death that occurred without someone there to witness it was automatically brought to the medical examiner for a determination of cause. It wasn't police procedure as much as human nature. We all want to know what went wrong, even when there isn't really an answer to that question.

● ● ●

The Monday after Jason Underhill's suicide, two psychologists were called to the high school to help students who needed to grieve. The hockey team took to wearing black armbands and won three straight, vowing to take the state title in homage to their fallen teammate. One entire page of the Portland paper's sports section was devoted to a memorial of Jason's athletic achievements.

That same day, Laura went out for groceries. She moved aimlessly through the store, picking up things like ugli fruit and bags of pitted prunes, slivered almonds, and balls of buffalo mozzarella. Somewhere in her purse she knew she had a list—ordinary items like bread and milk and dishwashing detergent—but there was a part of her that felt normal things didn't apply anymore and therefore there was no point in buying them. Eventually, she found herself in front of the freezer section, the door open and the cold spilling over the toes of her boots. There must have been a hundred different ice cream flavors. How could you pick, knowing that you'd have to go home and live with the choice you'd made?

She was reading the ingredients on a peach sorbet when she heard two women talking one aisle over, hidden by the freezers. "What a tragedy," one said. "That boy was going places."

"I heard that Greta Underhill can't get out of bed," the second woman added. "My pastor was told by her pastor that she might not even make it to the funeral."

A week ago, in spite of the rape accusations,

Jason had still been a hero to most of this town. But now death had swelled him to mythic proportions.

Laura curled her hands around the front bar of her grocery cart. She navigated around the corner, until she was face to face with the women who'd been talking. "Do you know who I am?" The ladies glanced at each other, shook their heads. "I'm the mother of the girl Jason Underhill raped."

She said it for the shock value. She said it on the off chance that these ladies might, out of sudden shame, apologize. But neither of them said a word.

Laura guided her shopping cart around the corner and toward an empty checkout line. The cashier had a skunk-streak of blue hair and a ring through her bottom lip. Laura reached into the basket and held up a box of plastic knives—when had she taken those off a shelf? "You know," she said to the cashier, "I actually don't need those."

"No biggie. We can reshelve them."

Six packets of powdered hollandaise sauce, suntan lotion, and wart remover medicine. "Actually," Laura said, "I'm going to pass on these, too."

She emptied the rest of her shopping cart: bacon bits and baby food and Thai coconut milk; a sippy cup and hair elastics and two pounds of green jalapeños; the peach sorbet. She stared at the items on the conveyor belt as if she were seeing them for the first time. "I don't want any of this," Laura said, surprised, as if it were anyone's fault but her own.

• • •

Dr. Anjali Mukherjee spent most of her time in the morgue, not just because she was the county medical examiner but also because when she ventured abovestairs at the hospital, she was continually mistaken for a med student or, worse, a candy striper. She was five feet tall, with the small, delicate features of a child, but Mike Bartholemew had seen her elbow-deep in a Y-shaped incision, determining the cause of death of the person who lay on her examination table.

"The subject had a blood alcohol level of point one two," Anjali said, as she rifled through a series of X-rays and headed toward the light box on the wall.

Legal intoxication was .10; that meant Jason Underhill was considerably trashed when he went over the railing of the bridge. *At least he wasn't driving*, Bartholemew thought. *At least he only killed himself.*

"There," the medical examiner said, pointing at an X-ray. "What do you see?"

"A foot?"

"That's why they pay you the big bucks. Come over here for a second." Anjali cleared off a lab table and patted it. "Climb up."

"I don't want—"

"Climb up, Bartholemew."

Grudgingly, he stood on top of the table. He glanced down at the top of Anjali's head. "And I'm doing this why?"

"Jump."

Bartholemew hopped a little.

"I meant jump *off.*"

He swung his arms, then went airborne, landing in a crouch. "Goddamn, I still can't fly."

"You landed on your feet," Anjali said. "Like most people who jump. When we see suicides like this, the X-rays show heel fractures and vertical compressions of the spine, which aren't present on this victim."

"Are you telling me he didn't fall?"

"No, he fell. There's contrecoup damage to the brain that suggests acceleration. When someone lands on the back of the skull, you'll see injury to the front of the brain, because it continues to fall after the skull stops and hits it hard."

"Maybe he jumped and landed on his head," Bartholemew suggested.

"Interestingly, I didn't see the types of fractures associated with that either. Let me show you what I did find, though." Anjali handed him two photographs, both of Jason Underhill's face. They were identical, except for the black eye and bruising along the temple and jaw of the second one.

"You been beating up the subjects, Angie?"

"That only works premortem," Anjali replied. "I took these ten hours apart. When you brought him in, he didn't have bruises . . . except for a subtle hemorrhage in the facial area that could have been caused by the fall. But he was lying on that side of his face when found, and the pooling of the blood might have obscured the contusions. When he was brought to the morgue and placed sunny-side up, the blood redistributed." She removed the

X-ray they'd been examining. "When I was doing an FP fellowship, we had a Jane Doe come in with no apparent external trauma, except for a slight hemorrhage in the strap muscles of the neck. By the time the autopsy was over, there were two obvious handprints on her throat."

"Couldn't he have banged himself up when he fell?"

"I thought you'd say that. Take a look at this." Anjali slid another X-ray onto the light box.

Bartholemew whistled softly. "That's his face, huh?"

"It was."

He pointed to a crack along the temple of the skull. "That looks like a fracture."

"That's where he landed," Anjali said. "But look closer."

Bartholemew squinted. On the cheekbone and the jaw were smaller, fainter fault lines.

"In the case of a blow and a subsequent fall, the fracture lines caused by the fall are blocked by those caused by the initial blow. An injury to the head caused by a fall is usually found around the level of the brim of a hat. However, a hard punch to the face usually hits below that."

The fracture at Underhill's temple radiated out toward the eye socket and the cheekbone but stopped abruptly at one of these hairline cracks.

"The subject also had extravasation of red blood cells on tissues around his jaw and ribs."

"Which means what?"

"It's a bruise that didn't get to happen. Meaning

there was trauma to that tissue, but before that blood could break down and go black and blue, the subject died."

"So maybe he was in a fight before he decided to jump," Bartholemew said, his mind running fast with possibilities.

"You might also be interested in this." Anjali passed him a microscopic slide with tiny filings on it. "We dug them out of the subject's fingertips."

"What are they?"

"Splinters consistent with the railing of the bridge. There were some wood slivers caught in the tails of his jacket, too." Anjali glanced at Bartholemew. "I don't think this kid killed himself by jumping off a bridge," she said. "I think he was pushed."

When Daniel heard sobbing, he immediately assumed it was Trixie. In the days since they'd heard the news about Jason, she would dissolve without any provocation—at the dinner table, while brushing her teeth, staring at a commercial on television. She was so firmly entrenched in memory that Daniel didn't know how to pry her loose and bring her back to the real world.

Sometimes he held her. Sometimes he just sat down next to her. He never tried to stop her tears; he didn't think he had that right. He just wanted her to know that he was there if she needed him.

This time, when the crying began, Daniel followed the sound upstairs. But instead of finding Trixie sobbing, he turned into his own bedroom to find his wife sitting on the floor, hugging a knot of clean laundry against her. "Laura?"

She turned at the sound of her name, wiping her cheeks. "I'm sorry . . . it's wrong, I know . . . but I keep thinking about him."

*Him.* Daniel's heart turned over. How long would it be until he could hear a sentence like that and not feel as if he'd been punched?

"It's just . . ." She wiped her eyes. "It's just that he was someone's child, too."

*Jason.* The immediate relief Daniel felt to know that Laura wasn't crying over the nameless man she'd slept with evaporated as he realized that she was crying, instead, for someone who didn't merit that kind of mercy.

"I've been so lucky, Daniel," Laura said. "What if Trixie had died last week? What if . . . what if you'd told me to move out?"

Daniel reached out to tuck Laura's hair behind her ear. Maybe you had to come close to losing something before you could remember its value. Maybe it would be like that for the two of them. "I would never have let you go."

Laura shuddered, as if his words had sent a shock through her. "Daniel, I—"

"You don't need to cry for us," he said, squeezing her shoulder, "because we're all going to be fine."

He felt Laura nod against him.

"And you don't have to cry for Jason," Daniel said. "Because Jason deserves to be dead."

He hadn't spoken the words aloud, the ones

he'd been thinking ever since Laura had taken that phone call days before. But this was exactly the sort of world he drew: one where actions had consequences, where revenge and retribution were the heartbeat of a story. Jason had hurt Trixie; therefore, Jason deserved to be punished.

Laura drew back and stared at him, wide-eyed.

"What?" Daniel said, defiant. "Are you shocked that I would think that?"

She was quiet for a moment. "No," Laura admitted. "Just that you said it out loud."

The minute Bartholemew entered the digital photo of the footprints on the bridge into his software program and compared it to an inking of Jason's boot, he got a match. However, there was another footprint with a tread on the sole that was different from Jason's, possibly from their suspect's shoe.

With a sigh, Bartholemew turned off his computer screen and took out the bag of evidence collected from the crime scene. He rummaged for the cell phone that Jerry had found near the victim. A Motorola, identical to the one Bartholemew carried—up here in Maine, you just didn't have all the cellular options available in a big city. Jason had probably bought it from the same store where he'd bought his. The same sales rep had probably programmed it for him.

Bartholemew started punching buttons. There were no messages, text or voice. But there was a memo.

He hit the shortcut button, *8, and suddenly the

sound of a fight filled the room. There were punches being landed, and grunts and moans. He heard Jason's voice, pleas that broke off at their edges. And another familiar voice: *If you ever, ever come near my daughter again, I will kill you.*

Bartholemew stood up, grabbed his coat, and headed out to find Daniel Stone.

"What do you think happens when you die?" Zephyr asked.

Trixie was lying on her stomach on her bed, flipping through the pages of *Allure* magazine and looking at purses and shoes that she would never be able to afford. She didn't *get* purses, anyway. She didn't want to ever be the kind of person who couldn't carry what she needed in her back pocket. "You decompose," Trixie said, and she turned to the next ad.

"That is so totally disgusting," Zephyr said. "I wonder how long it takes."

Trixie had wondered that too, but she wasn't going to admit it to Zephyr. Every night since his death, Jason had visited her in her bedroom in the darkest part of the night. Sometimes he just stared until she woke up; sometimes he talked to her. Finally he left by blasting through her middle.

She knew that he hadn't been buried yet, and maybe that was why he kept coming. Maybe once his body began to break down inside its coffin, he wouldn't show up at the foot of her bed.

Since Trixie had returned from the hospital, it had been like old times—Zephyr would come over after school and tell her everything she was missing: the catfight between two cheerleaders who liked the same guy, the substitute teacher in French who couldn't speak a single word of the language, the sophomore who got hospitalized for anorexia. Zephyr had also been her source of information about how Bethel High was processing Jason's death. The guidance counselors had led an assembly about teen depression; the principal had gotten on the PA during homeroom announcements to have a moment of memorial silence; Jason's locker had become a shrine, decorated with notes and stickers and Beanie Babies. It was, Trixie realized, as if Jason had grown larger than life after his death, as if it was going to be even harder now for her to avoid him.

Zephyr rolled over. "Do you think it hurts to die?"

*Not as much as it hurts to live*, Trixie thought.

"Do you think we go somewhere . . . after?" Zephyr asked.

Trixie closed her magazine. "I don't know."

"I wonder if it's like it is here. If there are popular dead people and geeky dead people. You know."

That sounded like high school, and the way Trixie figured it, that was more likely to be hell. "I guess it's different for different people," she said. "Like, if *you* died, there'd be an endless supply of Sephora makeup. For Jason, it's one big hockey rink."

"But do people ever cross over? Do the hockey players ever get to hang out with the people who eat only chocolate? Or the ones who play Nintendo twenty-four/seven?"

"Maybe there are dances or something," Trixie said. "Or a bulletin board, so you know what everyone else is up to, and you can join in if you want and blow it off if you don't."

"I bet when you eat chocolate in heaven it's no big deal," Zephyr said. "If you can have it whenever you want it, it probably doesn't taste as good." She shrugged. "I bet they all watch us down here, because they know we've got it better than them and we're too stupid to realize it." She glanced sideways at Trixie. "Guess what I heard."

"What?"

"His whole head was bashed in."

Trixie felt her stomach turn over. "That's just a rumor."

"It's totally not. Marcia Breen's brother's girlfriend is a nurse, and she saw Jason being brought into the hospital." She popped a bubble with her gum. "I hope that if he went to heaven, he got a big old bandage or plastic surgery or something."

"What makes you think he's going to heaven?" Trixie asked.

Zephyr froze. "I didn't mean . . . I just . . ." Her gaze slid toward Trixie. "Trix, are you truly glad he's dead?"

Trixie stared at her hands in her lap. For a moment, they looked like they belonged to someone else—still, pale, too heavy for the rest of her. She forced herself to open her magazine again, and she pretended she was engrossed in an ad about tampons so that she didn't have to give Zephyr a reply. Maybe after reading for a while, they would both forget what Zephyr had asked. Maybe after a while, Trixie wouldn't be afraid of her answer.

According to Dante, the deeper you got into hell, the colder it was. When Daniel imagined hell, he saw the vast white wasteland of the Yukon-Kuskokwim delta where he'd grown up. Standing on the frozen river, you might see smoke rising in the distance. A Yup'ik Eskimo would know it was open water, steaming where it hit the frigid air, but a trick of the light could make you believe otherwise. You might think you see the breath of the devil.

When Daniel drew the ninth circle of hell, it was a world of planes and angles, a synchronicity of white lines, a land made of ice. It was a place where the greater effort you made to escape, the more deeply entrenched you were.

Daniel had just put the finishing touches on the devil's face when he heard a car pull into the driveway. From the window of his office, he watched Detective Bartholemew get out of his Taurus. He had known it was coming to this, hadn't he? He had known it the minute he'd walked into that parking lot and found Jason Underhill with Trixie.

Daniel opened up the front door before the detective could knock. "Well," Bartholemew said. "That's what I call service."

Daniel tried to channel the easy repartee of social intercourse, but it was like he was fresh out of the village again, bombarded by sensations he didn't understand: colors and sights and speech he'd never seen or heard before. "What can I do for you?" he asked finally.

"I was wondering if we could talk for a minute," Bartholemew said.

*No*, Daniel thought. But he led the detective inside to the living room and offered him a seat.

"Where's the rest of the family?"

"Laura's teaching," Daniel said. "Trixie's upstairs with a friend."

"How'd she take the news about Jason Underhill?"

Was there a right answer to that question? Daniel found himself replaying possible responses in his head before he balanced them on his tongue. "She was pretty upset. I think she feels partially responsible."

"What about you, Mr. Stone?" the detective asked.

He thought about the conversation he'd had with Laura just that morning. "I wanted him to be punished for what he did," Daniel said. "But I never wished him dead."

The detective stared at him for a long minute. "Is that so?"

There was a thump overhead; Daniel glanced up. Trixie and Zephyr had been upstairs for about an hour. When Daniel had last checked on them, they were reading magazines and eating Goldfish crackers.

"Did you see Jason Friday night?" Detective Bartholemew asked.

"Why?"

"We're just trying to piece together the approximate time of the suicide."

Daniel's mind spiraled backward. Had Jason said something to the cops about the incident in the woods? Had the guy who'd driven by the parking lot during their fistfight gotten a good look at Daniel? Had there been other witnesses?

"No, I didn't see Jason," Daniel lied.

"Huh. I could have sworn I saw you in town."

"Maybe you did. I took Trixie to the minimart to get some cheese. We were making a pizza for dinner."

"About when was that?"

The detective pulled a pad and pencil out of his pocket; it momentarily stopped Daniel cold. "Seven," he said. "Maybe seven-thirty. We just drove to the store and then we left."

"What about your wife?"

"Laura? She was working at the college, and then she came home."

Bartholemew made a note on his pad. "So none of you ran into Jason?"

Daniel shook his head.

Bartholemew put his pad back into his breast pocket. "Well," he said, "then that's that."

"Sorry I couldn't help you," Daniel answered, standing up.

The detective stood too. "You must be relieved.

Obviously your daughter won't have to testify as a witness now."

Daniel didn't know how to respond. Just because the rape case wouldn't proceed didn't mean that Trixie's slate would be wiped clean as well. Maybe she wouldn't testify, but she wouldn't get back to who she used to be, either.

Bartholemew headed toward the front door. "It was pretty crazy in town Friday night, with the Winterfest and all," he said. "Did you get what you wanted?"

Daniel went still. "I beg your pardon?"

"The cheese. For your pizza."

He forced a smile. "It turned out perfect," Daniel said.

When Zephyr left a little while later, Trixie offered to walk her out. She stood on the driveway, shivering, not having bothered with a coat. The sound of Zephyr's heels faded, and then Trixie couldn't even see her anymore. She was about to head back inside when a voice spoke from behind. "It's good to have someone watching over you, isn't it?"

Trixie whirled around to find Detective Bartholemew standing in the front yard. He looked like he was freezing, like he'd been waiting for a while. "You scared me," she said.

The detective nodded down the block. "I see you and your friend are on speaking terms again."

"Yeah. It's nice." She wrapped her arms around herself. "Did you, um, come to talk to my dad?"

"I already did that. I was sort of hoping to talk to you."

Trixie glanced at the window upstairs, glowing yellow, where she knew her father was still working. She wished he was here with her right now. He'd know what to say. And what not to.

You had to talk to a policeman if he wanted to talk to you, didn't you? If you said no, he'd immediately know there was something wrong.

"Okay," Trixie said, "but could we go inside?"

It was weird, leading the detective into their mudroom. She felt like he was boring holes in the back of her shirt with his eyes, like he knew something about Trixie she didn't know about herself yet.

"How are you feeling?" Detective Bartholemew asked.

Trixie instinctively pulled her sleeves lower, concealing the fresh cuts she'd made in the shower. "I'm okay."

Detective Bartholemew sat down on a teak bench. "What happened to Jason . . . don't blame yourself."

Tears sprang into her throat, dark and bitter.

"You know, you remind me a little of my daughter," the detective said. He smiled at Trixie, then shook his head. "Being here . . . it didn't come easy to her, either."

Trixie ducked her head. "Can I ask you something?"

"Sure."

She pictured Jason's ghost: blued by the moon, bloody and distant. "Did it hurt? How he died?"

"No. It was fast."

He was lying—Trixie knew it. She hadn't realized that a policeman might lie. He didn't say anything else for such a long time that Trixie looked up at him, and that's when she realized he was waiting for her to do just that. "Is there something you want to tell me, Trixie? About Friday night?"

Once, Trixie had been in the car when her father ran over a squirrel. It came out of nowhere, and the instant before impact Trixie had seen the animal look at them with the understanding that there was nowhere left to go. "What about Friday night?"

"Something happened between your father and Jason, didn't it."

"No."

The detective sighed. "Trixie, we already know about the fight."

Had her father told him? Trixie glanced up at the ceiling, wishing she were Superman, with X-ray vision, or able to communicate telepathically like Professor Xavier from the X-Men. She wanted to know what her father had said; she wanted to know what *she* should say. "Jason started it," she explained, and once she began, the words tumbled out of her. "He grabbed me. My father pulled him away. They fought with each other."

"What happened after that?"

"Jason ran away . . . and we went home." She hesitated. "Were we the last people to see him . . . you know . . . *alive*?"

"That's what I'm trying to figure out."

It was possible that this was why Jason kept coming back to her now. Because if Trixie could still see him, then maybe he wouldn't be gone. She looked up at Bartholemew. "My father was just protecting me. You know that, right?"

"Yeah," the detective said. "Yeah, I do."

Trixie waited for him to say something else, but Bartholemew seemed to be in a different place, staring at the bricks on the floor of the mudroom. "Are we . . . done?"

Detective Bartholemew nodded. "Yes. Thanks, Trixie. I'll let myself out."

Trixie didn't know what else there was to say, so she opened the door that led into the house and closed it behind her, leaving the detective alone in the mudroom. She was halfway upstairs when Bartholemew reached for her father's boot, stamped the sole on an ink pad he'd taken from his pocket, and pressed it firmly onto a piece of blank white paper.

The medical examiner called while Bartholemew was waiting for his order at the drive-through window of a Burger King. "Merry Christmas," Anjali said when he answered his cell phone.

"You're about a week early," Bartholemew said.

The girl in the window blinked at him. "Ketchup-mustardsaltorpepper?"

"No, thanks."

"I haven't even told you what I've got yet," Anjali said.

"I hope it's a big fat evidentiary link to murder."

In the window of the drive-through, the girl adjusted her paper hat. "That's five thirty-three."

"Where are you?" Anjali said.

Bartholemew opened his wallet and took out a twenty. "Clogging my arteries."

"We started to clean off the body," the medical examiner explained. "The dirt on the victim's hand? Turns out it's not dirt after all. It's blood."

"So he scraped his hand, trying to hold on?"

The girl at the counter leaned closer and snapped the bill out of his fingers.

"I can ABO type a dried stain at the lab, and this was O positive. Jason was B positive." She let that sink in. "It was blood, Mike, but not Jason Underhill's."

Bartholemew's mind started to race: If they had the murderer's blood, they could link a suspect to the crime. It would be easy enough to get a DNA sample from Daniel Stone when he was least expecting it—saliva taken from an envelope he'd sealed or from the rim of a soda can tossed into the trash.

Stone's boot print hadn't been a match, but Bartholemew didn't see that as any particular deterrent to an arrest. There had been hundreds of folks in town Friday night; the question wasn't who had walked across the bridge, but who *hadn't*. Blood evidence, on the other hand, could be damning. Bartholemew pictured Daniel Stone on the icy bridge, going after Jason Underhill. He imagined Jason trying to hold him off. He thought back to his conversation with Daniel, the Band-Aid covering the knuckles of his right hand.

"I'm on my way," Bartholemew told Anjali.

"Hey," the Burger King girl said. "What about your food?"

"I'm not hungry," he said, pulling out of the pickup line.

"Don't you want change?" the girl called.

*All the time*, Mike thought, but he didn't answer.

"Daddy," Trixie asked, as she was elbow-deep in the sink washing dishes, "what were you like as a kid?"

Her father did not glance up from the kitchen table he was wiping with a sponge. "Nothing like you are," he said. "Thank God."

Trixie knew her father didn't like to talk about growing up in Alaska, but she was starting to think that she needed to hear about it. She had been under the impression that her dad was of the typical suburban genus and species: the kind of guy who mowed his lawn every Saturday and read the sports section before the others, the type of father who was gentle enough to hold a monarch butterfly between his cupped palms so that Trixie could count the black spots on its wings. But that easygoing man would never have been capable of punching Jason repeatedly, even as Jason was bleeding and begging him to stop. That man had never been so consumed by fury that it twisted his features, made him unfamiliar.

Trixie decided the answer must be in the part of

her father's life that he never wanted to share. Maybe Daniel Stone had been a whole different person, one who vanished just as Trixie arrived. She wondered if this was true of every parent: if, prior to having children, they all used to be someone else.

"What do you mean?" she asked. "Why am I so different from you?"

"It was a compliment. I was a pain in the ass at your age."

"How?" Trixie asked.

She could see him weighing his words for an example he was willing to offer out loud. "Well, for one thing, I ran away a lot."

Trixie had run away once, when she was little. She'd walked around the block twice and finally settled in the cool blue shadow beneath a hedgerow in her own backyard. Her father found her there less than an hour later. She expected him to get angry, but instead, he'd crawled underneath the bushes and sat beside her. He plucked a dozen of the red berries he was always telling her never to eat and mashed them in the palm of his hand. Then he'd painted a rose on her cheek and let her draw stripes across his own. He'd stayed there with her until the sun started to go down and then told her if she was still planning on running away, she might want to get a move on—even though they both knew that by that point, Trixie wasn't going anywhere.

"When I was twelve," her father said, "I stole a boat and decided to head down to Quinhagak.

There aren't any roads leading to the tundra—you come and go by plane or boat. It was October, getting really cold, the end of fishing season. The boat motor quit working, and I started drifting into the Bering Sea. I had no food, only a few matches, and a little bit of gas—when all of a sudden I saw land. It was Nunivak Island, and if I missed it, the next stop was Russia."

Trixie raised a brow. "You are totally making this up."

"Swear to God. I paddled like crazy. And just when I realized I had a shot at reaching shore, I saw the breakers. If I made it to the island, the boat was going to get smashed. I duct-taped the gas tank to myself, so that when the boat busted up, I'd float."

This sounded like some extravagant survival flashback Trixie's father would write for one of his comic book characters—she'd read dozens. All this time, she had assumed they were the products of his imagination. After all, those daring deeds hardly matched the father she'd grown up with. But what if he *was* the superhero? What if the world her father created daily—full of unbelievable feats and derring-do and harsh survival—wasn't something he'd dreamed up but someplace he'd actually lived?

She tried to imagine her father bobbing in the world's roughest, coldest sea, struggling to make it to shore. She tried to picture that boy and then imagine him fully grown, a few nights ago, pummeling Jason. "What happened?" Trixie asked.

"A Fish and Game guy who was taking one last look for the year spotted the fire I made after I washed up on the island and rescued me," her father said. "I ran away one or two times each year after that, but I never managed to get very far. It's like a black hole: People who go to the Alaskan bush disappear from the face of the earth."

"Why did you want to leave so badly?"

Her father came up to the sink and wrung out the sponge. "There was nothing there for me."

"Then you weren't really running away," Trixie said. "You were running *toward.*"

Her father, though, had stopped listening. He reached over to turn off the water in the sink and grasped her elbows, turning the insides of her arms up to the light.

She'd forgotten about the Band-Aids, which had peeled off in the soapy water. She'd forgotten to not hike up her sleeves. In addition to the gash at her wrist, which had webbed itself with healing skin, her father could see the new cuts she'd made in the shower, the ones that climbed her forearm like a ladder.

"Baby," her father whispered, "what did you do?"

Trixie's cheeks burned. The only person who knew about her cutting was Janice the rape counselor, who'd been ordered out of the house by Trixie's father a week ago. Trixie had been grateful for that one small cosmic favor: With Janice out of the picture, her secret could stay one. "It's not what you think. I wasn't trying to kill myself again.

It just . . . it's just . . ." She glanced down at the floor. "It's how *I* run away."

When she finally gathered the courage to look up again, the expression on her father's face nearly broke her. The monster she'd seen in the parking lot the other night was gone, replaced by the parent she'd trusted her whole life. Ashamed, she tried to pull away from his hold, but he wouldn't let her. He waited until she tired herself out with her thrashing, the way he used to when she was a toddler. Then he wrapped his arms so tight around Trixie she could barely breathe. That was all it took: She began to cry like she had that morning in the shower, when she had heard about Jason.

"I'm sorry," Trixie sobbed into her father's shirt. "I'm really sorry."

They stood together in the kitchen for what felt like hours, with soap bubbles rising around them and dishes as white as bones drying on the wire rack. It was possible, Trixie supposed, that everyone had two faces: Some of us just did a better job of hiding it than others.

Trixie imagined her father jumping into water so cold it stole his breath. She pictured him watching his boat break to pieces around him. She bet that if he'd been asked—even when he was sitting on that island, soaking wet and freezing—he'd tell you he would have done it all over again.

Maybe she was more like her father than he thought.

● ● ●

The secret recipe for Sorrow Pie had been passed down from Laura's great-grandmother to her grandmother to her mother, and although she had no actual recollection of the transfer of information to herself, by the time she was eleven she knew the ingredients by heart, knew the careful procedure to make sure the crust didn't burn and the carrots didn't dissolve in the broth, and knew exactly how many bites it would take before the heaviness weighing on the diner's heart disappeared. Laura knew that the shopping list in and of itself was nothing extraordinary: a chicken, four potatoes, leeks more white than green, pearl onions and whipping cream, bay leaves and basil. What made Sorrow Pie a force to be reckoned with was the way you might find the unlikely in any spoonful—a burst of cinnamon mixed with common pepper, lemon peel and vinegar sobering the crust—not to mention the ritual of preparation, which required the cook to back into the cupboard for her ingredients, to cut shortening only with the left hand, and, of course, to season the mixture with a tear of her own.

Daniel was the one who usually cooked, but when desperate measures were called for, Laura would put on an apron and pull out her great-grandmother's stoneware pie plate, the one that turned a different color each time it came out of an oven. She had baked Sorrow Pie for dinner the night Daniel got word of his mother's death—a funeral he would not attend and a woman he had, to Laura's knowledge, never cried for. She made Sorrow Pie the afternoon Trixie's parakeet flew into a bathroom mirror and drowned in the toilet. She made it the morning after she'd first slept with Seth.

Today, when she had gone to the grocery store to gather the ingredients, she found herself standing in the middle of the baking goods aisle with her mind blank. The recipe, which had always been as familiar to her as her own name, had been wiped out of her memory. She could not have said whether cardamom was part of the spice regimen, or if it was coriander. She completely forgot to buy eggs.

It was no easier when Laura came home and took out a stew pot, only to find herself wondering what on earth she was supposed to put inside it. Frustrated, she made herself sit down at the kitchen table and write what she remembered of the recipe, aware that there were huge gaps and missing ingredients. Her mother, who'd died when Laura was twenty-two, had told her that writing the recipe down was a good way to have it stolen; Laura hated to think that this magic would end with her own carelessness.

It was while she was staring at the blanks on the page that Trixie came downstairs. "What are you making?" she asked, surveying the hodgepodge of ingredients on the kitchen counter.

"Sorrow Pie," Laura answered.

Trixie frowned. "You're missing the vinegar. And the carrots. And half the spices." She backed into the pantry and began to pull jars. "Not to mention the *chicken*."

The chicken. How had Laura forgotten *that*?

Trixie took a mixing bowl out and began to measure the flour and baking powder for the crust. "You don't have Alzheimer's, do you?"

Laura couldn't remember ever teaching her daughter the way to make Sorrow Pie, yet here Trixie was passing the whisk to her left hand and closing her eyes as she poured the milk. Laura got up from the kitchen table and started peeling the pearl onions she'd bought, only to forget why she'd begun when she was halfway through.

She was too busy recalling the look on Daniel's face when he'd finished his first serving, after hearing of his mother's death. How the deep vertical lines between his eyes smoothed clear, how his hands stopped shaking. She was thinking of how many helpings this family would need to come close to approximating normal. She was wondering how her mother never thought it important enough to tell her that missing a step might have grave consequences, not only for the person dining but also for the chef.

The phone rang when they had just finished putting the top crust on the pie and painting their initials across it in vanilla. "It's Zeph," Trixie told Laura. "Can you hang up while I go upstairs?"

She handed Laura the phone, and moments later, Laura heard her pick up an extension. As tempted as Laura was to listen, she hung up.

When she turned around, she noticed the pie, ready and waiting to be baked.

It was as if it had been dropped down onto the counter from above. "Well," she said out loud, and she shrugged. She lifted it up to slide it into the oven.

An hour later, when the pie was cooling, Laura hovered in front of it. She had intended this to be supper but found herself digging for a fork. What was just a taste became a bite; what started as a bite turned into a mouthful. She stuffed her cheeks; she burned her tongue. She ate until there were no crumbs left in the baking dish, until every last carrot and clove and butter bean had disappeared. And still she was hungry.

Until that moment, she'd forgotten this about Sorrow Pie, too: No matter how much you consumed, you would not have your fill.

When Venice Prudhomme saw Bartholemew walking into her lab, she told him no before he'd even asked his question. Whatever he wanted, she couldn't do it. She'd rushed the date rape drug test for him, and that was difficult enough, but the lab was in transition, moving from an eight-locus DNA system to a sixteen-locus system, and their usual backlog had grown to enormous proportions.

*Just hear me out,* he'd said, and he started begging.

Venice had listened, arms crossed. *I thought this was a rape case.*

*It was. Until the rapist died, and suicide didn't check out.*

*What makes you think you've got the right perp?*

*It's the rape victim's father,* Bartholemew had said. *If your kid was raped, what would you want to do to the guy who did it?*

In the end, Venice still said no. It would take a while for her to do a full DNA test, even one that she put at the top of the pile. But something in his desperation must have struck her, because she told him that she could at least give him a head start. She'd been part of the validation team for a portion of the sixteen-locus system and still had some leftovers from her kit. The DNA extraction process was the same; she'd be able to use that sample to run the other loci once the lab came up for some air.

Bartholemew fell asleep waiting for her to complete the test. At four in the morning, Venice knelt beside him and shook him awake. "You want the good news or the bad news?"

He sighed. "Good."

"I got your results."

That was *excellent* news. The medical examiner had already told Bartholemew that the dirt and river silt on the victim's hand might have contaminated the blood to the point where DNA testing was impossible due to dropout. "What's the bad news?"

"You've got the wrong suspect."

Mike stared at her. "How can you tell? I haven't

even given you a control sample from Daniel Stone yet."

"Maybe the kid who got raped wanted revenge even more than her dad did." Venice pushed the results toward him. "I did an amelogenin test—it's the one we run on nuclear DNA to determine gender. And the guy who left your drop of blood behind?" Venice glanced up. "He's a *girl.*"

Zephyr gave Trixie the details. The service was at two o'clock at the Bethel Methodist Church, followed by an interment ceremony at the Westwind Cemetery. She said that school was closing early, that's how many people were planning on attending. The six juniors on the hockey team had been asked to serve as pallbearers. In memoriam, three senior girls had dyed their hair black.

Trixie's plan was simple: She was going to sleep through Jason's funeral, even if she had to swallow a whole bottle of NyQuil to do it. She pulled the shades in her room, creating an artificial night, and crawled under her covers—only to have them yanked down a moment later.

*You don't think I'm going to let you off the hook, do you?*

She knew he was standing there before she even opened her eyes. Jason leaned against her dresser, one elbow already morphing through the wood. His eyes had faded almost entirely; all Trixie could see were holes as deep as the sky.

"The whole town's going," Trixie whispered. "You won't notice if I'm not there."

Jason sat down on top of the covers. *What about you, Trix? Will you notice when I'm not here?*

She turned onto her side, willing him to go away. But instead she felt him curl up behind her, spooning, his words falling over her ear like frost. *If you don't come*, he whispered, *how will you know I'm really gone?*

She felt him disappear a little while after that, taking all the extra air in the room. Finally, gasping, Trixie got out of bed and threw open the three windows in her bedroom. It was twenty degrees outside, and the wind whipped at the curtains. She stood in front of one window and watched people in dark suits and black dresses exit their houses, their cars being drawn like magnets past Trixie's house.

Trixie peeled off her clothes and stood shivering in her closet. What was the right outfit to wear to the funeral of the only boy you'd ever loved? Sackcloth and ashes, a ring of thorns, regret? What she needed was an invisibility cloak, like the kind her father sometimes drew for his comic book heroes, something sheer that would keep everyone from pointing fingers and whispering that this was all her fault.

The only dress Trixie owned in a dark color had short sleeves, so she picked out a pair of black pants and paired it with a navy cardigan. She'd have to wear boots anyway, because of all the snow, and they'd look stupid with a skirt. She didn't know if she could do this—stand at Jason's grave while people passed his name around like a box of sweets—but she did know that if she stayed in her room during this funeral, as she'd planned to, it would all come back to haunt her.

She glanced around her room again, checking the top of the dresser and under the bed and in her desk drawers for something she knew was missing, but in the end, she had to leave without her courage or risk being late.

During her studies of rebellion, Trixie had learned which floorboards in the hallway screamed like traitors and which ones would keep a secret. The trickiest one was right in front of her father's office door—she sometimes wondered if he'd had the builder do that on purpose, thinking ahead. To get past him without making any noise, Trixie had to edge along the inside wall of the house, then slide in a diagonal and hope she didn't crash into the banister. From there, it was just a matter of avoiding the third and seventh stairs, and she was home free. She could take the bus that stopped three blocks away from her house, ride it downtown, and then walk to the church.

Her father's office door was closed. Trixie took a deep breath, crept, slid, and hopped her way silently down the stairs. The floor of the mudroom looked like the scene of a dismemberment: a mess of scattered boots and discarded jackets and tossed gloves. Trixie pulled what she needed from the pile, wrapped a scarf around the lower half of her face, and gingerly opened the door.

Her father was sitting in his truck with the motor running, as if he'd been waiting for her all along. As soon as he saw her exiting the house, he unrolled the power window. "Hop in."

Trixie approached the truck and peered inside. "Where are you going?"

Her father reached over and opened the door for her. "Same place you are." As he twisted in his seat to back out of the driveway, Trixie could see the collared shirt and tie he was wearing under his winter jacket.

They drove in silence for two blocks. Then, finally, she asked, "How come you want to go?"

"I don't."

Trixie watched the swirling snow run away from their tires to settle in the safe center of the divided highway. Dots between painted dashes, they spelled out in Morse code the unspoken rest of her father's sentence: *But you do.*

Laura sat in the student center, wishing she was even an eighth as smart as the advice ladies who wrote "Annie's Mailbox." They knew all the answers, it seemed, without even trying.

In the days after Jason's death, she'd become addicted to the column, craving it as much as her morning cup of coffee. *My daughter-in-law started her marriage as a size four, and now she's plus plus plus. She's a wonderful person, but her health is a concern for me. I've given her books and exercise videos, but none of it helps. What can I do? — Skinny in Savannah*

*My 14-year-old son has started replacing his boxer shorts with silky thong underwear he found in a catalog. Is this a style that hasn't hit my hometown yet, or should I be worried about cross-dressing? —Nervous in Nevada*

*On her deathbed, my great-aunt just confided a secret to me—that my mother was born as the result of an extramarital affair. Do I tell my mother I know the truth? —Confused in California*

Laura's obsession grew in part from the fact that she was not the only one walking around with questions. Some of the letters were frivolous, some cut through her heart. All of them hinted at a universal truth: At any crossroads in life, half of us are destined to take a wrong turn.

She opened the newspaper to the right page, skimming past the Marmaduke cartoon and the crossword puzzle to find the advice column, and nearly spilled her cup of coffee. *I've been having an affair. It's over, and I'm sorry it ever happened. I want to tell my husband so that I can start fresh. Should I? —Repentant in Rochester*

Laura had to remind herself to breathe.

*We can't say this enough,* the advice columnists answered. *What people don't know can't hurt them. You've already done your spouse a great disservice. Do you really think it's fair to cause him pain, just so you can clear your conscience? Be a big girl,* they wrote. *Actions have consequences.*

Her heart was pounding so hard she looked up, certain that everyone in the room would be staring.

She had been careful not to ask herself the question she should have: If Trixie hadn't gotten raped, if Daniel hadn't called her office the night

she'd been breaking off her affair with Seth—
would she ever have confessed? Would she have
kept it to herself, a stone in her soul, a cancer
clouding her memory?

*What people don't know can't hurt them.*

The problem with coming clean was that you
thought you were clearing the slate, starting over,
but it never quite worked that way. You didn't erase
what you'd done. As Laura knew now, the stain
would still be there, every time he looked at you,
before he remembered to hide the disappointment
in his eyes.

Laura thought of what she had not told Daniel,
the things he had not told her. The best decisions
in a marriage were based not on honesty but on
the number of casualties that the truth might
cause, versus the number saved by ignorance.

With great care, she folded the edge of the
newspaper and ripped it gently along the crease.
She did this until the advice column had been entirely cut out. Then she folded the article and
slipped it under the strap of her bra. The ink
smudged on Laura's fingers, the way it sometimes
did when she read the paper. She imagined a tattoo that might go through flesh and bone and
blood to reach her heart—a warning, a reminder
not to make the same mistake.

"Ready?" Daniel asked.

Trixie had been sitting in the truck for five minutes, watching townspeople crowd into the tiny
Methodist church. The principal had gone in, as

well as the town manager and the selectmen. Two local television stations were broadcasting from the steps of the church, with anchors Daniel recognized from the evening news. "Yes," Trixie said, but she made no move to get out of the truck.

Daniel pulled the keys out of the ignition and got out of the truck. He walked around to the passenger door and opened it, unbuckling Trixie's seat belt just like he used to when she was a baby. He held her hand as she stepped out, into the shock of the cold.

They took three steps. "Daddy," she said, stopping, "what if I can't do this?"

Her hesitation made him want to carry her back to the truck, hide her so securely that no one would ever hurt her again. But—as he'd learned the hard way—that wasn't possible.

He slid an arm around her waist. "Then I'll do it for you," he said, and he guided her up the steps of the church, past the shocked wide eyes of the television cameras, through an obstacle course of hissed whispers, to the place where she needed to be.

For a single moment, the focus of everyone in the church swung from the boy in the lily-draped coffin to the girl walking through the double doors. Outside, left alone, Mike Bartholemew emerged from behind a potbellied oak and crouched beside the trail of boot prints that Daniel and Trixie Stone had left in the snow. He lay a ruler down beside the best print of the smaller track and took a camera from his pocket for a few snapshots. Then he sprayed the print with aerosol wax and let the red skin dry on the snow before he spread dental stone to make a cast.

By the time the mourners adjourned to their cars to caravan to the cemetery for the interment service, Bartholemew was headed back to the police department, hoping to match Trixie Stone's boot to the mystery print left in the snow on the bridge where Jason Underhill had died.

"Blessed are those who mourn," said the minister, "for they will be comforted."

Trixie pressed herself more firmly against the back wall of the church. From here, she was completely blocked by the rest of the people who'd come for Jason's memorial service. She didn't have to stare at the gleaming coffin. She didn't have to see Mrs. Underhill, slumped against her husband.

"Friends, we gather here to comfort and support each other in this time of loss . . . but most of all we come here to remember and celebrate the mortal life of Jason Adam Underhill and his blessed future at the side of our Lord Jesus Christ."

The minister's words were punctuated by the tight coughs of men who'd promised themselves they wouldn't cry and the quick-silver hiccups of the women who'd known better than to make a promise they couldn't keep.

"Jason was one of those golden boys that the sun seemed to follow. Today, we remember him for the way he could make us laugh with a joke and the devotion he applied to everything he did. We remember him as a loving son and grandson, a caring cousin, a steadfast friend. We remember him as a gifted athlete and a diligent student. But most of all we remember him because Jason, in the short time we had with him, managed to touch each and every one of us."

The first time Jason touched Trixie, they were in his car, and he was illegally teaching her how to drive. *You have to let up on the clutch* while *you shift*, he explained, as she'd jerked the little Toyota around an empty parking lot. *Maybe I should just wait until I'm sixteen,* Trixie had said when she'd stalled for the bazillionth time. Jason had laced his fingers between hers on the stick shift, guiding her through the motions, until all she could think about was the temperature of his hand heating hers. Then Jason had grinned at her. *Why wait?*

The minister's voice grew like a vine. "In Lamentations 3, we hear these words: My soul is bereft of peace; I have forgotten what happiness is; so I say, 'Gone is my glory, and all that I had hoped for from the Lord.' We, whom Jason left behind, must wonder if these were the thoughts that weighed heavy on his heart, that led him to believe there was no other way out."

Trixie closed her eyes. She had lost her virginity in a field of lupine behind the ice rink, where the Zamboni shavings were dumped, an artificial winter smack in the middle of the September flowers. Jason had borrowed the key from the rinkmaster and taken her skating after the rink was closed for the day. He'd laced up her skates and told her to close her eyes. Then he'd reached for her hands, skating backward so fast she felt like she was falling to earth. *We're writing in cursive*, he told her as he pulled in a straight line. *Can you read it?* Then he looped the breadth of the rink, skated a circle, a right angle, a tinier loop, finishing with a curl. *I LOVE O?* Trixie had recited, and Jason had laughed. *Close enough,* he'd said. Later, in that field, with the pile of snow hiding them from sight, Jason had again been moving at lightning speed, and Trixie could not quite keep up. When he pushed inside her, she turned her head to watch the lupine tremble on their shivering stems, so that he wouldn't realize he'd hurt her.

"In the past few days, you who are Jason's family and friends have been struggling with the questions that surround his death. You are feeling a fraction of the pain, maybe, that Jason felt in those last, dark hours. You might be reliving the last time you spoke to him. You might be wondering, Is there anything I should have said or done that I didn't? That might have made a difference?"

Trixie suddenly saw Jason holding her down on Zephyr's white living room carpet. If she'd been brave enough to peek that night, would she have seen the bruises blooming on his jaw, the smile rotting off his face?

"Into your hands, O Savior, we commend your servant Jason Underhill. We pray for you to recognize this child of yours . . ."

His breath fell onto her lips, but he tasted of worms. His fingers bit so hard into her wrists that she looked down and saw only his bones, as the flesh peeled away from him.

"Receive him into your never-ending mercy. Grant him everlasting peace, and eternal life in your light."

Trixie tried to swim back to the minister's words. She craved light, too, but all she could see were the black and blue stripes of the nights when Jason came to haunt her. Or maybe she was seeing the nights when she had gone to him willingly. It was all mixed up now. She couldn't separate the real Jason from the ghost; she couldn't untangle what she'd wanted from what she didn't.

Maybe it had *always* been like that.

The scream started so deep inside of her that she thought it was just a resonance, like a tuning fork that could not stop trembling. Trixie didn't realize that the sound spilled through her seams, overflowing, bearing Jason's coffin like a tide and sweeping it off its stanchions. She didn't know that she'd fallen to her knees, and that every single eye in the congregation was on her, as it had been before the service began. And she didn't trust herself to believe that the savior the minister had been summoning had reached through the very roof of the church and carried her outside where she could breathe again—not until she found the courage to open her eyes and found herself safe and away, cradled in her father's arms.

• • •

Trixie's boot prints matched. Unfortunately, they were Sorels, which accounted for a large portion of all winter footwear sold in the state of Maine. They had no telltale crack of the sole, or a tack stuck into the rubber, to prove without any considerable doubt that it was Trixie's particular boot that had been on that bridge the night Jason Underhill had died, as opposed to anyone else who wore a size seven and happened to favor the same footwear.

As a rape victim, she had the motive to be a suspect. But a boot print alone—one that hundreds of townspeople shared—wouldn't be enough probable cause to convince a judge to swear out a warrant for Trixie's arrest.

"Ernie, get out of there," Bartholemew said, scolding the potbellied pig he'd brought out for a walk. To be perfectly honest, it wasn't wholly professional to bring a pig to a crime scene, but he'd been working round the clock and couldn't leave Ernestine at home alone any longer. He figured as long as he kept her away from the area that had been cordoned off by the techs, it was all right.

"Not near the water," Bartholemew called. The pig glanced at him and scooted down the riverbank. "Fine," he said. "Go drown. See if I care."

But all the same, Bartholemew leaned over the railing of the bridge to watch the pig walk along the edge of the river. The spot where Jason's body had broken the ice was frozen again, more translucent than the rest. A fluorescent orange flag stapled to a stake marked the northern edge of the crime scene.

Laura Stone's alibi had checked out: Phone records put her at the college, and then back at her residence. But several witnesses had noticed both Daniel and Trixie Stone at the Winterfest. One driver had even seen them both, in a parking lot, with Jason Underhill.

Trixie *could* have murdered Jason, in spite of the size difference between them. Jason had been drunk, and a well-placed shove might have tumbled him over the bridge. It wouldn't account for Jason's bruised and fractured face, but Bartholemew didn't hold Trixie responsible for that. Most likely, it had gone down this way: Jason saw Trixie in town and started to talk to her, but Daniel Stone stumbled onto their encounter. He beat the guy to a pulp, Jason ran off, and Trixie followed him to the bridge.

Bartholemew had believed, initially, that Daniel had lied about not seeing Jason in town that night, and that Trixie had told him about the fight to cover for her father. But what if it had been the other way around? What if Trixie had told the truth, and Daniel—knowing that his daughter had been in contact with Jason already that night—had lied to protect *her*?

Suddenly Ernestine began to root, her snout burrowing. God only knew what she'd found—the most she'd ever turned up was a dead mouse that had crawled under the foundation of his garage. He watched with mild interest as she created a pile of dirty snow behind her.

Then something winked at him.

Bartholemew slid down the steep grade of the riverbank, slipped on a plastic glove from his pocket, and pulled a man's wristwatch out of the snow behind Ernestine.

It was an Eddie Bauer watch with a royal blue face and a woven canvas band. The buckle was missing. Bartholemew squinted up at the bridge, trying to imagine the trajectory and the distance from there to here. Could Jason's arm have struck the railing and snapped the buckle? The medical examiner had found splinters in the boy's fingers— had he lost his watch while he was desperately trying to hang on?

He took out his cell phone and dialed the medical examiner's number. "It's Bartholemew," he said when Anjali answered. "Did Jason Underhill wear a watch?"

"He wasn't brought in wearing one."

"I just found one at the crime scene. Is there any way to tell if it's his?"

"Hang on." Bartholemew heard her rummage through papers. "I've got the autopsy photos here. On the left wrist, there's a band of skin that's a bit lighter than the rest of his arm's skin tone. Why don't you see if the parents recognize it?"

"That's my next stop," Bartholemew said. "Thanks." As he hung up and started to slide the watch into a plastic evidence bag, he noticed something he hadn't seen at first—a hair had gotten caught around the little knob used to set the time.

It was about an inch long, and coarse. There

seemed to be a root attached, as if it had been yanked out.

Mike thought of Jason's all-American good looks, of his dark hair and blue eyes. He held the watch up against the white canvas of his own dress shirt sleeve for comparison. In such stark relief, the hair was as red as a sunset, as red as shame, as red as any other hair on Trixie Stone's head.

"Twice in one week?" Daniel said, opening the door to find Detective Bartholemew standing on the porch again. "I must have won the lottery."

Daniel was still wearing his button-down shirt from the funeral, although he'd stripped off the tie and left it noosed around one of the kitchen chairs. He could feel the detective surveying the house over his right shoulder.

"You got a minute, Mr. Stone?" Bartholemew asked. "And actually . . . is Trixie here? It would be great if she could sit down with us."

"She's asleep," Daniel said. "We went to Jason's funeral, and she got pretty upset there. When we got home, she went straight to bed."

"What about your wife?"

"She's at the college. Guess I'm it for right now."

He led Bartholemew into the living room and sat across from him. "I wouldn't have expected you to attend Jason Underhill's funeral," the detective said.

"It was Trixie's idea. I think she was looking for closure."

"You said she got upset during the service?"

"I think it was too much for her, emotionally." Daniel hesitated. "You didn't come here to ask about this, did you?"

The detective shook his head. "Mr. Stone, on the night of the Winterfest, you said you never ran into Jason. But Trixie told me that you and Jason had a fistfight."

Daniel felt the blood drain from his face. When had Bartholemew talked to Trixie?

"Am I supposed to assume that your daughter was lying?"

"No, I was," Daniel said. "I was afraid you'd charge me with assault."

"Trixie also told me that Jason ran off."

"That's right."

"Did she follow him, Mr. Stone?"

Daniel blinked. "What?"

"Did she follow Jason Underhill to the bridge?"

He pictured the light of the turning car washing over them, and the minute Jason wrenched away. He heard himself calling for Trixie and realizing she wasn't there. "Of course not," he said.

"That's interesting. Because I've got boot prints, and blood, and hair that puts her at the crime scene."

"What crime scene?" Daniel said. "Jason Underhill committed suicide."

The detective just lifted his gaze. Daniel thought of the hour he'd spent searching for Trixie after she'd run away. He remembered the cuts he'd seen on Trixie's arms the day she was washing the dishes, scratches he'd assumed had been made by her own hand, and not someone else's, trying desperately to hold on.

Daniel had bequeathed Trixie his dimples, his long fingers, his photographic memory. But what about the other markers of heredity? Could a parent pass along the gene for revenge, for rage, for escape? Could a trait he'd buried so long ago resurface where he least expected it: in his daughter?

"I'd really like to speak to Trixie," Bartholemew said.

"She didn't kill Jason."

"Terrific," the detective replied. "Then she won't mind giving us a blood sample to compare with the physical evidence, so that we can rule her out." He clasped his hands together between his knees. "Why don't you see if she's about ready to wake up?"

Although Daniel knew life didn't work this way, he truly believed that he had the chance to save his daughter the way he hadn't been able to save her the night she was raped, as if there were some running cosmic tally of victory and defeat. He could get a lawyer. He could spirit her away to Fiji or Guadalcanal or somewhere they'd never be found. He could do whatever was necessary; he just needed to formulate a plan.

The first step was to talk to her before the detective did.

After convincing Bartholemew to wait in the living room—Trixie was, after all, still scared of her own shadow half the time—Daniel headed upstairs. He was shaking, terrified with what he would say to Trixie, even more terrified to hear her response. With every step up the stairs, he thought of escape routes: the attic, his bedroom balcony. Sheets knotted together and tossed out a window.

Daniel decided he'd ask her point-blank, when she was too wrapped in the silver veil of sleep to dissemble. Depending on her answer, he'd either take her down to Bartholemew to prove the detective wrong, or he'd carry Trixie to the far ends of the earth himself.

The door to Trixie's room was still closed; with his ear pressed against it, Daniel heard nothing but silence.

After they had come home from the funeral, Daniel had sat on Trixie's bed with her curled in his lap, the way he had once held her during bouts of stomach flu, rubbing her belly or her back until she slipped over the fine line of sleep. Now he turned the knob slowly, hoping to wake Trixie up by degrees.

The first thing Daniel noticed was how cold it was. The second was the window, wide open.

The room looked like the aftermath of a tropical storm. Clothes lay trampled on the floor. Sheets were balled at the foot of the bed. Makeup, looseleaf papers, and magazines had been dumped— the contents of a missing knapsack. Her toothbrush and hairbrush were gone. And the little clay jar where Trixie kept her cash was empty.

Had Trixie heard the detective downstairs? Had she left before Bartholemew even arrived? She was only a teenager; how far could she get?

Daniel moved to the window and traced the zigzag track of her flight on the snow from her room to the sloped roof, to the maple tree's out-stretched arm, across the lawn to bare pavement, at which point she simply disappeared. He thought of her words to him, a day before, when he'd seen the cuts on her arm: *It's how I run away.*

Frantic, he stared at the icy roof. *She could have killed herself.*

And on the heels of that thought: *She still might.*

What if Trixie managed to get someplace where, when she tried to swallow pills or cut her wrists or sleep in a cloud of carbon monoxide, nobody stopped her?

A person was never who you thought he was. It was true for him; maybe it was true for Trixie too. Maybe—in spite of what he wanted to believe, in spite of what he hoped—she *had* killed Jason.

What if Daniel wasn't the first one to find her?

What if he *was*?

# 6

It was late enough in December that all the radio stations played only Christmas carols. Trixie's hiding place was directly over the driver's seat, in the little jut of the box truck that sat over the cab. She had seen the truck at the dairy farm just past the high school athletic fields. With the doors wide open and no one around, she had climbed inside and hidden in that upper nook, drawing hay over herself for camouflage.

They'd loaded two calves into the truck—not down in the bottom, like Trixie had figured, but nearly on top of her in the narrow space where she was curled. This way, she supposed, they wouldn't stand up during the trip. Once they'd started under way, Trixie had poked her head out from the straw and looked at one calf. It had eyes as large as planets, and when she held out her finger, the calf sucked hard on it.

At the next stop, another farm not ten minutes down the road, an enormous Holstein limped up the ramp into the back of the truck. It stared right at Trixie and mooed. "Damn shame," the trucker said, as the farmer shoved the cow from behind.

"Ayuh, she went down on some ice," he said. "In you go, now." Then the door swung shut and everything went black.

She didn't know where they were headed and didn't particularly care. Prior to this, the farthest Trixie had ever been by herself was the Mall of Maine. She wondered if her father was looking for her yet. She wished she could phone him and tell him she was all right—but under the circumstances, she couldn't call. She might *never.*

She lay down on one calf's smooth side. It smelled of grass and grain and daylight, and with every breath, she felt herself rising and falling. She wondered why the cows were in transit. Maybe they were going to a new farm for Christmas. Or to be part of a Nativity play. She pictured the doors swinging open and farmhands in crisp overalls coming to lift down the calves. They would find Trixie and would give her fresh milk and homemade ice cream and they wouldn't even think to ask her how she'd wound up in the back of a livestock truck.

In a way, it was a mystery to Trixie, too. She had seen the detective at Jason's funeral, although he thought he'd been hiding. And then, when everyone thought she was asleep, she'd stood on the balcony and heard what he'd said to her father.

Enough to know that she had to get out of there.

She was, in a way, a little proud of herself. Who

knew that she'd be able to run away without a car, with only two hundred bucks in her pocket? She'd never considered herself to be the kind of person who was cool in the face of crisis—and yet, you never knew what you were capable of until you arrived at that given moment. Life was just a whole string of spots where you continued to surprise yourself.

She must have fallen asleep for a while, sandwiched between the knobby knees and globe bellies of the two calves, but when the truck stopped again they struggled to stand—impossible in that cramped space. Below them, the cow began to bellow, one low note that ricocheted. There was the sound of a seal being breached, a mighty creak, and then the doors to the back of the truck swung open.

Trixie blinked into the light and saw what she hadn't earlier: The cow had a lesion on her right foreleg, one that made it buckle beneath her. The Holstein calves on either side of her were males, no good for producing milk. She peered out the double doors and squinted so that she could read the sign at the end of the driveway: LaRue and Sons Beef, Berlin, NH.

This was not a petting zoo or Old MacDonald's Farm, as Trixie had imagined. This was a slaughterhouse.

She scrambled down from her ledge, startling the animals—not to mention the truck driver who was unhooking the tether of the cow—and took off like a shot down the long gravel driveway. Trixie ran until her lungs were on fire, until she had reached what passed for a town, with a Burger King and a gas station. The Burger King made her think of the calves, which made her think that she was going to be a vegetarian, if she ever got through the other side of this nightmare.

Suddenly, there was a siren. Trixie went still as stone, her eyes trained on the circling blue lights of the advancing police cruiser.

The car went screaming past her, on to someone else's emergency.

Wiping her hand across her mouth, Trixie took a deep breath and started to walk.

"She's gone," Daniel Stone said, frantic.

Bartholemew's eyes narrowed. "Gone?"

He followed Stone upstairs and stood in the doorway of Trixie's room, which looked as if a bomb had cut a swath through its middle. "I don't know where she is," Stone said, his voice breaking. "I don't know when she left."

It took Bartholemew less than a second to determine that this wasn't a lie. In the first place, Stone had been out of his sight for less than a minute, hardly long enough to tip off his daughter that she was under suspicion. In the second place, Daniel Stone seemed just as surprised as Bartholemew was to find Trixie missing, and he was skating the knife edge of panic.

For only a heartbeat, Bartholemew let himself wonder why a teenage girl who had nothing to hide would suddenly disappear. But in the next breath, he remembered what it felt like to discover that your daughter was not where you'd thought she was, and he switched gears. "When did you last see her?"

"Before she went to take a nap . . . about three-thirty?"

The detective took a notepad out of his pocket. "What was she wearing?"

"I'm not sure. She probably changed after the funeral."

"Have you got a recent photo?"

Bartholemew followed Stone downstairs again, watching him run a finger along the vertebrae of books on a living room shelf, finally pulling down an eighth-grade yearbook from Bethel Middle School. He turned pages until they fell open to the S's. A folio of snapshots—a 5-by-7 and some wallet-sized—spilled out. "We never got around to framing them," Stone murmured.

In the photographs, Trixie's smiling face repeated like an Andy Warhol print. The girl in the picture had long red hair held back with clips. Her smile was just a little too wide, and a tooth in front was crooked. The girl in that picture had never been raped. Maybe she had never even been kissed.

Bartholemew had to pry the pictures of Trixie from her father's hand. Both men were painfully aware that Stone was struggling not to break down. The tears you shed over a child were not the same as any others. They burned your throat and your corneas. They left you blind.

Daniel Stone stared at him. "She didn't do anything wrong."

"Sit tight," Bartholemew replied, aware that it was not an answer. "I'll find her."

The last lecture Laura gave before Christmas vacation was about the half-life of transgression. "Are there any sins Dante left out?" Laura asked. "Or any really bad modern-day behaviors that weren't around in the year 1300?"

One girl nodded. "Drug addiction. There's, like, no *bolgia* for crackheads."

"It's the same as gluttony," a second student said. "Addiction's addiction. It doesn't matter what the substance is."

"Cannibalism?"

"Nope, Dante's got that in there," Laura said. "Count Uggolino. He lumps it in with bestiality."

"Driving to endanger?"

"Filippo drives his horses recklessly. Early Italian road rage." Laura glanced around the silent hall. "Maybe the question we need to ask isn't whether there's any fresh twenty-first-century sin . . . but whether the people who define sin have changed, because of the times."

"Well, the world's completely different," a student pointed out.

"Sure, but look at how it's still the same. Avarice, cowardice, depravity, a need to control other people—these have all been around forever. Maybe nowadays a pedophile will start a kiddie-porn site instead of flashing in the subway tunnels, or a murderer will choose to use an electric chain saw to kill, instead of his bare hands . . . Technology helps us be more creative in the way we sin, but it doesn't mean that the basic sin is different."

A boy shook his head. "Seems like there ought to be a whole different circle for someone like Jeffrey Dahmer, you know?"

"Or the people who come up with reality TV shows," someone else interjected, and the class laughed.

"It's sort of interesting," Laura said, "to think that Dante wouldn't have put Jeffrey Dahmer as deep in hell as he would Macbeth. Why is that?"

"Because the skivviest thing you can do is be disloyal to someone. Macbeth killed his own king, man. That would be like Eminem taking down Dr. Dre."

The student was, at a literal level, correct. In the *Inferno,* sins of passion and despair weren't nearly as damning as sins of treachery. Sinners in the upper circles of hell were guilty of indulging their own appetites, but without malice toward others. Sinners in the middle levels of hell had committed acts of violence toward themselves or others. The deepest level of hell, though, was reserved for fraud—what Dante felt was the worst sin of all. There was betrayal to family—those who killed kin. There was betrayal to country—for the double agents and spies of the world. There was betrayal to benefactor—Judas, Brutus, Cassius, and Lucifer, all of whom had turned against their mentors.

"Does Dante's hierarchy still work?" Laura

asked. "Or do you think that in our world, the order of the damned should be shaken up?"

"I think it's worse to keep someone's head in your freezer than to sell national security secrets to the Chinese," a girl said, "but that's just me."

Another student shook her head. "I don't get why being unfaithful to your king is worse than being unfaithful to your husband. If you have an affair, you wind up only in the second level of hell. That's, like, getting off easy."

"Nice choice of words," the kid beside her joked.

"It's about intention," a student added. "Like manslaughter versus murder. It's almost as if you do something in the heat of the moment, Dante excuses you. But if you've got this whole premeditated scheme going on, you're in deep trouble."

In that moment, although she'd been a professor for this particular course—even this particular class topic—for a decade, Laura realized that there *was* a sin that Dante had left out, one that belonged in the very deepest pit of hell. If the worst sin of all was betraying others, then what about people who lied to themselves?

There should have been a tenth circle, a tiny spot the size of the head of a pin, with room for infinite masses. It would be overcrowded with professors who hid in ivy-covered towers instead of facing their broken families. With little girls who had grown up overnight. With husbands who didn't speak of their past but instead poured it out onto a blank white page. With women who pretended they could be the wife of one and the lover of another and keep the two selves distinct. With anyone who told himself he was living the perfect life, despite all evidence to the contrary.

A voice swam toward her. "Professor Stone? Are you okay?"

Laura focused on the girl in the front row who'd asked the question. "No," she said quietly. "I'm not. You can all . . . you can all go home a little early for vacation."

As the students disbanded, delighted with this windfall, Laura gathered her briefcase and her coat. She walked to the parking lot, got into her car, and began to drive.

The women who wrote "Annie's Mailbox" were wrong, Laura realized. Just because you didn't speak the facts out loud didn't erase their existence. Silence was just a quieter way to lie.

She knew where she was headed, but before she got there, her cell phone rang. "It's Trixie," Daniel said, and suddenly what he had to say was far more important than what she did.

Santa's Village in Jefferson, New Hampshire, was full of lies. There were transplanted reindeer languishing in a fake barn and phony elves hammering in a workshop and a counterfeit Santa sitting on a throne with a bazillion kids lined up to tell him what they wanted on the big day. There were parents pretending this was totally *real*, even the animatronic Rudolph. And then there was Trixie herself, trying to act like she was normal, when in fact she was the biggest liar of all.

Trixie watched a little girl climb onto Fake Santa's lap and pull his beard so hard that it ripped off. You'd think that a kid, even one so young, would get suspicious, but it never worked that way. People believed what they wanted to believe, no matter what was in front of their eyes.

That's why she was here, wasn't it?

As a kid, of course, Trixie had believed in Santa. For years, Zephyr—who was half Jewish and fully practical—pointed out the discrepancies to Trixie: How could Santa be in both Filene's and the Bon-Ton at the same time? If he really was Santa, shouldn't he *know* what she wanted without having to *ask*? Trixie wished she could round up the kids in this building and save them, like Holden Caulfield in the last book she'd read for English. *Reality check*, she would say. *Santa's a phony. Your parents lied to you.*

*And*, she might add, *they'll do it again.* Her own parents had said she was beautiful, when in fact she was all angles and bowlegs. They'd promised that she'd find her Prince Charming, but he'd dumped Trixie. They said if she came home by her curfew and picked up her room and held up her end of the bargain, they'd keep her safe—yet look at what had happened.

She stepped out from behind a fir tree that belched Christmas carols and glanced around to see if anyone was watching her. In a way, it would have been easier to get caught. It was hard to look over your shoulder every other second, expecting to be recognized. She'd worried that the truck driver who'd given her a lift would radio her whereabouts to the state police. She'd been sure that the man selling tickets at Santa's Village had glanced down to compare her face to the one on a Wanted poster.

Trixie slipped into the bathroom, where she splashed water on her face and tried to take deep, even, social-disaster-avoidance breaths, the way she'd done in science class when they were dissecting a frog and she was sure she would throw up on her lab partner. She pretended to have something in her eye and squinted into the mirror until she was the only person left in the restroom.

Then Trixie stuck her head under the faucet. It was the kind you had to push down to get the water going, so she had to keep pounding the knob for a continuous stream. She took off her sweatshirt and wrapped it around her hair, then went into a stall and sat on the toilet, shivering in her T-shirt while she rummaged through her backpack.

She'd bought the dye at Wal-Mart when the trucker stopped for cigarettes. The color was called Night in Shining Armor, but it looked plain old black to Trixie. She opened the box and read the instructions.

With any luck no one would think it weird that she was sitting in the bathroom for thirty minutes. Then again, no one else should *be* in the bathroom for thirty minutes. Trixie slipped on the plastic gloves and mixed the dye with the peroxide, shook, and squirted the solution onto her hair. She rubbed it around a little and pulled the plastic bag over her scalp.

Was she supposed to dye her eyebrows, too? Was that even possible?

She and Zephyr used to talk about how you could be an adult way before you hit twenty-one. The age wasn't as important as the milestones: taking a trip sans parents, buying beer without getting carded, having sex. She wished she could tell Zeph that it was possible to grow up in an instant, that you could look down and see the line in the sand dividing your life now from what it used to be.

Trixie wondered if, like her father, she'd never go back home again. She wondered how big the world was, really, when you crossed it, instead of traced it with your finger on a map. A little rivulet of liquid ran down her neck; she smeared it with a finger before it reached the collar of her shirt. The dye came away as dark as motor oil. For just a moment she pretended she was bleeding. It would be no surprise to her if inside she'd gone as black as everyone suspected.

Daniel parked in front of the wide-eyed windows of the toy store and watched Zephyr hand some bills and small change back to an elderly woman. Zephyr's hair was in braids, and she was wearing two long-sleeved shirts, one layered over the next, as if she'd planned to be cold no matter what. Through the shadows and the stream of the glass, it was almost possible to pretend that she was Trixie.

There was no way Daniel planned to sit inside his house and wait for the police to find Trixie and bully an explanation out of her. To that end, the minute Bartholemew had gone—and Daniel checked to make sure he wasn't just lurking at the end of the block—Daniel had begun to consider what he knew about Trixie that the cops didn't. Where she might go, whom she might trust.

Right now, there were precious few people who fell into that category.

The customer left the store, and Zephyr noticed him waiting outside. "Hey, Mr. S," she said, waving.

She wore purple nail polish on her fingers. It was the same color Trixie had been wearing this morning; Daniel realized that they must have put it on together the last time Zephyr was over at the house. Just seeing it on Zephyr, when he so badly wanted to see it on Trixie, made it hard to breathe.

Zephyr was looking over his shoulder. "Is Trixie with you?"

Daniel tried to shake his head, but somewhere between the thought and the action the intent vanished. He stared at the girl who knew his daughter maybe better than he'd ever known her himself, as much as it hurt to admit it. "Zephyr," he said, "have you got a minute?"

For an old guy, Daniel Stone was *hot*. Zephyr had even said that to Trixie once or twice, although it totally freaked her out, what with him being her father and everything. But beyond that, Mr. Stone had always fascinated Zephyr. In all the years she'd known Trixie, she had never seen him lose his temper. Not when they spilled nail polish remover on Mrs. S's bedroom bureau, not when Trixie failed her math test, not even when they were caught sneaking cigarettes in Trixie's garage. It was against human nature to be that calm, like he was some kind of Stepford dad who couldn't be provoked. Take Zephyr's own mother, for example. Zephyr had once found her hurling all of their dinner plates against the backyard fence, when she found out that this loser she was dating was two-timing her. Zephyr and her mom had screaming matches. In fact, her mother had been the one to teach her the best curse words.

On the other hand, Trixie had learned them from Zephyr. Zephyr had even tried to lure Trixie into objectionable behaviors simply for the purpose of trying to get a rise out of Mr. Stone, but nothing had ever worked. He was like some kind of soap opera actor whose tragic story line you fell madly for: beautiful to look at, but all the same, you knew what you were seeing wasn't all it was cracked up to be.

Today, though, something was different. Mr. Stone couldn't concentrate; even as he grilled Zephyr, his eyes kept darting around. He was so far from the even-keeled, friendly father figure she'd envied her whole life that if Zephyr didn't know better, she would have assumed it wasn't Daniel Stone standing across from her at all.

"The last time I talked to Trixie was last night," Zephyr said, leaning across the glass counter of the toy store. "I called her around ten o'clock to talk about the funeral."

"Did she tell you that she had somewhere to go after that?"

"Trixie isn't really into going out these days." As if her father didn't already know that.

"It's really important, Zephyr, that you tell me the truth."

"Mr. Stone," she said, "why would I lie to you?"

An unspoken answer hovered between them: *because you have before.* They were both thinking about what she'd told the police after the night of the rape. They both knew that jealousy could rise like a tide, erasing events that had been scratched into the shore of your memory.

Mr. Stone took a deep breath. "If she calls you . . . will you tell her I'm trying to find her . . . and that everything's going to be okay?"

"Is she in trouble?" Zephyr asked, but by then Trixie's father was already walking out of the toy store.

Zephyr watched him go. She didn't care that he thought she was a lousy friend. In fact, she was just the opposite. It was *because* she'd already wronged Trixie once that she'd done what she had.

Zephyr punched the key on the cash register that made the drawer open. Three hours had passed since she'd stolen all the twenty-dollar bills and had given them to Trixie. Three hours, Zephyr thought, was a damn good head start.

HAVE GONE TO LOOK FOR TRIXIE, the note said. BRB.

Laura wandered up to Trixie's room, as if this was bound to be a big mistake, as if she might open the door and find Trixie there, silently nodding to the beat of her iPod as she wrestled with an algebraic equation. But she wasn't there, of course, and the small space had been overturned. She wondered if that had been Trixie or the police.

Daniel had said on the phone that this was suddenly a homicide investigation. That Jason's death had not been accidental after all. And that Trixie had run away.

There was so much that had to be fixed that Laura didn't know where to start. Her hands shook as she sorted through the leftovers of her daughter's life—an archaeologist, looking over the artifacts and trying to piece together an understanding of the young woman who'd used them. The Koosh ball and the Lisa Frank pencil—these belonged to the Trixie she thought she had known. It was the other items that she couldn't make sense of: the CD with lyrics that made Laura's jaw drop, the sterling silver ring shaped like a skull, the condom hidden inside a makeup compact. Maybe she and Trixie still had a lot in common: Apparently, while Laura was turning into a woman she could barely recognize, her daughter had been, too.

She sat down on Trixie's bed and lifted the receiver of the phone. How many times had Laura cut in on the line between her and Jason, telling her that she had to say good night and go to bed? *Five more minutes,* Trixie would beg.

If she'd given Trixie those minutes, all those nights, would it have added up to another day for Jason? If she took five minutes now, could she right everything that had gone wrong?

It took Laura three tries to dial the number of the police station, and she was holding for Detective Bartholemew when Daniel stepped into the room. "What are you doing?"

"Calling the police," she said.

He crossed in two strides and took the receiver from her hand, hung up the phone. "Don't."

"Daniel—"

"Laura, I know why she ran away. I was accused of murder when I was eighteen, and I took off, too."

At this confession, Laura completely lost her train of thought. How could you live with a man for fifteen years, feel him move inside you, have his child, and not know something as fundamental about him as this?

He sat down at Trixie's desk. "I was still living in Alaska. The victim was my best friend, Cane."

"Did you . . . did you do it?"

Daniel hesitated. "Not the way they thought I did."

Laura stared at him. She thought of Trixie, God knows where right now, on the run for a crime she could not have committed. "If you weren't guilty . . . then why—"

"Because Cane was still dead."

In Daniel's eyes, Laura could suddenly see the most surprising things: the blood of a thousand salmon slit throat to tail, the blue-veined crack of ice so thick it made the bottoms of your feet hurt, the profile of a raven sitting on a roof. In Daniel's eyes she understood something she hadn't been willing to admit to herself before: In spite of everything, or maybe because of it, he understood their daughter better than she did.

He shifted, hitting the computer mouse with his elbow. The screen hummed to life, revealing several open windows: Google, iTunes, Sephora.com, and the heartbreaking rapesurvivor.com, full of poetry by girls like Trixie. But MapQuest? When Trixie wasn't even old enough to drive?

Laura leaned over Daniel's shoulder to grasp the mouse. FIND IT! the site promised. There were empty boxes to fill in: address, city, state, zip code. And at the bottom, in bright blue: *We are having trouble finding a route for your location.*

"Oh, Christ," Daniel said. "I know where she is."

Trixie's father used to take her out into the woods and teach her how to read the world so that she'd always know where she was going. He'd quiz her on the identification of trees: the fairy-tale spray of needles on a hemlock, the narrow grooves of an ash, the paper-wrapped birch, the gnarled arms of a sugar maple. One day, when they were examining a tree with barbed wire running through the middle of its trunk—*how long do you think* that *took*?—Trixie's eye had been caught by something in the forest: sun glinting off metal.

The abandoned car sat behind an oak tree that had been split by lightning. Two of the windows had been broken; some animal had made its home in the tufted stuffing of the backseat. A vine had grown from the bottom of the forest floor through the window, wrapping around the steering wheel.

*Where do you think the driver is?* Trixie had asked.

*I don't know,* her father replied. *But he's been gone for a long time.*

He said that the person who'd left the car behind most likely didn't want to bother with having it towed away. But that didn't keep Trixie from making up more extravagant explanations: The man had suffered a head wound and started walking, only to wander up a mountain and die of exposure, and even now the bones were bleaching south of her backyard. The man was on the run from the Mob and had eluded hit men in a car chase. The man had wandered into town with amnesia and spent the next ten years completely unaware of who he used to be.

Trixie was dreaming of the abandoned car when someone slammed the door of the bathroom stall beside her. She woke up with a start and glanced down at her watch—surely if you left this stuff in your hair too long it would fall out by the roots or turn purple or something. She heard the flush of the toilet, running water, and then the busy slice of life as the door opened. When it fell quiet again, she crept out of the stall and rinsed her hair in the sink.

There were streaks on her forehead and her neck, but her hair—her red hair, the hair that had inspired her father to call her his chili pepper when she was only a baby—was now the color of a thicket's thorns, of a rosebush past recovery.

As she stuffed the ruined sweatshirt into the bottom of the trash can, a mother came in with two little boys. Trixie held her breath, but the woman didn't look twice at her. Maybe it was really *that* easy. She walked out of the bathroom, past a new Santa who'd come on duty, toward the parking lot. She thought of the man who'd left his car in the woods: Maybe he had staged his own death. Maybe he'd done it for the sole purpose of starting over.

If a teenager wants to disappear, chances are he or she will succeed. It was why runaways were so difficult to track—until they were rounded up in a drug or prostitution ring. Most teens who vanished did so for independence, or to get away from abuse. Unlike an adult, however, who could be traced by a paper trail of ATM withdrawals and rental car agreements and airline passenger lists, a kid was more likely to pay in cash, to hitchhike, to go unnoticed by bystanders.

For the second time in an hour, Bartholemew pulled into the neighborhood where the Stones lived. Trixie Stone was officially registered now as a missing person, not a fugitive from justice. That couldn't happen, not even if all signs pointed to the fact that the reason she'd left was because she knew she was about to be charged with murder.

In the American legal system, you could not use a suspect's disappearance as probable cause. Later on, during a trial, a prosecutor might hold up Trixie's flight as proof of guilt, but there was never going to be a trial if Bartholemew couldn't convince a judge to swear out a warrant for Trixie Stone's arrest—so that at the moment she was located, she could be taken into custody.

The problem was, had Trixie not fled, he wouldn't be arresting her yet. Christ, just two days ago, Bartholemew had been convinced that Daniel Stone was the perp . . . until the physical evidence started to prove otherwise. *Prove,* though, was a dubious term. He had a boot print that matched Trixie's footwear—and that of thousands of other town residents. He had blood on the victim that belonged to a female, which ruled out only half the population. He had a hair the same general color as Trixie's—a hair with a root on it full of uncontaminated DNA, but no known sample of Trixie's to compare it to and no imminent means of getting one.

Any defense attorney would be able to drive a Hummer through the holes in that investigation. Bartholemew needed to physically find Trixie Stone, so that he could specifically link her to Jason Underhill's murder.

He knocked on the Stones' front door. Again, no one answered, but this time, when Bartholemew tried the knob, it was locked. He cupped his hands around the glass window and peered into the mud-room.

Daniel Stone's coat and boots were gone.

He walked halfway around the attached garage to a tiny window and peered inside. Laura Stone's Honda, which hadn't been here two hours ago, was parked in one bay. Daniel Stone's pickup was gone.

Bartholemew smacked his hand against the ex-terior wall of the house and swore. He couldn't prove that Daniel and Laura Stone had gone off to find Trixie before the cops did, but he would have bet money on it. When your child is missing, you don't go grocery shopping. You sit tight and wait for the word that she's being brought safely home.

Bartholemew pinched the bridge of his nose and tried to think. Maybe this was a blessing in disguise. After all, the Stones had a better chance of finding Trixie than he did. And it would be far easier for Bartholemew to track two adults than their fourteen-year-old daughter.

And in the meantime? Well, he could get a war-rant to search the house, but it wouldn't do him any good. No lab worth its salt would accept a toothbrush from Trixie's bathroom as a viable known sample of DNA. What he needed was the girl herself and a lab-sanctioned sample of her blood.

Which, in that instant, Bartholemew realized he already had—sitting in a sealed rape kit, evidence for a trial that wasn't going to happen.

• • •

In eighth grade, as part of health class, Trixie had had to take care of an egg. Each student was given one, with the understanding that it had to remain intact for a week, could not ever be left alone, and had to be "fed" every three hours. This was supposed to be some big contraceptive deterrent: a way for kids to realize how having a baby was way harder than it looked.

Trixie took the assignment seriously. She named her egg Benedict and fashioned a little carrier for it that she wore around her neck. She paid her English teacher fifty cents to babysit the egg while she was in gym class; she took it to the movies with Zephyr. She held it in the palm of her hand during classes and got used to the feel of it, the shape, the weight.

Even now, she couldn't tell you how the egg had gotten that hairline fracture. Trixie first noticed it on the way to school one morning. Her father had shrugged off the F she received—he said it was a stupid assignment, that a kid was nothing like an egg. Yet Trixie had wondered if his benevolence had something to do with the fact that in real life, he would have failed too: how else to explain the difference between what he thought Trixie was up to and what she actually was doing?

Now, she inched up the wrist of her coat and looked at the loose net of scars. It was her hairline crack, she supposed, and it was only a matter of time before she completely went to pieces.

"Humpty freaking Dumpty," she said out loud.

A toddler bouncing on his mother's lap next to Trixie clapped his hands. "Dumpty!" he yelled. "Fall!" He lurched himself backward so fast that Trixie was sure that he'd smash his head on the floor of the bus station.

His mother grabbed him before that happened. "Trevor. Cut it out, will you?" Then she turned to Trixie. "He's a big fan of the Egg Man."

The woman was really just a girl. Maybe she was a few years older than Trixie, but not by much. She wore a ratty blue scarf wrapped around her neck and an army surplus coat. From the number of bags around them, it looked like they were making a permanent move—but then again, for all Trixie knew, this was how people with kids had to travel. "I don't get nursery rhymes," the girl said. "I mean, why would all the king's horses and all the king's men try to put an egg back together anyway?"

"What's the egg doing on the wall in the first place?" Trixie said.

"Exactly. I think Mother Goose was on crack." She smiled at Trixie. "Where are you headed?"

"Canada."

"We're going to Boston." She let the boy wriggle off her lap.

Trixie wanted to ask the girl if the baby was hers. If she'd had him by accident. If, even after you make what everyone considers to be the biggest mistake of your life, you stop thinking it's a mistake and maybe see it as the best thing that ever could have happened.

"Ew, Trev, is that you?" The girl grabbed the baby around the waist and hauled him toward her face, rump first. She grimaced at the collection of duffels littering their feet. "Would you mind watching my stuff while I do a toxic waste removal?"

As she stood up, she banged the diaper bag against her open backpack, spilling its contents all over the floor. "Oh, shit . . ."

"I'll get it," Trixie said as the girl headed for the restroom with Trevor. She started jamming items back into the diaper bag: plastic keys that played a Disney song, an orange, a four-pack of crayons. A tampon with the wrapper half off, a hair scrunchie. Something that might, at one time, have been a cookie. A wallet.

Trixie hesitated. She told herself she was only going to peek at the girl's name, because she didn't want to ask and run the risk of striking up a conversation.

A Vermont driver's license looked nothing like one from Maine. In the first place, there wasn't a photograph. The one time Zephyr had convinced Trixie to go to a bar, she'd used a Vermont license as fake ID. "Five foot six is close enough," Zephyr said, although Trixie was four inches shorter. Brown eyes, it read, when she had blue.

Fawn Abernathy lived at 34 First Street in Shelburne, Vermont. She was nineteen years old. She was the same exact height as Trixie, and Trixie took that as an omen.

She left Fawn her ATM card and half of the cash. But she slipped the American Express card and the license into her pocket. Then Trixie hurried out of the Vermont Transit Bus terminal and threw herself into the first cab at the side of the curb. "Where to?" the driver asked.

Trixie looked out the window. "The airport," she said.

"I wouldn't be asking if it wasn't an emergency," Bartholemew begged. He glanced around Venice Prudhomme's office, piled high with files and computer printouts and transcripts from court testimony.

She sighed, not bothering to look up from her microscope. "Mike, for you, it's always an emergency."

"Please. I've got a hair with a root on it that was found on the dead kid's body, and I have Trixie's blood preserved all nice and neat in her rape kit. If the DNA matches, that's all I need to get a warrant for her arrest."

"No," Venice said.

"I know you've got a backlog and—"

"That's not why," she interrupted, glancing at Bartholemew. "There's no way I'm opening up a sealed rape kit."

"Why? Trixie Stone consented to having her blood drawn for it already."

"As a victim," Venice pointed out. "Not to prove she committed a crime."

"You've got to stop watching *Law and Order*."

"Maybe you ought to start."

Bartholemew scowled. "I can't believe you're doing this."

"I'm not doing anything," Venice said, bending over her scope again. "At least not until a judge says so."

Summer on the tundra was dreamlike. Since the sun stayed out until two A.M., people didn't sleep much in Akiak. Kids would cluster around bootleg booze and weed if they could get it, or leave behind the skins of their candy bars and spilled cans of pop if they couldn't. Younger children splashed in the foggy green water of the Kuskokwim, even though by August they would still lose feeling in their ankles after only a few moments of submersion. Every year, in one of the Yup'ik villages, someone would drown; it was too cold for anyone to stay in the water long enough to learn how to swim.

The year Daniel was eight, he spent July walking barefoot along the banks of the Kuskokwim. A wall of alders and willows lined one side of the river, on the other, sod sloughed into the water from a ten-foot-high embankment. Mosquitoes beaded on the planes of his face every time he stopped moving; sometimes they'd fly into his ears, loud as a bush plane. Daniel would watch the fat backs of king salmon rise like miniature sharks in the center of the river. The men in the village were off in their aluminum fishing boats, the ones that had been sleeping on the shore like beached whales all winter. Yup'ik fish camps dotted the bank: single-celled cities made of whitewalled tents, or knobby poles nailed together and covered with blue tarps that flapped like the aprons of flustered old women. On plywood tables, the women cut kings and reds into strips, then hung them on the racks to dry as they called out to their children: *Kaigtuten- qaa? Are you hungry? Qinucetaanrilgu kinguqliin!* Don't try to provoke your little brother!

He picked up a crusted twig, a fan belt, and a binder clip before he saw it—a pitted peak jutting out of the silt. It couldn't be . . . could it? It took a trained eye to look past the soaked driftwood to pick out an ivory tusk or a fossilized bone, but it had happened, Daniel knew. Other kids in school—the ones who teased him because he was *kass'aq*, who laughed when he didn't know how to shoot a ptarmigan or couldn't find his way back from the bush on a snow-go—had found mast- odon teeth along the banks of the river.

Crouching, Daniel dug around the base, even as the river rushed into the hole and buried his progress. It was an honest-to-God tusk, right here, under his hands. He imagined it reaching past the water table, bigger even than the one on display in Bethel.

Two ravens watched him from the bank, chatter- ing a play-by-play commentary as Daniel pulled and heaved. Mammoth tusks could be ten or twelve feet long; they might weigh a couple hun- dred pounds. Maybe it wasn't even a mammoth but a *quugaarpak.* The Yupiit told stories of the huge creature that lived under the ground and came out only at night. If it was caught above the ground when the sun was up—even the slightest part of it—its entire body would turn into bone and ivory.

Daniel spent hours trying to extricate the tusk, but it was stuck too firm and wedged too deep. He would have to leave it and bring back reinforcements. He marked his site, trampling tall reeds and leaving a hummock of stones piled onto the bank to flag the spot where the tusk would be waiting.

The next day, Daniel returned with a shovel and a block of wood. He had a vague plan of building a dam to stave off the flow of water while he dug his tusk out of the silt. He passed the same people working at fish camp, and the bend where the alder trees had fallen off the bank right into the water, the two ravens cackling—but when he came to the spot where he'd found the tusk yesterday, it was gone.

It's said that you can't step into the same river twice. Maybe that was the problem, or maybe the current was so strong it had swept away the pile of rocks Daniel had left as a marker. Maybe it was, as the Yup'ik kids said, that Daniel was too white to do what they could do as naturally as breathing: find history with their own two hands.

It was not until Daniel reached the village again that he realized the ravens had followed him home. Everyone knew that if one bird landed on your roof, it meant company. A tiding of ravens, though, meant something else entirely: that loneliness would be your lot, that there was no hope of changing your course.

Marita Soorenstad looked up the minute Bartholemew entered her office. "Do you remember a guy named David Fleming?" she asked.

He sank down into the chair across from her. "Should I?"

"In 1991, he raped and attempted to kill a fifteen-year-old girl who was riding her bike home from school. Then he went and killed someone in another county, and there was a Supreme Court case about whether or not the DNA sample taken for the first case could be used as evidence in the next case."

"So?"

"So in Maine, if you take a blood sample from a suspect for one case, you can indeed use it for subsequent tests in a different case," Marita said. "The problem is that when you took blood from Trixie Stone, she consented because she was a victim, and that's very different from consenting because she's a suspect."

"Isn't there some kind of loophole?"

"Depends," Marita said. "There are three situations when you're talking about an individual sample that was given based on consent, as opposed to based on a warrant. In the first, the police tell the individual the sample will be used for any investigation. In the second, the police tell the individual the sample will be used only for a certain investigation. In the third, the police obtain consent after saying that the sample will be used to investigate one particular crime, but they don't make any mention of other uses. You with me so far?"

Bartholemew nodded.

"What exactly did you tell Trixie Stone about her rape kit?"

He thought back to the night he'd met the girl and her parents in the hospital. Bartholemew could not be entirely sure, but he imagined that he said what he usually did with a sexual assault victim: that this was going to be used for the purposes of the rape case, that it was often the DNA evidence that a jury would hang their hat on.

"You didn't mention using it for any other potential case, did you?" Marita asked.

"No," he scowled. "Most rape victims have enough trouble with the current one."

"Well, that means the scope of consent was ambiguous. Most people assume that when the police ask for a sample to help solve a crime, they aren't going to use the sample indefinitely for other purposes. And a pretty strong argument could be made that in the absence of explicit consent, retaining the sample and reusing it is constitutionally unreasonable." She pulled off her glasses. "It seems to me you have two choices. You can either go back to Trixie Stone and ask for her permission to use the blood sample you've got in the rape kit for a new investigation, or you can go to a judge and get a warrant for a new sample of her blood."

"Neither one's going to work," Bartholemew said. "She's missing."

Marita glanced up. "Are you kidding?"

"I wish."

"Then get more creative. Where else would there be a sample of her DNA? Does she lick envelopes for the drama club or Teen Democrats?"

"She was too busy carving up her arms for any other extracurriculars," Bartholemew said.

"Who treated her? The school nurse?"

No, this had been Trixie's big secret; she would have gone to great pains to hide it, especially if she was cutting herself during school hours. But it did beg the question: What did she use to stanch the flow of blood? Band-Aids, gauze, tissue?

And was any of that in her locker?

The bush pilot from Arctic Circle Air had been hired to fly in a veterinarian headed to Bethel for the K300 sled dog race. "You going there too?" the vet asked, and although Trixie had no idea where it was, she nodded. "First time?"

"Um, yeah."

The vet looked at her backpack. "You must be a JV."

She was; she'd played junior varsity soccer this fall. "I was a striker," Trixie said.

"The rest of the JVs headed up to the checkpoints yesterday," the pilot said. "You miss the flight?"

He might as well have been speaking Greek. "I was sick," Trixie said. "I had the flu."

The pilot hauled the last box of supplies into the belly of the plane. "Well, if you don't mind riding with the cargo, I don't mind giving a pretty girl a lift."

The Shorts Skyvan hardly looked airworthy—it resembled a Winnebago with wings. The inside was crammed with duffels and pallets.

"You can wait for the commuter flight out tomorrow," the pilot said, "but there's a storm coming. You'll probably sit out the whole race in the airport."

"I'd rather fly out now," Trixie said, and the pilot gave her a leg up.

"Mind the body," he said.

"Oh, I'm okay."

"Wasn't talking about *you.*" The pilot reached in and rapped his knuckles against a pine box.

Trixie scrambled to the other side of the narrow cargo hold. She was supposed to fly to Bethel next to a coffin?

"At least you know he won't talk your ear off." The pilot laughed, and then he sealed Trixie inside.

She sat on the duffels and flattened herself against the riveted metal wall. Through the mesh web that separated her from the pilot and the vet, she could hear talking. The plane vibrated to life.

Three days ago, if someone had told her she'd be riding in a flying bus beside a dead body, she would have flat-out denied it. But desperation can do amazing things to a person. Trixie could remember her history teacher telling the class about the starving man in a Virginia settlement who'd killed, salted, and eaten his wife one winter before the rest of the colonists ever noticed she was missing. What you'd deem impossible one day might look promising the next.

As the plane canted off the ground, the pine box slid toward Trixie, jamming up against the soles of her shoes. *It could be worse,* she thought. He might not be in a coffin but in a body bag. He might not be some random dead guy but Jason.

They climbed into the night, a rich batter mixed with stars. Up here, it was even colder. Trixie pulled down the sleeves of her jacket.

*Ooooh.*

She leaned toward the mesh to speak into the front of the cockpit. The vet was already asleep. "Did you say something?" she called to the pilot.

"Nope!"

Trixie settled back against the side of the plane and heard it again: the quiet long note of someone singing his soul.

It was coming from underneath the lid of the pine box.

Trixie froze. It had to be the engine. Or maybe the veterinarian snored. But even louder this time, she could trace the origin to the coffin: *Ohhhhh.*

What if the person wasn't dead at all? What if he'd been stapled into this box and was trying to get out? What if he was scratching at the insides, splinters under his fingernails, wondering how he'd ever wound up in there?

*Ohhh,* the body sighed. *Noooo.*

She came up on her knees, grabbing through the mesh at the bush pilot's shoulder. "Stop the plane," she cried. "You have to stop right now!"

"You should have gone before we left," the pilot yelled back.

"That body . . . it's not dead!"

By now, she'd awakened the vet, who turned around in the passenger seat. "What's the matter—"

Trixie couldn't look back at the coffin; if she did there would be an arm reaching out of that box, a face she couldn't lose in her nightmares, a voice telling her that he knew the secret she hadn't told anyone else.

*Ooooh.*

"There," Trixie said. "Can't you hear that?"

The vet laughed. "It's the lungs expanding. Like when you take a bag of potato chips on a plane and it puffs up after liftoff? That's all you're hearing—air going over the vocal cords." He grinned at her. "Maybe you ought to lay off the caffeine."

Mortified, Trixie turned back toward the coffin. She could hear the pilot and the vet bonding over her stupidity, and her cheeks burned. The body—dead as could be, dead as the wood it was surrounded by—continued to sing: one lonely note that filled the hold of the plane like a requiem, like the truth no one wanted to hear.

"This really is a shock," said Jeb Aaronsen, the principal of Bethel High. "Trixie seemed to be getting along so well in school."

Bartholemew didn't even spare him a sideways glance. "Before or after she stopped coming altogether?"

He didn't have a lot of patience for this principal, who hadn't noticed any change in his own daughter's behavior, either, when she'd been a student here. Aaronsen always put on his tragedy face but couldn't seem to keep the next one from happening.

Bartholemew was tired. He'd traced the Stones to the airport, where they'd boarded a plane to Seattle. That would connect to one that landed in Anchorage just shy of midnight. They'd paid $1,292.90 per ticket, according to the American Express agent who'd given the detective the lead.

Now he knew where Trixie was headed. He just had to convince a judge that she needed to be brought home.

Bartholemew had awakened the principal and waved the search warrant. The only other people in the school at this time of night were the janitors, who nodded and pushed their rolling trash receptacles out of the way as the men passed. It was strange—almost eerie—to be in a high school that was so patently devoid of commotion.

"We knew the . . . incident was . . . difficult on her," the principal said. "Mrs. Gray in guidance was keeping an eye on Trixie."

Bartholemew didn't even bother to answer. The administration at Bethel High was no different from any other group of adults in America: Rather than see what was right under their noses, they pretended that everything was exactly like they wanted it to be. What had Mrs. Gray been doing when Trixie was carving up her skin and slitting her wrists? Or, for that matter, when Holly had skipped classes and stopped eating?

"Trixie knew she could have come to us if she was feeling ostracized," the principal said, and then he stopped in front of a drab olive locker. "This is the one."

Bartholemew lifted the bolt cutters he'd brought from the fire department and snipped the combination lock. He opened the metal latch, only to have dozens of condoms spring out of the locker like a nest of snakes. Bartholemew picked up one string of Trojans. "Good thing she wasn't being ostracized," he said.

The principal murmured something and disappeared down the hallway, leaving Bartholemew alone. He snapped on a pair of rubber gloves and pulled a paper bag out of his coat pocket. Then he brushed the remaining condoms from the innards of the locker and stepped closer to investigate.

There was an algebra textbook. A dog-eared copy of *Romeo and Juliet.* Forty-six cents in assorted change. A ruler. A broken binder clip. Mounted on the swinging door underneath a sticker that said HOOBASTANK was a tiny compact mirror with a flower painted in the corner. It had been smashed hard enough to crack, and the bottom left corner was missing.

Bartholemew found himself looking at it and wondering what Trixie Stone had seen in there. Did she picture the girl she'd been at the beginning of ninth grade—a kid, really, checking out what was going on in the hall behind her and wishing she could be a part of it? Or did she see the shell she'd become—one of the dozens of faceless adolescents in Bethel High who made it through the day by praying, one step at a time, they wouldn't attract anyone's notice?

Bartholemew peered into Trixie's locker again. It was like a still life, without the life.

There was no gauze or box of Band-Aids. There was no shirt crumpled into the corner, stained with Trixie's blood. Bartholemew was about to give up when he noticed the edge of a photo, jammed down into the joint between the back metal wall and the floor of the locker. Pulling a pair of tweezers out of his pocket. Bartholemew managed to inch it free.

It was a picture of two vampires, their mouths dripping with blood. Bartholemew did a double take, then looked again and realized the girls were holding a half-eaten bucket of cherries. Zephyr Santorelli-Weinstein was on the left. Her mouth was a bright crimson, her teeth stained, too. The other girl must have been Trixie Stone, although he would have been hard-pressed to make an identification. In the photo, she was laughing so hard her eyes had narrowed to slits. Her hair was nearly the same color as the fruit and fell all the way down her back.

Until he saw that, he'd forgotten. When Bartholemew had first met Trixie Stone, her hair had reached down to her waist. The second time they'd met, those locks had been brutally shorn. He remembered Janice the rape advocate telling

him that it was a positive step, a donation Trixie
had made to a charity that made wigs for cancer
patients.

A charity that would have taken, recorded, and
labeled Trixie Stone's hair.

Daniel and Laura sat in an airport bar, waiting. A
snowstorm in Anchorage had delayed the connecting flight out of Seattle, and so far three hours
had passed, three hours that Trixie was getting farther away from them.

Laura had tossed back three drinks already.
Daniel wasn't sure if it was because of her fear of
heights and flying in general, or her worry about
Trixie, or a combination of both. There was, of
course, the chance that they had been wrong—
that Trixie was heading south to Mexico, or sleeping in a train station in Pennsylvania. But then
again, Trixie wouldn't be the first kid in trouble to
turn to Alaska. So many folks on the run from the
law wound up there—the last great frontier—that
states had long ago given up spending the money
to come pick them up. Instead, the Alaska state
troopers hunted down fugitives from justice. Daniel
could remember reading newspaper stories about
people who were dragged out of cabins in the
bush and extradited on charges of rape or kidnapping or murder. He wondered if Trixie's picture was
being e-mailed to sergeants around Alaska, if
they'd already started to search.

There was a difference, though, between
searching and hunting, one he'd learned with Cane

and his grandfather. *You have to clear your mind of the thoughts of the animal*, the old man used to say, *or he'll see you coming.* Daniel would focus, wishing he was less white and more like Cane— who, if you told him, "Don't think of a purple elephant," could truly *not* think of a purple elephant.

The difference here was that if Daniel wanted to find Trixie, he couldn't afford to *stop* thinking about her. That way, she'd know that he was looking.

Daniel moved a martini glass that had been on the bar when they first sat down—someone's leftovers. You didn't have to clean up after yourself; there was always waitstaff to do it for you. That was one difference between Eskimo culture and white culture he'd never quite understood—people in the lower forty-eight had no responsibility to anyone else. You looked out for number one; you fended for yourself. If you interfered in someone else's business—even with the best of intentions— you might suddenly be held accountable for whatever went wrong. The good Samaritan who pulled a man from a burning car could be sued for injuries caused during the process.

On the other hand, the Yupiit knew that everyone was connected—man and beast, stranger and stranger, husband and wife, father and child. Cut yourself, and someone else bled. Rescue another, and you might save yourself.

Daniel shuddered as more memories passed through him. There were disjointed images, like the Kilbuck Mountains in the distance flattened by an air inversion in the utter cold. There were unfamiliar sounds, like the plaintive aria of sled dogs waiting for their dinner. And there were distinctive smells, like the oily ribbon of drying salmon that blew in from fish camp. He felt as if he were picking up the thread of a life he had forgotten weaving and being expected to continue the pattern.

And yet, in the airport were a thousand reminders of how he'd been living for the past two decades. Travelers belched out of jetways, dragging wheeled carry-ons and hauling wrapped presents in oversized department store bags. The smell of strong coffee drifted from the Starbucks stand across the way. Carols played in an endless loop on the speaker system, interrupted by the occasional call for a porter with a wheelchair.

When Laura spoke, he nearly jumped out of his seat. "What do you think will happen?"

Daniel glanced at her. "I don't know." He grimaced, thinking of all that could go wrong from this point on for Trixie: frostbite, fever, animals she could not fight, losing her way. Losing herself. "I just wish she'd come to me instead of running off."

Laura looked down at the table. "Maybe she was afraid you'd think the worst."

Was he that transparent? Although Daniel had told himself Trixie hadn't killed Jason, although he'd say this till he went hoarse, there was a seed of doubt that had started to blossom, and it was choking his optimism. The Trixie he knew could not have killed Jason; but then, it had already been proved that there was a great deal about Trixie he didn't know.

Here, though, was the remarkable thing: It didn't matter. Trixie could have told him that she killed Jason with her bare hands, and he would have understood. Who knew better than Daniel that everyone had a beast inside, that sometimes it came out of hiding?

What he wished he had been able to tell Trixie was that she wasn't alone. Over the past two weeks, this metamorphosis had been happening to him, too. Daniel had kidnapped Jason; he'd beaten the boy. He'd lied to the police. And now he was headed to Alaska—the place he hated more than anywhere else on earth. Daniel Stone was falling away, one civilized scale at a time, and before long he'd be an animal again—just like the Yupiit believed.

Daniel would find Trixie, even if it meant he had to walk across every mile of Alaska to do it. He'd find her, even if he had to slip into his old skin—lying, stealing, hurting anyone who stood in his way. He'd find Trixie, and he'd convince her that nothing she could do or say would make him love her any less.

He just hoped when she saw what he'd become for her, she'd feel the same way.

The race headquarters for the K300 were already in full swing when Trixie arrived with the veterinarian shortly after six o'clock. There were lists posted on dry-erase boards: the names of the mushers, with grids to post their progress at a dozen race checkpoints. There were rule books and maps of the course. Behind one table a woman sat at a bank of phones, answering the same questions over and over. Yes, the race started at eight P.M. Yes, DeeDee Jonrowe was wearing bib number one. No, they didn't have enough volunteers.

People who arrived by snow machine stripped off several layers the minute they walked into the Long House Inn. Everyone wore footwear with soles so thick they looked like moon boots, and sealskin hats with flaps that hung down over the ears. There were one-piece snowsuits and elaborately embroidered fur parkas. When the occasional musher came in, he was treated like a rock star—people lined up to shake his hand and wish him the best of luck. Everyone seemed to know everyone else.

You'd think that in this environment, Trixie would have looked ridiculously out of place, but if anyone noticed her presence, they didn't seem to care. She wasn't stopped when she took a bowl of stew from the Crock Pot on the back table and then went back seconds later for another helping. It wasn't beef—frankly, she was a little scared to find out *what* it was—but it was the first food she'd eaten in almost two days, and at that point, anything would have been delicious.

Suddenly the woman behind the table stood up and started toward Trixie. She froze, anticipating a moment of reckoning. "Let me guess," she said. "You're Andi?"

Trixie forced a smile. "How'd you know?"

"The other JVs called from Tuluksak and said you were new and you'd gotten snowed in Outside."

"Outside where?"

The woman grinned. "Sorry, that's what we call all the other states. We'll get someone to run you to the checkpoint before the mushers arrive."

"Tuluksak," Trixie repeated. The word tasted like iron. "I was hoping to get to Akiak."

"Well, Tuluksak's where we stick all the Jesuit Volunteers who work up here. Don't worry—we haven't lost one yet." She nodded toward a box. "I'm Jen, by the way. And it would be really great if you could help me carry that down to the starting line."

Trixie hefted the box, which was full of camera equipment, as Jen pulled her face mask up over her nose and mouth. "You might want your coat," she said.

"This is all I brought," Trixie replied. "My, um, friends have my stuff with them."

She didn't know if this lie would even make sense, since she hadn't understood any of Jen's comments about Jesuit Volunteers and Tuluksak in the first place. But Jen just rolled her eyes and dragged her toward a table covered with K300 merchandise for sale. "Here," she said, tossing her a big fleece jacket and mittens and a hat that Velcroed under the chin. She took a pair of boots and a heavy anorak from behind the headquarter tables. "These'll be too big, but Harry'll be too drunk later to notice they're missing."

As Trixie followed Jen out of the Long House, winter smacked her with an open hand. It wasn't just cold, the way it got in Maine in December. It was bone-deep cold, the kind that wrapped around your spine and turned your breath into tiny crystals, the kind that matted your eyelashes together with ice. Snow was piled on both sides of the walkway, and snow machines were parked at right angles in between a few rusted trucks.

Jen walked toward one of the pickups. It was white, but one of the doors was red, as if it had been amputated from a different junk heap for transplant onto this one. Tufts of stuffing and coils sprang out from the passenger side of the bench. There were no seat belts. It looked nothing like Trixie's father's truck, but as she slid into the passenger seat, homesickness slipped like a knife between her ribs.

Jen coaxed the truck's engine into turning over. "Since when did the Jesuit Volunteers start recruiting on playgrounds?"

Trixie's heart started to pound. "Oh, I'm twenty-one," she said. "I just look way younger."

"Either that, or I'm getting too damn old." She nodded toward a bottle of Jägermeister jammed into the ashtray. "Feel free to have some, if you want."

Trixie unscrewed the cap of the bottle. She took a tentative sip, then spit the liquor across the dashboard.

Jen laughed. "Right. Jesuit Volunteer. I forgot." She watched Trixie furiously trying to wipe the mess up with her mitten. "Don't worry, I think that it's got enough alcohol in it to qualify as cleaning fluid."

She took a sharp right, turning the pickup over the edge of a snowbank. Trixie panicked—there was no road. The truck slid down an icy hill onto the surface of a frozen river, and then Jen began to drive to the center of it.

A makeshift start and finish line had been erected, with two long chutes cordoned off and a banner overhead proclaiming the K300. Beside it was a flatbed truck, on which stood a man testing a microphone. A steady stream of dilapidated pickups and snow machines pulled onto the ice, parking in ragged lines. Some pulled trailers with fancy kennel names painted across them; others had a litter of barking dogs in the back. In the distance was a belching hovercraft, one that Jen explained brought the mail downriver. Tonight it was serving free hot dogs, in honor of the race.

A pair of enormous flood lamps illuminated the night, and for the first time since she'd landed in Bethel, Trixie got a good look at the Alaskan tundra. The landscape was layered in pale blues and flat silvers; the sky was an overturned bowl of stars that fell into the hoods of the Yup'ik children balanced on their fathers' shoulders. Ice stretched as far as she could see. Here, it was easy to understand how people once thought you could fall off the edge of the world.

It all looked familiar to Trixie, as impossible as

that might be. And then she realized it *was*. This was exactly how her father drew hell.

As mushers hooked dogs to their sleds, a crowd gathered around the chute. All the people looked immense and overstuffed in their outside gear. Children held their hands out to the dogs to sniff, getting tangled in the lead lines.

"Andi. Andi?"

When Trixie didn't answer—she forgot that was the name she'd been given this time—Jen tapped her on the shoulder. Standing beside her was a Yup'ik Eskimo boy not much older than Trixie. He had a wide face the color of hazelnuts, and amazingly, he wasn't wearing a hat. "Willie's going to take you up to Tuluksak," Jen said.

"Thanks," Trixie answered.

The boy wouldn't look her in the eye. He turned away and started walking, which Trixie assumed was the cue that she was supposed to follow. He stopped at a snow machine, nodded at it, and then walked away from her.

Willie disappeared quickly into the dark ring of night outside the flood lamp. Trixie hesitated beside the snow machine, not sure what she was supposed to do. Follow him? Figure out how to turn this thing on herself?

Trixie touched one of the handlebars. The snow machine smelled like exhaust, like her father's lawn mower.

She was about to look for an On switch when Willie returned, holding an oversized winter parka with black wolf fur sewn into the hood. Still averting his glance, he held it out to her. When she didn't take it, he mimed putting it on.

There was still heat trapped inside. Trixie wondered whom he'd taken this jacket from, if he or she was shivering now in the cold. Her hands were lost in the sleeves, and when she pulled up the hood, it blocked the wind from her face.

Willie climbed onto the snow machine and waited for Trixie to do the same. She glanced at him—what if he didn't know his way to Tuluksak? Even if he did, what was she going to do when everyone realized Trixie wasn't the person they were expecting? Most important, how was she supposed to get on the back of this thing without having to lean up against this boy?

With all of their layers, it was a tight fit. Trixie pushed herself back to the very edge of the seat, holding on to the rails at the sides with her mittened hands. Willie pulled the rip cord to start the machine and they groaned forward slowly, to keep the dogs from startling. He maneuvered around the chute and then gunned the engine, so that they flew across the ice.

If it was cold standing around, it was fifty times colder on a snow machine blasting at full throttle. Trixie couldn't imagine not having the parka; as it was, she was shivering inside it and had curled her hands into fists.

The headlamp on the front of the machine cut a tiny visible triangle in front of them. There was no road whatsoever. There were no street signs, no traffic lights, no exit ramps. "Hey," Trixie yelled into the wind. "Do you know where you're going?"

Willie didn't answer.

Trixie grasped onto the handholds more firmly. It was dizzying, going at this speed without being able to see. She listed to the left as Willie drove up a bank, through a narrow copse of trees, and then back out onto a finger of the frozen river.

"My name's Trixie," she said, not because she expected an answer but because it kept her teeth from chattering. After she spoke, she remembered that she was supposed to be someone else. "Well, it's Trixie, but they call me Andi." *God,* she thought. *Could I sound any more stupid if I tried?*

The wind blew into Trixie's eyes, which—as they started tearing—froze shut. She found herself huddling forward, her forehead nearly touching Willie's back. Heat rose off him in waves.

As they drove, she pretended that she was lying prone in the back of her father's pickup, feeling it vibrate underneath her as he bounced into the parking lot of the drive-in. The metal flatbed pressed against her cheek was still warm from a whole day of sun. They would eat so much popcorn that her mother would be able to smell it on their clothes even after she'd put them through the wash.

A frigid blast of air hit her full in the face. "Are we going to be there soon?" Trixie asked, and then, at Willie's silence, "Do you even speak *English*?"

To her surprise, he ground the brakes, until the snow machine came to a stop. Willie turned around, still avoiding her gaze. "It's fifty-five miles," he said. "Are you going to yap the whole time?"

Stung, Trixie turned away and noticed the eerie light that had spilled onto the surface of the river up ahead. She traced it to its overhead origin—a wash of pink and white and green that reminded her of the smoke trails left behind by fireworks on the Fourth of July.

Who knew that when you cut a slit in the belly of the night sky, it bled color?

"That's beautiful," Trixie whispered.

Willie followed her gaze. *"Qiuryaq."*

She didn't know if that meant *Shut up* or *Hold on* or maybe even *I'm sorry.* But this time when he started the sled, she tilted her face to the Northern Lights. Looking up here was hypnotic and less harrowing than trying to squint at the imaginary road. Looking up here, it was almost easy to imagine they were nearly home.

# 7

Max Giff-Reynolds had made a career out of focusing on the things most people never saw: a carpet fiber trapped on the inside edge of a victim's coat, a grain of sand left at a crime scene that was indigenous to a certain part of the country, the dust of a coffee grinder on the makings of a dirty bomb. As one of two hundred forensic microscopists in the country, he was in high demand. Chances were that Mike Bartholemew would never have gotten anywhere close to him for an analysis of Trixie's hair sample—if he hadn't known Max when he was a skinny little geek in college, back when they were roommates and Bartholemew served as bodyguard in return for private tutorials in chemistry and physics.

He'd driven to Boston that night with a hank of Trixie Stone's hair on the seat beside him. The salon, Live and Let Dye, hadn't even sent the sample in to Locks of Love yet; it had been languishing in a drawer in the back room near the peroxide and the paraffin wax. Now he was sitting on top of a counter, waiting for Max to tell him something useful.

The lab was piled with boxes of dust and hair and fiber for comparison. A poster of Max's hero, Edmond Locard, hung over his polarized-light microscope. Bartholemew could remember Max reading books about Locard, the father of forensic science, even back at U Maine. "He burned off his fingerprints," Max had told him once with admiration, "just to see if they grew back in the same patterns!"

It had been almost thirty years since they'd graduated, but Max looked the same. Balder, but still skinny, with a permanent curve to his back that came from bending over a microscope. "Huh," he said.

"What's that mean?"

Max pushed back from his workspace. "What do you know about hair?"

Bartholemew grinned at the other man's gleaming pate. "More than you do."

"Hair's got three layers that are important, in terms of forensics," Max said, ignoring his comment. "The cortex, the cuticle, and the medulla. If you think of a piece of hair as a pencil, the medulla is the graphite, the cortex is the wood, and the paint on the outside is the cuticle. The medulla is sometimes in pieces and differs from hair to hair on the same human head. The cells in the cortex have pigment, which is pretty much what I'm trying to match up between your two samples. You with me so far?"

Bartholemew nodded.

"I can tell you, by looking at a hair, if it's human or not. I can tell you if it came from someone of Caucasian, Negroid, or Mongolian origin. I can tell you where it came from on the body and whether the hair was forcibly removed or burned or crushed. I can tell you that a hair excludes a suspect, but I can't use it to pinpoint a particular one."

He spoke as he bent over the microscope again. "What I'm seeing in both samples is a moderate shaft diameter and diameter variation, medulla continuous and relatively narrow, soft texture. That means they're both hairs from a human head. The hue, value, and intensity of the color are nearly identical. The tip of your known sample was cut with a pair of scissors; the other still has a root attached, which is soft and distorted—telling me it was yanked out. Pigment varies a bit between the two samples, although not enough for me to draw any conclusion. However, the cortex of the hair you found on the victim's body is much more prominent than the hairs in the known sample."

"The known sample came from a haircut three weeks before the murder," Bartholemew said. "Isn't it possible that during those three weeks, the cortex got more . . . what did you say again?"

"Prominent," Max answered. "Yeah, it's possible, especially if the suspect had some kind of chemical hair treatment or was excessively exposed to sunlight or wind. Theoretically, it's also possible for two hairs from the same human head to just plain look different. But there's also the chance, here, that you're talking about two different heads." He looked at Bartholemew. "If you asked me to get up in front of a jury, I couldn't tell them conclusively that these two hairs came from the same person."

Bartholemew felt like he'd been punched in the chest. He'd been so certain that he'd been on the right track here, that Trixie Stone's disappearance flagged her involvement in the murder of Jason Underhill.

"Hey," Max said, looking at his face. "I don't admit this to many people, but microscopy's not always an exact science. Even when I think I *do* see a match, I tell detectives to get a DNA analysis to back up what the scope says."

Mike sighed. "I have a root on only *one* of the hairs. That rules out DNA."

"It rules out *nuclear* DNA," Max corrected. He leaned over and took a card out of his desk. He scribbled something on the back and handed it to Bartholemew. "Skip's a friend of mine, at a private lab in Virginia. Make sure you say I sent you."

Bartholemew took the card. SKIPPER JOHANSSEN, he read. GENETTA LABS. MITOCHONDRIAL DNA.

By the time the storm blew in, Trixie had already lost feeling in her toes. She was nearly catatonic, lulled by the cold and the exhaust of the snow machine. At the first strike of ice against her cheek, Trixie blinked back to awareness. They were still somewhere on the river—the scenery looked no different than it had an hour ago, except that the lights in the sky had vanished, washed over by gray clouds that touched down at the line of the horizon.

Snow howled. Visibility grew even worse. Trixie began to imagine that she had fallen into one of her father's comic book panels, one filled with Kirby crackle—the burst of white bubbles that Jack Kirby, a penciler from years ago, had invented to show an energy field. The shapes in the darkness turned into villains from her father's art—twisted trees became the clawed arms of a witch; icicles were the bared fangs of a demon.

Willie slowed the snow machine to a crawl and then stopped it altogether. He shouted to Trixie over the roar of the wind. "We have to wait this out. It'll clear up by morning."

Trixie wanted to answer him, but she'd spent so long clenching her jaw shut that she couldn't pry it open wide enough for a word.

Willie moved to the back of the machine, rummaging around. He handed her a blue tarp. "Tuck this under the treads," he said. "We can use it to get out of the wind."

He left her to her own devices and disappeared into the whorls of snow. Trixie wanted to cry. She was so cold that she couldn't even classify it as cold anymore; she had no idea what he meant by *treads*, and she wanted to go home. She clutched the tarp against her parka, not moving, wishing that Willie would come back.

She saw him moving in and out of the beam cast by the snow machine's headlight. He seemed to be snapping off the branches of a dead tree next to the riverbank. When he saw her still sitting on the snow machine, he walked up to her. She expected him to scream about not pulling her weight, but instead his mouth tightened and he helped her off. "Get under here," he said, and he had her sit with her back to the snow machine before he wrapped it in the tarp and pulled it over her, an awning to cut the wind.

It wasn't perfect. There were three large slits in the tarp, and the snow and ice unerringly found those gashes. Willie crouched down at Trixie's feet and peeled some of the bark off the birch branches he'd gathered, tucking it between lengths of cottonwood and alder. He poured a little gas from the snow machine on top of the pile and ignited it with a lighter from his pocket. Only when she could feel the fire against her skin did she let herself wonder how cold it might be out here.

Trixie remembered learning that the human body was, like, sixty percent water. How many degrees below zero did it have to get before you literally froze to death?

"Come on," Willie said. "Let's get some grass."

The last thing Trixie wanted to do right now was smoke weed. She tried to shake her head, but even that set of muscles had stopped working. When she didn't get up, he turned away, as if she wasn't even worth bothering with. "Wait," she said, and although he didn't look at her, he stopped moving. She wanted to explain how her feet felt like blocks and her fingers stung so bad that she had to keep biting down on her lower lip. She wanted to tell him how her shoulders hurt from trying not to shiver. She wanted to tell him she was scared and that when she imagined running away, this hadn't entered into it. "I c-can't move," Trixie said.

Willie knelt beside her. "What can't you feel?"

She didn't know how to answer that. Comfort? Safety?

He began unlacing Trixie's boots. Matter-of-factly, he cupped his hands around one of her feet. "I don't have a sleeping bag. I let my cousin Ernie take it, he's one of the mushers, and the officials check to see if you have one before you start the race." Then, just when Trixie could move her toes again, just as a searing burn shot from her nails to the arch of her foot, Willie stood up and left.

He came back a few minutes later with an armful of dead grass. It was still dusted with snow; Willie had dug it out from the edge of the riverbank. He packed the grass in Trixie's boots and mittens. He told her to stuff some under her parka.

"How long will it snow?" Trixie asked.

Willie shrugged.

"How come you don't talk?"

Willie rocked back on his heels, his boots crunching in the snow. "How come you think you have to talk to say something?" He pulled off his mittens and toasted his hands over the fire. "You've got frostnip."

"What's that?"

"Frostbite, before it happens."

Trixie tried to remember what she knew about frostbite. Didn't the affected body part turn black and fall off? "Where?" she panicked.

"Between your eyes. On your cheek."

Her *face* was going to fall off?

Willie gestured, almost delicately, in a way that let her know he wanted to move closer to her, to place his hand on her. It was at that moment that Trixie realized she was in the company of a boy who was stronger than she was, in the middle of nowhere, a good twenty-five miles away from anyone who'd hear her scream. She leaned away from him, shaking her head, as her throat closed like a rose after dark.

His fingers caught her at the wrist, and Trixie's heart started hammering harder. She closed her eyes, expecting the worst, thinking that maybe if you'd lived a nightmare once it wasn't quite as bad the second time around.

Willie's palm, hot as a stone in the sun, pressed against her cheek. She felt his other hand touch her forehead, then sweep down the side of her face to cup her jaw.

She could feel calluses on his skin, and she wondered where they'd come from. Trixie opened her eyes and, for the first time since she'd met him, found Willie Moses looking right at her.

Skipper Johanssen, the mitochondrial DNA expert, was a woman. Bartholemew watched her pour sugar into her coffee and look over the notes on the case that he'd brought. "Unusual name," he said.

"Mom had a Barbie thing going on."

She was beautiful: straight platinum hair that swept the middle of her back, green eyes hidden behind her thick-framed black glasses. When she read, sometimes her mouth formed the words. "What do you know about mitochondrial DNA?" she asked.

"That you can hopefully use it to compare two hairs?"

"Well, yeah, you can. The real question is what you want to do with that comparison." Skipper leaned back in her chair. "Thanks to *C.S.I.*, everyone's heard about DNA analysis. Most of the time they're talking about nuclear DNA, the kind that comes, in equal halves, from your mother and your father. But there's another kind of DNA that's the up-and-comer in the forensic community—mitochondrial DNA. And even though you may not know a lot about it, you—and the rest of the world—know the largest case in history where it was used: 9/11."

"To identify the remains?"

"Exactly," Skipper said. "Traditional efforts didn't work—they couldn't find intact teeth, or bones that weren't crushed, or even anything to X-ray. But mtDNA can be used to profile samples that have been burned, pulverized, you name it. All scientists need is a saliva sample from a family member of the deceased in order to make a comparison."

She picked up the hair sample that Max had scrutinized under a microscope the previous day. "The reason we can test this for DNA—without a root attached—is that a cell isn't made up of just a nucleus. There are many more parts—including the mitochondria, which are basically the powerhouses that keep the cell functional. There are hundreds of mitochondria in a cell, as compared to a single nucleus. And each mitochondrion contains several copies of the mtDNA we're interested in."

"If there's so much more mtDNA than nuclear DNA, why isn't it used all the time for criminal profiling?" Bartholemew asked.

"Well, there's a catch. Typically, when you get a nuclear DNA profile, the chances of finding another person with that profile are one in six billion. Mitochondrial DNA stats are far less discriminating, because unlike nuclear DNA, you inherit mtDNA only from your mom. That means that you and your brothers and sisters all have the same mtDNA she does . . . and that *her* mom and siblings do, and so on. It's actually fascinating—a female egg cell possesses tons of mitochondria, as compared to the sperm cell. At fertilization, not only are the few sperm mitochondria totally outnumbered, they're actually destroyed." Skipper smiled brightly. "Natural selection at its finest."

"It's a pity you have to keep us around for that

whole fertilization thing in the first place," Bartholemew said dryly.

"Ah, but you should see what's going on next
door to me in the cloning lab," Skipper replied.
"Anyway, my point is that mtDNA isn't helpful if
you're choosing between two biological siblings to
pinpoint a suspect, but it's a nice tool if you're
looking to exclude someone nonrelated from an investigation. Statistically, if you test fifteen spots on
the DNA strand, there are more than an octillion
nuclear DNA profiles, which is awfully nice when
you're in front of a jury and trying to pin down a
particular individual. But with mtDNA, there are
only forty-eight hundred sequences logged to
date . . . and another six thousand reported in scientific literature. With mtDNA, you might wind up
with a relative frequency of point one four or something like that—basically, a subject will share a profile with four percent of the world's population. It's
not specific enough to nail a perp without reasonable doubt in front of a jury, but it would allow you
to rule someone out as a suspect because he or
she *doesn't* have that particular profile."

"So if the mtDNA profile of the hair found on the
victim's body *doesn't* match the one for Trixie
Stone's hair," Bartholemew said, "then I can't link
her to the murder."

"Correct."

"And if it does match?"

Skipper glanced up. "Then you've got reasonable cause to arrest her."

•  •  •

The sun skipped the Alaskan tundra. At least, that's how it seemed to Laura, or why else would it be pitch-dark at nine in the morning? She anxiously waited for the flight attendant to open the hatch of the plane, now that they had landed in Bethel. It was bad enough that she had a fear of heights and hated flying, but this was only half a plane, really—the front end was devoted to cargo.

"How are you doing?" Daniel asked.

"Fantastic," Laura said, trying to lighten her voice. "It could have been a Cessna, right?"

Daniel turned just as they were about to exit the plane and pulled up the hood of her jacket. He tugged on the strings and tied them under her chin, just like he used to do when Trixie was tiny and headed out to play in the snow. "It's colder than you think," he said, and he stepped onto the rollaway staircase that led to the runway.

It was an understatement. The wind was a knife that cut her to ribbons; the act of breathing felt like swallowing glass. Laura followed Daniel across the runway, hurrying into a small, squat building.

The airport consisted of chairs arranged in narrow rows and a single ticket counter. It wasn't manned, because the lone employee had moved to the metal detector, to screen passengers on the outbound flight. Laura watched two native girls hugging an older woman, all three of them crying as they inched toward the gate.

There were signs in both English and Yup'ik. "Does that mean *bathroom*?" Laura asked, pointing to a doorway with the word ANARVIK overhead.

"Well, there's no Yup'ik word for bathroom," Daniel said, smiling a little. "That actually translates to 'the place to shit.' "

The single door split off to the right and the left. The men's and women's rooms were not marked, but she could glimpse a urinal in one direction, so she walked the opposite way. The sinks were operated by push pedals; she pumped one to start the flow of water and then splashed some on her face. She looked at herself in the mirror.

*If someone else walks into the bathroom*, she thought, *I will stop being a coward.*

*If the family outside has made it through security, to the gate.*

*If Daniel is facing forward, when I come out.*

She used to play this game with herself all the time. If the light changed before she counted to ten, then she would go Seth's after class. If Daniel picked up before the third ring, she would stay an extra five minutes.

She'd take these random occurrences and elevate them to oracles; she'd pretend that they were enough to justify her actions.

Or lack therof.

Wiping her hands on her jacket, she stepped outside to find the family still crying near the metal detector and Daniel facing out the window.

Laura sighed with relief and walked toward him.

Trixie was shivering so hard that she kept shaking off the quilt of dead grass Willie had used to cover them for warmth. It wasn't like a blanket you could just pull over yourself; you had to burrow down and think warm thoughts and hope for the best. Her feet still ached and her hair was frozen against her head. She was consciously awake—somehow she thought that sleeping was too close to the line of being blue and stiff and dead, and that you might pass from one side to the other without any fanfare.

Willie's breath came out in little white clouds that floated in the air like Chinese lanterns on a string. His eyes were closed, which meant Trixie could stare at him as much as she wanted. She wondered what it was like to grow up here, to have a snowstorm hit like this and to know how to save yourself, instead of needing someone to do it for you. She wondered if her father knew this sort of stuff too, if elemental knowledge about living and dying might be underneath all the other, ordinary things he knew, like how to draw a devil and change a fuse and not burn pancakes.

"Are you awake?" she murmured.

Willie didn't open his eyes, but he nodded the tiniest bit, and a stream of white flowed out of his nostrils.

There was a warm zone connecting them. They were lying two feet apart, with grass heaped in the space between their bodies, but every time Trixie turned his way she could feel heat conducting through the dried straw, pulsing like light from a star. When she thought he might not notice, she inched infinitesimally closer.

"Do you know anyone who ever died out here?" Trixie asked.

"Yeah," Willie said. "That's why you don't make a cave in a snowbank. If you die, no one can ever find you, and then your spirit won't ever rest."

Trixie felt her eyes get damp, and that was awful, because almost immediately her lashes sealed shut again. She thought of the ladders she'd cut on her arms, the way she'd wanted to feel real pain instead of the hurt gnawed on her heart. Well, she'd gotten what she wanted, hadn't she? Her toes burned like fire; her fingers had swollen like sausages and ached. The thought of that delicate razor blade being drawn across her skin seemed, by comparison, ridiculous, a drama for someone who didn't really know what tragedy was.

Maybe it took realizing that you *could* die to keep you from wanting to do it.

Trixie wiped her nose and pressed her fingertips against her eyelashes to dissolve the ice. "I don't want to freeze to death," she whispered.

Willie swallowed. "Well . . . there is *one* way to get warmer."

"How?"

"Take off our clothes."

"Yeah, right," Trixie scoffed.

"I'm not bullshitting you." Willie glanced away. "We both get . . . you know . . . and then huddle together."

Trixie stared at him. She didn't want to be pressed up against him; she kept thinking of what had happened the last time she was this close to a boy.

"It's just what you do," Willie said. "It's not like it means anything. My dad's stripped down naked with other guys, when they get stuck overnight."

Trixie pictured her father doing this—but stopped abruptly when she got to the part where she had to imagine him without clothes.

"Last time it happened, my dad had to cuddle up to old Ellis Puuqatak the whole night. He swore he'd never leave home again without a sleeping bag."

Trixie watched Willie's words crystallize in the cold, each as differentiated as a snowflake, and she knew he was telling her the truth. "You have to close your eyes first," she said, hesitant.

She shucked off her jeans, anorak, and sweater. She left on her bra and panties, because she *had* to.

"Now you," Trixie said, and she looked away as he pulled off his coat and his shirt. She peeked, though. His back was the color of the outside of an almond, and his shoulder blades flexed like pistons. He took off his jeans, hopping around and making little sounds, like a person at the town pool who makes a big deal when he finally manages to get into the cold water.

Willie spread some grass on the ground, then lay down and motioned for Trixie to do the same. He drew their jackets over them, like a blanket, and then covered these with more grass.

Trixie squeezed her eyes shut. She could feel

the rustle of the straw as he moved closer and the
itch of the grass on her bare skin as it caught between them. Willie's hand touched her back, and
she stiffened as he came up behind her, curling his
knees into the hollow bowl made by the bend of
her own. She took deep breaths. She tried not to
remember the last boy she'd touched, the last boy
who'd touched her.

The inferno began where his fingers rested on
her shoulder and spread to every spot where their
skin was touching. Pressed up against Willie, Trixie
didn't find herself thinking about Jason, or the
night of the rape. She didn't feel threatened or
even frightened. She simply felt, for the first time in
hours, warm. "Did you ever know someone who
died?" she asked. "Someone our age?"

It took Willie a moment, but he answered. "Yes."

The bitter wind beat against their tarp and made
its loose tongue rattle like a gossip's. Trixie un-
clenched her fists. "Me too," she said.

Bethel was technically a city, but not by any normal standards. The population was less than six
thousand, although it was the closest hub for fifty-
three native villages along the river. There were
only about thirteen miles of roads, most of them
unpaved. Daniel opened the terminal's door and
turned to Laura. "We can get a taxi," he said.

"There are *taxis* here?"

"Most people don't have cars. If you've got a
boat and a snow-go, you're pretty much set."

The cab driver was a tiny Asian woman with a

massive bun perched on her head like an avalanche waiting to happen. She wore fake Gucci sunglasses, although it was still dark outside, and was listening to Patsy Cline on the radio. "Where you go?"

Daniel hesitated. "Just drive," he said. "I'll tell you when to stop."

The sun had finally broken over the horizon like the yolk of an egg. Daniel stared out the window at the landscape: pancake flat, windswept, opaque with ice. The rutted roads had houses pitted along them, ranging from tiny shacks to modest 1970s split-levels. On the side of one road sat a couch with the cushions missing and its overstuffed arms dusted with frost.

They drove past the neighborhoods of Lousetown and Alligator Acres, the Alaska Commercial Company store, the medical center where Yup'ik Eskimos received free treatment. They passed White Alice, a huge curved structure that resembled a drive-in movie screen but that actually was a radar system built during the Cold War. Daniel had broken into it a hundred times as a kid—climbed up through the pitch-black center to sit on top and get drunk on Windsor Whiskey.

"Okay," he told the cab driver. "You can stop here."

The Long House Inn was covered with ravens. There were at least a dozen on the roof, and another group battled around the remains of a torn Hefty bag in the Dumpster off to the side. Daniel paid the driver and stared at the renovated building. When he'd left, it was on the verge of being condemned.

There were three snow machines parked out front, something Daniel filed away in the recesses of his mind. He'd need one, after he figured out what direction to head to find Trixie. He could hotwire one of these, if he still remembered how, or take the honorable route and charge one to his MasterCard. They were sold in the Alaska Commercial store, at the end of the dairy aisle, past the $6.99 gallons of milk.

"Did you know a group of ravens is called an *unkindness*?" Laura said, coming to stand beside him.

He looked at her. For some reason, the space between them seemed smaller in Alaska. Or maybe you just had to get far enough away from the scene of a crime to start to forget the details. "Did you know," he replied, "that ravens like Thai food better than anything else?"

Laura's eyes lit up. "You win."

A banner had been strung across the doorway: K300 HEADQUARTERS. Daniel walked inside, stamping his boots to get the snow off. He'd been a kid when this dogsled race was just getting organized, when locals like Rick Swenson and Jerry Austin and Myron Angstman had won the pot of a few thousand dollars. Now the winnings were $20,000, and the mushers who came were stars with corporate backing for their dog kennels—Jeff King and Martin Buser and DeeDee Jonrowe.

The room was crowded. A knot of native kids

sat on the floor, drinking cans of Coke and passing around a comic book. Two women answered phones, another was carefully printing the latest splits on a white board. There were Yup'ik mothers carrying moon-faced babies, elderly men reading the scrapbooks of newspaper clippings, schoolgirls with blue-black braids giggling behind their hands as they helped themselves to the potluck stews and cobblers. Everyone moved pendulously in layers of winter clothing, astronauts navigating the surface of a distant planet.

Which, Daniel thought, this might as well be.

He walked up to the desk where the women were answering phones. "Excuse me," he said. "I'm trying to find a teenage girl . . ." One woman held up a finger: *Just a moment.*

He unzipped his jacket. Before they'd left, he'd packed a duffel full of winter gear; he and Laura were pretty much wearing everything they'd brought all at once. It was cold in Maine, but nothing compared to what it would be like in the Eskimo villages.

The woman hung up. "Hi. Can I—" She broke off as the phone rang again.

Frustrated, Daniel turned away. Impatience was a trait you developed in the lower forty-eight, an attribute that a child who grew up here didn't possess. Time wasn't the same on the tundra; it stretched to elastic lengths and snapped back fast when you weren't looking. The only things that really operated on a schedule were school and church, and most Yupiit were late to those anyway.

Daniel noticed an old man sitting on a chair, staring. He was Yup'ik, with the weathered skin of a person who'd spent his life outside. He wore green flannel pants and a fur parka. *"Aliurturua,"* the man whispered. I'm seeing a ghost.

"Not a ghost." Daniel took a step toward him. *"Cama-i."*

The man's face wrinkled, and he reached for Daniel's hand. *"Alangruksaaqamken."* You amazed me, showing up unexpectedly.

Daniel had not spoken Yup'ik in fifteen years, but the syllables flowed through him like a river. Nelson Charles had, in fact, taught him his very first Yup'ik words: *iqalluk* . . . fish, *angsaq* . . . boat, and *terren purruaq* . . . you suck the meat off an asshole, which is what Nelson told him to say to kids who made fun of him for being *kass'aq.* Daniel reached for Laura, who was watching the exchange with amazement. *"Una arnaq nulirqaqa,"* he said. This is my wife.

"That kind's pretty," Nelson said in English. He shook her hand but didn't look her in the eye.

Daniel turned to Laura. "Nelson used to be a substitute teacher. When the native kids got to go on field trips to Anchorage that were subsidized by the government, I wasn't allowed to go because I was white. So Nelson would take me on my own little field trip to check out fishnets and animal traps."

"Don't teach these days," Nelson said. "Now I'm the race marshal."

That would mean, Daniel realized, that Nelson

had been here since the start of the K300. "Listen," he said, and he found himself slipping back into Yup'ik because the words, thorny on his tongue and in his throat, didn't hurt quite as much as they did in English. *"Paniika tamaumauq."*

My daughter is lost.

He didn't have to explain to Nelson why he thought that his child, who lived a whole country away, might have wound up in Alaska when she went missing. The Yupiit understood that the person you were when you went to sleep at night might not necessarily be the person you were when you woke up. You could have become a seal or a bear. You might have crossed into the land of the dead. You might have casually spoken a wish aloud in your dreams and then found yourself living in the middle of it.

"She's fourteen," Daniel said, and he tried to describe Trixie, but he didn't know what to say. How could her height or weight or the color of her hair convey that when she laughed, her eyes narrowed shut? That she had to have the peanut butter on the top side of the sandwich and the jelly on the bottom? That she sometimes got up and wrote poetry in the middle of the night because she'd dreamed it?

The woman who had been on the phone stepped out from behind the table. "Sorry about that—the calls have been crazy. Anyway, the only kids coming through here I didn't know are the Jesuit Volunteers. One girl flew in late, because of the snowstorm, but by now, they're all up at Tuluksak, manning the checkpoint."

"What did she look like?" Laura asked. "The girl who was late?"

"Skinny little thing. Black hair."

Laura turned to Daniel. "It's not her."

"This girl didn't have a warm coat," the woman said. "I thought that was pretty crazy for a kid who knew she was coming to Alaska. She didn't even have a *hat.*"

Daniel remembered Trixie sitting in the passenger seat of his truck in the middle of the winter as they drove up to the high school entrance. *It's freezing out*, he'd said, and he handed her a hunter-orange wool stocking cap he'd used when he was out cutting wood. *Wear this.* And her response: *Dad, do you want people to think I'm a total freak?*

There had been times, when he lived in Akiak, that he would know things before they happened. Sometimes it was as simple as thinking of a red fox and then looking up and seeing one. Sometimes it was more profound: sensing a fight building up behind him, so that he could turn in time to throw the first punch. Once it had even wakened him out of his sleep: the sound of a gunshot and the echo of basketballs thudding when the bullet upset the cart they were stored on.

His mother had called it coincidence, but the Yupiit wouldn't. People's lives were as tightly woven as a piece of lace, and pulling on one string might furrow another. And although he'd dis-

missed it when he was a teenager in Akiak, he recognized now the tightening of the skin at his temples, the way light moved too fast in front of his
eyes a moment before he pictured his daughter,
*not* wearing a hat, or anything else for that matter,
shivering in what seemed to be a haystack.

Daniel felt his heart jump. "I have to get to Tuluksak."

*"Ikayurnaamken,"* Nelson said. Let me help you.

The last time he'd been here, Daniel hadn't
wanted anyone's help. The last time he'd been
here, he'd actively pushed it away. Now he turned
to Nelson. "Can I borrow your snow machine?" he
asked.

The checkpoint in Tuluksak was at the school,
close enough to the river for mushers to settle their
dogs in straw on the banks and then walk up to the
building for hot food. All mushers racing the K300
passed through Tuluksak twice—once on the way
up to Aniak and once on the way back. There was
a mandatory four-hour rest and vet check during
one of those stops. When Trixie and Willie arrived,
a team of dogs was idling without its musher down
at the bank of the river, being watched over by a
kid with a clipboard who asked if they'd run into
anyone else on the trail. All but one of the mushers
had passed through Tuluksak, detained, presumably, by the storm. No one had heard from him
since he'd checked in at Akiak.

Trixie hadn't really spoken much to Willie this
morning. She had awakened with a start a little af-

ter six A.M., noticing first that it wasn't snowing and second that she wasn't cold. Willie's arm was draped over her, and his breath fell onto the nape of her neck. Most humiliating, though, was the hard thing Trixie could feel pressing up against her thigh. She had inched away from Willie, her face burning, and focused on getting herself fully dressed before he woke up and realized he had a boner.

Willie parked outside the school and climbed off the snow machine. "Aren't you coming in?" Trixie asked, but he was already tinkering with the engine, not seeming the least bit inclined to finesse an introduction for her. "Whatever," she muttered under her breath, and she walked into the building.

Directly in front of her was a trophy case that held a wooden mask decorated with feathers and fur and a loving cup with a basketball etched onto it. A tall boy with a long, horsey face was standing next to it. "You're not Andi," he said, surprised.

The Jesuit Volunteers who were in charge of the checkpoint at Tuluksak were a group of college-age kids who did Peace Corps–style service work at the native clinic in Bethel. Trixie had thought Jesuits were priests—and these kids clearly weren't. She asked Willie why they were called that, and he just shrugged.

"I don't know about Andi," Trixie said. "I was just told to come here."

She held her breath, waiting for this boy to point a finger at her and scream *Imposter!* but before he could, Willie walked inside, stamping off his boots.

"Hey, Willie, what's up," the tall boy said. Willie nodded and walked into one of the classrooms, heading toward a table set up with Crock Pots and Tupperware. He helped himself to a bowl of something and disappeared through another doorway.

"Well, I'm Carl," the boy said. He held out his hand.

"Trixie."

"You ever done this before?"

"Oh, sure," Trixie lied. "Tons of times."

"Great." He led her into the classroom. "Things are a little crazy right now, because we've got a team that just came in, but here's a five-second orientation: First and most important, that's where the food is." He pointed. "The locals bring stuff all day long, and if you haven't had any, I recommend the beaver soup. On the other side of the door where you came in is another classroom; that's where the mushers sleep when they come in for their layover. They basically grab a mat and tell you when they want to be woken up. We rotate shifts—every half hour someone's got to sit out on the river, which is cruel and unusual punishment in this kind of weather. If you're the one on duty when a musher comes in, make sure you tell him his time and call it into headquarters, then show him which plywood corral has his gear in it. Right now everyone's a little freaked out because one team hasn't made it in since the storm."

Trixie listened to Carl, nodding at the right places, but he might as well have been speaking Swahili. Maybe if she watched someone else doing what she was supposed to do, she could copy when it came her turn.

"And just so you know," Carl said. "Mushers are allowed to drop dogs here."

*Why?* Trixie wondered. *To see if they land on their feet?*

A cell phone rang, and someone called out Carl's name. Left alone, Trixie wandered around, hoping to avoid Willie, who was doing such an effortless job of avoiding *her.* It seemed that the entire school consisted of two classrooms, and Trixie thought of Bethel High's complex layout, a map she had memorized all summer before starting ninth grade.

"You made it."

Trixie turned to find the vet who'd been on the bush plane with her from Anchorage. "Go figure."

"Well, I guess I'll see you outside. I hear there's a nasty case of frostbite out there with my name on it." He zipped up his coat and waved as he walked out the door.

Trixie was starving, but not enough to want to eat something that might have beaver in it. She gravitated toward the oil stove at the corner of the room and held her hands out in front of it. It was no warmer than Willie's skin had been.

"You all set?"

As if her thoughts had conjured him, Willie was suddenly standing next to her. "For what?"

"This."

"Oh, yeah," she said. "Piece of cake." He smirked

and started to walk away. "Hey. Where are you going?"

"Home. This is my village."

Until that moment, it hadn't occurred to Trixie that she was going to be by herself again. As a teenager, she was always part of a greater whole—a family, a class, a peer group—and there was always someone sticking a nose in her business. How many times had she stormed off after a fight with her mother, yelling that she just wanted to be left alone?

*Be careful what you wish for*, Trixie thought. After a single day spent on her own, here she was getting all upset about losing the company of a total stranger.

She tried to wipe all the emotion off her face, so that it reflected back at Willie the same indifference he was showing her. Then she remembered she was still wearing a coat that belonged to someone he knew, and she struggled to unfasten it.

Willie pushed her hands away from the zipper. "Keep it," he said. "I'll come back for it later."

She followed him out of the school building, feeling the cold rake the hair from her scalp. Willie headed toward a cluster of small houses that seemed two-dimensional, sketched in shades of smoky brown and gray. His hands were dug deep into his pockets, and he spun around so that he wouldn't have to bear the bite of the wind. "Willie," Trixie called out, and although he didn't look up, he stopped walking. "Thanks."

He ducked his head deeper, an acknowledgment, then kept moving backward toward the village. It was exactly how Trixie felt: If she was getting anywhere on this journey, it was still the wrong way. She watched Willie, pretending she could see him even when she couldn't, until she was distracted by the sound of barking near the river.

The JV they'd seen when they pulled up in their snow-go was still on the ice, watching over the same dog team, which panted in small frosty bites of punctuation. He grinned when he saw Trixie and passed her the clipboard. "Are you my relief? It's brutal out here. Hey, listen, Finn Hanlon's up taking a leak while the vet finishes checking out the team."

"What do I have to do?" Trixie said, but the boy was already halfway up the hill, making a beeline for the warmth of the school. Trixie looked around, nervous. The vet was too busy to pay attention to her, but there were a few native kids kicking a Sprite can, and their parents, who hopped from foot to foot to ward off the cold and talked about who would win the race this year.

The lead dog looked tired. Trixie couldn't blame the poor thing; she'd traveled the same route on the back of a snow machine and it had nearly killed her; what would it be like to do that barefoot and naked? Taking a glance at the vet—he could keep an eye out, just in case that last musher came in, couldn't he?—she walked away from the team to a set of plywood lockers. Rummaging inside one, she grabbed a handful of kibble and walked back to the husky. She held out her palm, and the dog's tongue, rough and warm, rasped against her skin to devour the treat.

"Jesus," a voice yelled. "You trying to get me disqualified?"

Staring down at her was a musher wearing a bib with the number 12 on it. She glanced at her clipboard: FINN HANLON.

"You're feeding my dogs!"

"S-sorry," Trixie stammered. "I thought—"

Ignoring her, Hanlon turned to the vet. "What's the verdict?"

"He's going to be fine, but not if you race him." The vet stood up, wiped his hands on his coat.

The musher knelt beside the dog and rubbed him between the ears, then unhooked his traces. "I'm dropping him," he said, handing the neck line to Trixie. She held it and watched Hanlon reconfigure the tug line of the dog that had been Juno's partner, so that the sled would pull straight. "Sign me out," he ordered, and he stepped on the runners of his sled, holding on to the handle bow. "All right," he called, and the team loped north along the river, gaining speed, as the spectators on the bank cheered.

The vet packed up his bag. "Let's get Juno comfortable," he said, and Trixie nodded, holding the neck line like a leash as she started to walk the dog toward the school building.

"Very funny," the vet said.

She turned around to find him in front of a stake hammered into the grass along the edge of the river. "But it's so cold out here . . ."

"You noticed? Tie him up, and I'll get the straw."

Trixie clipped the dog's neck line onto the stake. The vet returned, carrying a slice of hay in his arms. "You'd be surprised how cozy this is," he said, and Trixie thought of the night she'd spent with Willie.

A current suddenly energized the small tangle of spectators, and they began to point to the spot on the horizon where the river became a vanishing point. Trixie gripped the clipboard with her mittened hands and looked at the pinprick in the distance.

"It's Edmonds!" a Yup'ik boy cried. "He made it!"

The vet stood up. "I'll go tell Carl," he said, and he left Trixie to fend for herself.

The musher was wearing a white parka that came down to his knees and the number 06 on his bib. "Whoa," he called out, and his malamutes slowed to a stop, panting. The swing dog—the one closest to the sled—curled up like a fiddlehead on the ice and closed her eyes.

The children spilled over the riverbank, tugging at the musher's coat. "Alex Edmonds! Alex Edmonds!" they shouted. "Do you remember me from last year?"

Edmonds brushed them off. "I have to scratch," he said to Trixie.

"Um. Okay," she answered, and she wondered why he thought he had to make an itch common knowledge. But Edmonds took the clipboard out of her hands and drew a line through his name. He handed it back and pulled the sleeping bag off the basket of the sled, revealing an old Yup'ik man who reeked of alcohol and who was shaking even as he snored. "I found him on the trail. He must have passed out during the storm. I gave him mouth to mouth last night to get him breathing again, but the weather was too bad to get him back to the medical center in Bethel. This was the closest checkpoint . . . can someone help me get him inside?"

Before Trixie could run up to the school, she saw Carl and the other volunteers hurrying down to the river. "Holy cow," Carl said, staring at the drunk. "You probably saved his life."

"Whatever *that's* worth," Edmonds replied.

Trixie watched the other volunteers drag the old man out of the dogsled and carry him up to the school. The bystanders whispered and clucked to each other, snippets of conversation in Yup'ik and English that Trixie caught: *Edmonds used to be an EMT . . . Kingurauten Joseph ought to pay for this . . . damn shame.* One Yup'ik woman with owl eyeglasses and a tiny bow of a mouth came up to Trixie. She leaned over the clipboard and pointed to the line splitting Edmonds's name. "I had ten bucks riding on him to win," she complained.

With all the dog teams accounted for, the on-lookers dispersed, heading into the village where Willie had gone. Trixie wondered if he was related to any of those little kids who'd been cheering for Edmonds. She wondered what he'd done when he got home. Drunk orange juice out of the container, like she might have? Taken a shower? Lay down on his bed, thinking of her?

Just as suddenly as all the activity had arrived, there was nobody on the bank of the river. Trixie looked north, but she couldn't see Finn Hanlon and his team anymore. She looked south, but she couldn't tell where she and Willie had come from. The sun had climbed almost directly overhead, washing out the ice so that it made her eyes burn even to pick out the trail from the field of white.

Trixie sank down beside Juno on the straw and scratched the dog's head with her glove. The husky stared up at her with one brown eye and one blue, and when he panted, it looked like he was smiling. Trixie imagined what it was like to be a sled dog, to have to pull your weight or realize you'd be left behind. She pictured how it would feel to trust your instincts in a strange land, to know the difference between where you had been and where you were going.

When the river froze in the winter, it got its own highway number, and at any given time you would see rusted trucks and dogsled teams driving over the ice in no particular direction or parallel course. Like most Yup'ik Eskimos, Nelson didn't believe in a helmet or goggles; to brace himself against the wind on the old man's snow machine, Daniel had to crouch down close to the windshield. Laura sat behind him, her face buried against the back of his coat.

In the middle of the river was a stationary white

truck. As Daniel slowed the snow-go, he could feel Laura relax—she was freezing, even if she wasn't complaining. "This must be a checkpoint," he said, and he got off the machine with his thighs still thrumming from the power of the engine.

A dreadlocked white woman unrolled the driver's side window. "Kingurauten Joseph, for the love of God, go pass out in someone else's backyard."

*Kingurauten* was Yup'ik for *too late.* Daniel pulled down the neck warmer that covered his nose and mouth. "I think you've got me confused with someone else," he began, and then realized that he knew the woman in the truck. "Daisy?" he said hesitantly.

Crazy Daisy, that was what they'd called her when she used to run the mail out to the native villages by dogsled back when Daniel was a kid. She frowned at him. "Who the hell are you?"

"Daniel Stone," he said. "Annette Stone's son."

"That wasn't the name of Annette's kid. He was—"

"Wassilie," Daniel finished.

Daisy scratched her scalp. "Didn't you bug out of here because—"

"Nah," Daniel lied. "I just left for college." It was common knowledge that Crazy Daisy had gotten that way by running with Timothy Leary's crowd in the sixties, and that she'd pretty much fried the functioning parts of her brain. "Did you happen to see a snow-go pass by here with a *kass'aq* girl and a Yup'ik boy?"

"This morning?"

"Yeah."

Daisy shook her head. "Nope. Sorry." She jerked her thumb toward the back of the truck. "You want to come in and warm up? I got coffee and Snickers bars."

"Can't," Daniel said, lost in thought. If Trixie hadn't come past Akiak, then how had he missed her on the trail?

"Maybe later," Daisy yelled, as he turned the ignition on the snow machine again. "I'd love to catch up."

Daniel pretended not to hear her. But as he circled around the truck, Daisy started waving like a madwoman, trying to get his attention. "No one's passed by this morning," she said, "but a girl and boy came through last night, before the storm hit."

Daniel didn't answer, just gunned the engine and drove up the riverbank into Akiak, the town he'd run away from fifteen years earlier. The Washeteria—the place they'd gone with their laundry and for showers—was now a convenience store and video rental shop. The school was still a squat, serviceable gray building; the house beside it where he'd grown up had two dogs staked out front. Daniel wondered who lived there now, if it was still the schoolteacher, if she had children. If basketballs still sometimes started to bounce in the gymnasium without being set in motion, if the last one to lock up the school building ever saw the old principal who'd killed himself, still hanging from the crossbeam in the only classroom.

He stopped in front of the house next door to the school, a shack with a slight pedigree. A snow-go sat in front of the building, and an aluminum boat peeked out from beneath a blue tarp. Paper snowflakes had been taped to the windows, as well as a red metallic crucifix. "Why are we stopping?" Laura asked. "What about Trixie?"

He got off the snow machine and turned to her. "You're not coming with me."

She wasn't used to this kind of cold, and he couldn't slow down for her and risk losing Trixie for good. And a part of him wanted to be alone when he found Trixie. There was so much he needed to explain.

Laura stared at him, struck dumb. Her eyebrows had frosted over, her eyelashes were matted together with ice, and when she finally spoke, her sentence rose like a white banner between them. "Please don't do this," she said, starting to cry. "Take me with you."

Daniel pulled her into his arms, assuming that Laura thought this was a punishment, retribution for leaving *him* behind when she had her affair. It made her seem vulnerable; it made him remember how easy it was for them to still hurt each other. "If we had to walk through hell to find Trixie, I'd follow you. But this is a different kind of hell, and I'm the one who knows where he's going. I'm asking you . . . I'm *begging* you to trust me."

Laura opened her mouth, and what might have been a reply came out only as a smoke ring full of what she could not say. Trust was exactly what they no longer had between them. "I can go faster if I don't have to worry about you," he said.

Daniel saw true fear in her eyes. "You'll come back?" she asked.

"We *both* will."

Laura glanced around at the rutted street with snow-go tracks, at the public water receptacles at the base of the street. The community was silent, windswept, frigid. It looked, Daniel knew, like a dead end.

"Come with me." He led Laura up the set of wooden stairs and opened the door without knocking, entering a little antechamber. There were plastic bags stuck on nails in the frame overhead, and stacks of newspaper. A pair of boots toppled to the right, and a tanned hide was stretched on the back wall, beside the door that led into the house. Lying on the linoleum was a severed moose hoof and a half rack of frozen ribs.

Laura stepped hesitantly over them. "Is this . . . is this where you used to live?"

The interior door opened, revealing a Yup'ik woman about sixty years old, holding an infant in her arms. She took one look at Daniel and backed away, her eyes bright with tears.

"Not me," Daniel said. "Cane."

Charles and Minnie Johnson, the parents of Daniel's one and only childhood friend, treated him with the same sort of deference they might have given any other ghost who sat down at their kitchen table to share a cup of coffee. Charles's skin was as dark and lined as a cinnamon stick; he wore creased jeans and a red western shirt and called Daniel Wass. His eyes were clouded with cataracts, as if life were something poured into a body, a vessel that could hold only so much before memories floated across the windows of consciousness.

"It's been a long time," Charles said.

"Yes."

"You've been living Outside?"

"With my family."

There was a long silence. "We wondered when you'd come home," Minnie said.

The Yupiit did not speak of the dead, and because of that, neither would Daniel. But he had less practice with silence. In a Yup'ik household, ten minutes might pass between a question and the answer. Sometimes you didn't even have to reply out loud; it was enough to be thinking your response.

They sat around the kitchen table in the quiet, until a young woman walked through the front door. She was clearly Minnie's daughter—they had the same wide smile and smooth hickory skin—but Daniel remembered her only as a young girl who liked to storyknife—using a butter knife in the soft mud to illustrate the tales she'd tell. Now, though, she held in her arms her own fat, squirming baby, who took one look at Laura and pointed at her and laughed.

"Sorry," Elaine said shyly. "He's never seen anyone with that color hair before." She unwound her scarf and unzipped her coat, then did the same for the baby.

"Elaine, this is Wass," Charles said. "He lived here a long time ago."

Daniel stood at the introduction, and when he did, the baby reached for him. He grinned, catching the boy as he twisted out of his mother's arms. "And who's this?"

"My son," Elaine said. "His name's Cane."

Elaine lived in the same house as her parents, along with her two older children and her husband. So did her sister Aurora, who was seventeen years old and heavily pregnant. There was a brother, too, in his late twenties; Laura could see him in the only bedroom in the house, feverishly playing Nintendo.

On the kitchen table was a hunk of frozen meat in a bowl—if Laura had to guess, she would have said it was intimately related to the moose parts in the arctic entry. There was a stove but no sink. Instead, a fifty-five-gallon drum in the corner of the kitchen area was filled with water. Dusty ice-fishing lures and antique hand-carved kayak paddles were suspended from the ceiling; five-gallon buckets filled with lard and dried fish were stacked beside the threadbare couch. The walls were covered with religious paraphernalia: programs from church services, plaques of Jesus and Mary, calendars printed with the feast days of saints. Anywhere there was a spare square of paneling, a photograph had been tacked: recent pictures of the baby, old school portraits of Elaine and Aurora and their brother, the boy Daniel had been accused of murdering.

There was a curious irony to being left behind here, even if the very thought of it made Laura break into a sweat. She kept remembering what Daniel had said about the Alaskan bush: It was a place where people tended to disappear. What did that bode for Trixie, or for Daniel? And what might it mean for Laura herself?

In Maine, when Laura's life had been jolted off course, it had been terrifying and unfamiliar. Here, though, she had no standard for comparison—and not knowing what came next *was* the norm. She didn't know why no one would look her in the eye, why the boy playing video games hadn't come out to introduce himself, why they even *had* state-of-the-art video equipment when the house itself was little more than a shed, why a family that at one point had believed you'd killed their son would welcome you into their home. The world had been turned inside out, and she was navigating by the feel of its seams.

Daniel was speaking quietly to Charles, telling him about Trixie. "Excuse me," Laura said, leaning toward Minnie. "Could I use your restroom?"

Minnie pointed down the hall. At its end was a flattened cardboard refrigerator box, erected like a screen. "Laura," Daniel said, getting to his feet.

"I'm fine!" she said, because she thought if she could make Daniel believe it, then maybe he'd convince her of it as well. She slipped behind the screen, and her jaw dropped. There was no bathroom; there wasn't even a toilet. Only a white bucket—like the ones in the living room that stored dried fish—with a toilet seat balanced on top of it.

She peeled off her ski pants and squatted, holding her breath the whole time, praying nobody was listening. When Laura and Daniel had moved in together, there had still been a certain shyness between them. After all, she was pregnant, and that had speeded along a relationship that might have otherwise taken years to reach that level of commitment. Laura could remember Daniel separating his laundry from hers for the first few months, for example. And she had studiously avoided going to the bathroom if Daniel happened to be in there taking a shower.

She couldn't recall when, exactly, all their shirts and jeans and underwear had mixed in the washer together. Or when she'd been able to pee while he was two feet away from her, brushing his teeth. It was simply what happened when the histories of two people dovetailed into one.

Laura straightened her clothes—washing her hands wasn't even an option—and stepped out from behind the partition. Daniel was waiting for her in the narrow hallway. "I should have warned you about the honey bucket."

She thought of how Daniel couldn't bear to run the dishwasher if it wasn't overflowing, how his showers lasted less than five minutes. She'd always considered it thrifty; now she saw that when you grew up with water as a luxury and plumbing a distant wish, it might simply be a habit too deeply rooted to break.

"I need to get going," Daniel said.

Laura nodded. She wanted to smile at him, but she couldn't find it in herself. So much could happen between now and the next time she saw him. She wrapped her arms around Daniel and buried her face against his chest.

He led her into the kitchen, where he shook Charles's hand and spoke in Yup'ik: *"Quyana. Pi-urra."*

When Daniel walked into the arctic entry, Laura followed. She stood at the front door, watching him start the snow machine and climb aboard. He lifted one hand, a farewell, and mouthed words he knew she would not hear over the roar of the engine.

*I love you.*

"I love you, too," Laura murmured, but by then, all that remained of Daniel was what he'd left behind: a trail of exhaust, hatched tracks in the snow, and a truth neither of them had spoken for some time.

Bartholemew stared at the sheet of results that Skipper Johanssen had given him. "How sure are you?" he asked.

Skipper shrugged. "As sure as this particular typing can be. One-hundredth of one percent of the world's population has the same mito DNA profile as your suspect. You're talking about six hundred thousand people, any of whom could have been at the scene of the crime."

"But that also suggests that ninety-nine point ninety-nine percent of the population *wasn't* there."

"Correct. At least not based on that piece of hair you found on the victim."

Bartholemew stared at her. "And Trixie Stone doesn't fall into that ninety-nine point ninety-nine percent?"

"Nope."

"So I can't exclude Trixie Stone."

"Not mitochondrially speaking."

The odds were looking better, when you glanced at them from this angle, Bartholemew thought. "Even though Max said—"

"No insult to Max, but no court is going to put stock in an analysis done by the human eye, as compared to a validated scientific test like mine." Skipper smiled at him. "I think," she said, "you've got yourself a suspect."

The Johnsons were addicted to the Game Show Network. They especially liked Richard Dawson, who kissed anything on two legs while hosting *Family Feud.* "One day," Minnie kept saying, elbowing her husband, "I'm gonna run away with Richard."

"He'll run, all right, when he sees you coming after him." Charles laughed.

They had a satellite dish, a flat-screen TV, a PlayStation and a GameCube, as well as a DVD/VCR player and a stereo system that would have put Laura's own to shame. Roland, the antisocial brother, had bought all the equipment with his check this year from the Alaska Permanent Fund— the dividends on oil that every Alaskan was paid by the government since 1984. The Johnsons had lived the entire year on the $1,100 of Charles's check alone, supplemented by hunting expeditions for caribou and dried salmon caught during the summer at fish camp. Roland had told her that Akiak residents could even get wireless Internet for free—they qualified for government-funded technology because they were both rural and native— but that no one could afford it. A person had to have a computer first, which would cost nearly a whole year's Permanent Fund check.

When Laura had had her fill of Richard Dawson, she put on her coat and walked outside. On a telephone pole, someone had nailed a basketball hoop; the ball itself was half buried in a hummock of snow. She pulled it free and bounced it, amazed at how the sound echoed. Here there were no lawn mowers or blaring radios or rap music. No slamming of SUV doors, no clatter of kids spilling out of a school bus, no hum from a nearby highway. It was the sort of place where you could hear the tumblers of your mind falling into place as you pieced thought together, as you tried to match it to action.

Although Laura knew without a doubt that Trixie had not murdered Jason, she didn't understand what had made her daughter run away. Was Trixie just scared? Or did she know more about what had happened that night than she'd let on?

Laura wondered if it was possible to run away forever. Daniel had certainly managed to do it. She knew that his childhood had been foreign, but she never could have envisioned something as stark as this. If she'd believed that there was a vast dichotomy between the man she'd met in college and the one she lived with now—well, there was an even greater gap between who Daniel had been when she met him and where he had started. It made Laura wonder where all of Daniel's jettisoned personalities had gone. It made her wonder if you could know a person only at a single moment in time, because a year from now or a day from now, he might be different. It made her wonder if everyone reinvented himself or herself, if that was as natural as other animals shedding skin.

If she was going to be honest now—and wasn't it time for that, already?—Laura would have to admit that Trixie had changed, too. She had wanted to believe that behind that closed bedroom door, her daughter was still playing God with the denizens of her dollhouse; but in fact Trixie had been keeping secrets, and pushing boundaries, and turning into someone Laura didn't recognize.

On the other hand, Daniel had been keeping a vigil for Trixie's metamorphosis. He'd been so nervous about the thought of their daughter getting older, taking on the world, being flattened by it. As it turned out, though, Trixie had grown up during the one instant Daniel had turned away, momentarily distracted by his wife's betrayal.

It wasn't what you didn't know about the people

you loved that would shock you; it was what you didn't want to admit about yourself.

When the door opened, Laura jumped, her thoughts scattering like a flock of crows. Charles stood on the steps, smoking a pipe. "You know what it means if you go outside and there are no Yupiit around?"

"No."

"That it's too damn cold to be standing here." He took the basketball from Laura's hands and sank a neat basket; together they watched it roll into a neighbor's yard.

Laura dug her hands into her pockets. "It's so quiet," she said. *How ironic*, she thought, *to make conversation about the lack of it.*

Charles nodded. "Every now and again someone will move to Bethel, and then come back because it's too loud. Down there, there's too much going on."

It was hard to imagine this: Bethel was the last place Laura would ever have considered a metropolis. "New York City would probably make their heads explode."

"I was there once," Charles said, surprising her. "Oh, I been lots of places you wouldn't think: to California, and to Georgia, when I was in the army. And to Oregon, when I went to school."

"College?"

Charles shook his head. "Boarding school. Back before they made it a law to have education in every village, the government used to ship us off to learn the same things the whites did. You could pick your school—there was one in Oklahoma, but I went to Chemawa in Oregon because my cousins were already there. I got sick like you can't imagine, eating all that white food . . . melting in that heat. One time I even got in trouble for trying to snare a rabbit with one of my shoelaces."

Laura tried to imagine what it would be like to be sent away from the only home you'd ever known, just because somebody else thought it was best for you. "You must have hated it."

"Back then, I did," Charles said. He dumped the contents of his pipe and kicked snow over the embers. "Now, I'm not so sure. Most of us came back home, but we got to see what else was out there and how those folks lived. Now some kids don't ever leave the village. The only *kass'aqs* they meet are teachers, and the only teachers who come up here either can't get hired in their own towns or are running away from something—not exactly role models. The kids today, they all talk about getting out of the village, but then when they do, it's like Bethel—only a hundred times worse. People move too fast and talk too much, and before you know it, they come back to a place they don't want to be—except now they know there's nowhere left to run." Charles glanced at Laura, then tucked the pipe into his coat pocket. "That's how it was for my son."

She nodded. "Daniel told me about him."

"He wasn't the first. The year before him, a girl took pills. And earlier still, two ball players hanged themselves."

"I'm sorry," Laura said.

"I knew all along that Wass wasn't the one who killed Cane. Cane would have done that, no matter what, all by himself. Some people, they get down in a hole so deep they can't figure out what to hold on to."

*And some people*, Laura thought, *make the choice to let go.*

Although it was only two o'clock, the sun was already sagging against the horizon. Charles headed back up the steps. "I know this place must seem like Mars to you. And that you and me, we're about as different as different could be. But I also know what it feels like to lose a child." He turned at the top landing. "Don't freeze to death. Wassilie'd never forgive me."

He left Laura outside, watching the night sky bloom. She found herself lulled by the lack of sound. It was easier than you'd think to grow accustomed to silence.

When the Jesuit Volunteers tried to raise Kingurauten Joseph's body temperature by cutting off his frozen clothes and covering him with blankets, they found a dove fashioned delicately out of bone, a carving knife, and three hundred dollars in his boot. This was a cash economy, Carl told Trixie. That was Joseph's health insurance, wadded up in his sock.

Trixie had just come in from her rotation on the riverbank, and she was still frozen to the core.

"Why don't you two warm up together?" Carl suggested, and he left her watching over the old man.

She didn't mind, actually. While the mushers raced from Tuluksak to Kalskag and Aniak and back, the volunteers were mostly catching some sleep. But Trixie was wide awake; she'd slept on the trail with Willie, and her body was all mixed up with jet lag. She remembered how every year when it was time to turn the clocks back, her father would insist that he was going to stay on daylight saving time and keep the extra hour, so that he'd get more work done. The problem was, when he took the additional minutes every morning, he'd conk out in front of the television earlier at night. Finally he'd give in and live on the same schedule as the rest of the world.

She wished her father was here right now.

"I've missed you," he answered, and Trixie whirled around in the dark classroom. Her heart was pounding, but she couldn't see anyone there.

She looked down at Joseph. He had the broad, chiseled features of a Yup'ik and white hair that was matted down in whorls. His beard stubble glinted silver in the moonlight. His hands were folded over his chest, and Trixie thought they couldn't have looked more different from her father's—Joseph's were blunt and calloused, the tools of a laborer; her father's were smooth and long fingered and ink stained, an artist's.

"Aw, Nettie," he murmured, opening his eyes. "I came back."

"I'm not Nettie," Trixie said, moving away.

Joseph blinked. "Where am I?"

"Tuluksak. You nearly froze to death." Trixie hesitated. "You got really drunk and passed out on the K300 trail, and a musher quit the race to bring you in here. He saved your life."

"Shouldn't have bothered," Joseph muttered.

There was something about Joseph that seemed familiar to Trixie, something that made her want to take a second look at the lines around his eyes and the way his eyebrows arched. "You one of those juveniles for Jesus?"

"They're Jesuit Volunteers," Trixie corrected. "And no. I'm not."

"Then who are you?"

Well, wasn't *that* the $64,000 question. Trixie couldn't have answered that if Joseph had held a gun to her head. It wasn't even a matter of giving her name, because that didn't explain anything. She could remember who she used to be—that picture was like an image sealed into a snow globe, one that went fuzzy when she shook it too hard but then, if she held her breath, might see clearly. She could look down at herself now and tell you how surprised she was that she had come this distance, how strange it was to discover that lying came as easily as breathing. What she couldn't put into words was what had happened in between to change her from one person into the other.

Her father used to tell her the story of how, when she was eight, she'd awakened in the middle of the night with her arms and legs burning, as if they'd been tugged from their sockets. *It's growing pains*, he'd told her sympathetically, and she'd burst into tears, certain that when she woke up in the morning, she'd be as big as him.

The amazing thing was, it *did* happen that quickly. All those mornings in middle school she'd spent scrutinizing her chest to see if it had budded the slightest bit, all the practice kisses she'd given her bathroom mirror to make sure her nose didn't get in the way on D-day; all the waiting for a boy to notice her—and as it turned out, growing up was just as she'd feared. One day when your alarm clock rang, you got up and realized you had someone else's thoughts in your head . . . or maybe just your old ones, minus the hope.

"Are you sure you're not Nettie?" Joseph said when Trixie didn't answer.

It was the name he'd called her before. "Who is she?"

"Well." He turned his face to the wall. "She's dead."

"Then chances are pretty good I'm not her."

Joseph seemed surprised. "Didn't you ever hear about the girl who came back from the dead?"

Trixie rolled her eyes. "You're still trashed."

"A young girl died," Joseph replied, as if she hadn't spoken at all, "but she didn't know it. All she knew is that she went on a journey and reached a village. Her grandmother was at the village, too, and they lived together there. Every now and then, they went to another village, where the girl's father would give her fur parkas. What she didn't know was that he was really giving them to her name-sake, the girl who'd been born just after his daughter had died."

Joseph sat up gingerly, sending a potent wave of alcohol fumes toward Trixie. "One day, they were going home from that other village, and the girl's grandmother said she'd forgotten some things. She asked the girl to go get them. She told her that if she came to a fallen evergreen tree, even though it might look like she could go under it or around it, she had to go over it instead."

Trixie folded her arms, listening in spite of her best intentions.

"The girl backtracked to the village, and sure enough, she came to a fallen tree. She tried to do what her grandmother had told her, but when she climbed over it she tripped, and that was the last thing she remembered. She couldn't figure out the way back to her grandmother, and she started to cry. Just then, a man from the village came out of the *qasgiq* and heard weeping. He followed the noise and saw the girl who had died years ago. He tried to grab on to her, but it was like holding only air."

*Of course*, Trixie thought. *Because the more you changed, the less of you there was.*

"The man rubbed his arms with food, and then he could grab her, even when the girl fought him. He carried her into the *qasgiq*, but they kept rising off the floorboards. An elder rubbed the girl with drippings from a seal oil lamp, and then she was able to stand without floating away. They all saw that this girl was the same one who had died. She was wearing the parkas her father had given to her namesake, all those years. And wouldn't you know it, after she came back, her namesake died not long after that." Joseph pulled the blanket up to his chest. "She lived to be an old woman," he said. "She told people what it had been like in *Pamaalirugmiut*—the place back there, obscured from their view."

"Oh really," Trixie said, not buying a word of the story. "Let me guess: There was a white light and harp music?"

Joseph looked at her, puzzled. "No, she used to say it was dry. People who die are always thirsty. That's why we send the dead on their way with fresh water. And why, maybe, I'm always looking for a little something to wet my throat."

Trixie drew her knees into her chest, shivering as she thought of Jason. "You're not dead."

Joseph sank back down on the mat. "You'd be surprised," he said.

"It's not too cold to keep me from going for a walk," Aurora Johnson said to Laura in perfect, un-accented English, and she stood there, waiting for Laura to respond, as if she'd asked her a question.

Maybe Aurora wanted someone to talk to and didn't know how to ask. Laura could understand that. She got to her feet and reached for her coat. "Do you mind company?"

Aurora smiled and pulled on a jacket that fell to her knees but managed to zip up over her swollen belly. She stepped into boots with soles as thick as a fireman's and headed outside.

Laura fell into step beside her, moving briskly against the cold. It had been two hours since Daniel had left, and the afternoon was pitch-dark now—there were no streetlamps lighting their way, no glow from a distant highway. From time to time the green cast of a television set inside a house would rise like a spirit in the window, but for the most part, the sky was an unbroken navy velvet, the stars so thick you could cut through them with a sweep of your arm.

Aurora's hair was brown, streaked with orange. Long tendrils blew out from the edges of her parka's hood. She was only three years older than Trixie, yet she was on the verge of giving birth. "When are you due?" Laura asked.

"My BIB date is January tenth."

"BIB date?"

"Be-in-Bethel," Aurora explained. "If you live in the villages and you're pregnant, you have to move into the prematernal home in the city six weeks or so before you're due. That way, the docs have you where they need you. Otherwise, if there's some kind of complication, the medical center has to get the *anguyagta* to fly in a Blackhawk. It costs the National Guard ten thousand bucks a pop." She glanced at Laura. "Do you just have the one? Baby, I mean?"

Laura nodded, bowing her head as she thought of Trixie. She hoped that wherever Trixie was now, it was warm. That someone had given her a bite to eat, or a blanket. She hoped that Trixie was leaving markers the way she had learned ages ago in Girl Scouts—a twig broken here, a cairn of rocks there.

"Minnie's my second mom, you know," Aurora said. "I was adopted out. Families are like that here. If a baby dies, your sister or aunt might give you her own. After Cane died, I was born and my mom sent me to be Minnie's daughter too." She shrugged. "I'm adopting out this baby to my biological mom's cousin."

"You're just going to give it away?" Laura said, shocked.

"I'm not giving her away. I'm making it so she'll have both of us."

"What about the father?" Laura asked. "Are you still involved with him?"

"I see him about once a week," Aurora said.

Laura stopped walking. She was talking to a Yup'ik girl who was heavily pregnant, but she was seeing Trixie's face and hearing Trixie's voice. What if Laura had been around when Trixie had met Jason, instead of having her own affair? Would Trixie have ever dated him? Would she have been as crushed when they broke up? Would she have been at Zephyr's house the night of the party? Would she have gotten raped?

For every action, there was an opposite reaction. But maybe you could undo your wrongs by keeping someone else from making the same mistakes of misjudgment. "Aurora," Laura said slowly, "I'd love to meet him. Your boyfriend."

The Yup'ik girl beamed. "Really? Now?"

"That would be great."

Aurora grabbed her hand and dragged her through the streets of Akiak. When they reached a long, low gray building, Aurora clattered up the wooden ramp. "I just need to stop off at the school for a sec," she said.

The doors were unlocked, but there was nobody inside. Aurora flipped on a light switch and hurried into an adjoining room. Laura unzipped her jacket and glanced toward the gymnasium on the right, its polished wooden floors gleaming. If she looked closely, would she still see Cane's blood? Could she retrace the steps Daniel had taken all those years ago, when he ran away and into her own life?

Laura was distracted by the sound of . . . well, it couldn't be a toilet flushing, could it? She pushed through the door that Aurora had entered, marked *Nas'ak.* Aurora was standing in front of a serviceable white porcelain sink with *running water.* "That one's sitting on my bladder," Aurora said, smiling.

"There's *plumbing* here?" Laura glanced around. On the upper lip of the bathroom stall, various items of clothing had been draped: bras and panties, long-sleeved T-shirts, socks.

"Just in the school," Aurora said. "On any given day, the line'll be out the door with girls waiting to wash their hair. This is the only place it won't freeze solid."

She gave Laura a chance to use the facilities— *use* wasn't really the word as much as *relish* or *give thanks for*—and then they struck outside again.

"Does your boyfriend live far away?" Laura asked, wondering what might happen if Daniel returned to find her missing.

"He's just over that hill," Aurora said, but as they crested the rise, Laura didn't see any homes at all. She followed Aurora inside a picket fence, careful to stay on the trodden path instead of hiking through the drifts that were hip-high. In the dark, it took her a moment to realize that they were walking to the far end of a tiny cemetery, one scattered with white wooden crosses that were almost entirely buried in snow.

Aurora stopped at a cleared grave. A name was engraved on the wooden cross: ARTHUR M. PETERSON, June 5, 1982–March 30, 2005. "He was mushing, but it was the end of March, and he went through the ice. His lead dog chewed through the lead and came to our house. I knew the minute I saw the dog that something was wrong, but by the time we got to the river, Art and the sled had both gone under." She faced Laura. "Three days later I found out I was pregnant."

"I'm so sorry."

"Don't be," Aurora said, matter-of-fact. "He was probably drinking when he went out on the trail, like usual." As she spoke, though, she leaned down and gently swept the cross clean of its most recent dusting of snow.

Laura turned away to give Aurora privacy and saw one other grave that had been carefully cleared. In front of the marker was a collection of ivory—full mammoth tusks and partial ones, some nearly as tall as the wooden cross. On each tusk, numerous flowers had been carved in exquisite detail: roses and orchids and peonies, lupine and forget-me-nots and lady's slippers. It was a garden that had been bleached of its color and none of its beauty, flowers that would never die, flowers that could bloom even in the most inhospitable climate.

She imagined the artist who'd crafted these, walking through sleet and hail and ice storms to plant this endless garden. It was exactly the sort of romance and passion she would have expected of Seth, who had tucked poems into the flustered leaves of her date book and the prim mouth of her change purse.

Wistfully, Laura let herself imagine what it was like to be loved that deeply. She envisioned a wooden cross labeled with her own name. She saw someone fighting the elements to bring gifts to her grave. But when she pictured the man weeping over what he'd lost, it wasn't Seth.

It was Daniel.

Laura brushed the snow off the marker, wanting to know the identity of the woman who had inspired such devotion.

"Oh, I was going to show you that one," Aurora said, just as Laura read the name: ANNETTE STONE. Daniel's mother.

Trixie had gone AWOL. She couldn't say why she felt guilty about this, especially since it wasn't like she was really supposed to be working the Tuluksak checkpoint in the first place. She ran beside

Willie in the dark, small puffs of her breath leaving a dissipating trail.

As promised, Willie had come back to the school, although Trixie hadn't really expected him to. She had planned to leave his coat behind with one of the volunteers when she got ready to leave—whenever and toward wherever that would be. But Willie had arrived while Trixie was still babysitting Joseph. He'd knelt down on the other side of the snoring old man and shook his head. He knew Joseph—apparently everyone did in an eight-village radius, since Joseph didn't discriminate when it came to where he'd go on a bender. The Yupiit called him *Kingurauten*—Too Late— Joseph because he'd promised a woman he'd return, only to turn up a week after she'd died.

Willie had come to invite Trixie to steam. She didn't know what that meant, but it sounded heavenly after shivering for nearly two days straight. She'd followed Willie, tiptoeing past Joseph, past the sleeping Jesuit Volunteers, and out the front door of the school.

They ran. The night was spread like icing over the dome of the sky; stars kept falling at Trixie's feet. It was hard to tell if it was the uncovered beauty of this place that took her breath away, or the seize of the cold. Willie slowed when they came to a narrow road lined with tiny homes. "Are we going to your house?" Trixie asked.

"No, my dad's there, and when I left he was drinking. We're going to my cousin's. He was having a steam with some of his buddies, but they're leaving for a city league basketball game down-river."

Several dogs that were chained up outside houses started to bark. Willie fumbled for her hand, probably to get her to move faster, but if that was the intent it didn't work. Everything slowed inside Trixie: her heartbeat, her breathing, her blood.

Although Janice had tried to tell her otherwise, Trixie had believed she would never want another guy to lay hands on her again. But when Willie touched her, she couldn't really remember what it had felt like to touch Jason. It was almost as if one canceled out the other. She knew this: Willie's skin was smoother than Jason's. His hand was closer to hers in size. The muscles in his forearms weren't thick, the product of a million slap shots—they were lean and ropy, almost sculpted. It made no sense, given their upbringings, but she had this weird feeling that she and Willie were equals, that neither of them was in control, because they were both so skittish in each other's company.

They stopped behind one of the houses. Through the buttery light of the windows, Trixie could see a sparse living room, a single couch, and a few young men putting on their coats and boots. "Come on," Willie said, and he tugged her away.

He opened the door to a wooden shack not much bigger than an outhouse. It was divided into two rooms—they had entered the larger one; the other room lay through the closed door directly ahead of Trixie. Once the sound of his cousin's snow machine winnowed away, Willie shrugged out of his coat and boots, gesturing to Trixie to do the same. "The good news is, my cousin already did all the hard work tonight—hauling water and chopping wood. He built this *maqi* a few years ago."

"What do you do in it?"

Willie grinned, and in the dark his teeth gleamed. "Sweat," he said. "A lot. The men usually go in first, because they can handle the real heat. Women go in later."

"Then how come we're here together?" Trixie asked.

Willie ducked his head. She knew he was blushing, even if she couldn't see it.

"I bet you take girls here all the time," she said, but she was only half joking, waiting for his answer.

"I've never been with a girl in the steam before," Willie said, and then he shucked off his skirt. Trixie closed her eyes, but not before she saw the bright white flash of his underwear.

He opened a door and disappeared inside the adjoining room. Trixie waited for him to come back, but he didn't. She heard the hiss of rising steam.

She stared at the wooden door, wondering what was on the other side. Was he trying to show her how tough he was, by taking the *real heat*? What did he mean when he said that he hadn't been with a girl in the steam before? Did he take them other places, or was that an invitation for her to follow? She felt like she had fallen into one of her father's comic book universes, where what you said was not what you meant, and vice versa.

Hesitantly, Trixie pulled off her shirt. The action—and Willie's proximity—immediately made her think about playing strip poker the night of Zephyr's party. But nobody was watching this time; there were no rules to the game; no one was telling her what she had to do. It was entirely different, she realized, when the choice was up to her.

If she went in there in her bra and panties, that was just like wearing a bikini, wasn't it?

She shivered only a moment before she opened the stunted door and crawled inside.

The heat slammed into her, a solid wall. It wasn't just heat. It was a sauna and a steam room and a bonfire all rolled together, and then ratcheted up a notch. The floor beneath her bare feet was slick plywood. She couldn't see, because of all the steam.

As the clouds drifted, she could make out a fifty-five-gallon oil drum on its side with a fire burning hot in its belly. Rocks were nestled in birdcage wire on top, and a metal container of water sat beside it. Willie was hunkered down on the plywood, his knees drawn up to his chest, his skin red and blotched.

He didn't say anything when he saw her, and Trixie understood why—if she opened her mouth, surely her throat would burst into flame. He wasn't wearing anything, but the region between his thighs was only a shadow, and somehow, she was the one who felt overdressed. She sat down beside him—in that small a space there wasn't much choice—and felt him wrapping something around her head. A rag, she realized, that had been dipped in water, to cover her ears and keep them from burning. When he knotted it, the skin of his upper arm stuck to hers.

The orange light that spilled through the cracks in the stove door illuminated Willie. His silhouette glowed, lean and feline; at that moment, Trixie wouldn't have been surprised to see him turn into a panther. Willie reached for a ladle, a wooden stick wired to a soup can. He dipped it into the bucket of water, pouring more over the rocks and causing a fresh cloud of steam to fill the chamber. When he settled down beside Trixie, his hand was so close to hers on the plywood that their pinkies touched.

It hurt, almost past the point of pain. The room had a pulse, and breathing was nearly impossible. Heat rose off Trixie's skin in the shape of her soul. Perspiration ran down her back and between her legs: her entire body, crying.

When Trixie's lungs were about to explode, she ran through the door into the cold room again. She sat down on the floor, warmth rolling off her in waves, just as Willie burst in with a towel wrapped around his waist. He sank down beside her and passed her a jug.

Trixie drank it without even knowing what was inside. The water cooled the lining of her throat. She passed the jug to Willie, who tipped his head back against the wall and drank deeply, the knot of his Adam's apple following each swallow. He turned to her, grinning. "Crazy, huh?"

She found herself laughing, too. "Totally."

Willie leaned against the wall and closed his eyes. "I always kind of figured that's what Florida's like."

"Florida? It's nothing like this."

"You've been to Florida?" Willie asked, intrigued.

"Yeah. It's just, you know, another state."

"I'd like to see an orange growing on a tree. I'd pretty much like to see anything that's somewhere other than here." He turned to her. "What did you do when you went to Florida?"

It was so long ago, Trixie had to think for a moment. "We went to Cape Canaveral. And Disney World."

Willie started picking at the wooden floor. "I bet you fit in there."

"Because it's so tacky?"

"Because you're like that fairy. The one who hangs out with Peter Pan."

Trixie burst out laughing. "*Tinker Bell*?"

"Yeah. My sister had that book."

She was about to tell him he was crazy, but then she remembered that Peter Pan was about a boy who didn't want to grow up, and she decided she didn't mind the comparison.

"She was so pretty," Willie said. "She had a light inside her."

Trixie stared at him. "You think I'm pretty?"

Instead of answering, Willie got up and crawled back into the hot room. By the time she followed, he'd already poured water over the rocks. Blinded by steam, she had to find her way by touch. She drew her fingers over the rough run of the wooden floor, up the joints of the walls, and then she brushed the smooth curve of Willie's shoulder. Before she could pull away, Willie's hand came up to capture hers. He tugged her closer, until they were facing each other on their knees, in the heart of a cloud. "Yeah, you're pretty," Willie said.

Trixie felt like she was falling. She had ugly chopped black hair and scars up and down her arms, and it was like he didn't even notice. She looked down at their interlaced fingers—a weave of dark and pale skin—and she let herself pretend that maybe there *could* be a light inside of her.

"When the first white folks came to the tundra," Willie said, "the people here thought they were ghosts."

"Sometimes that's what I think I am, too," Trixie murmured.

They leaned toward each other, or maybe the steam pushed them closer. And just as Trixie was certain that there wasn't any air left in the room, Willie's mouth closed over hers and breathed for her.

Willie tasted like smoke and sugar. His hands settled on her shoulders, respectfully staying there even when she itched to have him touch her. When they drew back from each other, Willie looked down at the ground. "I've never done that before," he confessed, and Trixie realized that when he'd said he'd never been with a girl in a steam, he'd meant that he'd never *been* with a girl.

Trixie had lost her virginity a lifetime ago, back when she thought it was a prize to give to someone like Jason. They'd had sex countless times—in the backseat of his car, in his bedroom when his parents were out, in the locker room at the hockey rink after hours. But what she had done with him compared in no way to the kiss she had just experienced with Willie; it was impossible to draw a line to connect the two. She couldn't even say that her own participation was the common denominator, because the girl she was back then was completely different from the one here now.

Trixie leaned toward Willie, and this time, *she* kissed *him*. "Me neither," she said, and she knew she wasn't lying.

When Daniel was eleven, the circus had come for the first and only time to the tundra. Bethel was the last stop for the Ford Brothers Circus, on an unprecedented tour of bush Alaska. Cane and Daniel weren't going to miss it for the world. They worked odd jobs—painting an elder's house, putting a new roof on Cane's uncle's steam bath—until they each had fifteen dollars. The flyers, which had been put up in all the village schools, including Akiak, said that admission would be eight bucks, and that left plenty of money for popcorn and souvenirs.

Most of the village was planning to go. Daniel's mother was going to hitch a ride with the principal, but at the last minute, Cane invited Daniel to go in his family's boat. They sat in its belly, the aluminum sides cold against their backs and bottoms, and told each other elephant jokes on the way down.

*Why is an elephant gray, large, and wrinkled?*

*Because if he was small, white, and round, he'd be an aspirin.*

*Why does an elephant have a trunk?*

*Because he'd look stupid with a glove compartment.*

Six thousand people from all over the delta showed up, many coming just after midnight so that they could see the MarkAir Herc fly in at dawn with the performers and the animals. The circus was going to take place at the National Guard Armory gym, with the bathrooms converted to costume changing areas. Cane and Daniel, running ragged around the edges of the activity, even got to hold a rope as the big top was pitched.

During the show, there were trained dogs in ratty tutus, and two lions named Lulu and Strawberry. There was a leopard, which waited for its cue outside the big top, drinking from a mud puddle. There was calliope music and peanuts and cotton candy, and for the little children, an inflatable house to jump in and Shetland pony rides. When Shorty Serra came thundering out to do rope tricks with his monstrous horse, Juneau, the beast stood on his hind legs to tower over everyone, and the crowd shrieked.

A group of Yup'ik boys sitting behind Daniel and Cane cheered, too. But when Daniel leaned over to say something to Cane, one of them spit out a slur:

"Look at that: I always knew *kass'aqs* belonged in the circus."

Daniel turned around. "Shut the fuck up."

One Yup'ik boy turned to another. "Did you hear something?"

"Want to feel something instead?" Daniel threatened, balling his hand into a fist.

"Ignore them," Cane said. "They're assholes."

The ringmaster appeared, to the roar of applause. "Ladies and gentlemen, I'm afraid we have some disappointing news. Our elephant, Tika, is too ill for the show. But I'm delighted to introduce . . . all the way from Madagascar . . . Florence and her Amazing Waltzing Pigeons!"

A tiny woman in a flamenco skirt walked out with birds perched on each shoulder. Daniel turned to Cane. "How sick could an elephant be?"

"Yeah," Cane said. "This sucks."

One of the Yup'ik boys poked him. "So do you. And I guess you like white meat."

All of his life, Daniel had been teased by the village kids—for not having a father, for being *kass'aq*, for not knowing how to do native things like fish and hunt. Cane would hang out with him, but the Yup'ik boys in school let that slide, because after all, Cane was one of them.

These boys, though, were not from his village.

Daniel saw the look on Cane's face and felt something break loose inside of him. He stood up, intent on leaving the big top. "Hang on," Cane said.

Daniel made his gaze as flat as possible. "I didn't invite you," he said, and he walked away.

It didn't take him long to find the elephant, penned up in a makeshift fence with no one to watch over it. Daniel had never seen an elephant up close; it was the one thing that he had in common with kids who lived in normal places. The elephant was limping and throwing hay in the air with its trunk. Daniel ducked under the wire and walked up to the animal, moving slowly. He touched its skin, warm and craggy, and laid his cheek along the haunch.

The best part about his friendship with Cane was that Cane was an insider, and that made Daniel one by association. He'd never realized that it could go the other way, too, that their acquaintance might make Cane a pariah. If the only way to keep Cane from being ostracized was to stay away from him, then Daniel would.

You did what you had to, for the people you cared about.

The elephant swung its massive head toward Daniel. Its dark eye winked; the loose-lipped drip of its mouth worked soundlessly. But Daniel could hear the animal perfectly, and so he answered out loud: *I don't belong here either.*

It was still dark out the next morning when the cargo plane arrived, puddle-jumping from village to village to pick up the dogs that had been dropped by mushers along the trail. They'd be flown back to Bethel where a handler could pick them up.

Willie was driving his cousin's pickup truck to the airstrip, and Trixie was in the passenger seat. They held hands across the space between them.

In the flatbed were all of Alex Edmonds's dogs, Juno, and Kingurauten Joseph, who was being transported back to the medical center. Willie parked the truck and then began to pass the dogs to Trixie, who walked them over to the chain-link fence and tethered them. Every time she returned for another one, he smiled at her, and she melted as if she were back in the steam again.

Last night, after the steam had died out, Willie bathed her with a rag dipped in warm water. He'd run the makeshift sponge right over her bra and her panties. Then they'd gone back to the cold room, and he'd toweled her dry, kneeling in front of her to get the backs of her knees and between her toes before they'd dressed each other. Fastening and tucking seemed so much more intimate than unbuttoning and unzipping, as if you were privy to putting the person back together whole, instead of unraveling him. "I have to take my uncle's coat back," Willie had said, but then he had given her his own lined canvas jacket.

It smelled like him, every time Trixie buried her nose in the collar.

The lights on the airstrip suddenly blazed, magic. Trixie whirled around, but there was no control tower anywhere nearby. "The pilots have remotes in their planes," Willie said, laughing, and sure enough ten minutes hadn't passed before Trixie could hear the approach of an engine.

The plane that landed looked like the one that had flown Trixie into Bethel. The pilot—a Yup'ik boy not much older than Willie—jumped out. "Hey," he said. "Is this all you've got?"

When he opened the cargo bay, Trixie could see a dozen dogs already tethered to D rings. As Willie loaded the sled dogs, she helped Joseph climb down from the back of the pickup. He leaned on her heavily as they walked to the runway, and when he stepped into the cargo bay, the animals inside started barking. "You remind me of someone I used to know," Joseph said.

*You already told me that,* Trixie thought, but she just nodded at him. Maybe it wasn't that he wanted her to hear it but only that he needed to say it again.

The pilot closed up the hatch and hopped back into his plane, accelerating down the airstrip until Trixie could not tell his landing lights apart from any given star. The airstrip blinked and went black again.

She felt Willie move closer in the dark, but before her eyes could adjust, another beacon came at them. It glinted directly into her eyes, had her shielding them from the glare with one hand. The snow machine pulled up, its engine growling before it died down completely and the driver stood up on the runners.

"Trixie?" her father said. "Is that you?"

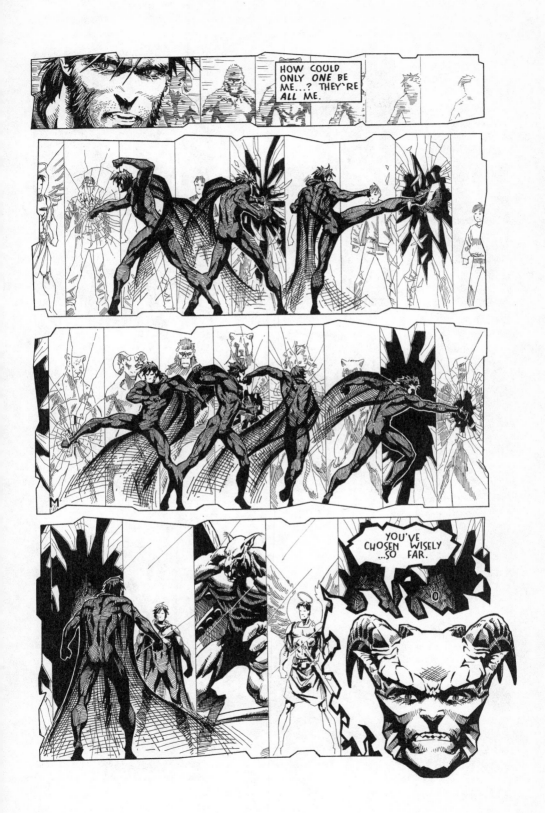

# 8

In the middle of the Alaskan tundra, staring at a daughter he could barely recognize, Daniel thought back to the moment he'd known that everything between him and Trixie was bound to change.

It was, like so many of those minutes between a father and a little girl, unremarkable. The season might have been summertime, or it could have been fall. They might have been bundled up in winter coats, or wearing flip-flops. They could have been heading to make a deposit at the bank, or leaving the bookstore. What stuck in Daniel's mind was the street—a busy one, in the middle of town—and the fact that he was walking down it with Trixie, holding her hand.

She was seven. Her hair was French-braided—badly, he'd never quite gotten the hang of that—and she was trying not to walk on the breaks in the sidewalk. They reached the intersection, and like always, Daniel reached for Trixie's hand.

She very deliberately slipped it free and stepped

away from him before she looked both ways and crossed by herself.

It was a hairline crack, one you might never have noticed, except for the fact that it grew wider and wider, until there was a canyon between them. A child's job, ostensibly, was to grow up. So why, when it happened, did a parent feel so disappointed?

This time, instead of a busy street, Trixie had crossed an entire country by herself. She stood in front of Daniel, bundled in an oversized canvas coat, with a wool cap pulled over her head. Beside her was a Yup'ik boy with hair that kept falling into his eyes.

Daniel didn't know what was more shocking: seeing a girl he'd once carried on his shoulders and tucked into bed and wondering if she'd committed murder, or realizing that he'd hide in the Alaskan bush with Trixie for the rest of his life if that was what it took to keep her from being arrested.

"Daddy . . . ? " Trixie launched herself into his arms.

Daniel felt a shudder work down his spine; relief, when you came right down to it, was not all that different from fear. "You," he said to the boy who stood a distance apart, watching them with a guarded expression. "Who are you?"

"Willie Moses."

"Can I borrow your rig?" Daniel tossed him the keys to the snow-go, a trade.

The boy looked at Trixie as if he was about to speak, but then he dropped his gaze and walked to the snow machine. Daniel heard the lion's growl of its engine, and the high-pitched whine as it sped away, and then led Trixie to the truck. Like most Alaskan vehicles, this one would never have passed inspection in the lower forty-eight. It was rusted clean through on the side panels; its speedometer was stuck at 88 mph, and first gear didn't work at all. But the light over the rearview mirror did, and Daniel turned that on to scrutinize his daughter.

With the exception of dark circles under her eyes, she seemed to be all right. Daniel reached up and pulled off her wool cap, revealing a sleek cap of black hair. "Oh," she said when his eyes widened. "I forgot about that."

Daniel slid across the bench seat and pulled her into his arms. God, was there anything more solid, more *right*, than knowing your child was where she ought to be? "Trixie," he said, "you scared the hell out of me."

He felt her grab a fistful of his coat. He had a thousand questions for her, but one sprang to the surface first, the one that he couldn't help but ask. "Why *here*?"

"Because," Trixie murmured, "you said it's where people disappear."

Daniel drew away from her slowly. "Why did you want to?"

Her eyes filled with tears, until finally one spilled over and ran to the point of her chin. She opened her mouth to speak, but nothing came out. Daniel held on to her, as her thin body started to shake. "I didn't do what everyone thinks . . ."

Daniel threw his head back and winged a prayer to a God he'd never quite believed in: *Thank you.*

"I wanted him back. I didn't really want to fool around like Zephyr told me to, but I was willing to do anything if it got things back to the way it was before Jason broke up with me." She swallowed hard. "When everyone left, he was so nice at first, I thought maybe it had worked. But then everything started happening so fast. I wanted to talk, and he didn't. When he started . . . when *we* started . . ." She took a ragged breath. "He said that this was exactly what he needed—a friend with benefits. And that's how I realized that he didn't want me back. He just wanted me for fifteen minutes."

Daniel didn't move. Surely if he did, he'd shatter.

"I tried to get away, but I couldn't. It felt like I was underwater, like when I told my arms and legs to move, they didn't work fast enough, strong enough. He thought it was a game, me fighting just a little bit, like I was still playing hard to get. He pinned me down and . . ." Trixie's skin was flushed and damp. "He said, *Don't tell me you don't want this.*" She looked up at Daniel in the halo of the overhead light. "And I . . . I didn't."

Trixie had once seen a science fiction movie that suggested we all had doppelgängers, we just couldn't ever run into them because our worlds would collide. It was like that, now that her father had come to rescue her. Just this morning, walking back with Willie from the *maqi,* she had entertained the thought of what it would be like to stay in Tuluksak. Maybe they needed someone to be a teaching assistant. Maybe she could move in with one of Willie's cousins. But with her father's arrival, the world had jarred to a stop. He didn't fit here, and neither did she.

She had told him her secret: that she was a liar. Not just about being a virgin and playing Rainbow . . . but even more. She'd never said no to Jason that night, although she'd told the DA she had.

And the drugs?

She was the one who'd brought them.

She hadn't realized, at the time, that the guy at the college who sold pot to the high school kids was sleeping with her mother. She'd gone to buy some for Zephyr's party, in the hopes that she could take the edge off. If she was going to be as wild as Zephyr planned for her to be, she needed a little pharmaceutical help.

Seth was out of pot, but Special K was supposed to be like Ecstasy. It would make you lose control.

Which, in a completely different way, she had.

This much wasn't a lie: She hadn't taken it that night, not on purpose. She and Zephyr had planned to get high together, but it was a real drug, not pot, and at the last minute, Trixie had chickened out. She'd forgotten about it, until the DA brought up the fact that she might have had a drug in her system. Trixie didn't really know what Zephyr had done with the vial: if she'd used it herself, if she'd left it sitting on the kitchen counter, if someone else at the party had found it first. She couldn't say for a fact that Jason had slipped it into her drink. She'd had so *much* to drink that night—half-empty cans of Coke left lying around, screwdrivers with the ice cubes melting—it was possible that Jason had had nothing to do with it at all.

Trixie hadn't known that adding drugs into the legal mix would mean Jason was tried as an adult. She hadn't been looking to ruin his life. She'd only wanted a way to salvage her own.

It was not a coincidence, Trixie thought, that *no* and *know* sounded the same. You were supposed to be able to say the magic word, and that was enough to make your wishes—or lack of them—crystal clear. But no one ever said *yes* to make sex consensual. You took hints from body language, from the way two people came together. Why, then, didn't a shake of the head or a hand pushing hard against a chest speak just as loudly? Why did you have to actually say the word *no* for it to be rape?

That one word, spoken or not, didn't make Jason any less guilty of taking something Trixie hadn't wanted to give. It didn't make her any less foolish. All it did was draw a line in the sand, so that the people who hadn't been there to witness it—Moss and Zephyr, her parents, the police, the district attorney—could take sides.

But somewhere along the line, it also made her realize that she couldn't blame Jason, not entirely, for what had happened.

She had thought of what it would be like when the trial started, when it was a hundred times worse than it was now, and Jason's lawyer would get up in court and paint Trixie as a complete slut and a liar. She had wondered how long it would be before she just gave in and admitted they were right. She'd started to hate herself, and one night, when the dark had folded itself around Trixie like the wings of a heron, she wished that Jason Underhill would drop dead. It was just a secret, silent thought, and she knew better than anyone at this point that what was not said aloud didn't count. But then one thing led to another: Jason was charged as an adult, not a minor. Jason ran into her at the Winterfest. And then, before she knew it, her wish had come true.

Trixie knew the police were looking for her. *We'll take care of it*, her father kept saying. But Jason was dead, and it was her fault. Nothing she said now—or didn't say—was going to bring him back.

She wondered if she would be sent to jail in Jason's place, and if it would be horrible there, like you saw in the movies, or if it would be full of people like Trixie, people who understood that there were some mistakes you never got to erase.

While her father explained to the Jesuit Volunteers that they were about to lose a fake staff member, Trixie sat in the truck and cried. She had thought that by now, she would have been bone dry, a husk, but the tears didn't ever stop. All she had wanted was for something to feel right again in her life, and instead, everything had gone impossibly wrong.

There was a knock at the window of the truck, and she looked up to see Willie, his fingers stuck in a bowl of something pink. He scooped out a bit with his middle and index fingers as she unrolled the window.

"Hey," he said.

She wiped her eyes. "Hey."

"You okay?"

Trixie started to nod, but she was so sick of lying. "Not so much," she admitted.

It was nice, the way Willie didn't even try to say something to make her feel better. He just let her sadness stand. "That's your dad?" he asked.

She nodded. She wanted to explain everything to Willie, but she didn't know how. As far as Willie had been concerned, she was a Jesuit Volunteer, one who had been stranded by the storm. With him, she had not been a rape victim or a murder suspect. How did you tell someone that you weren't the person he thought you were? And more importantly, how did you tell him that you'd meant the things you'd said, when everything else about you turned out to be a lie?

He held out the dish. "Want some?"

"What is it?"

"*Akutaq.* Eskimo ice cream." Trixie dipped her finger in. It wasn't Ben & Jerry's, but it wasn't bad—berries and sugar, mixed with something she couldn't recognize.

"Seal oil and shortening," Willie said, and she

wasn't in the least surprised that he could read her mind.

He looked down at her through the window. "If I ever get to Florida, maybe you could meet me there."

Trixie didn't know what was going to happen to her tomorrow, much less after that. But she found that in spite of everything that had happened, she still had the capacity to pretend, to think her future might be something it never actually would. "That would be cool," she said softly.

"Do you live nearby?"

"Give or take fifteen hundred miles," Trixie said, and when Willie smiled a little, so did she.

Suddenly Trixie wanted to tell someone the truth—all of it. She wanted to start from the beginning, and if she could make just one person believe her, at least it was a start. She lifted her face to Willie's. "At home, I was raped by a guy I thought I loved," Trixie said, because that was what it was to her and always would be. Semantics didn't matter when you were bleeding between your legs, when you felt like you'd been broken from the inside out, when free will was taken away from you.

"Is that why you ran away?"

Trixie shook her head. "He's dead."

Willie didn't ask her if she was responsible. He just nodded, his breath hanging on the air like lace. "I guess sometimes," he said, "that's the way it works."

• • •

It was bingo night at the village council offices, and Laura had been left alone in the tiny house. She had read every *Tundra Drums* newspaper twice, even the ones stacked in the entryway for disposal. She'd watched television until her eyes hurt.

She found herself wondering what kind of person would choose to live in a place like this, where conversation seemed abnormal and where even the sunlight stayed away. What had brought Daniel's mother here?

Like Annette Stone, Laura was a teacher. She knew you could change the world one student at a time. But how long would you be willing to sacrifice your own child's happiness for everyone else's?

Maybe she hadn't *wanted* to leave. Daniel had told Laura about his wandering father. There were some people who hit your life so hard, they left a stain on your future. Laura understood how you might spend your whole life waiting for that kind of man to come back.

It was a choice Daniel's mother had made for both of them, one that immediately put her son at a disadvantage. To Laura, it seemed selfish, and she ought to know.

Was it tough love, putting your child through hell? Or was it the best of parenting, a way to make sure your child could survive without you? If Daniel hadn't been teased, he might have felt at home on the tundra. He might have become one of the faceless kids, like Cane, who couldn't find a way out.

He might have stayed in Alaska, forever, waiting for something that didn't come.

Maybe Annette Stone had only been making sure Daniel had an escape route, because she didn't herself.

Outside, a truck drove into the yard. Laura jumped up, running out the arctic entry to see if Daniel and Trixie had returned. But the truck had a bar of flashing blue lights across the top of the cab, casting long shadows on the snow.

Laura straightened her spine. You'd do whatever it took to protect your child. Even the things that no one else could possibly understand.

"We're looking for Trixie Stone," the policeman said.

Trixie fell asleep on the ride back to Akiak. Daniel had wrapped Trixie in his own balaclava and parka; she rode the snow machine with her arms around his waist and her cheek pressed up against his back. He followed the setting sun, a showgirl's tease of pink ribbon trailing off the stage of the horizon.

Daniel didn't really know what to make of his daughter's confession. In this part of the world, people believed that a thought might turn into an action at any moment; a word held in your mind had just as much power to wound or to heal as the one that was spoken aloud. In this part of the world, it didn't matter what Trixie had or had not said: What Jason Underhill had done to Trixie *did* count as rape.

He was also painfully aware of the other things Trixie had not said out loud: that she hadn't killed Jason; that she was innocent.

In Akiak, Daniel revved up the riverbank and past the post office to reach Cane's house. He turned the corner and saw the police truck.

For just a moment, he thought, *I have reinvented myself before, I can do it again.* He could drive until the gas ran out of the snow-go, and then he would build a shelter for himself and Trixie. He'd teach her how to track and how to hunt and, when the weather turned, where to find the salmon.

But he could not leave Laura behind, and he couldn't send for her later. Once they left, he would have to make sure they could never be found.

He felt Trixie stiffen behind him and realized that she had seen the policemen. Even worse, when the officer got out of the car, he understood that they'd been seen, too.

"Don't talk," he said over his shoulder. "Let me take care of this."

Daniel drove the snow-go toward Cane's house and turned off the ignition. Then he got off the vehicle and stood with his hand on Trixie's shoulder.

When you loved someone, you did whatever you thought was in her best interests, even if—at the time—it looked utterly wrong. Men did this for women; mothers did it for sons. And Daniel knew he'd do it for Trixie. He'd do anything. What made a hero a hero? Was it winning all the time, like Superman? Or was it taking on the task reluctantly, like Spider-Man? Was it learning, like the X-Men had, that at any moment you might fall from grace to become a villain? Or, like Alan Moore's Rorschach, was it being human enough to enjoy watching people die, if they deserved it?

The policeman approached. "Trixie Stone," he said, "you're under arrest for the murder of Jason Underhill."

"You can't arrest her," Daniel insisted.

"Mr. Stone, I've got a warrant—"

Daniel didn't take his eyes off his daughter's face. "Yes," he said. "But I'm the one who killed him."

Trixie couldn't talk, she couldn't breathe, she couldn't think. She was frozen, rooted to the permafrost like the policeman. Her father had just confessed to murder.

She stared at him, stunned. "Daddy," she whispered.

"Trixie, I told you. Not a word."

Trixie thought of how, when she was tiny, he used to carry her on his shoulders. She, like her mother, got dizzy up high—but her father would anchor her legs in his hands. *I won't let you fall*, he said, and because he never did, the world from that vantage point stopped being so scary.

She thought of this and a thousand other things: how for one entire year, he'd cut her lunch box sandwiches into letters so that they spelled out a different word each week: BRAVE, SMART, SWEET. How he'd always hide a caricature of her in one of the pages of his comic books. How she would rummage in her backpack and find, tucked in a pocket, peanut M&M's that she knew he'd left for her.

Her eyes filled with tears. "But you're lying," she whispered.

The policeman sighed. "Well," he said, "*somebody* is."

He glanced toward the truck, where Trixie's mother already sat in the passenger seat, staring at them through the glass.

It had been almost comical, getting the call. The state troopers in Alaska had served the arrest warrant for Trixie Stone, they told Bartholemew. But in doing so, two other people had confessed to the crime. What did they want him to do?

Short of getting governor's warrants, the detective had to fly out there himself, interview the Stones, and decide who—if anyone—he wanted to arrest.

Daniel Stone had been brought into the conference room at the Bethel Police Station, where he and his wife had been taken following their individual confessions. Trixie, a minor, was in custody at the Bethel Youth Center, a juvenile detention facility. A radiator belched out erratic heat, stirring tinsel that had been draped above its casing.

Tomorrow, he realized, was Christmas.

"You know this doesn't change anything," Bartholemew said. "We still have to hold your daughter as a delinquent."

"What does that mean?"

"After we go back to Maine, she stays at a juvy

lockup until she's certified to be tried as an adult for murder. Then if she doesn't get bail—which she won't, given the severity of the charge—she'll be sent back there after the arraignment."

"You can't hold her if I'm the one who committed the crime," Daniel pointed out.

"I know what you're doing, Mr. Stone," Bartholemew said. "I don't even blame you, really. Did I ever tell you about the last conversation I had with my daughter? She came downstairs and told me she was going to watch a high school football game. I told her to have a good time. Thing is, it was May. Nobody was playing football. And I *knew* that," Bartholemew said. "The people who were at the scene said she never even braked as she went around the curve, that the car went straight over at full speed. They said it rolled three, maybe four times. When the medical examiner told me she'd OD'd before she went over the railing, I actually said *thank God.* I wanted to know she didn't have to feel any of that."

Bartholemew crossed his arms. "Do you know what else I did? I went home, and I tossed her room, until I found her stash, and the needles she used. I buried them in the bottom of the trash and drove to the dump. She was already dead, and I still was trying to protect her."

Stone just stared at him. "You can't prosecute all of us. Eventually, you'll let her go."

"I've got evidence that puts her at the bridge."

"There were a thousand people there that night."

"They didn't leave behind blood. They didn't get their hair caught in Jason Underhill's watchband."

Stone shook his head. "Trixie and Jason were arguing, near the convenience store parking lot. That's when her hair must have gotten caught. But I showed up just as he grabbed Trixie, and I went after him. I was already a suspect once. I told you I got into a fight with the kid. I just didn't tell you what happened afterward."

"I'm listening," Bartholemew said.

"After he ran off, I tracked him to the bridge."

"And then?"

"Then I killed him."

"How? Did you sock him in the jaw? Hit him from behind? Give him a good shove?" When the other man remained silent, Bartholemew shook his head. "You can't tell me, Mr. Stone, because you weren't there. You're excluded by the physical evidence . . . and Trixie isn't." He met Stone's gaze. "She's done things before that she couldn't tell you about. Maybe this is one more."

Daniel Stone glanced down at the table.

Bartholemew sighed. "Being a cop isn't all that different from being a father, you know. You do your damnedest, and it's still not good enough to keep the people you care about from hurting themselves."

"You're making a mistake," Stone said, but there was a thread of desperation in his voice.

"You're free to go," Bartholemew replied.

• • •

In juvenile jail, the lights did not go out. In juvenile jail, you weren't in cells. You all slept single-sex in a dormitory that reminded Trixie of the orphans in *Annie*.

There were girls in here who'd stolen cash from the stores where they worked, and one who had thrown a knife at her principal. There were drug addicts and battered girlfriends and even an eight-year-old who was everyone's mascot—a kid who had hit her stepfather in the head with a baseball bat after he finished raping her.

Because it was Christmas Eve, they had a special dinner: turkey with cranberry sauce, gravy, mashed potatoes. Trixie sat next to a girl who had tattoos up and down her arms. "What's your story?" she asked.

"I don't have one," Trixie said.

After dinner, a church group came to give the girls presents. The ones who'd been in the longest got the biggest packages. Trixie got a colored pencil set with Hello Kitty on the plastic cover. She took them out, one by one, and drew on her fingernails.

If she were at home now, they'd have turned off all the lights in the house except for the ones on the Christmas tree. They'd open one present—that was the tradition—and then Trixie would go to bed and fake being asleep while her parents traipsed up and down the attic stairs with her gifts, the semblance of Santa for a girl who'd grown up years before they wanted her to.

She wondered what the fake Santa at the

amusement park in New Hampshire was doing tonight. Probably it was the only day of the year he got off.

After lights out, someone in the dorm started to sing "Silent Night." It was thready at first, a reed on the wind, but then another girl joined in, and another. Trixie heard her own voice, disembodied, floating away from her like a balloon. *All is calm. All is bright.*

She thought she would cry her first night in juvenile jail, but it turned out she didn't have any tears left. Instead, when everyone forgot the extra verses, she listened to the eight-year-old who sobbed herself to sleep. She wondered how trees became petrified, if the same process worked with a human heart.

In the small holding cell where Laura had been for the past four hours, there was nothing soft, only cement and steel, and right angles. She'd found herself dozing off, dreaming of rain and cirrus clouds, of angel food cake and snowflakes—things that gave way the moment you touched them.

She wondered how Trixie was, where they'd sent her. She wondered if Daniel was on the other side of this thick wall, if they had come to question him as they had questioned her.

When Daniel came into the room, on the heels of a policeman, Laura stood up. She pressed herself against the bars and reached out to him. He waited until the policeman left, then walked up to the bars and reached inside to Laura. "Are you okay?"

"They let you go," she breathed.

He nodded and rested his forehead against hers.

"What about Trixie?"

"They've got her at a juvenile center down the road."

Laura let go of him. "You didn't need to cover for Trixie," she said.

"I don't think either one of us was about to let her get sent to jail."

"She won't be," Laura said. "Because I'm the one who killed Jason."

Daniel stared at her, all the breath leaving his body. *"What?"*

She sank onto the metal bench in the cell and wiped her eyes. "The night of the Winterfest, when Trixie disappeared, we said that I'd go home and wait there, in case she turned up. But when I headed back to my car, I saw someone on the bridge. I called out her name, and Jason turned around."

She was crying in earnest now. "He was drunk. He said . . . he said that my bitch of a daughter was ruining his life. Ruining *his* life. He stood up and started coming toward me, and I . . . I got scared and pushed him away. But he lost his balance, and he went over the railing."

Laura unconsciously brought her hand up to her ear as she spoke, and Daniel noticed that the small gold hoop earring she usually wore was gone. *The blood. The red hair on the watchband. The boot prints in the snow.* "It caught on his sweater. He ripped it out when he fell," she said, following Daniel's gaze. "He was hanging on to the railing with one hand and reaching up with the other. Looking down—I was so dizzy. He kept yelling for me to help. I started to reach for his hand . . . and then . . ." Laura closed her eyes. "Then I let him go."

It was no coincidence that fear could move a person to extremes, just as seamlessly as love. They were the conjoined twins of emotion: If you didn't know what was at stake to lose, you had nothing to fight for.

"I went home, and I waited for you and Trixie. I was sure the police were going to find me before you got there. I was going to tell you . . ."

"But you didn't," Daniel said.

"I tried."

Daniel remembered bringing Trixie home from the Winterfest, how Laura had been so shaken. *Oh, Daniel*, she had said. *Something happened.* He'd thought at the time that his wife was just as frantic about Trixie's disappearance as he had been. He thought Laura had been asking him a question when, in fact, she'd been trying to give him an answer.

She hugged her arms across her middle. "At first, they said it was a suicide, and I thought maybe I'd only dreamed it, that it hadn't happened the way I thought at all. But then Trixie ran away."

*And made herself look guilty*, Daniel thought. *Even to me.*

"You should have told me, Laura. I could have—"

"Hated me." She shook her head. "You used to

stare at me like I'd hung the stars in the sky, Daniel. But after you found out about . . . you know, that I'd been with someone else . . . it was different. You couldn't even look me in the eye."

When a Yup'ik Eskimo met another person, he averted his glance. It wasn't out of disrespect, but rather, the opposite. Sight was something to be conserved for the moments when you really needed it—when you were hunting, when you needed strength. It was only when you looked away from a person that you had the truest vision.

"I just wanted you to look at me like you used to," Laura said, her voice breaking. "I just wanted it to be the way it used to be. That's why I couldn't tell you, no matter how many times I tried. I'd already been unfaithful to you. What would you have done if I'd told you I'd *killed* someone?"

"You didn't kill him," Daniel said. "You didn't mean for that to happen."

Laura shook her head, her lips pressed tightly together, as if she was afraid to speak out loud. And he understood, because he'd felt this himself: Sometimes what we wish for actually comes true. And sometimes that's the very worst thing that can happen.

She buried her face in her hands. "I don't know what I meant and what I didn't. It's all mixed up. I don't even recognize myself anymore."

Life could take on any number of shapes while you were busy fighting your own demons. But if you were changing at the same rate as the person

beside you, nothing else really mattered. You became each other's constant.

"I do," Daniel said.

It was possible, he decided, that even in today's
day and age—even thousands of miles away from
the Yup'ik villages—people could still turn into animals, and vice versa. Just because you chose to
leave a place did not mean you could escape taking it with you. A man and a woman who lived together long enough might swap traits, until they
found parts of themselves in each other. Jettison a
personality and you just might find it taking up residence in the heart of the person you loved most.

Laura lifted her face to his. "What do you think
is going to happen?"

He did not know the answer to that. He wasn't
even certain he knew the right questions. But he
would get Trixie, and they would go home. He'd
find the best lawyer he could. And sooner or later,
when Laura came back to them, they'd reinvent
themselves. They might not be able to start over,
but they could certainly start again.

Just then, a raven flew past the police station,
soaring in the courtyard, imitating the sound of
running water. Daniel watched carefully, the way
he had learned to a lifetime ago. A raven could be
many things—creator, trickster—depending on
what form it felt like taking. But when it looped in a
half circle and turned upside down, it could mean
only one thing: It was dumping luck off its back—
anyone's for the taking, if you happened to see
where it landed.

Dear Reader:

In *The Tenth Circle,* Daniel Stone—a comic book penciler—woos his future wife, Laura, by drawing a sketch of her and including a hidden message in the background: letters that spell out a place to meet. In this spirit, I've included a hidden message for you to find in the artwork in this novel. Beginning on page 12, each page of art has several letters hidden in the background—two or three per page, eighty-six letters in all. The letters spell out a quotation that sums up the theme of *The Tenth Circle*, and the name of the quotation's author. Readers can go to my website, www.jodipicoult.com, to see if they're right. (If you're eagle-eyed enough to be successful, please don't spoil the fun for someone else . . . keep the answer a secret!)

Jodi Picoult